I0761149
Get on board the Elsewhere Express—the train that takes you to your life's purpose. As you color in this illustration, let your mind wander and your heart open. What are the colors of your daydreams? What picture do you want to paint of your future? And what kind of life can you create if you dare to color outside the lines? Enjoy this activity on long train rides and journeys of all kinds.

BY SAMANTHA SOTTO YAMBAO

Before Ever After

Love and Gravity

A Dream of Trees

The Beginning of Always

Water Moon

The Elsewhere Express

THE ELSEWHERE EXPRESS

THE ELSEWHERE EXPRESS

A NOVEL

SAMANTHA SOTTO YAMBAO

NEW YORK

Del Rey
An imprint of Random House
A division of Penguin Random House LLC
1745 Broadway, New York, NY 10019
randomhousebooks.com
penguinrandomhouse.com

Hardcover ISBN 978-0-593-72502-3
Ebook ISBN 978-0-593-72503-0
International ISBN 979-8-217-09433-2

Printed in Canada

2 4 6 8 9 7 5 3 1

First Edition

BOOK TEAM: Production editor: Cara DuBois • Managing editor: Paul Gilbert • Production manager: Richard Elman • Copy editor: Sheryl Rapée-Adams • Proofreaders: Julie Ehlers, Tricia Wygal

Book design by Alexis Flynn

Adobe Stock illustrations: tarakacraft (ticket shape), ronnarid (parchment texture), Roverto (flourish), magicpics1806 (train), biancaoddi (eternity knot), petrrgoskov (hanging sign silhouette)
Case art direction and sprayed edges design: Regina Flath
Case illustration: Haylee Morice
Sprayed edges image: Shutterstock

The authorized representative in the EU for product safety and compliance is Penguin Random House Ireland, Morrison Chambers, 32 Nassau Street, Dublin D02 YH68, Ireland. https://eu-contact.penguin.ie

For Nico and Cai,
and everyone trying to find their way and why

Author's Note

This is a work of fiction that touches on the subject of gradual loss of sight. Reader discretion is advised.

THE ELSEWHERE EXPRESS

THE FIRST LEG

EVERYWHERE

The soul which has no fixed purpose in life is lost; to be everywhere is to be nowhere.

—Michel de Montaigne

WELCOME ABOARD

Dearest Guest,

Thank you for choosing the Elsewhere Express. We hope that you had a pleasant boarding experience and find your accommodations to your liking. As you begin your journey, we would like to remind you that while we do our best to ensure your utmost comfort and safety, you must remain mindful of your personal belongings. We cannot be responsible for any valuables, baggage, or souls that are lost.

On behalf of the crew, welcome aboard.

Sincerely yours,
The Conductor

YOUR ITINERARY

MEET THE PASSENGERS

"Who can board the Elsewhere Express?"

Frequently Asked Questions
THE ELSEWHERE EXPRESS
PASSENGER HANDBOOK

Hiraya Sia
(hee-rah-yah)

Some names are heavier than others. But the tiny premature girl had been weighed before being given one, so her official weight on record was only four and a half pounds.

Despite her small size, or perhaps because of it, she charmed the hospital's entire neonatal intensive care unit. Mary Beth, a nurse on the night shift, enjoyed humming an old, nameless lullaby to her, a song Mary Beth's mother had sung to her, and that Mary Beth had sung to her daughter. It scented the air with sugared almonds and vanilla, and flowed into the girl like warm milk, carrying a wordless wish that every heart, no matter how small, could understand.

Live. Breathe. Be.

The girl did her best not to disappoint the voice that filled her evenings. Its song was her whole world and she wanted to keep it close. When she learned how to move her tiny fingers, she held the lullaby singer's calloused hand as tightly as she could. Mary Beth had never felt a more stubborn grip. This girl, the nurse thought, would need someone to teach her how to let things go.

The girl's strength proved useful on the day of her baptism, when, upon receiving her name, she was made to carry the full weight of her parents' hopes. Unlike most people who spent their lives searching for meaning, the girl was given a premade one, no assembly required. In her name was a single simple instruction: Save your brother's life. If, on the off chance, she ever forgot her purpose, her name reminded her exactly why she had been conceived.

Her father, Dr. Jason Sia, a linguistics professor, had come up with the idea to call her *Hiraya,* an ancient Tagalog word commonly translated as "imagination." Its actual meaning was more complex. *Hiraya* was the power of the mind to bring that which did not exist into being. The professor could not think of a name that suited his new daughter more. Hiraya was a desperate wish. A dream come true. The one chance he and his wife, Cristina, had to save their eldest child's life.

Their son, Jace Sia, was meant to be an only child, but his blood disorder, thalassemia major, had other plans. He had received over seventy blood transfusions before he turned four, and unless his parents found a genetically matched bone marrow donor for him, he was going to need more.

Hiraya did not disappoint them. Growing up, she joked that her name was just a nicer way of saying that she had been born for spare parts. Her parents did not appreciate her humor, even as they kept chips, cookies, and soda out of her reach. Her mother packed her lunch box with apples, whole-grain crackers, and low-fat cheese, along with little notes on pink Post-its reminding her not to trade any of her snacks for candy. After all, it was prudent to be prepared in case Jace ever required a piece of her liver. Or any other part of herself he happened to need more than she did.

But Hiraya didn't mind: Jace was an excellent cookie thief and giggled as much as she did when they gobbled them up in her closet in the middle of the night. Their crumb-filled laughter fed the old lullaby that had taken root inside her, making it bear new melodies like fruit. When Hiraya learned how to spell, she gave her songs words and wrote them down to keep herself from bursting. Some songs smelled like springtime, others, like fresh bread. Her favorite ones coated her tongue with clover honey. Each song, though distinct, ferried the same wish.

Live. Breathe. Be.

Jason and Cristina weren't too worried about the hours Hiraya spent setting the wish to music, playing her glittery sticker-covered guitar, and filling purple notebooks with songs. She was young and had plenty of time to find a real dream like her brother's. There was no doubt that Jace was going to make an excellent oncologist, but music was far too slippery and big a dream for their daughter's small hands. Hiraya would need to learn that the only place her songs would lead her was the corner of nowhere and disappointment. Jason and Cristina were thankful that they had no such concerns about Jace.

That is, until the night all their dreams tumbled out of his cold, limp hands.

Quentin Chen Philips Jr.

The day after his father, Quentin Philips Sr., killed himself, a thirteen-year-old Quentin Jr. insisted that everyone start calling him "Q." His mother, Connie Chen Philips, did not need another reason to cry. Lying to everyone about her husband's death was hard enough. Lying to herself that it had been an accident was harder. Sparing his mother from having to say her late husband's name each time she called her only child down to dinner was the sole comfort Q could give her.

But he could not do anything about his eyes.

Though Q inherited most of his features from his mother, his irises resembled his father's, borrowing their somber palette from an overcast sky. Q hated that they stood out from the rest of his face and made him look like a mistake. When Quentin Sr. died, however, Q discovered that gray eyes had their uses—they camouflaged his dark days and most shades of sadness. But while he was reticent about his pain, Q made sure that his clients' portraits told the whole truth. His father's suicide had blindsided him and Q refused to let anyone lie to him ever again. He was particularly wary of smiles.

Smiles were the easiest of deceptions and the prettiest of open wounds. Quentin Sr. had worn a bright and gummy one every day of his life until the morning he didn't. Q's paintings were the opposite, revealing everything his clients tried their best to hide. Considering how much they paid him, Q did his best to give them their money's worth no matter how much or loudly they complained. At the end of the day, their portrait's appraised value trumped their pride. After all, scarcity drives prices up, and there was nothing more limited than the time Q had left to paint.

Q stood at the doorway of his home studio, surveying the room with what remained of his sight. His degenerative eye disease had shrunk his tunnel of vision to the size of a pinhole, but his home was a place where memory was the only walking stick he required.

He was going to miss this place and the way it smelled of sharpened pencils, paint, and sunshine. He had bought the apartment because of its large windows and had sold it for the same reason. Feeling the sun on his skin without seeing its light turned his blood cold on the warmest of days. The studio was chillier now that it was empty.

His tools and supplies had already been donated, and his business manager had picked up all the paintings for his final collection, save one. Q strode over to the small painting resting on an easel in the middle of his studio, navigating the paint-splattered, scuffed wooden floors like someone with perfect vision. Q might have gotten more when he sold his apartment if he had worked over a drop cloth, but he was always in too much of a hurry to paint to bother covering his hardwood floor.

And his sessions with the sole subject of his final collection never lasted long—this was the biggest challenge when trying to paint a woman who existed only in his dreams. When he woke up, only fragments of her remained: The corner of a lip. The tip of a nose. The shadow in the well of a collarbone.

No matter how hard Q tried to remember her, he could not collect enough details to assemble her face. The song that wafted through his dreams, the same melody that had filled his nights since he was a young boy, however, was unforgettable. It kept him company while he slept and leaked into his days, its message a record on repeat.

Live. Breathe. Be.

Trying to live by the peace it prescribed, though, proved to be difficult. Painting through his window of vision was like trying to build a seashore one grain of sand at a time. But as the imaginary woman was the last sitter he would ever have, he promised to show up for her for as long as she showed up for him.

Speck by speck, he captured what he could, and in those moments, with all his focus and energy flowing through the tip of his paintbrush, he couldn't let his anger boil over. Being angry all the time was tiring. Still, he preferred being furious about losing his sight to mourning the loss of his dreams. Tears choked you. Rage kept you breathing. Anger needed air to fan its flames.

Q ran his fingertips over his final painting. It was meant to capture the woman's left eye, but he had run out of time to finish it. All he could do was trust his manager's word that even if the piece wasn't done, it was good enough. His show was opening this evening and he needed to deliver its missing piece. It would be a shame not to include the painting since it fit the collection's theme perfectly.

Unfinished

A Silent Auction of the Final Works of Q Chen Philips Jr.

All proceeds to be donated to blindness research.

Q took the painting from the easel and wrapped it in brown paper. He did not have time to have it framed, but it was just as well. Frames were doorways into a painter's truth and this piece only led to a dream's end. His patrons would simply assume that this was yet another piece where he broke the rules, just like the swarms of scorched moths he vigorously denied spray-painting on the city's walls.

YOUR ITINERARY

BOARDING

"Where do I board the Elsewhere Express?"

Frequently Asked Questions
THE ELSEWHERE EXPRESS
PASSENGER HANDBOOK

Raya

It had been ten years to the day since Raya had sat by Jace's hospital bed, holding his bandaged hand. (She no longer went by the name Hiraya, but it was still the name printed on her first-year medical school ID.) She had squeezed her brother's fingers harder than she should have, convinced that if she held on to him tightly enough, he would stay. Their parents stood at the foot of his bed, unable to speak or cry. They had braced themselves for the cruel twists of his disease but failed to foresee that what would actually leave their teenage son brain-dead would be a drunk driver in a red pickup, a few blocks away from their home. This, however, was only half of the truth of what had happened that night.

The other half hung above Raya's head, hovering in the hospital room's arctic air, a secret only she could know.

Raya kept her eyes on Jace's bandaged face, aware of how every breath the blinking machines forced inside him extracted every drop of meaning from her bones. She ground her guilt between her teeth, counting down the last moments she could call herself "Hiraya." She did not care to be reminded of what she had become: She was now a wasted wish. A pile of useless spare parts. She had had one purpose. And now he was gone.

She clung to Jace's hand more tightly than she had held on to anything before. Mary Beth had been right about the strength of her grip.

Tonight, as she rushed to catch her train home, Raya used that grip to clutch the straps of the overstuffed bag swinging from her shoulder. The blue tote was made from ocean trash and shimmered like the sea. Raya was not too proud to admit that she envied the bag: The plastic bottles it used to be had been given a second chance to be new.

At twenty-five, Raya swore her bones creaked as loudly as the steps to her sixth-floor walk-up apartment. She didn't have to be a doctor to know that her diet of candy bars, sour gummies, and energy drinks did not do her any favors. But if living off simple sugars and caffeine was what it took to stay awake for the next four years of medical school, diabetes, osteoporosis, and renal failure would just have to sit in the waiting room and flip through old magazines until she could see them.

A man ran into her bag and scampered away. Raya apologized when she had meant to swear. Saying sorry and smiling were default responses that came with living on autopilot. They had their uses but sometimes left her mouth coated in ash. Raya grimaced and took a quick inventory of her belongings. A dented laptop, a dog-eared textbook, a binder containing her anatomy notes, and a purple notebook peeked through an assortment of ultra-processed snacks that had no business being called food.

As far as she could tell, nothing was missing. Her upcycled bag still strained to carry a downcycled dream. Raya conceded that she was never going to be half the doctor her brother would have been, but holding on to half of a dream was better than letting go of a dead one.

Raya transferred the tote to her other shoulder even if it didn't make a difference—invisible loads were at least twice as heavy as any that you could see. She slipped the bag off and then returned it to its bruised home. Her skin welcomed it back with a silent sigh. Old pain trained the body to miss it. Over time, flesh forgot the difference between what it had learned to tolerate and what gave it relief.

Wind blew through the subway tunnel, whipping Raya's newly dyed lavender hair. She slipped a hair tie off her wrist and secured her hair in a messy ponytail. The electric-blue elastic had matched her previous hair color but clashed with the pale purple. She made a mental note to replace it. Though she never colored her hair the same shade twice, she could not bring herself to throw any of her old hair ties out. The rainbow of retired elastics in her drawer grew each year, always a few days before Jace's death anniversary. Raya insisted that it was a coincidence just as staunchly as she denied that changing her appearance was the only way she could stand looking in the mirror. But today, despite her new hair, she took pains to avoid her reflection. The lavender only reminded her of Claire, a cadaver who shared her hair color.

Claire was not the corpse's real name. Following protocol, the bodies donated to Raya's gross anatomy class were anonymous. Naming her group's cadaver had not been Raya's idea, but she didn't care enough to object. Dissecting a dead body for the first time was just another item on her to-do list, no different from doing the laundry or organizing her notes. Numbness was the sole perk of living in the hollow of someone else's life and Raya took full advantage of it. It came in handy in class when it steadied her fingers as she unzipped the black body bag containing Claire.

Hollow eyes. Ashen skin. Purple hair. The elderly woman's cadaver was as cold and lifeless as the rest of the laboratory's equipment. Raya groaned in her head when her groupmates decided that thanking the corpse before dissecting it was the right thing to do. No one else seemed to notice that the body on the stainless steel table couldn't hear them. Nothing lived inside it anymore. Perhaps, Raya thought as she stared down at the dead body, only husks saw other husks for the empty shells that they were.

Thank you, Claire. The name's single syllable rolled off Raya's tongue without ceremony. Raya regarded the cadaver, shifting her weight on her feet. Its face remained just as sunken, stiff, and gray as it was before its christening. Giving it a name had changed nothing.

Then everything was churning inside Raya all at once.

A breath hissed between Raya's teeth as sharp as the truth that lodged behind her tonsils like a fish bone. She coughed twice but couldn't spit it out, and so she forced herself to swallow the reality whole: Names weren't spells cast on those given them, they bewitched those who said them out loud. While Raya's eyes still saw a dead body, her mind could not stop seeing the woman who had lived.

Wrinkles recorded the smiles that had reached Claire's eyes, along with all the frowns that didn't. The deep creases around her mouth logged a lifetime of laughter while the finer ones documented the words she spoke. But if Claire had felt any sorrow when she passed, death had taken great care to erase every trace of it.

Raya pursed her lips, struggling to describe what remained on the woman's face. She couldn't remember the last time she had seen anything like it in the mirror, not even when she dyed her hair the prettiest of pinks.

Contentment. Composure. Peace. Raya pasted each word over Claire like a label, only to then peel them off. She needed a word with more weight. Dying had stripped Claire of many things, but not the gravity that came with knowing that even in death, she was a gift with meaning and mass, and that not an inch of her was a waste of space.

Raya clasped her hands behind her back, resisting the urge to brush a stray strand of purple hair from Claire's temple. Their choice of hair dye, Raya thought, was the only thing they had in common. Serenity made its home in a lived life's marks, and without a place to nestle on Raya's face, it rolled off her cheeks and chin like tears.

Her brown eyes watered. She dried them on her lab coat's sleeve, blaming the formaldehyde lingering in the laboratory's filtered air. When fresh tears stung her eyes hours later at the subway station, Raya convinced herself that it must be on account of the preservative clinging to her clothes. She wiped them away with the back of her hand before squeezing through the subway car's doors.

Raya made her way through the crowd, her eyes flitting over their faces. She found a seat and began a timer in her head, counting down the seconds the passengers would share the train with her. Soon, each one of them was going to disappear, just as they did every evening.

Q

Q kicked himself for forgetting to top up his metro card. The musky perfume of the man in line in front of him at the top-up machine lanced his nose. Losing his sight had heightened his other senses, but this was one of those instances that he wished it had not.

He held his breath until the man left, adjusting the brown-paper-wrapped painting tucked under his arm. It would have been easier to deliver the piece to the gallery by cab, but he was stubborn that way. Only tourists used taxis. He stepped in front of the machine and squinted through his thick glasses, trying to make out the words on the screen one letter at a time. Cold sweat beaded on his nape. The woman in line behind him came to his rescue. Q thanked her, unable to tell from what he could see of her lips if she was wearing a smile or a frown.

Q made his way to the platform, tracing the guiding strip along the tiled floor with his walking stick. A blue blur darted in front of him and tripped over the stick, breaking it in two. Q tumbled to the floor, taking his painting with him. The blur mumbled an apology and ran off. A man helped Q to his feet and handed his painting back along with the pieces of his cane.

"Thank you." Q ran his hand over the painting. Its wrapper was torn, but the canvas was intact.

"Are you hurt?" The rasp in the man's voice gave Q the impression that the man either was twice his age or smoked two packs of cigarettes a day. The hint of cloves on his breath made Q inclined to believe that it was the latter and that his cigarette of choice was the same brand of Indonesian cigarettes his father used to hoard.

"I'm fine." Q put on a smile that he would have ripped off his own face if he had known how much it mimicked his father's. "Thanks."

A tinny voice crackled over the loudspeaker and announced that Q's train was going to be delayed. Q checked his watch, forgetting that he no longer wore one. He clenched his fists around his broken walking stick and squeezed his eyes shut even though he didn't have to. He already lived in the dark. Tears watered his throat. He imagined that tonight, after people bid on the last pieces of his dream, he would spend his final evening in his empty apartment staring up at a ceiling he could no longer see.

He was never going to know if the blue blur had meant his apology or if the stranger who had just helped him had smiled before he walked away. He was never going to be able to look anyone in the eye and see their true intentions. The world would blindside him just as his father had and all he could do was brace himself and wait to be knocked down.

Wind howled through the tunnel and blew across the platform. The gray storm raging behind Q's eyelids wailed over it. He pulled his shoulders back and took a step forward, with neither a walking stick nor the will to keep himself from falling. He gripped his unfinished painting and hurled it onto the tracks and into the waiting dark.

"What time does the Elsewhere Express depart?"

Frequently Asked Questions
THE ELSEWHERE EXPRESS
PASSENGER HANDBOOK

Raya

Meandering thoughts carried their owners farther than any subway line could. The woman seated next to Raya was in the process of boarding a daydream without having to buy a ticket or swipe a card.

A small smile played over the woman's glossy, overlined lips as she stroked the orange cat purring on her lap with her glittery acrylic extensions. Each of her fingernails contained a galaxy, and every star in them, a wish. Her fondest one was to put up an animal shelter. No, a sanctuary. On a sprawling piece of land where animals could roam free. Cats. Dogs. Bunnies. Horses. She scratched behind her cat's ears, strolling through a moonlit meadow only she could see. She strode past a clear pond where unwanted goldfish didn't turn gray or grow monstrously big. She paused mid-step. Fish, she thought, would be nice for dinner. She had a couple of sole fillets in her freezer that she could bake with a creamy sauce of butter, garlic, and lemon. Oh, and mustard. It was her secret ingredient. And the name of her orange cat. Mustard rubbed its head against her palm and purred.

Across from Mustard, a man with a neatly trimmed beard contemplated the mud splattered on his right pant leg, not because it was particularly interesting, but because the largest of the stains resembled a black hole. He and Lily had watched a movie about black holes on their third date. The movie was terrible. The date was not. It ended in her bed, their clothes in a tangle around their ankles. Six months later, Lily would tattoo his name in cursive on the inside of her right wrist. Though the bright scarlet letters were as fine as silk thread, they clanked inside his skull like iron chains whenever Lily held his hand. It was at that precise moment, he realized, that he and Lily had started to rust. He wondered if Lily was married now and if she had any kids, and what would have happened if he had not left her for a job that took him as far away from the chain on her arm as possible. He thought about the little mole on her collarbone, her perfectly shaped toes, and all the wonderful things she could do with her tongue. *Lily. Lily. Lily.* If he closed his eyes, he could smell the coconut shampoo in her untamable red hair.

Standing in front of the man daydreaming of an ex-lover named Lily, a young man with more piercings along his shaved brow than Raya had on her entire body slipped on a pair of black headphones. Haydn's String Quartet in E-flat Major, opus 20, number 1, swept away the noise of the day, making room for all the formulas he would need for his two-hour-long actuarial math exam the next morning. An oak tree's thick canopy rustled above him, heavy with bright, glowing numbers where there should have been leaves. He stretched across the grass and ran his palms over a patch of wildflowers, stirring a scent reminiscent of roses and mint.

Raya did not have to hear the music flowing through the man's headphones to know that it had carried him to a place far beyond the subway line's last stop. His gaze was like everyone else's around her: glazed over and distant, regardless of whether they stared into space or at their phones. Unlike her fellow passengers, Raya kept her thoughts on a much shorter leash, never allowing them to go farther than two seats away. They made do with strolls through a stranger's brown coat buttons, another person's hearing aid, and the downward turn of the mouth on a girl who looked much too young to be wearing a permanent frown.

But today their leash was even shorter. Raya kept a closer eye on her thoughts at this time of year—they were always extra fidgety around Jace's death anniversary. She ordered them to sit down while she switched on her earphones' noise-canceling mode.

Soft static flooded her ears. Raya couldn't bear to listen to music, not since she had stopped writing it. Songs were terrible houseguests. They never took off their shoes, they poked around drawers without permission, and they always left a mess. White noise had far better manners and had the good sense to stay out of locked cabinets and rooms. Raya closed her eyes. A fresh floral fragrance drifted past her nose. Someone close by, she thought, had the most incredible rose-and-mint perfume. It slipped inside her, painting a moonlit scene behind her eyelids.

Wildflowers.

Grass.

An oak tree heavy with branches of glowing math formulas instead of leaves.

Raya usually banished daydreams before they whisked her away, but tonight, she made an exception. Her station was close and a reverie about a strange number tree could not possibly take her very far. A symphony of birdsongs and violins broke through the earphones' static. Raya's eyes flew open.

She was no longer in the subway car. An empty vintage train had taken its place.

YOUR ITINERARY

MEET THE CONDUCTOR

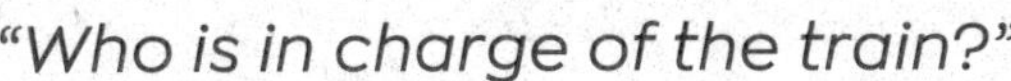

Frequently Asked Questions
THE ELSEWHERE EXPRESS
PASSENGER HANDBOOK

Lily

"Good evening." An angular woman walked up to the Elsewhere Express's newest passenger dressed in a crisp, black uniform, her thick, wavy red hair threatening to burst free from her gold-banded felt cap. A cherry-tinted smile lit her hazel eyes.

"Welcome aboard the Elsewhere Express." She extended a white-gloved hand. A delicate tattoo peeked out from her glove, spelling out a man's name on her wrist in a cursive script that looked like red thread. "I'm Lily, the train's conductor."

Declaring that her name was Lily was both a lie and the truth. Lily was indeed the name of the woman whose likeness she wore like a coat, but it was not the name she was born with. That name did not matter, not as much as giving the Elsewhere Express's newest arrival the best boarding experience possible. The conductor tugged her felt cap lower over her borrowed forehead, trying to contain Lily's thick hair. The man who had daydreamed of Lily while riding the subway had done an excellent job of fleshing out his ex-lover. Every detail, from the inked name on her wrist to each rebellious strand of red hair, was exceptionally clear. Though the conductor wasn't a fan of Lily's fiery hair color, she did enjoy the smell of her organic, coconut-scented shampoo. The fragrance was what ultimately swayed her to choose to look like Lily this evening instead of someone else.

Selecting a face to wear for the night shift never took the conductor long. Her options were limited to the daydreams of the passengers in the train car the Elsewhere Express's newest arrival departed from. She browsed through the reveries like clothes on a vintage store's rack, searching for ones that were clean, smelled nice, and didn't have any holes. Faces of lovers were always a great find and the conductor did not hesitate to snap them up. They were sharp and very detailed, almost as vivid as the teary daydreams about loves that were lost.

At first, the conductor didn't understand why it was necessary to don a fresh face each time she welcomed a passenger on board. As the years passed, it became clearer. With so few memories left of her life before boarding the train, slipping on the semblance of a person from the world outside the Elsewhere Express helped the conductor to remember that once, just like the rest of the crew, she had been a new passenger too. This allowed her to offer new arrivals empathy like a welcome drink, minus the alcohol, miniature paper umbrella, and fancy straw.

The passenger scrambled off an emerald-green velvet couch. "Where am I? What's going on? What happened to the subway?"

"I understand how strange all of this must seem," Lily said in the tone that grown-ups used when speaking to young children. "I'll explain everything at the passenger orientation. I just need to see your train ticket first."

The passenger backed away and tripped on a hand-knotted Persian rug. She fell to the marquetry floor, scattering the contents of her blue tote.

Lily rushed over and knelt by her side, avoiding two chocolate-and-peanut-butter candy bars and a binder bursting with handwritten notes. A canned orange-flavored energy drink rolled past her knee. "Are you all right?"

"Oh god." Color drained from the passenger's face. "I'm going crazy."

"You're not." Lily picked up one of the passenger's six blue pens from the floor and handed it back. "You've switched trains."

The passenger dropped the pen. "I . . . I don't remember getting off the subway."

"Wonderful." Lily's smile grew brighter. "I'll make sure to let the boarding team know."

"The boarding team?" The passenger's lips paled as though she was about to either faint or vomit.

"They're the team responsible for making the boarding experience as smooth as possible. And what could be more seamless than not having any memory of how you got here?"

"This isn't happening." The passenger drew her legs to her chest and tucked her head to her knees. "Wake up. Wake up."

"You're awake. Look around you." Lily admired the vintage train car's interior. A backlit, curved, onyx ceiling cast a soft glow over the car, warming its cherrywood walls. Couches upholstered in lush velvet stood in place of the subway's blue plastic seats. Ornate gilded frames of varying sizes leaned against the wall at the far end of the train car, waiting for painted worlds to fill them. "I think that you'll find that the Elsewhere Express is quite the upgrade from the subway. And this is just the boarding car. Wait until you see the rest of the train."

The passenger looked up, her eyes wild and flashing. "If this is real, prove it. Stop the train." She shoveled her things back into her bag and got to her feet. "Let me off right now."

"I'm sorry, but I can't do that." Lily stood up and smoothed her blazer. "The Elsewhere Express doesn't make any stops."

"Then how could I have boarded it?" The passenger's knuckles hardened around her bag's straps.

"The Elsewhere Express doesn't pick up passengers at stations." Lily repeated a script that lived on her tongue. "You boarded it at the end of all your dreams at a quarter past your heaviest sigh. The train caught you when you floated away."

"Floated away?" The passenger's voice climbed in pitch. "Are you serious? If you won't stop this train then I'm going to find someone who will."

Lily straightened her cap. "Be my guest, but that might be a bit difficult without a door."

The passenger's eyes darted around the carriage's doorless walls. "What the hell is going on?"

"Even before you got here, you'd drifted away from your own life. Everyone on this train had." Lily flicked a piece of lint from her shoulder and watched it float away. "It might surprise you how little a person without purpose weighs."

"Are the Elsewhere Express's tickets refundable?"

Frequently Asked Questions
THE ELSEWHERE EXPRESS
PASSENGER HANDBOOK

Raya

Both of Raya's parents suffered from hypertension, and she had always known that it was just a matter of time before genetics caught up with her artery walls. She did not, however, expect it to happen this soon. Still, it seemed that death was here, and she was grateful that her passing had been painless and quick. It was far more than she deserved.

Lily motioned to a velvet couch. "Perhaps you should sit down."

Raya gripped the seat's carved arm and lowered herself into the plush, green cushion, barely able to hear the woman over the blood pounding in her ears.

"Can I get you some water?" Lily offered.

Raya fixed her eyes on the looping marquetry design on the floor, a crisscrossing knot without a beginning or an end. It was, she thought, a fitting symbol for an afterlife she did not believe in until now. "How did it happen?"

"How did what happen?" Lily took a seat across from her.

"How did I die? Was it a stroke?"

"Oh. No, no. You misunderstand." A bemused smile teased the corners of Lily's mouth. "You aren't dead."

"I'm not?" Raya winced, hating that she sounded disappointed. "But you said that I floated away from my life."

"You did, but not because you died. You drifted away because you were too light."

Raya squeezed her eyes shut, rubbing her temples. "None of this makes any sense."

"And yet here you are." Lily laced her gloved hands over her lap.

"Where is 'here'?" Raya threw a glance at the train car's windows. Thick black curtains, embroidered with the same pattern of golden knots as the design on the floor, hid the view.

"As I said," Lily stated with a practiced patience, "you're on the Elsewhere Express."

Raya pushed herself off the couch. "There's been a mistake. I'm not supposed to be here."

Lily nodded. "I understand."

"You do?"

"Completely. I've been doing this job for a very long time. I've met many passengers who insisted that they didn't belong here. Like you, they were convinced that they had a purpose too. *What do you do? What do you want to be? What are your plans for the future?* The Elsewhere Express is full of people who whipped out answers to these questions like some form of identification, believing this was proof that the train had mixed them up with someone else. But purpose has little to do with 'what' and everything to do with 'why,' don't you think?"

"I'll tell you what I think." Raya gripped her tote's straps, digging her fingernails into her palm. "I think that if you don't let me off right now, I'm going to—"

"You missed something." Lily reached beneath the emerald couch. She stood up, a purple notebook in her hand. Raya snatched it from her.

Raya had not opened the notebook since Jace died, but she could not bear to discard her old songs. A piece of rectangular black paper stuck out from between its pages and brushed the side of her thumb. She tugged it free. Shimmering gold ink swirled over it like oil in water and twisted into intersecting loops. "It . . . it's moving."

"It's called the eternal knot." Lily pointed to the identical design embroidered onto her blazer's breast pocket. "It's the train's symbol. You'll find it all around the Elsewhere Express. Floors. Curtains. Tableware. Linens." Her gaze fell on the piece of paper in Raya's hand. "Train tickets."

Raya's fingers trembled over the twisting knot. Beneath it, elegant letters twinkled like stars and spelled out her name in gold. A simpler font printed along the bottom of the ticket stated the name of the subway station she had caught her train from and the date and time she had boarded it.

"May I?" Lily said.

Raya dropped the ticket into Lily's palm as though it were on fire.

Lily ran her eyes over it. "Everything appears to be in order. I'm very happy to officially welcome you aboard, Ms. Sia. As you can see, there hasn't been any mistake. You're supposed to be here. This proves it." She held the ticket out to Raya.

"It proves nothing." Raya folded her arms over her chest. "I've never seen that thing in my life. I don't want it."

"The ticket has been issued in your name." Lily tucked the ticket into Raya's bag. "It's yours."

"I don't care." Raya yanked the ticket out and crumpled it. Her hand tingled. She opened her fingers and caught the paper melting into her palm, leaving its gold knot and words imprinted on her skin. She gasped and frantically rubbed her hand.

"Convenient, isn't it?" Lily peeled off her glove and turned her hand over. An identical knot shimmered and coiled on her palm like a living tattoo. "This way, no one needs to worry about losing their ticket. The previous conductor came up with it. He's quite the tinkerer. Now, if you'll follow me, we can head to—"

"I'm not going anywhere with you." Raya lifted her chin. "None of this is real."

"That depends on how you define 'real,' Ms. Sia." Lily pulled her glove back on and strode over to the empty picture frames at the end of the carriage. She picked one up and held it at arm's length in front of the paneled wall. "Is what's real what you can see and touch?" She peered through the frame and moved it an inch to the left. "Or does it include things that are invisible and intangible?" she said, alternately looking through the frame and adjusting its position over the wall. "Like thoughts?"

"I'm not listening. You're not here. We're not having this conversation."

"As you wish." Lily let go of the frame.

Raya flinched. There were few things that she hated more than hearing things shatter. She had not been with Jace when his car flipped over twice, but this did not stop the sound of crumpling metal from grating in her skull whenever it got too quiet. Real memories and made-up ones sounded the same in the dark.

"If you're waiting for the frame to fall," Lily said, "it won't."

Raya flung her gaze to the empty frame. It hung in the air as though held steady by an invisible hook. A moonlit meadow stretched inside it. A bird flew out of the frame, darting past Raya. She jumped back.

"I won't say another word if you don't want me to, Ms. Sia." Lily looked through the frame. "But first, allow me to show you what 'real' means on the Elsewhere Express."

"Where are the train's doors located?"

Frequently Asked Questions
THE ELSEWHERE EXPRESS
PASSENGER HANDBOOK

Raya

A breeze blew through the frame's gilded borders, perfuming the vintage train car with roses and mint. "That scent." Raya inhaled deeply. "I've smelled it before." A wispy, fragrant memory wafted across her mind. "On the subway."

"Ah, yes. That can happen sometimes when Mr. Nakamura and his team set up the boarding car. Incoming passengers catch glimpses of it. Some can hear and smell it. I just love the scent of wildflowers."

Raya surveyed the meadow through the frame, her heart racing faster than the train. A large oak tree stood to the left of the scene, its canopy of glowing numbers rustling in time with a chorus of unseen birds and a violin quartet. A golden retriever ran past the oak and chased a husky around a pond. Black-and-white kittens tumbled over one another a few feet from them. If the scene was an illusion, it was a convincing one.

And if it was the truth, then Raya was much farther from home than she had thought. "What is all this?"

"It's the product of a lot of hard work. The boarding team outdid themselves tonight." Lily puffed her chest out. "The passengers in your subway car deserve a lot of credit too, of course."

"What do the passengers have to do with anything?" Raya said.

"The boarding team's work is only as good as the daydreams that are available to use as décor. Last night's setup was lovely, but not as charming as today's. A woman on the Singapore MRT had been thinking about a Yayoi Kusama exhibit she had just visited. And so Mr. Nakamura and his team brought it to life. The giant polka-dot trail was gorgeous. Hopping from dot to dot, however, was a bit tricky." Lily let out a small laugh. "But don't worry, we shouldn't have any problems walking over grass."

Lily's words scattered in Raya's mind like ten different jigsaw puzzles tossed onto the floor.

"I know it's a lot to process." Lily selected a second empty frame from the collection leaning against the train car's wall and handed it to Raya. "It will all make sense soon."

Raya frowned at the frame. "What am I supposed to do with this?"

"Just hold on to it for now." Lily set her hands on the bottom border of the floating frame and pushed down, expanding it until it was the shape and size of a door. She stepped through it and looked over her shoulder. "Coming, Ms. Sia? The boarding car's exit is this way."

Lily had been wrong about how easy it would be to walk over grass.

Though Raya was standing on solid ground, she was adrift. Each step led her deeper into a flood of questions steadily rising above her neck. The world inside the gilded frame refused to fit in any of her mind's premade boxes, no matter how hard she tried to shove it in. Its grass was green, its air crisp, and the large chestnut-colored horse that had galloped over to say hello smelled like grain and warm hay. While her senses agreed that the meadow was real, a tingling deep in her bones challenged all she heard, saw, touched, and smelled. "What is this place?"

"The boarding car," Lily said. "Stunning, isn't it?"

"I thought the carriage we came from was the boarding car?" Raya glanced back at the frame they had just stepped through. A star-filled horizon stared back at her.

"We haven't left it." Lily patted the oak's trunk. "But now you can view and appreciate the décor the boarding team meticulously prepared to welcome you on board. Do you like it?"

A force, the kind that pushed against you when you took a sharp turn, shoved Raya to the grass. The ground rumbled against her cheek. She sat up, her palms pressed to the vibrating soil. "We're moving."

"Like I said, the train never stops."

Raya stood up and spat out dirt. "This isn't a train."

"Do you ride the subway often, Ms. Sia?"

"Yes. Why?"

"Good. That makes my job a lot easier. A stranger to trains would have a harder time understanding what the Elsewhere Express is. A regular rider such as yourself should be more than familiar with the vacant stares that fill a train car."

The glazed stares of the subway passengers who had left their seats and disappeared into their daydreams flashed in Raya's mind. "What if I am?"

"This means that you already know the truth about trains," Lily said. "Every train, no matter how full, is—"

"Empty." The word slipped from Raya's lips so quietly that she wondered if she had said it out loud.

Lily nodded. "Thoughts carry people away. Once created, thoughts don't just vanish into thin air. They can't. They need a place to go." Lily looked out at the meadow. "And so, those thoughts come here."

Raya's head throbbed.

"Some passengers find it easier to grasp what the Elsewhere Express is when it's broken up into parts." Lily gazed up at the canopy of glowing numbers. "This tree, for example, grew from the imagination of a young man pondering his math exam."

"You're telling me that this whole place is someone's daydream?"

Lily shook her head. "No, that would be impossible. There aren't any daydreams this large. This tree is from the young man, but the meadow is from a daydream of a passenger who was picturing the animal sanctuary she's hoping to build one day. Mr. Nakamura, in my opinion, couldn't have made a better choice. Many on the Elsewhere Express see the train as a kind of sanctuary too."

Lily's words screeched like fingernails down a chalkboard in Raya's ears.

"Is something wrong, Ms. Sia?"

Bile churned in Raya's stomach. "The Elsewhere Express is a sanctuary . . ."

Lily smiled. "That's correct."

"A place where the lost and helpless go." The edges of Raya's voice hardened and hissed like iron quenched in water.

Lily's smile slipped off. "That's not what I meant."

Raya pulled her spine as straight as she could. "I didn't ask to be rescued."

"Neither did anyone force you to board this train, Ms. Sia. All the Elsewhere Express did was open its doors." Lily refastened her smile, tugging it wider than before. "And speaking of doors, the boarding car's exit is over there." She gestured to an empty stretch of grass to the left of the tree.

Raya squinted at the fluttering leafy shadows. "There's nothing there."

"That's why we brought the frame. Do you mind holding it up?"

Raya kept the frame firmly at her side. She had clung to the edge of reason from the moment she found herself inside a strange vintage train car. To do as Lily asked was to pry her fingers from this cliff and fall. "Then what? We step into another train car that looks nothing like a train car? I drown in more questions that you'll continue to ignore?"

"The sooner we leave the boarding car, the sooner you'll have your answers, Ms. Sia. I'll tell you everything you need to know at the passenger orientation."

Raya clenched and unclenched her jaw. If she was going to have any hope of finding her way home, she needed to know where she was. Her fingers trembled around the gilded frame. She lifted it to the level of her eye, copying what she had seen Lily do. Blurry golden strings coiled, twisted, and twirled inside it.

"They're threads of thought," Lily said.

"Threads of what?"

"Every thought that passes through your mind is connected to something else. Memories. Lies. Truths. They're all woven together. No idea or daydream stands alone. It's the fabric this train and everything you see around you is made of. Including the door that leads out of this boarding car."

Raya's insides twisted as the threads did. As strange as the sight was, it was the first thing that felt truly familiar since she had found herself on the Elsewhere Express. Her thoughts were just as tangled, binding her to the night she lost the very reason she was born. Three memories twisted around one another to form a noose: a stolen tube of lipstick, a song, and frantic knocking on her childhood bedroom's door. It tightened around her neck each time she dared to dream of a life other than the one stuffed inside her upcycled bag. "I still don't see a door."

"It's difficult to see through the clearest glass when the window is shaking as much as this frame is. Allow me." Lily took the frame from Raya.

Raya shoved her trembling hands as deep as they would go into her pockets, remembering how just a few hours ago, she had gripped a scalpel and pressed it into a cadaver's flesh without the slightest quiver. She was used to living her life from a distance, watching herself from the back row as she mouthed someone else's lines on a stage. Acting brave was easy as a stand-in, but much less so without the costume of someone else's dream.

"The frames you'll find around the Elsewhere Express serve the same purpose as they do on a gallery's walls. They give the person who looks through them perspective." Lily lifted the frame an inch higher and left it to hover in the air. "And focus."

Raya looked through the frame. A short distance from the oak, a circular patch of wildflowers cast a silver-blue light. "All I see are some very strange flowers."

"Congratulations. You've found the exit." Lily beamed like someone whose puppy had just learned a new trick. "The doors on the Elsewhere Express look a bit different from the doors that you're familiar with."

"A bit different?"

Lily laughed. "All right. Maybe a lot. The train's doors can look like anything, really, and tend to move around when they get bored."

Raya quirked a brow. "Sorry?"

"Have you ever had a thought that stayed perfectly still, Ms. Sia? Thoughts are as alive as the people who created them. On this train, we can shape thoughts into the most amazing things, but we cannot change their nature. Any thought, big or small, short or long, pretty or monstrous, can lead you anywhere. You don't have to be a passenger on the Elsewhere Express to know that a song can be a rabbit hole to your childhood, a heartbreak, or your first love. The thoughts curling up from a cup of hot cocoa can be a tunnel to the day you learned that Santa wasn't real. The picture frames reveal the doors hiding in plain sight."

"But you saw the door without using one." Raya stared at the glowing wildflowers, unable to look away.

"I didn't," Lily said. "I heard it. The doors are scattered around the train. They sing to each other to keep themselves from feeling lonely. Most passengers can't hear them. That's why the Elsewhere Express has a team whose sole task is to make sure that there are frames available in every train car for those who need it. Not everyone has an ear for music."

A heaviness poured into Raya's chest like plaster, molding itself in the cavity left by a withered lullaby.

"Ms. Sia? Is everything all right?"

Raya avoided Lily's eyes. "I . . . was just wondering how a wildflower door worked."

"It works the same way all doors do." Lily smiled. "We go through it."

YOUR ITINERARY

WELCOME DRINKS AT
THE LOTUS LOUNGE

"Is alcohol allowed on the train?"

Frequently Asked Questions
THE ELSEWHERE EXPRESS
PASSENGER HANDBOOK

Raya

Raya blinked.

And wished she hadn't. Had her eyes been open, she might have been able to explain how she had fallen through a patch of wildflowers and was now lying on her back, staring up at two luminescent whale sharks swimming across a purple sky. She tried to stand. Her limbs refused. Every bone and muscle in her body felt as though they had just been pulled, stretched, squeezed, and then poured out.

Lily stood over her, offering a hand. "Passing through the train's doors can make you dizzy."

Raya clutched Lily's hand, a part of her hoping that her fingers would pass through Lily like smoke. But Lily's palm was solid and warm, leaving no doubt that she was made of flesh, blood, and bone.

"You look disappointed." Lily helped Raya to her feet. "Were you still hoping to prove that I was some kind of hallucination?"

A wave of nausea washed over Raya. She leaned against a round table for two and closed her eyes. She drew slow breaths and waited for the room to stop spinning. She peeked through her lashes. Towering white petals grazed the purple sky, framing a kaleidoscope of iridescent fish swimming through cotton-candy-pink clouds. The whales circled the school and swam away. A rainbow-colored jellyfish, larger than both whales combined, took their place. It floated over Raya, a wishing star just beyond her reach.

Lily gazed up at the galaxy of fish. "The sky's my favorite thing about the Lotus."

"The Lotus?" Raya struggled not to be entranced by the lights swimming in her eyes.

"The Elsewhere Express's award-winning rice wine bar." Lily grinned. "It's one of the most popular cars on the train."

"We're at a bar?" Raya tore her eyes from the sky. "You said that we were headed to the passenger orientation."

"We are, but the welcome drinks are part of our boarding tradition. I didn't want you to miss out."

Raya planted her hands on her hips and groaned. "Let's just get this over with."

"You'll love the cocktails here." Lily picked up a black ceramic rice wine bottle lying on its side on a nearby table. "Let me just put this door back in place first," she said, righting the bottle. "It's one of the few on the train that doesn't wander around. I think it knows that the view of the sky doesn't get much better than this. This door usually takes the shape of a bottle, but occasionally, it shifts into a vase or bowl depending on its mood." Lily held the bottle to her ear, nodding to music only she could hear. "And it likes to sing love songs."

Raya folded her arms over her chest, stopping herself from trying to catch a note. "Look, I really don't feel like having a drink right now. Since you've already found the door, why don't we just use it and head to wherever we're supposed to have the orientation?"

"You can't exit the Lotus through this door." Lily set the bottle down. "The train's doors only work in one direction."

"Of course." Raya sighed. "How efficient."

"Good evening, ladies, what can I get you tonight?" A voice, effervescent like a vodka tonic, drifted over Raya's shoulder.

Raya spun its way.

A smiling spindly young man in a smart dark shirt and matching vest walked up to a long granite counter. His sleeves were rolled up to his elbows, exposing the host of angels tattooed in black and white over his arms. The tip of a wing curled up on his neck behind his collar. "Welcome to the Lotus." He rested his palms on the counter. "I'm Aki, your bartender this evening."

"Aki, this is Ms. Sia," Lily said. "Our newest passenger."

"It's a pleasure to meet you, Ms. Sia." Aki poured a milky white liquid from a gold makgeolli kettle into a cocktail shaker with ice. "Please, make yourself comfortable." He gestured to the red barstools in front of the counter, exposing the golden knot twisting over his palm.

Raya slid onto one of the stools without saying a word. If she had met Aki at any other bar, she would have forgotten him as soon as she had paid her tab. Aki was stylish, but not original; friendly, but not obtrusive; personable, but seamlessly blended into the bar's décor. He suited his job perfectly. It was always better if you couldn't remember the face of the person you poured sorrows out to over too many shots of tequila. It was the same reason priests hid behind a confessional box's screen. But Raya had met Aki inside a giant lotus flower beneath a purple sky, a place where the mundane and forgettable stood out. The utterly ordinary bartender made everything around her feel stranger.

"Can I offer you a makgeolli margarita?" Aki said. "We also have an excellent selection of tapuey, sake, brem, sato, and Shaoxing wine, if you'd like to try something else."

Lily hopped onto the stool next to Raya's. "Aki also distills his own spirits. Happiness, melancholy, restlessness. Name it. He won't tell me what he mixes into his pear-ginger saketini, but whatever it is, it's incredible. My guess is that it's a jigger of calm."

"Sorry, it's a trade secret." Aki winked. "But speaking of ginger"—Aki eyed Lily's hair—"I think this is the first time I've ever seen you as a redhead."

"My choices were rather limited this evening," Lily said. "But I do love the scent of her shampoo. And her name."

Aki set a bowl of spicy lotus root crisps on the counter. "What is it?"

"Lily."

Raya stiffened. "I thought you were Lily."

"I am. For now."

"What's that supposed to mean?" Raya jumped off the barstool. Names were important. They told you and others who you were. When she called herself "Hiraya," she had been a dream come true. When she dropped her old name, she had acknowledged her failure to live up to everything she was meant to be. People lied about many things, but those who lied about who they were were the worst of them. You could not trust anyone who did not own their misery. "If you aren't really Lily, then who are you? What else are you lying about?"

Aki and Lily exchanged small smiles.

Raya glared at them. "Did I say something funny?"

"I'm sorry," Aki said. "I just remembered that I said exactly the same thing to Lily when I boarded. Lily wasn't Lily then, of course." He looked at her, rubbing his chin. "I think you were 'Felipe' that evening. Or was it 'Fred'?"

"I've had so many names. I honestly can't remember." Lily turned to Raya. "I told you who I am, Ms. Sia. Tonight, my name is Lily. Tomorrow evening, when I welcome the train's next passenger, it will be something else. What people call me doesn't matter. I'm the conductor of this train, whatever my name is." She reaffixed her smile. "Have you decided what you'd like to drink?"

"I don't want a damn drink." Raya slammed her fist on the counter, rattling the bowl of lotus crisps. "I want answers."

"And you'll have them," Lily said. "But having a drink or two before the orientation might help to—"

A loud crash cut Lily off. She jumped in her seat and elbowed a cocktail shaker, sending a waterfall of ice cubes, rice wine, and a measure of joy cascading over the floor.

Raya twisted around. A chair lay broken in the shadow of a petal wall partially hiding a dark figure behind it.

"What in the—" Aki leapt over the bar and ran toward the crumpled man.

"I apologize for this disturbance, Ms. Sia." Lily dabbed a napkin on the wet spot on her sleeve. "Why don't you pour yourself a drink while I get this sorted? I won't be long." She set her jaw and marched over to the figure on the floor.

"Wait." Raya hurried after her. "What's going on?"

"It appears that we have a stowaway."

Aki helped the man to his feet. At full height, the man stood a foot taller than the bartender. The jellyfish's pulsing glow alternately lit and hid his face, revealing his features in varying combinations. Brooding eyebrows and a sharp jawline. A widow's peak and a mouth resting in a slight curl. A slim nose and hooded, almond-shaped gray eyes. A strong neck and layers of dark waves that fell just above his broad shoulders. Depending on where the shadows fell, the young man looked either beautiful or broken. In full light, Raya thought, he was both.

The thickest pair of eyeglasses dangled from the bridge of the man's slightly crooked nose. He pushed the glasses up, squinting through their cracked lenses. He pulled them off. His eyes quivered, growing large. His hand flew over a gasp. The jellyfish reached down and flicked his hair from his forehead. The man jumped back, stumbling against a petal wall.

Lily strode up to him. "How did you get on board?"

He scrambled to his feet. "Who are you? Where am I?"

Raya's heart stopped and started, unsure if it should be racing or slowing down. There was a guilty comfort in finding someone who looked and sounded as lost as she felt. She lowered her gaze to hide her relief and found the stowaway's shoes. One sneaker was a shade lighter than charcoal, the other, midnight blue.

"I'm asking the questions," Lily said. "How did you get here?"

Raya held her breath. If the man had managed to stow away on the Elsewhere Express, then he had to know the way off it.

His gray eyes shifted. "I don't remember."

Lily squeezed the strap of the satchel slung across her chest. "*Try.*"

"I'm sorry, but I honestly don't know how I got here. I don't even know where 'here' is. All I know is that I was—" The man's gaze retreated to the tips of his mismatched shoes.

"You were what?" Lily folded her arms over her blazer, wrinkling it.

"I was on a train." The stranger kept his eyes down.

Raya leaned forward on her toes, straining to hear him over the rush of blood in her head. "And?"

"And then I . . . wasn't. It's difficult to describe, but I felt as though I was . . . um . . ."

"Poured out?" Raya said, remembering how she had felt like a puddle on a floor.

His eyes widened. "How did you know?"

"Aki, look." Lily pointed to a sake bottle behind the toppled chair's shattered leg. "The back door. That's how he boarded."

"That's impossible. I locked it." Aki scooped up the bottle, squeezed one eye shut, and peered into its mouth. Color drained from his thin lips. "I'm sorry. It won't happen again."

"Leave us," Lily said.

"But—"

"Now."

"I'll be in the back room if you need anything." Aki slunk away, his thin fingers wringing the sake bottle's neck.

Raya did not understand how doors on a giant lotus flower worked, but she was almost certain that if Aki could have squeezed himself through the sake bottle's mouth and hidden there, he would have.

Lily's eyes bored into the man. "I'd like to see your ticket."

"What ticket?" he said.

Raya spied a sliver of black paper sticking out from the man's coat pocket. "That ticket."

The man glanced down, raising his sharp brows. He pulled the paper out, gaping at the eternal knot twisting over it.

"May I see that?" Lily said.

The man handed the ticket to her, his eyes anchored on the moving knot.

Lily looked up from the ticket with a smile so broad and bright that it made Raya question if it had ever slipped off. "It's a pleasure to welcome you aboard the Elsewhere Express, Mr. Philips. I'm Lily, the train's conductor. I apologize for the confusion. We weren't expecting you. This is the first time I've had the pleasure of welcoming more than one passenger in one evening. I'll have the manifest updated immediately." She handed the ticket back to him. It melted into his palm, leaving a golden knot shimmering over his skin. "Luckily, you're just in time for the orientation."

Q

"Lucky" was not a word Q would ever use to describe himself. He was born in the Year of the Goat, the unluckiest of all the signs in the Chinese zodiac. His mother made sure he was never dressed in green, blue, or black, or accessories made of wood. Spicy and oily foods were harder to avoid, but Connie was determined to counter as much of the bad luck her only son was born with as she could. A part of Q always wondered if the reason she had shipped him off to boarding school was so that four years' worth of bland dining hall fare would chase away whatever bad luck remained. A bigger part guessed that it was because he reminded her too much of his late father. Whatever the reason, anyone who followed Q's career as one of the world's most celebrated portraitists had to agree that Connie's plan had worked. For a while.

Q had never introduced himself with a lie before, but when the woman who called herself Lily had asked him where he had come from, it had slipped off his tongue faster than the truth could. Truths were heavy and rough around the edges, and his truth was more cumbersome than most. Explaining where he had really come from was not something that he was prepared to admit to strangers. Or himself. And even if he were, he had neither the time nor the inclination to tell a story that began when he was a boy. The odd scene inside a giant Lotus flower was the kind of dream that he didn't want to waste a second of. Dreams were the only places left where he could see.

Q was thirteen when the stars vanished, but the loss of his night vision wasn't anything a flashlight and a good memory couldn't fix. The biggest consequence of not being able to see in the dark was tripping over his easel and breaking his nose. His bridge had not healed straight, but he wasn't concerned. Other people's faces fascinated him infinitely more than his own. Lily's face was no exception.

Lily, Q suspected, would be the type of client to fidget while sitting for him. As someone who had made a name for himself capturing a face's truth, he was quick to spot masks. The one Lily wore seemed new and ill fitting, her neck's taut sinews betraying the struggle she waged to keep it on. Q doubted that Lily was even her real name.

The young woman standing next to the woman who was claiming to be Lily, however, appeared to be her opposite. Her brown eyes didn't bother to lie when they openly stared at him with an odd mix of confusion and relief. They were either not afraid to be honest or not used to being seen. The portraitist in him itched to discover which, but a more urgent question demanded an answer. He looked at Lily. "Sorry, but did you say that this was a train?"

"Finally." The woman with naked eyes extended her hand. "I'm Raya, the only other person here who can see that this is anything but a train."

"Q." He shook her hand. Nothing in his dreams had ever felt this warm. He held it tighter. Dreams were fleeting and fragile and he had learned to scour them for anything that could keep the morning from dragging him back into the dark. No detail was too small. His eyes were starved and content with scraps. Once, he clung to a blade of grass and bought himself an extra ten minutes of sleep and then woke up profoundly regretting all the different shades of green he had taken for granted.

Raya winced.

"I'm sorry." Q dropped her hand, realizing how hard he had been squeezing it. Dreaming did not give him permission to be rude.

"The Elsewhere Express is a train just like the one you departed from, Mr. Philips," Lily said, "but also so much more. I'll explain everything in more detail at the orientation. I just have to fetch a few things we'll need." Lily slipped through a curtain behind the granite counter.

Q smiled at the glowing jellyfish floating in the purple sky. "I've outdone myself."

"Sorry?" Raya said.

"I've outdone myself with this dream." A smile crinkled the corners of his eyes. "It reminds me of the ones I used to have as a boy. I thought that I had outgrown them, but I guess I was wrong." Words slipped out easily when he didn't have to worry if they made him look silly or made sense. When he woke up, nothing he said or did inside this giant flower was going to matter in the slightest. So he was going to steal as much imagined happiness as he could. He had the rest of his life to be angry.

"You aren't dreaming," Raya said.

Q smirked. "If only that were true."

"Listen to me." Raya gripped his arms. "This is real. *I'm* real. I'm trapped here. And so are you."

"Trapped?" Q choked on a chuckle, remembering his dark prison. "Hardly."

"Lily told me that the train's passengers are people who don't have purpose. Without it, we become too light and float away."

"I'm . . . um . . . sorry." Q wrestled down a smile. "I know that this is my dream and it's not your fault, but nothing you said makes anything clearer."

Raya looked over her shoulder at the curtain to the back room. "We don't have time for this, Q. I need to know if you remember anything else about how you boarded." She leaned closer to his ear.

"Anything at all. We need to find a way out of here before Lily comes back."

Q caught the ghost of her perfume. Orange flowers, brown sugar, and notes of ripe pears. He blinked, forgetting what he had meant to say next. His heightened senses were a blessing when he was awake and blind. In a dream where he could see, they overwhelmed him. Without his walking stick to keep things at a safe distance, even an imaginary woman felt too close. He took a step back from her.

Lily returned carrying three bright orange life vests and a gold makgeolli kettle. She set the rice wine kettle on the counter and handed Q and Raya a vest each. "Make sure you fasten them securely and don't take them off until I tell you to."

"Why do we need to wear life vests?" Q shrugged the vest on. A black moth, its wings half burned away, peeked out from his left collarbone. He had planned to get the tattoo on his nape, but when he learned that inking it over his clavicle would hurt more, he changed his mind. The scorched moth was a message that he couldn't allow himself to forget. "How do you drown on a train?"

"Quite easily. People drown all the time. In their beds, in their heads, in other people. Why not on a train?" Lily set the kettle on the table and lifted its lid. "The venue's right through here. Watch your step. It can be slippery on the other side."

YOUR ITINERARY

PASSENGER
ORIENTATION ON
THE DECK

"Does the train have a set route?"

Frequently Asked Questions
THE ELSEWHERE EXPRESS
PASSENGER HANDBOOK

Raya

The inside of a rice wine kettle and grief had one thing in common: They were both pitch-black.

Lily had called the kettle a doorway, but the inky darkness that filled it hid any promise of an exit. Raya floated around, certain that she had wandered back to the winding tunnel of days she was lost in after Jace's death. A chill snaked up her spine and spread through her limbs. "Lily?" The tremble in her voice echoed around her. "Q?"

A hand closed around Raya's wrist, the golden knot on its palm shining in the darkness. "I'm here."

Raya's breath hitched. Q's voice sounded different in the dark. In a place without gravity, she could hear and feel its weight. It felt strong enough to stand on and was the closest thing around her to solid ground.

"I think we're almost out," Q said.

"How do you know?" Raya strained to see him, but the darkness concealed everything but his warmth. It spread up her arm, thawing it. "I can't see a thing."

"I can feel it."

"You can? How?"

"I—" He weaved his long fingers through hers, holding her more securely. "I've had some practice." Light poured over Q's face. He shielded his eyes with his arm. A thick rope dangled inches from Q's shoulder.

"Mr. Philips? Ms. Sia?" Lily's voice called down from the window of light. "Climb up."

"Go." Q released Raya's hand. "I'll be right behind you."

Her palms burned. Raya grunted and pulled herself higher, her tote hanging from her side. Dropping the bag would have been the practical thing to do, but Raya refused to entertain the thought. The recycled bag helped her believe that no matter how many dark and strange doorways she crossed, fell through, or climbed up, she was going to find her way back home. She put one hand over the other and pulled herself into the light. She drew a breath and tasted salt. She squinted, waiting for her eyes to adjust to the light. Swaths of red rippled above her. She forced her eyes open.

Five crimson battened sails caught the wind from massive bamboo masts. The train's gold knot twisted over each sail, coiling like a serpent without a head or a tail. Raya might have been mesmerized by their scale if they had not been overshadowed by a sky that was split in two. A clear, blue morning stretched over one half, a cloudless, starry night over the other. Raya jerked her head, knocking the base of her skull against the rim of a large clay pot. She bit down the pain. Lily hooked her arm around her and helped her climb out. She glanced around, ignoring the lump swelling on the back of her head. Either she was standing on the deck of the largest Chinese junk she had ever seen or she had hit her head harder than she thought.

"Be careful, Ms. Sia." Lily steered her from a puddle of seawater. "The deck's wet."

Q emerged from the pot, his eyes on the halved sky. "What happened to the sky? Why does it look like that?"

"It's the border between waking and dreaming," Lily said. "The train follows it."

"For the love of god." Raya threw up her hands. "Can we please stop calling whatever this is a train? It's pretty obvious that it's not."

"Is it?" Lily said. "Tell me, Ms. Sia, does wearing a coat when it's cold or a summer dress when it gets hot change who you are? We adapt to the seasons; the train adapts to its route. Would you like to see the tracks? We can view them from the bow."

A silver railway shimmered just beneath the waves and disappeared into the horizon. It dawned on Raya just how long this ride might last if she didn't find a way to escape. She wobbled from the ship's bow, pressure building behind her eyes. She slipped on a puddle and fell backward.

Q caught her by the elbow. "Watch your step."

"Sorry." She pulled away from him. "I think I'm a bit seasick."

"I can give you something to help with that." Lily lifted the flap of her satchel.

Raya waved Lily's offer away. "I don't want anything from you."

Lily closed the satchel. "If you change your mind, just let me know. Mr. Goh, the train's pharmacist, makes sure that I always carry a kit of his concoctions. But I'll be honest. Most of them taste horrible. His seasickness syrup, however, is surprisingly delicious. The latest version tastes like a liquid lemon drop. When I boarded the train, it tasted worse than vomit." She stepped up to the bow and looked out at the silver railway. "But drinking it was worth it, to enjoy this view."

Q's gray coat flapped in the wind. "Where do the tracks go?"

Lily's gaze settled on the point where the railway met the two skies. "Nowhere."

Raya scowled. "What's the point of any of this then? Why are we even here?"

"Does a journey require a destination to be worthwhile, Ms. Sia?"

"You can't call something a journey if you're just running around in circles," Q said.

"I wasn't aware there was such a rule." Lily folded her arms, hiding a smirk behind a cough. "What would you rather call it, Mr. Philips? I'm open to suggestions."

"A complete waste of time." Raya raised her voice over the wind.

"You can't waste something that doesn't exist, Ms. Sia. As Mr. Philips accurately pointed out, the Elsewhere Express travels in circles. But also in squares, triangles, and every shape you can imagine. It goes forward, backward, up, down, around, and through. It's not uncommon for it to loop through some days twice."

Q bent down to whisper in Raya's ear. "Did any of that make sense to you or am I just slow?"

"This is your dream." Raya caught a whiff of his scent. Springtime and soap. And the faintest suede. "You tell me."

"Given what it's built from, the Elsewhere Express doesn't really care about breaking time's rules," Lily said.

"Here we go." Raya looked at Q. "Brace yourself."

"As I explained to Ms. Sia earlier, the Elsewhere Express is made from spools of daydreams, plans, ideas, memories, poems, and songs."

A crease dug between Q's eyes as though he were trying to grip something slippery between them. "Er, could you say that again?"

"I told you to brace yourself," Raya said.

"The Elsewhere Express is made up of thoughts. Waking thoughts, to be precise," Lily said. "The thoughts people dream of while they sleep are theirs to keep." She knocked on the side of a mast. "This bamboo is created from a list a woman made of all the reasons why she's divorcing her husband." Lily lifted her eyes to the sail. "And the sails are woven from an extremely detailed vacation itinerary an accountant was planning. They're impossible to tear and have absolutely no holes."

Q squeezed his eyes shut and pinched the bridge of his nose. "Let's pretend I understood that. I still don't see how being made from thoughts exempts the Elsewhere Express from time's rules."

"Have you ever reminisced about your childhood, Mr. Philips? Or revisited a particular day in your head?"

A cold hospital room's door creaked open in the darkest corner of Raya's mind. She shook her head, slamming it shut.

"Of course," Q said. "Who hasn't?"

"We can relive decades in the span of a train ride home and pluck a second from a day and freeze it, rewind it, speed it up, and turn it inside out. Time has no power over thoughts. When you have eternity as your railway, having a destination sounds rather trite, don't you think?" A wave crashed into the ship, knocking Lily off her feet. Her cap flew off. A cascade of red hair escaped from under it and fell over her shoulders.

Raya stumbled against Q. He fell backward, hitting his elbow on the deck. He groaned and clutched his arm. Raya crawled over to him. "I'm sorry," she said, trying to remember her pre-college EMT training on how to make a sling. "Are you all right?"

Q pulled his lips into a shape between a wince and a smile. "I'm fine."

"Do you still think this is a dream?" Raya stood up and helped Q to his feet.

"I apologize about the Echoes." Lily slipped her cap back on and looked over the side of the ship beneath the night sky. "Thankfully, they appear to be calming down. But keep your vests on. You never know when they'll act up. They get restless when they sense passengers are on the deck."

"What are Echoes?" Raya leaned over the side of the ship. The moon's reflection broke apart over dark waves. "All I see is the moon."

Lily's eyes followed the ripples of pale light. "That's not the moon, Ms. Sia."

"How much baggage am I allowed to bring?"

Frequently Asked Questions
THE ELSEWHERE EXPRESS
PASSENGER HANDBOOK

Lily

Spectral faces with hollowed-out eyes emerged inches from the surface of the ocean, coalescing from ribbons of silver light. Their translucent mouths moved in unison, whispering words drowned by the waves.

Lily retreated from the water, motioning for Raya and Q to follow her. Explaining the train's baggage policy to new arrivals was her least favorite part of the orientation, but also the most necessary one. Due to space and safety considerations, excess baggage, emotional or otherwise, was strictly not allowed. Those who complied with the rules enjoyed their time on the train the most. Those who didn't got lost.

"What were those things?" Raya said.

"They're the next topic in the orientation." Lily opened her satchel and pulled out a slim booklet. "I only brought one copy of the passenger handbook, so you'll have to share. I'll do my best to cover everything you need to know about the train's excess baggage policy, but if you want to review it, you'll find all the details in here. What I'm about to tell you is extremely important so please, pay attention."

Memory was like a suitcase and Lily had learned how to travel light.

She did not hesitate to toss things she didn't use, but admitted that sometimes she got carried away. There were quite a few passengers on the Elsewhere Express, however, who had difficulty complying with its luggage regulations. Even though the policy was discussed during the orientation, there were still those who failed to grasp how a memory's length had nothing to do with its weight. Only a handful understood how the briefest of kisses could weigh twice as much as a decade's worth of routine.

As much as the train wanted to accommodate everything its passengers brought with them, it could not. On another train, solving such a problem would have fallen to its engineers. On the Elsewhere Express, the task landed squarely on the shoulders of its onboard pharmacist.

Mr. Goh, a compact, box-shaped man who had a more-than-average interest in mustache wax, threw himself into the challenge. If a train's pharmacy couldn't solve the problem of excess baggage, then what was it for? He toiled for weeks, well into the night, twirling the ends of his pencil-thin mustache while experimenting with poetry that made the entire train car smell of sewage and sage. The pharmacy's poems, bottled as drafts or packed in tins as minty balms, promised everything from a good night's sleep to more energy. Its haikus were especially popular and known throughout the train to be good for hangovers and indigestion. The poems, though not equally palatable, were all pretty. And Mr. Goh's excess baggage remedy was as thick as stubborn phlegm but the loveliest shade of blue.

Lily took a small vial from her satchel. A thick sea-blue liquid sloshed inside it. "It's quite potent for something that's only eight verses long."

Q looked at Raya. "That settles it."

"Settles what?" Raya said.

"That this is a dream. Most likely a fevered one."

"Is it really that hard to believe that poems can relieve pain?" Lily said. "I don't remember much of my life before boarding the Elsewhere Express, but I do remember that poetry has always been widely accepted as good for the soul."

"The soul, yes," Raya said. "The stomach, not as much."

"Memory, even less," Q added.

"Fortunately, this is a debate that we can easily settle." Lily offered the vial to Raya. "One dose is enough to rid yourself of any memories you have in excess of your luggage allowance. Just memories you won't be needing anymore, of course. You know, things like family, friends, the project due next week. Nothing that you'll miss. The serum will let you keep important ones such as this orientation as well as everything you've seen and heard since boarding. The trick to keeping it down is to pinch your nose while swallowing. It's best to do it in one gulp."

Raya clutched her tote. "You're out of your mind if you think I'm drinking that."

"How about you, Mr. Philips?" Lily looked his way.

"Um . . . no, thank you. I'll pass."

"As you wish. I can't force you to do anything you don't want to do." Lily tucked the vial into her satchel. "Just as I couldn't compel the Echoes."

"You never told us what the Echoes were," Raya said.

"Oh, didn't I?" Lily directed her gaze to the lights swirling in the ocean. "They're the faces in the water, the passengers who fell from the train when they refused to let their excess baggage go."

"What type of accommodations does the Elsewhere Express provide?"

Frequently Asked Questions
THE ELSEWHERE EXPRESS
PASSENGER HANDBOOK

Q

Every scary movie had gotten it wrong. Q had learned at thirteen that ghosts didn't haunt crumbling houses in cul-de-sacs or forests at the edge of foggy, remote towns. Real ghosts lived in kitchen drawers, clothes dryers, and bathroom sinks. And sometimes they moved into bookshelves, tucking themselves between the dog-eared pages of yellowing novels.

After Q's father woke up one morning and decided to step in front of a train, his ghost lingered in the most mundane corners of their home. His favorite haunt was a closet filled with all his old clothes that Q's mother refused to clean out. But what surprised Q more than his father's hiding places was learning that ghosts were not phantoms nor floating bedsheets with cut-out holes. The scariest ones were dusty memories that had gone feral and grown thorns.

Quentin Sr. had left at least a hundred such barbed traps for his wife to find. An unopened pack of cigarettes. A blue toothbrush. A leftover box of the Darjeeling tea that only he drank. They ambushed Connie when she made dinner or folded the laundry, slicing her open and making her cry. One night, a month after her husband's death, she locked herself in her bedroom after his favorite plaid jacket had smothered her with his scent: leather, cedar, and musk. Those who didn't know Connie well thought she looked the same when she emerged two days later and carried on the business of living with her perfect posture and South Sea pearls. Only Q, despite his failing vision, saw the truth.

The woman who left her room each day was a mere facsimile of Q's mother, with eyes as empty as its smile. This is why Q was inclined to believe that despite lying about who she really was, Lily was telling the truth about what happened to passengers who insisted on clinging to suitcases filled with ghosts. Ghosts had hollowed out his mother and turned her into an echo of herself too.

"I don't care what the baggage policy is," Raya said. "I'm not erasing a single memory. I don't even want to be here."

"The choice is entirely yours, Ms. Sia. If you find your compartment and change your mind about lightening your luggage, you'll find Mr. Goh's serum inside your amenity kit next to the shampoo."

"*If* we find our compartment?" Lily's word choice was little more than a puff of air, but it struck the center of Q's chest like a fist. "What do you mean *if*? Why wouldn't we find our compartments?"

"You'll have to search for your compartments on your own, Mr. Philips. I cannot assist you. No one on the train can. Finding your place isn't a journey someone else can take for you."

"You can't be serious." Q furrowed his brow at the train ticket details swirling over his hand. "The ticket doesn't even say what compartment we're assigned to. How are we supposed to find our way around a place where doors don't even look like doors?"

"The same way I did and all the passengers before you have. You say that the train's doors don't look like doors. I say that everything on the Elsewhere Express appears as it truly is. You don't recognize them because you're viewing them through an old, broken lens. The world you left is the illusion, not this train. Until you boarded, you lived with your eyes closed."

Q tensed up from his ankles to the top of his head. He wondered if Lily knew more about him than she let on.

"What are you even talking about?" Raya said. "What illusions?"

"Wealth. Prestige. Fame. Failure. Guilt. Grief. Past. Present. Future." Lily shrugged. "Just to name a few. They color your world and make some things appear shinier or larger than they are, camouflaging others so that they're easier to overlook."

"And this place doesn't?" Raya said. "I haven't seen a single thing here that isn't masquerading as something else. This mast. That sail. You."

"What makes you say that?" Lily tilted her head. "Why wouldn't thoughts that make a woman decide to stand strong and tall look exactly like a ship's mast? Why wouldn't a man's plan for reclaiming his freedom appear like a sail that could take you anywhere you wanted to go? Why are you so certain that I don't look like someone's greatest regret? The world you left drapes people in gold to make you believe that they're more valuable than a person wearing the skin they were born in. It builds houses with more rooms than people who live in them because you're taught that an excess of emptiness makes a better home. Please tell me, Ms. Sia, which of these two worlds is hiding behind a mask and playing pretend?"

Raya parted her lips as though she was about to speak and clamped them before she uttered a sound.

"I know how the idea of navigating a train made of thoughts can seem daunting. I've gone through it," Lily said. "But how is this different from what you did each day prior to boarding? You woke up in pajamas a stranger designed, drank a brand of coffee an entire department of people convinced you was essential to start your day, and made your way around a city shaped by the ideas and beliefs of generations that came before you. The only difference between finding your place in that world and this train is this: To be able to see things for what they truly are and to know where you fit in, one of them requires that you present yourself as your true self too."

Lily directed her attention to Q's and Raya's hands. "The knot on your palms isn't just your ticket. It's a reminder that you can't hold on to two things at the same time. The past and the future pull you in opposite directions. The Elsewhere Express's baggage policy isn't a rule that was made up for fun. A train that never stops carries a lot of weight. Do you have any idea how heavy eternity is and how much space it takes up? As wondrous as the Elsewhere Express is, it does not have the capacity to accommodate the combined load of all its passengers' infinite tomorrows and the weight of their past. Choosing to remember one means losing your memory of the other. And trust me, clinging to your past and forgetting that you need to locate your compartment isn't a situation you want to find yourself in. The knot will unravel if you forget what you're searching for. It can happen slowly or fast, depending on the weight of the baggage pulling on it. If the knot comes undone, you will lose your bond to the train." Her eyes fell on the ghostly lights in the water. "And tumble from it."

"There's a simple solution to that." An old anger that Q usually kept sheathed whittled his words to sharp points. "Why don't you just let the passengers who've fallen off back on? For god's sake. They're right there. Do something. Anything. Throw them a lifeline. Save them."

"Do you think we enjoy the way they batter the ship, Mr. Philips? Do you think we like keeping the curtains closed and ignoring their constant scratching and wails? The Elsewhere Express does not reissue train tickets, no matter how hard you hurl yourself against it or how loud you scream." Lily flicked her smile back on like a light. "But as I said, this isn't something that should concern you. Passengers who travel light usually find their compartments right away."

Q caught Raya wringing her overstuffed bag's straps in the corner of his eye.

"The key to finding your compartment is to keep moving forward, searching one car after another, without looking back," Lily said, "and never going through locked doors."

"Why?" Raya creased her forehead. "What happens if you go through a locked door?"

"Nothing good." Lily's tone made it clear she had no intentions of elaborating on the subject.

"And what happens after we've found our compartments?" Q said.

"Then that means that the Elsewhere Express has truly welcomed you on board. You become a part of the train and the train becomes a part of you. One passenger. One compartment. One bond. Like a person's place and purpose in life—and on this train—it is uniquely yours. It is the eternal knot manifested." Lily grinned. "And secured."

"Does that mean once we find our compartments we won't turn into Echoes and fall off the train?" Raya said.

Lily nodded. "The compartment will anchor you to the train and keep you from drifting off it. You'll be able to explore the train at your leisure and find your role in it. The Elsewhere Express is a train run by its passengers. No one here is a dead weight. I'm looking forward to seeing where both of you apply your talents. Think of this train as your second chance to find what eluded you before you boarded it. And of course, the best part about finding your accommodations is that you get to enjoy the chocolate-covered strawberries and the bottle of champagne housekeeping has left for you by the minibar."

Q turned toward the water, wondering how useful a painter might be on a train made of thoughts and if he would be thrown off once Lily learned he had nothing to contribute. His ribs squeezed his heart. Even with his sight, he was useless.

Lily walked over to a wooden chest and lifted its lid. An assortment of gilded frames peeked out from inside it. She picked one up. "I've taught Ms. Sia how to use these but allow me to quickly demonstrate how they work one more time." She closed her eyes, a smile lighting her face as though her favorite song had come on the radio.

Q lowered his lips to Raya's ear. "What's she doing?"

"I need both of you to be quiet, please." Lily moved the frame to the right, keeping her eyes shut. She tilted the frame up the length of a mast until the top of its sail fluttered within its borders. She opened her eyes. "Ah. There you are." She released the frame, leaving it hanging in the air.

Q's mouth fell open. "How—"

"It's a bit of a climb, but once you go through the door, the rest of your search should be much easier," Lily said. "So, who wants to go first?"

Lightning did not care to wait for their answers. It cleaved the sky and struck the sail, sending it crumpling to the deck in a heap of scarlet, gold, and flames.

"What should I do in the event of an emergency on the Elsewhere Express?"

Frequently Asked Questions
THE ELSEWHERE EXPRESS
PASSENGER HANDBOOK

Raya

Raya hated surprises. She was like Jace that way. An old atmospheric pressure barometer he had made for a science fair stood guard by his window to make sure that he was never ambushed by rain. When Jace went off to college, the barometer kept Raya company while she wrote songs in a purple notebook on his bedroom floor.

Their house had never felt emptier than when Jace was away, but also never as full of questions. Every moment beyond the second Raya stood on was hidden. Her present had been intertwined with Jace's from the moment she was conceived, but their tomorrows were not bound. Raya could not help but wonder what would happen when they finally came undone. She sought answers in a song she wrote about a barometer that could predict more than just the rain. It gave her one reply.

Live. Breathe. Be.

But not even the most magical barometer could have predicted the detour her subway ride home would take.

A large wave slammed into the Elsewhere Express and extinguished the burning sail.

"Thank god." Q clung to the large clay pot.

Raya nodded, unable to shape her lips into anything that resembled relief. A heaviness replaced the salt in the wind and made it difficult to breathe, much less smile. She looked up at the dark clouds. If her magical barometer appeared and told her a torrent of tears was about to fall, she would have believed it.

"It's not just me, right?" Thunder cracked over Q's voice. "Am I imagining things or does the air suddenly feel . . . um . . . thick? And sad?"

"I feel it too." Raya pushed past the tears welling in her throat. "It's making my chest hurt."

Lily stared up at the brewing storm. "You need to get off this deck now."

"How?" Raya's eyes fell on the crumpled sail. "The door's gone."

Lily gripped the rim of the clay pot. "Use this one."

"The pot? Again? But you told me that the train's doors only go in one direction."

"They only go in one direction *reliably,*" Lily said.

Q arched a brow. "What's that supposed to mean?"

"It means that there's no way to know where you'll end up if you go through a door the wrong way." Lily squinted in the wind.

"And you want us to use it?" Raya yelled over the crashing waves. "Crossing it the right way was horrible enough."

"Isn't there another door we can use?" Q said.

"I'm afraid not." Lily turned her collar up to the squall. "But don't worry. Passengers are allowed to use any unlocked door in the event of an emergency. You won't be breaking any rules."

"Who cares about the rules?" Lightning streaked across Raya's eyes. "That door could take us anywhere. Or nowhere. What if we get lost?"

"Just stay together," Lily said. "If you get lost, I'll come and find you. I promise."

"You're not coming with us?" Raya frowned.

Lightning pierced a cloud, casting shadows over Lily's face. "No."

"Why not?" Q's expression turned as dark as Lily's.

"Because it's my job to keep this train safe. Yours is to find your place in it."

"I think I'll take my chances here." Raya folded her arms. "I'm not going through that doorway again."

"We don't have time to argue about this, Ms. Sia." Lily eyed Raya's hand. "Look at your ticket."

Raya glanced at her palm. The edges of the knot frayed as it twisted, sending gold flakes swirling over her skin.

"Your knot is unraveling fast," Lily said. "Your baggage is too heavy. You can either take Mr. Goh's serum right now or get off this deck and find your compartment before it's too late."

The emergency doorway inside the clay pot was awash with a bright white light that made Raya miss the dark. Fear was worse when you could see exactly what was going to happen next. A current of white paint swept her closer to the waterfall at the river's end. Q fell over the frothing edge, followed by the upcycled bag containing all Raya had left of her brother.

"Q!" Raya swallowed paint. She sputtered and tilted her face up, trying to keep her head above the irony raging around her. As desperately as she needed to find a way off the train, she had to bind herself to it. She could not keep Jace's dream alive if the weight of his memory dragged her into the sea.

"What type of weather should I pack for?"

Frequently Asked Questions
THE ELSEWHERE EXPRESS
PASSENGER HANDBOOK

Lily

The handbook clearly stated that using a door as an emergency exit was left to a passenger's personal judgment. The footnote that train tickets included a complimentary funeral service and a wide selection of urns was mentioned in finer print.

Lily dragged the scorched sail to a corner of the ship. Though the sail was drenched and burnt black, Lily was confident that the maintenance crew would have it looking as good as new.

Maintenance could fix everything on the Elsewhere Express with one exception: Nothing could be done about Train Rot. This unstoppable black, putrid, creeping rot was not the common sort that soured milk or made garbage reek. Train Rot took root and spread, corrupting and consuming every thought the train was built from.

But this was not a concern that Lily spent any time thinking about. As her predecessor had pointed out, you needed to worry about rot only when it rained, and it never rained on the Elsewhere Express.

A torrent poured over the deck, plastering Lily's hair over her freckles. She might have sought shelter if she weren't fully convinced that this was a mistake. Whatever was streaming into her eyes and down her cheeks was not rain. It couldn't be. It didn't rain on the Elsewhere Express.

Because if it did rain, it could mean only two things: There was a danger on board the train that needed to be washed off. And that she had failed at her job miserably.

THE SECOND LEG

ELSEWHERE

The happiness of your life depends upon the quality of your thoughts, therefore, guard accordingly.

—Marcus Aurelius

YOUR ITINERARY

PAINTING
WORKSHOP AT THE
SKY ART STUDIO

"What are the passenger activities on board the train?"

Frequently Asked Questions
THE ELSEWHERE EXPRESS
PASSENGER HANDBOOK

Q

Gasping for air, Q climbed out of a can of white paint sitting on a worktable. He stood up and tore off his life jacket. He held out his hands, fully expecting them to be coated in a shade of white darker than rice but lighter than alabaster. His arms were dry and paint-free. And so was the rest of him. He exhaled through a smile, glancing around the large room. "Raya?"

Metal shelves were arranged along its walls, heavy with cans of paint. Pulleys and ropes dangled from a high ceiling. The room reminded Q of the backstage area of his old boarding school's theater that he had once vandalized. He might have gotten away with his crime if he painted something other than burnt black moths. Everyone knew that he was responsible for all the moth paintings that randomly appeared every week on the school's walls. But Q could not be bothered to paint anything else. He and moths were kindred spirits, creatures that lived in the dark.

"Raya?" Q's smile faded.

Paint splashed behind him. He spun around. Raya's overstuffed tote tumbled from the paint can and landed on the floor. Raya burst out after it.

"You scared me." Q pulled her the rest of the way out of the can. "For a second, I thought—"

Raya lunged from his grasp and hurriedly gathered her things from the floor. She hugged her bag tight, her chest heaving against it.

"Watch out for the holes." A woman whose balmy voice was a smooth meld of terra-cotta orange and pomegranate red pointed to the floor. Square-shaped holes were scattered around the room, the darkness filling them blending into the black-painted floorboards.

Q quickly backed away from a hole an inch from the tip of his shoe. "Thanks."

The woman wiped a paint-splattered hand over her stained overalls. A faded maroon bandanna kept her tight curls off her face. Her wide smile needed all the space that it could get. "I'd shake your hands, but I don't think you'd want me to." She flashed a gap-toothed grin. "I'm Astrid."

"I'm Q."

"Raya."

"It's lovely to meet you both. Go ahead and sit anywhere you like while I get your materials."

"Materials?" Raya said. "For what?"

"Your painting lesson. Isn't that why you're here?"

"Er, no, sorry." Q shook his head. "The doorway just led us here."

"You didn't sign up for the workshop?" Astrid looked from Q to Raya.

"No. We're still looking for our compartments," Raya said.

"Oh." Astrid smiled. "Welcome aboard. I remember popping into unexpected places when I was searching for my compartment too. You better get going then. It was nice meeting you. You should sign up for a painting workshop once you've settled in."

"I don't suppose you could point us in the right direction?" Q said.

"I'd love to but that would be against the train's rules. However"—Astrid lowered her voice—"I suppose that telling you where the compartments *aren't* located would be okay." She winked. "I've been painting this train car's ocean and sky since I boarded and so I know that you definitely won't find any accommodations up here or on the island."

Q's mind played catch-up with Astrid's words. "I'm sorry, but did you say that you've been painting the sky and ocean?"

"Oops." Astrid giggled. "Sometimes I forget how different things are off this train. Before I confuse you more, you should probably see what I'm talking about." She gestured to the holes in the floor. "Take your pick. They all have great views."

Q knelt on the floor and peered into a hole. Beneath him, moonlit waves rolled to the shore of a crescent-shaped island. "If that's the ocean—"

"You're standing on the night sky," Astrid said. "Until we paint the sunrise over it. We'll also be touching up the ocean to lighten it and reflect the sun. We pour out the sun, moon, clouds, and stars we've painted through the holes on the floor. That ocean you're looking at is the best on the train." Astrid smiled. "No matter what the painting crew of the fishing car says."

Q angled his head to stare at the sky through the hole. "It looks so real."

"Thanks. We try our best. But I'll admit that even after all this time, I'm still terrible at painting stars. I cannot, for the life of me, make them twinkle. I leave the stars to the more talented painters. I used to help paint the sun, but I've discovered that my forte is water. I've found that with the right blend of ultramarine blue, viridian green, and titanium white, the ocean stays nice and warm the whole day. It's the perfect temperature for swimming even in the evenings."

"You can swim in a painting?" Raya said.

"Of course. Why not?"

"I saw an ocean during the passenger orientation. And a border across the sky. Were those paintings too?" The phantom faces in the water swam in Q's mind. His stomach turned cold at the possibility that everything Lily had told them had been an elaborate lie, not because Lily was dishonest, but because he had believed her. A simmering rage rolled to a boil.

"No," Astrid said. "Those weren't paintings. Passenger orientations are always held outdoors. The conductor believes that seeing the train's route helps passengers understand what the Elsewhere Express is."

Lights appeared through the holes in the floor. Q crouched to get a closer look. Glowing spheres bobbed over the waves. Q pressed his hand over his mouth, breathing hard into the knot twisting over his palm.

"What is it?" Raya said.

"I . . . I've seen those spheres before."

"*You have?* When?"

"Remember when I told you that I used to have strange dreams as a boy?"

"Yes. You mentioned it at the Lotus."

"This sounds mad." Q gnawed his lower lip. "But I think I dreamt about this place. And those spheres."

"That's not as crazy as you think it sounds." Astrid retied her bandanna. "The Elsewhere Express has a very strict baggage policy."

"What does the baggage policy have to do with Q's dreams?" Raya said.

"The train can only carry so much." Astrid looked over a hole and watched the spheres roll over the painted waves. "Just look at the water. Can you imagine how much an ocean of thoughts weighs? And this isn't the only ocean on the train. There are seas, rivers, lakes, and fjords too."

Astrid straightened. "Every thought has weight, and night dreams—the thoughts we have in our sleep—are no exception. To keep the train light, we take a draft from the pharmacy before going to bed to cast our night dreams off before we wake up. It tastes like cough syrup, but housekeeping gives everyone warm brown-butter cookies, so we don't complain. Much." Astrid chuckled.

"Night dreams need to go somewhere after they're sent away from the train in the same way wandering daydreams board the Elsewhere Express from the world off it. It's almost like an exchange." Astrid looked at Q. "The dreams you had as a boy most likely belong to a passenger on this train, someone who dreamt about this ocean and those spheres. Once a night dream finds you, it leaves a trail for others to find. The dreams that visit you will always come from the same passenger. People outside the train call it inspiration. We call it excess weight."

Q gazed down at the water. "In my dreams, the spheres weren't just balls of light."

Sixteen Years Ago

The words that spilled out of the phone's receiver made no sense. Connie Chen Philips told the voice on the other end of the line that it had the wrong number and set the phone down. Surely, the caller could not have said that her husband had gotten struck by a train and was dead. Either the line must have been garbled or if the news was true, it was meant for someone else.

The phone rang again.

"Hello?" Connie answered, arranging fresh pink peonies in her favorite crystal vase. This time around, the police officer spoke slower, pounding each syllable into her skull like a long, rusty nail. Connie dropped the phone and collapsed next to it. She curled up on the Italian marble, staring at the painting hanging above a tufted, cream sofa.

Her son was seven when he had given the painting to her on her birthday. Critics praised his pieces as mature and complex, even as he insisted that each piece was only a means to remember the strange world he visited in his dreams. Before he switched to canvas, he used to jump out of bed first thing in the morning to sketch on the nearest surface he could find. Walls always happened to be close by. Connie wasn't too happy when he ruined them.

Connie's husband, an artist himself, was more understanding. He sat Quentin down on his knee with a smile that crinkled the corners of his gray eyes and suggested that Quentin might be able to remember his impossible world better if he used canvases that weren't constantly scrubbed clean. The painting above the sofa was the first one Q had made after his father convinced him to make the change.

According to the brass label Connie had made for the piece, the painting was called *Sky filled with stars*. It was not the most creative title in the world, but she admitted that her son was more articulate with his brush than with words. She blamed herself for this, having insisted that he be raised trilingual. Quentin Sr. spoke to him in English, while she spoke to him in Math and Mandarin. When he was younger, Quentin often mixed the three languages up.

So when he told her that her birthday present was of water singing, she assumed that he meant to say "xīngxīng," the word for stars. And since stars were not found in the sea, she taught Quentin the correct word for "sky," making him repeat it until he got it right. Tiānkōng. Tiānkōng. Tiānkōng. Names, she reminded him, were important. The perfect title could make a painting sell for twice the price.

Now, as she viewed the painting with her cheek pressed against cold marble and hot tears streaming down her face, she realized that Quentin had been right about the painting's original title. From this angle, she gazed upon an ocean, watching little moons shimmer over painted waves. Her son's gentle brushstrokes strummed her soul, playing a silent song that even shattered hearts could feel. Connie closed her eyes and let the music ferry its silent wish inside her.

Live. Breathe. Be.

Connie told herself that after she buried her husband she would have the painting's correct title etched on a new brass plate.

"Why do I need to sign safety waivers?"

Frequently Asked Questions
THE ELSEWHERE EXPRESS
PASSENGER HANDBOOK

Raya

According to Astrid, there were only two ways to get down from the painted sky, and Raya did not like either of them. Ladders made her knees hurt and Raya couldn't even begin to imagine how a star would take her to the island below. But as the only door leading out of the train car was located on the island, she was forced to choose. "Stars," Raya said, trusting her fate to the unknown.

"Good choice." Astrid nodded. "That's what most passengers pick. The ladders are terrifying. I avoid them as much as I can. I hate it when they creak or when a rung gives way. There's just one problem. We're all out of stars. Everything we painted today is already hanging in the night sky."

Raya grimaced at the rickety-looking ladders leaning against the brick wall. "Would it be possible to paint some more? How many do we need?"

"Just one. I could try to make it for you, but I can't promise that it will work as well as the ones that my colleagues paint."

Raya looked at Q. "What do you think?"

"I'm game if you are." He pulled a wry smile. "I'm not a big fan of ladders that look like they're one half-hearted gust of wind away from falling apart."

"Neither am I," Raya said.

"I'll get started then." Astrid gathered paints and brushes from a metal shelf. "But this might take a while."

Raya turned her palm over. One of the loops of the golden knot was noticeably looser. Her heart dropped to her ankles. "I . . . um . . . think we should probably use the ladder instead."

Q stepped forward. "I'll do it."

"Do what?"

"I'll paint the star. I'm used to painting things in a hurry."

"I don't think that's such a good idea." Astrid arranged the painting supplies on a stained worktable. "Stars are extremely difficult to paint. It takes a long time to master even the simplest one."

"I can do it." Q's eyes flitted over the brushes and paints Astrid had selected. "I have some experience."

"I'm sure you do." Astrid slipped her hands into her overalls' pockets. "But have you ever painted without a canvas?"

Painting over thin air might have daunted most people, Raya thought, but not Q. He relished it. His brush flew over the air like a horse that had broken free from its reins and was racing the wind. Raya watched him work, refusing to blink. Genius was too rare of a sight to miss. Each of Q's brash and bold strokes made it clear that he cared little about painting within lines. Or on canvases. He painted as though in a trance, his will surging into the star from his soul.

The star floated around the room, drifting past jugs of clouds, around a bottle of twilight, and into the mason jar that Astrid held open. She covered the jar and set it on a worktable, her eyes flickering and wide. "I'm impressed."

Q nodded with a small smile.

"That was magical," Raya said breathlessly.

"Magic's only a trick you've practiced a lot." Q massaged the bruise he had gotten on his elbow when Raya knocked him onto the deck.

A familiar pang stabbed Raya between the ribs. Guilt was a knife permanently wedged in her heart, indistinguishable from her own tissue. It took very little to twist it. "Does it hurt?"

"No." Q shook his head. "I just strained it a bit while I was painting."

"I'm really sorry about—"

"Raya," he said, looking into her eyes. "It wasn't your fault."

"I've never seen anyone learn how to paint stars so quickly." Astrid admired the star twinkling inside the jar. "And so well."

"You're a great teacher," Q said.

"I wish." Astrid laughed. "Anyway, I know you're supposed to take your time deciding which department to join, but I want you to know there's a place for you here if you want it."

Raya looked at the knot on her hand, thinking how much simpler it would be if she found a place for herself on the train and believed that people like her deserved a second chance.

"You've exceeded the luggage limit, haven't you?" Astrid said quietly.

Raya clutched the straps of her bag. "Nothing I can't carry."

"Of course." Astrid cracked a smile that fell short of her eyes. "You should get going. Come." She strode to the worktable and picked up the jar containing the star. She twisted its lid open. The star popped out and hovered by a hole in the floor. Astrid gave it a nudge. It dove through the hole, leaving a trail of stardust on its way down. It landed on the island's shore, flickered, and faded away.

Raya looked up from the glittering stardust slide and caught Q lingering over what remained of his painting. She didn't need to ask him how he felt about watching it dim. His eyes gave him away. Those less acquainted with longing might have looked at them and seen nothing but the reflection of stardust, but Raya saw every hue of sadness no matter how well Q blended them in. His was a combination of pensiveness and melancholy, and the smallest drop of mourning.

"You're all set." Astrid held out a clipboard. "I'll just need you to sign this waiver and you can be on your way." She took a pen from behind her ear and tapped the paper attached to the board with it.

"A waiver for what?" Raya scanned the page.

"Just standard safety stuff."

"I thought that using a star was supposed to be safe?" Q peered down at the stardust flickering in the sky.

"It is. The waiver isn't for sliding down the star. It's protocol for high-risk activities like painting. I should have made you sign this before you painted the star, but I honestly didn't think that you were going to be able to do it. But the conductor is strict about admin stuff like this. Sorry."

"How is painting a high-risk activity?" Raya said.

"You're on a train made of thoughts and standing on a painted sky." Astrid handed the waiver and pen to Q. "There are no limits to what our minds can create here. Q just made a star with a flick of his wrist. Can you imagine what someone with dark thoughts could conjure? On a train that brings thoughts to life"—Astrid's gaze fell on Raya's bag—"we need to be very careful about the thoughts that we bring on board."

Raya lowered her eyes, grateful that she had no talent for painting. Jace died in her mind over and over again because an air freshener that smelled like rain or an ad for the brand of milk they had dunked their cookies in was a one-way ticket to her blackest night. On a spectrum of darkness, there was no bleaker shade than grief-tinted guilt.

But this was not something Raya felt that she needed to confess, as she had no intentions of ever picking up a paintbrush. She might have been more worried if she still wrote music. The last song she had ever written was for Jace. It was meant to be a quiet goodbye, but all it did was drown the lullaby inside her with tears until it decayed.

Raya was keenly aware that the shadows that lived in her songs were more of a danger to the Elsewhere Express than anything Q could ever paint. She kept her gaze on the floor, blinking back fresh tears.

If she had looked up, she would have seen that Q was hiding something too.

Q

Q did not consider himself a dangerous man unless vandalizing school property counted as a violent crime against walls. His career as a young vandal began on his first day at boarding school, with a tiny moth he drew in the corner of his desk. It ended months later with the swarm he painted by the school chapel's largest window, their wings burning in the sun. It would have been more prudent to have kept his paintings hidden in the shadows, but as his vision worsened, he needed more light.

This was, at least, the standard answer Q gave whenever his school records came up during media interviews. In truth, he painted each burnt wing to remind himself that bad things happened when you wanted things you couldn't have. Moths that chased fire got burned. Blind men who missed the light floundered and grew bitter in the dark. There was nothing he could do about going blind, and the sooner he taught himself not to long for the light, the less rage he needed to hide. His darkest thoughts would come later, in the hours before he boarded the Elsewhere Express. Astrid's warning about the dangers of such thoughts made it clear that joining the train's painting crew was never going to be an option. It was too easy to give a swarm of his old thoughts wings. No waiver, even if he signed it in blood, would be able to keep the train safe from his imaginings.

"Ready?" Raya crouched by a hole in the floor.

Q wiped his icy palms on his coat. "No."

"Do you want me to go first?" Raya looked up at him.

Her eyes were just as naked as when Q first saw them. Their rims quivered, putting her fear on full display. Q would have offered her a robe if fear could be clothed, but the quiet courage that flickered behind her irises like a small flame told him that she did not need it. This woman, he thought, was not a stranger to being selfless. Perhaps even to a fault. "I made the star. I should test it before you get on."

"Are you sure? I can—"

Q jumped through the hole before he could change his mind. It seemed only right that the person who went first was the one who had more experience hurtling to their doom.

YOUR ITINERARY

STARLIGHT SERENADE
AT THE BEACH

"Who do I call to make repairs in my compartment?"

Frequently Asked Questions
THE ELSEWHERE EXPRESS
PASSENGER HANDBOOK

Raya

Had the trip down the stardust slide been a song, it would have tasted like fresh lychees and laughter. Raya landed feetfirst on the powdery, pale-pink sand wishing that the shimmering trail were longer.

"That was quite the ride." Q smiled brighter than the spheres surfing the waves to shore. "I'm glad we decided not to use a ladder."

The wind scattered the stardust, sprinkling it through Raya's hair and making it sparkle. "Me too. It's just sad that your painting's gone."

Q smiled at her twinkling hair. "Not entirely."

"And I took photos in case you want something to remember it by." A man with silver threaded through his dark hair strode over, a vintage Leica camera hanging from a strap around his neck. He extended his tanned hand and rough fingers. "I'm Dev."

Raya shook his hand, no longer surprised that it felt solid and warm. The Elsewhere Express was beginning to feel as real as the world she had left behind. "I'm Raya and this is Q."

Dev narrowed his eyes at her. "Have we met?"

"Who?" Raya pointed to herself. "Me?"

"Were you at Scrabble night?" Dev scratched the gray stubble on his cleft chin. "Or maybe at happy hour at the Lotus last week?"

Raya shook her head. "No, sorry. We just boarded."

"You did? I must have misheard then."

"Misheard what?" Q said.

"That you painted the star that took you to the island."

"He did." Raya gestured to Q. "You heard correctly."

Dev's heavy brows shot up. "Really? That's quite the feat for a newcomer. Well done. You should consider joining the painting crew."

Q fidgeted as though his shirt made him itch. "Desperation's a great motivator."

Dev tilted his head. "Sorry?"

"The painting crew was out of stars," Raya said. "And we weren't keen on using a ladder."

Dev chuckled. "Falling ladders make great photos, though. I've got quite the collection. It helps with my memory." He tapped the side of his head. "I'm terrible at remembering things. Well, I won't keep you from your search for your compartments. And if you're looking for the picture frames, they're behind"—he scanned the shore—"where were they again?" He laughed. "Sorry. Oh. Wait. I remember. They're behind the fifth palm tree on your left."

"Thanks for the tip. It was great meeting you." A glowing sphere rolled past Raya's heel. Followed by another. And three more. They washed up on the crescent beach like little moons, making the pinkish sand shimmer like fairy dust.

"Finally." Dev planted his hands on his hips. "Well, I better get to work. I don't want to be here all night."

"Work?" Q said.

"I know, I know." Dev flashed a grin. "A lot of people on this train don't think that strolling on the beach and listening to the songs that wash ashore is a real job."

"Did you say *songs*?" Raya shot a glance at Q. His eyes mirrored her shock.

She had wanted to believe him when he had told her about his strange dreams, but all the dreams she had about Jace being alive had taught her that dreams were nothing more than lies you told yourself while you were sleeping.

"This wouldn't be the maintenance department without them, would it?" Dev said. "I've heard that they tried using pastry recipes to patch things up back in the day, but while they were okay for quick fixes, even repairs made using the best chocolate cake ideas didn't last long."

A wrinkle wedged itself between Raya's eyes. "I don't understand."

"Thoughts come in a variety of shapes and sizes. Not every thought is suitable for the same task. Using a cupcake recipe versus a song is like slapping on a Band-Aid instead of treating a wound. Songs heal. But they don't pick themselves up." Dev smirked. "It's a tough job, but someone's got to do it. Would you like to hear one before you go? I can crack one open for you. It won't take long."

After years of avoiding music, waiting to listen to a song filled Raya's stomach with ice. It was like meeting up with an old friend who she wasn't very confident would be happy to see her.

"Are you sure you want to do this?" Q looked at Raya's hand. "We don't have to wait for Dev to come back with his tools. We should keep searching for our compartments."

Raya turned her palm over. "The knot doesn't seem to have changed much since we left the sky. I think it's unraveling more slowly. Look."

"I wonder what's changed?" Q inspected her hand, his fingertips grazing the knot on her skin. "Why did it slow down?"

"I'm not sure." Raya cast her eyes down the glowing shore. She had no idea what songs inside spheres were supposed to sound like, but their lights warmed her and made the path ahead easier to see. "I just know it means we can afford to stay a little longer and listen to one song."

"Don't get me wrong," Q said, "I'm glad that the knot isn't unraveling, but I don't understand why you want to do this. It's still a delay. I know why hearing the song matters to me, but if I were in your shoes, I'd be more interested in finding my compartment as quickly as possible."

"I want to hear the song because the fact that we're standing on a beach you dreamt of as a child can't be a coincidence." Raya watched the beach glow in Q's eyes like a new day. "That has to mean something, don't you think? The more we know about this place, the better. It's the only way I'll be able to find my way home."

"Is that still what you want?" Q picked up a sphere. "To go home?"

"Don't you?"

Glowing specks swirled inside the sphere like glitter in a snow globe and made shadows dance over Q's face. "When I was a boy, there was nothing I wanted more than for this place to be real."

"And now?"

"My head is bursting trying to understand how this place actually exists." He clutched the sphere tighter. "And how I can make sure that I never leave it."

Dev jogged back to the shore with a red toolbox. "Which song do you want to open?" He set the toolbox on the sand.

Q looked at Raya. "Why don't you pick?"

Raya surveyed the shore. The spheres were identical, but some exerted a greater pull on her. A sphere by the edge of the water drew her its way. She resisted the urge to sprint. She walked over to the sphere, unsure if it had selected her or if she had chosen it. She picked it up and made her way back to the group. The sphere's light seeped into her skin, finding and filling the spaces music used to live.

"Interesting choice." Dev held his hand out.

Raya's will wrestled with her fingers, refusing to let the sphere go.

Dev plucked it from her palm, taking its soothing heat with it. "Come on, kids." He sat down next to his toolbox. "Gather round."

Raya folded her legs beneath her. She pressed her bag against the chill in her chest. Q sat next to her, close enough to lend her some of his warmth.

Dev shook the sphere and brought it to his ear. "I think we'll need a number eight and eleven to crack this open." He set the sphere in the middle of the group and opened the toolbox.

"Do all thoughts board the Elsewhere Express this way?" Raya said, arranging words into a sentence she would have never uttered before this night.

"Just the songs." Dev rummaged through an assortment of silver tools. "Thoughts board the train through different cars depending on what kind they are. There's a sink in the back room of the Lotus, for example, that grudges and worries gurgle up from, and a beehive in the back of the bakery car that memories of first kisses drip out of. I have yet to find anything better to sweeten my tea." He pulled out a silver hammer and chisel and looked up at Raya and Q. "Care to give it a try?"

Raya raised her hand. "I'll do it."

Dev handed her the tools. "Just position the chisel over the sphere and give it a good whack."

Raya gripped the tools, surprised by how well they fit in the curves and shallows of her hand. The last thing that had felt as comfortable against her skin was her old guitar. And Q's hand, if she counted how he had found her in the darkness of a kettle. She positioned the chisel over the sphere. "How's this?"

Dev gave her a thumbs-up.

Raya raised the hammer, turning her head away to avoid shards. She brought the hammer down, striking the chisel squarely on the handle. The sphere rippled like a soap bubble and quietly popped. A luminous, rainbow-colored butterfly flew out, strewing notes in the air with every flap of its wings. Raya gaped at it, the tools slipping from her fingers.

"Lovely song," Dev said. "You have a knack for this."

Raya clamped her lips to keep a smile from spreading. It had been a long time since music had made her feel good. She couldn't let it happen again.

The winged song flew by Q's ear, trailing a story about winter giving way to spring. "It's beautiful."

"And quite fragile compared to other thoughts that board the train. Grudges are especially tough." Dev lifted his hand. The song landed on his index finger. "That's why songs are encased in spheres when they board. To keep them safe." He examined the melody's wings. "Some songs are more resilient than others. I throw the flimsier ones back and only pick the ones I know will last. I would hate to have to constantly replace them."

"Replace them?" Raya said.

"A train on an endless journey goes through a lot of wear and tear. We use specific songs to repair particular parts of the train. Sad songs are perfect for fixing leaks because sadness starts out soft, sticks to things, and hardens over time. If the train had mice, I imagine that such songs would also make excellent traps. Anyway, the train's plumbers need to be careful about not getting them into the pipes. No one likes bitter water." Dev brought the song close to his lips and whispered. It glowed bright and took flight.

"You're just letting it go?" Raya's throat squeezed her voice.

"Don't worry." Dev smiled. "It won't get lost. It knows what it needs to do. You won't find a clearer map than purpose."

The song landed on a palm tree's withered leaf. Its light intensified, growing brighter until it engulfed the whole palm. When it dimmed, a rainbow-colored frond took the dead leaf's place. The frond's colors shifted between different shades of green before settling into the most vibrant one.

"I've been meaning to fix that leaf." Dev snapped a photo of the palm. "You chose the perfect song for it. Songs may shed their wings and change their appearance depending on the train part they repair, but no matter what they look like, their essence doesn't change. The more hopeful the song, the healthier the leaf. The more tragic the song, the harder the seal. There isn't a part of the Elsewhere Express that a song hasn't touched up or repaired."

"How about passengers?" Raya stole a glance at Q's bruised elbow. "Can songs fix people too?"

"Some love songs can," Dev said, "but they can only work on simple things like cuts and bumps. The train has a healer made from new beginnings for more serious injuries. Not that anyone ever gets really hurt on the Elsewhere Express." He stuck his hand in his pocket and pulled out a small linen pouch.

"What's that?" Q asked.

Dev opened the pouch and poured a little mound of tiny black seeds over his palm. "The train's emergency services number."

"Sorry?" Q said.

"They're lavender seeds. They're made from calm thoughts, the ones that pass through your mind right before you nod off on your commute. Love songs are drawn to their scent. Lavender is like catnip for them. It reminds them of the quiet they were born in. Plant it and a song or two will be on its way to patch you right up." Dev poured the seeds back into the pouch and returned the pouch to his pocket. "It's the nature of songs to soothe."

A sphere glimmered in the corner of Raya's eye. She picked it up. "May I open this one?"

"Be my guest." Dev eyed the song. "The tools you used earlier should be able to open it."

"Are you sure that's a good idea?" Q glanced at the knot on Raya's hand.

"I'll be quick." Raya gave the sphere a swift whack. A song burst from the sphere.

The melody, a song about fated love, fluttered by Q's injured arm, stirring the air like the breath before a kiss. It landed on his elbow, grew bright, and vanished along with his bruise. Q gasped. "How did you know the song could do that?"

"I . . . I'm not sure." Raya stared at his unmarked skin. "I just did."

"Well done." Dev trained the camera on Raya and took her picture. "I hope that you'll seriously consider joining the maintenance crew. I think you'll be great at this kind of work."

Q looked at Raya as though seeing her for the first time. "I think so too."

"What's it like, Dev?" Raya said.

"For starters"—Dev rubbed his jaw—"no two days are alike. I never know what songs will wash up. And the rest of the crew's a fun bunch. I'm sure you'll—"

"Sorry." Raya shook her head. "That's not what I meant. I'd like to know what it feels like to erase your old life. Do you have any regrets about leaving it behind?"

Dev laughed. "Why would I have any regrets?"

"You don't miss anything? Your family? Friends?"

"You can't miss what you don't remember. Besides, if our old lives were worth missing, then we wouldn't have drifted away from them, would we?"

"But what makes the Elsewhere Express different from the world we came from?" Raya squeezed a fistful of sand. "Why would someone be able to find their purpose here when they failed to find it before boarding?"

"It's simple." Dev shrugged. "The world outside the train likes to think of purpose as though it were this mystical, sacred thing. Here, things couldn't be more straightforward. A passenger's purpose is to keep the Elsewhere Express running. That's it. No mystery. No ambiguity. No uncertainty. If we don't play our part, the train falls into disrepair, grinds to a halt, and everyone on board perishes."

"I . . . see." Raya released the sand.

"But how do we find what we're supposed to do here?" Q said.

"The same way you painted a star and Raya found the right songs to fix that palm and your arm," Dev said. "There are no magical quests or monsters to slay on the Elsewhere Express. The only thing standing between you and your purpose is your own thoughts. You will either master them and shape them into whatever you need them to be, or they will master you."

Two chimes rang through the beach. A loudspeaker crackled to life.

"Good evening, passengers. We would like to request Mr. Philips Jr. and Ms. Sia to proceed to the Dragonfly dining car. The conductor will meet you there. Thank you."

YOUR ITINERARY

THE
DOORWAY DISCOVERY
EXPERIENCE

"What is the fastest way to get to the Dragonfly?"

Frequently Asked Questions
THE ELSEWHERE EXPRESS
PASSENGER HANDBOOK

Raya

The sweet and tangy fragrance of mangosteen tea coiled around the spiral paper stairway, following Raya and Q as they climbed seemingly endless steps. Dev's directions to the Dragonfly had taken them through the hot springs in the spa car, across giant mahjong tiles in the game lounge, and inside a dictionary sitting next to a pot of freshly made mangosteen tea. Words, along with their definitions, silently crept up the paper stairs and snaked across paper walls, parting and swerving to avoid being stepped on and crushed.

"Peristeronic." Raya read a word slithering down the banister. "Adjective. Suggestive of pigeons."

"Extremely useful." Q grinned. "You never know when you'll see something that's pigeon-like, but not actually a pigeon."

"Here's another good one. 'Ucalegon.'" Raya pointed to a word climbing up a step.

"Noun. A neighbor whose house is on fire." Q read its definition out loud. "I'll keep that in mind in case I ever see smoke coming from your compartment."

A chuckle burst from Raya's lips. She snapped her mouth shut and picked up her pace. It was easy to get distracted on a train filled with wonders, in the company of a man who delighted in each of them.

"Hey," Q said. "Did I say something wrong?"

Raya tugged her tote higher over her shoulder. "We should hurry up and see what Lily wants."

"I can carry that for you, if you like," Q offered.

"Thanks, but it's not that heavy. Just some notes. A laptop. The usual."

"I can see why you don't think you belong here."

Raya's spine stiffened. "You can?"

"You're carrying around your weight in dreams. Med school, right?"

Raya paused on a step. "How did you know?"

"I have a sixth sense about these things." He smiled at the ID card sticking out from the binder containing her anatomy notes.

Raya shoved the card deeper into her bag and climbed two steps at a time. "Apparently, studying to be a doctor doesn't count as purpose on this train."

Q caught up with her. "I'm sorry, Raya. No one should be here if they don't want to be."

Raya twisted the bag's straps. "But you want to stay."

"I can't think of a better place to retire, can you?"

"Aren't you a bit young to retire?"

"What can I say?" Q shrugged. "I followed some great financial advice."

Raya smirked. "Maybe the train has a financial consulting department you can join."

Q laughed. "Maybe."

"What did you do before retiring? No. Wait. Let me guess. You painted. There's no way that anyone who paints the way you do is an amateur."

Q's eyes roamed over the words scrolling across the curved wall. "That's behind me now."

"It didn't seem that way when you were painting the star. You looked like a person who was enjoying what he was doing. A lot."

"We needed a star and so I made one."

Raya looked him in the eye. "So you're saying that being set for life is the only reason you stopped painting?"

"Is there a better reason to retire that I don't know of?"

"Maybe not." Raya's gaze dropped to the broken eyeglasses tucked into Q's coat pocket. "But there are worse," she said quietly.

He glanced down. "You noticed."

"I'm sorry. I know it's none of my business but they're hard to miss. Just like your—" She bit her lip.

"Mismatched shoes?"

Raya sighed. "Sorry."

"I'm guessing that you already know the reason I stopped painting then."

"We don't have to talk about it if you don't want to." Though Raya whispered the words, they seemed to echo around her.

"Have you ever looked through a keyhole?" Q said.

Raya nodded, dreading what he was going to say next.

"Halve it." Q gripped the paper banister, crumpling it. A small letter "s" narrowly avoided getting squished. It crawled away, catching up to the word it belonged to. *Accismus.* The word went on its way without pausing or looking back. "Then halve it again."

"Q—" She reached out to him and stopped, reminding herself that they were nothing more than strangers in a stairwell a long way from home.

"That's what I could see before I boarded," Q continued. "That's why I was so convinced that all of this was just a dream. How could it possibly be anything else? I never dared to imagine that I would be able to see again. I guess you might say that I was—" He tried to smile, but the corners of his mouth only managed to lift a fourth of the way and tremble. "A *ucalegon.*"

"A neighbor whose house is on fire?" Raya said.

"And surrounded by so much smoke that he was convinced that it would be less painful to breathe all of it in and just get it over with."

Q

The most difficult part about painting was knowing when a piece was done. There was no finish line to cross or horn that blared, no conclusion arrived at or answer reached. There was only a decision, a declaration that what was on canvas had told the truth as best it could, and that it was time to take a step back, put down the brush, and stop.

When Q had stood on the edge of the train station's platform earlier that evening, he thought about all the paintings he had decided were done and the decision his father had made on a similar platform. For the first time since he passed, Q wondered if Quentin Sr. knew something that he did not. Who got to declare when a life was finished? Was deciding to put his brush down that much different from choosing to pick it up? People plotted their lives down to the minute but left their final hour to chance. Q had not intended to share his secrets with Raya, but they rushed out of him, hungry for light and air. Or maybe he shared them because a journey to nowhere was not a trip he wanted to take on his own. He recounted his path to a train platform, sparing no detail about his father's death, the faceless woman who visited his dreams, and the darkness that had taken everything from him.

"Did you—" Raya's voice dissolved into a breath.

"Kill myself?" Q looked at Raya, feeling like he was one of his sitters, and she, the painter holding the brush, coaxing the truth from the shadows of his face. Her question was neither abstract nor difficult, one answerable by a simple yes or no. After sharing an endless stairwell's worth of his life's story, a monosyllabic answer should have been easy. That is, if he knew what the answer was. If death was your darkest point, the ending of all your dreams, then he had crossed its door. And yet, he was also more alive than he had ever been, his sight restored by a magical train, his aches healed by a lavender-haired woman and a song.

"Q?" Raya said.

"I . . ." he stammered, as if he were peeling off a mask that he was afraid to ruin in case he needed to wear it again. He had witnessed this unmasking take place in his studio, though always on someone else's face. Tonight, he was the client, disrobing his defenses in front of a woman who was supposed to be a stranger, but in all the ways that mattered on a train made of thoughts, was not. Here, where he was reborn, he had known her his entire life. "I wanted to."

His mask fell off, revealing his greatest shame. When so many others had built meaningful lives without sight, falling into despair at the loss of his vision made him no better than a spoiled child screaming because their toy was taken away. His eyes drifted over the words moving across the stairwell. It was a pity, he thought, that dictionaries only provided the definition of words and not people. It would have saved him a lot of grief if he could have looked up who he was supposed to be.

Q Chen Philips.

Proper noun.

Not his father.

In the absence of such a dictionary, it took a train's bright headlights to illuminate the truth hidden in the dark. Q didn't want to die. He wanted to see.

"But I couldn't go through with it," Q confessed. "I realized that I wasn't finished. I wasn't even close to being done. I backed away from the edge of the platform and boarded my train. Or so I thought. The next thing I knew, I was lying on the floor at the Lotus, staring up at a purple sky."

"And you could see," Raya said.

"The Elsewhere Express is my miracle, Raya. My second chance."

"I'm happy for you, Q. I really am."

"Don't you think you could learn to be happy here too?" Q said.

"It's not a question of being happy here. I mean, who wouldn't be? It's like the most amazing dream." Raya clutched her bag. "But it's not a dream that's meant for me."

"Do you really believe that?" Q held her gaze.

Raya stared back without flinching. "You think I'm lying?"

"I think sometimes, we hide things so deep that we forget they're there."

YOUR ITINERARY

TEATIME
AT THE DRAGONFLY
DINING CAR

"What are the dining options on the Elsewhere Express?"

Frequently Asked Questions
THE ELSEWHERE EXPRESS
PASSENGER HANDBOOK

Lily

Lily weaved through a small forest with a black umbrella hooked over her arm. A thick carpet of dry pine needles crunched beneath the soles of her polished, lace-up boots. She stopped at the foot of the tallest tree in the grove and pulled off a freshly laundered white glove. She sucked in a breath, stuck two fingers in the corners of her mouth, and whistled. A silver rope dropped inches from her nose, dangling from a branch that was too high up for her to see. She tugged it twice, took a step back, and opened her umbrella. Gold ink twisted into intersecting and infinite loops over the umbrella's panels. The tree shook and sent a shower of pine cones bouncing off the umbrella and onto the ground. When the last of the cones ricocheted to a neighboring pine, Lily leaned the umbrella against the tree's trunk and secured the brim of her gold-banded cap firmly over her forehead. A branch rustled, scooped her up, and handed her off to the branch above it.

Lily bobbed from branch to branch, holding on to the worn leather satchel slung across her chest. The Leaf Lift was her favorite among the previous conductor's inventions. Before he had come up with it, passengers who used this doorway needed to climb. Lily recalled how Rasmus's pale blond eyebrows nearly flew off his face when she suggested that, for greater convenience, the pinewood birdhouse containing the Dragonfly dining car be set on the ground. He promptly sat her down for an hour-long lecture on why rearranging cars was not the best idea on a train that never stopped.

A branch deposited Lily next to a little city of birdhouses complete with a post office and a school. The one Lily was looking for had a little sign on its red roof.

The Dragonfly

Open all day.

Lily peeked inside the birdhouse. A hanging bridge spanning two limestone cliffs greeted her. Lily stepped onto it.

The bridge, if a silky path spun from silver cobwebs could be called such, swayed in the wind. The swarm of golden dragonflies that held it up by tiny bejeweled harnesses did their best to keep it steady. Buzzing filled Lily's ears. She closed her eyes, distilling the sound.

I hate my job.

The rent's due.

I'll never forgive her.

He's cheating. I'm sure of it.

God, I need to pee.

The chatter never varied, regardless of where the thoughts that made up the bridge came from. The Hong Kong MTR. The London Underground. The Manila LRT. The worries buzzing inside people's skulls were more similar than they were different. Building a bridge out of these concerns and grudges, Lily thought, was a stroke of engineering genius. Stubborn thoughts were a thousand times stronger than carbon steel.

A small group of passengers inched their way down the bridge, their gaze locked on the mountain cavern waiting on the other end. From the way they gripped the bridge's gossamer railing, Lily could tell that they had not paid attention during the orientation or reviewed the train's handbook. Longtime passengers knew that the fastest way to cross a bridge made of anxieties and resentments was to let go of it. Lily strode past the new passengers, her hands clasped behind her back, her eyes in front of her. This was not a bridge you wanted to linger on.

Lily stepped off the bridge and walked into the large limestone cave that housed the Dragonfly's dining area. She greeted diners with a perfunctory nod, avoiding as many as she could. After what had just happened on the deck, she was not in the mood for pleasantries. The savory promise of lemongrass, ginger, garlic, coconut, chilies, and kaffir lime drifting through the cave from the buffet stations and open kitchen, however, made it difficult not to smile.

There was no question in Lily's mind that the Elsewhere Express's menu was its crowning achievement. The train's chefs were exceptionally creative, transforming the most ordinary thoughts into culinary masterpieces. From behind the glass window of the restaurant's kitchen, diners could watch them pull and stretch the mental grocery lists people made on their morning commute into fresh egg noodles and turn the most persistent intrusive thoughts into a spicy beef tendon stew. No thought that boarded the train ever went to waste.

Lily's smile grew wider at the sight of a song fluttering behind one of the maintenance crew's electricians. She tipped her cap at the electrician as the tall woman made her way to the dining car's kitchen, reserving a proper grin for the glowing song. The song circled back, grazing the tip of Lily's nose to say hello. Lily let out a small laugh despite the storm howling in her mind. The song's wings were thinner than paper, but they were strong enough to lift the corners of her lips into a wide smile. Lily could tell from its bright lyrics that it was meant to repair one of the Dragonfly's light bulbs. The song flew after the electrician, disappearing behind a broad-shouldered sous chef. The smile on Lily's face vanished with it, the storm growing louder in her head.

Lily filled a cup with oolong tea at the drinks station and chose a spot tucked away in a quiet corner of the cave. She set her tea down on a carved rosewood table more suited for an emperor's palace than a dining car. She settled into an equally ornate chair and warmed her hands around the steaming tea, keenly aware that the small cup contained the last moments of peace she was going to enjoy for a while. She lifted it to her lips and sipped it slowly.

Raya

The silence that filled the stairwell followed Raya out of the doorway and drowned every sound. Raya had no answer to give Q about why she needed to return to a life that had not made her smile as much as she had since she boarded the Elsewhere Express. None of the words in the stairwell helped. No matter how she arranged and rearranged them, nothing could explain the crime she had committed nor the sentence that she needed to serve.

"I think it's coming from over there." Q pointed to a cobweb bridge gently swinging between limestone cliffs.

Raya surfaced from her thoughts. "What is?"

"That buzzing. Don't you hear it?"

She angled her ear, becoming aware of the sound. "You're right. It's from the bridge."

Q squinted.

"What is it?" Raya said.

"Are those dragonflies?"

The cobweb bridge swayed beneath Raya's feet. Here, the buzzing was so loud, it vibrated in her teeth. Her heart pounded louder, demanding that she turn around and run back. She reached for the railing. A large hand grabbed her arm. Raya glanced up. A man the size of a bear, his pale hair flopping over a brown leather eyepatch, stared down at her with one clear blue eye. Raya yanked her arm free.

"Back off." Q jumped between Raya and the man, rocking the bridge.

Raya grabbed on to the railing.

"Just trying to help." The man's soft-spoken tone did not match his size, but compelled Raya to pay attention to his lips and listen closely, lest she miss a word. "Getting stuck to the bridge can be a bother, especially if you're hungry. I heard they're serving Hainanese chicken rice tonight."

Raya tried to let go of the railing. Her fingers were stuck. She tugged harder.

"Allow me." The man pulled out a metal ladybug, half the size of his palm, from his satchel. "Or I should say, 'allow Beatrice.' I named her after the woman whose thoughts I made her out of. She was very upset after catching her fiancé cheating. Beatrice has very sharp teeth. Don't move." He set the insect on the railing. "Off you go, B." It crawled over to Raya and nibbled at the cobwebs around her hand.

Raya's fingers came free, silver residue dripping from them. "Thank you," she said, trying to shake the residue off. The ladybug flew away and crawled back into the man's pocket. "What is this stuff?"

The man shut his good eye and turned an ear toward her hand. "It sounds like someone grumbling about their boss. You can wash it off when you get to the dining area."

"Sorry?" Raya said.

"I'll explain while we walk." The man proceeded down the bridge. "The railing's the stickiest part of the bridge, but the other parts get stickier the longer you linger. It's the nature of anything built from worries and grudges. If you don't let go of it, the stronger it will hold on to you. Didn't the conductor mention this during your orientation?"

Raya shook her head. "No."

"She might have been a bit distracted during our orientation," Q said.

"*Our* orientation?" The man stopped. "You had the passenger orientation at the same time?"

Raya nodded. "We both boarded this evening and that got us off to a bit of a chaotic start. Q boarded through the back door and so his name wasn't on the manifest."

The man raised eyebrows so pale, they vanished against his skin.

"And then lightning set a sail on fire," Q added.

"I see." The man nodded, his tone flat.

"We're on the way to meet up with the conductor." Q held his arms out slightly, balancing on the swaying bridge. "I'm guessing she asked to see us so we can cover the topics we missed."

"That's not the reason for the meeting," the man said.

Raya tilted her head up to look at him. "How do you know?"

"Because the conductor asked to see me too. I'm Other Rasmus, by the way, but you can just call me Rasmus since you probably haven't met my other versions yet."

"Other versions?" Q said.

"It's one of the quirks of being on a train that loops around time." Rasmus tapped the gold knot embroidered on the collar of his jacket. "The Elsewhere Express is a wonder, but it's not perfect. Sometimes, it picks up the same passenger when the tracks twist and double back. I believe there are three versions of me now. Or is it four?" He scratched his beard. "We also have quite a few versions of our pharmacist, Mr. Goh, which is wonderful. The pharmacy never has to close."

Raya's neck and shoulders tightened. She had enough trouble looking at her own face in the mirror. Another version of herself would know all the thoughts she kept locked away. The hardest words to hear weren't those uttered by other people. They were the words you refused to say out loud.

"Anyway, even if you had met the other *Rasmi,*" Rasmus said with a smirk, "you wouldn't have been able to tell that we were the same person. It isn't just the conductor who changes faces. Some of the passengers do too. It helps pass the time when you're traveling across eternity, trying to get as far as possible from who you used to be."

YOUR ITINERARY

STORYTELLING AT THE STEW

"What's in the stew?"

Frequently Asked Questions
THE ELSEWHERE EXPRESS
PASSENGER HANDBOOK

Raya

Raya had seen the look on Lily's face before. It was the face a person wore when they knew the words to apologize, but not quite the right ones to set things right. Children learned it when they knocked over glass vases or lost their new lunch box at school. Some people grew up and perfected it after years in medical school, donning it when they walked into waiting rooms and told parents that their dreams were shattered beyond all hope of repair. Whatever Lily was about to say was not going to be good.

"Red hair." Rasmus took a seat at the rosewood table. "I thought you were never going to do that again."

"It was unavoidable." Lily set her teacup down and looked at Raya and Q. "I'm glad that both of you were able to find your way here so quickly. I trust that your trip through the emergency exit wasn't too terrible?"

"What's this about, Lily?" Raya sat stiffly. "Why are we here?"

"Believe me, Ms. Sia, this isn't something I wanted to do." She glanced at Raya's hand. "I know that locating your compartment should be top priority but finding it won't matter if we don't"—her eyes darted around the dining area—"address the train's current predicament." She lowered her voice.

"Raya and I just boarded," Q said. "How does this have anything to do with us?"

"It's best if we continue this conversation in the Stew, Mr. Philips. I've asked the kitchen to prepare it. It should be ready by now."

"What's the Stew?" Raya said. "Is it a meeting room or something?"

"Or something." Rasmus stood up and made his way to the dining car's kitchen.

Q

A slightly built chef with a half-moon-shaped birthmark on his pointed chin silently tended to the stew gently bubbling in a corner of the Dragonfly's large kitchen. It was a task that Q was quite familiar with even if the only kitchen appliances he ever used were his microwave and refrigerator. His talent for painting was rivaled only by his skill at keeping his anger from boiling over.

His mother thought it was one of his best traits and told him that he was a lot like his father that way. While other children threw embarrassing tantrums, Q was content to sit quietly and simmer. He blended his more inconvenient feelings into the darkest pigments he could find, using them to paint singed moths in places where he shouldn't. He ran a thumb under his collar, grazing the insect inked into his skin.

"The Stew is made up of unspoken thoughts. Rage. Love. Grief. The kitchen staff reduces it into a spicy dip for dumplings." Lily bent over the stew and sniffed it. "Anything you say while you're inside the Stew will never leave this room." She straightened and patted the shoulder of the chef minding the stew. "Thank you, Olly. This is perfect."

Olly kept his eyes on the pot.

"Excellent work." Rasmus put his arm around Olly's narrow,

hunched shoulders, dwarfing him. He drew Olly away from the stove and walked him over to the kitchen's main area. "Thank you."

A gray-haired chef nodded at Rasmus and led Olly to one of the kitchen's other stoves. He placed a cooking spoon in Olly's hand and gently closed Olly's fingers around it. Olly gripped the spoon's handle and blinked, becoming aware of what he was supposed to do. He set the spoon inside a large soup pot, his eyes growing distant as he stirred.

"Is he all right?" Q's fingers twitched the way they did when they ached to hold a brush. Olly had one of those faces he would have painted for free. Paying Olly for this privilege, however, was out of the question. Purchasing the truth turned it into a performance and Q had no interest in buying a ticket to see a show. The only thing he cared to capture was the story hiding behind the curtains of Olly's eyes. If he squinted, he could almost make out its shape.

"Olly entered a locked door and got lost." Lily fixed her gaze on the bubbling stew. "And it took us a very long time to find him."

"How long?" Raya asked.

Rasmus exhaled heavily. "Too long."

"We don't use calendars or clocks here." Lily looked up from the pot. "But my best guess was that he was gone for what would be called twenty years in the world outside the train."

"Or a hundred," Rasmus said, his voice swallowed by his beard. "There's no way to know for sure."

"That's terrible." Raya pressed her hand over her mouth. "Where was he all that time?"

Lily took a sip of the stew. "The maintenance crew found him when they were repairing a broken clothes rack in the cloakroom," she said, adding a sprinkle of salt to the pot. "Coats had fallen from the rack and were scattered over the floor. Olly rolled out of the inner pocket of one of the coats. He had been in the MMD the whole time."

"The MMD?" Q inhaled the stew's heady aroma, salivating at the blend of garlic, chilies, and ginger.

"The Missed and Misplaced Department." Lily cracked pepper into the pot. "It's the Elsewhere Express's version of the lost and found. It includes things people long for alongside the things they've mislaid."

"And because that train car is meant for storage," Rasmus said, "it's the one place on the train where we don't keep frames. Without one, Olly couldn't find the door."

"Olly's never been able to explain how he found his way out of the MMD but we guess he must have stumbled on a doorway by accident," Lily added.

"Why didn't anyone bother to look for him there?" Raya asked.

"The items in the MMD aren't things the Elsewhere Express's passengers have lost, Ms. Sia. They're thoughts that board the train, worries people have when they lose their things. It isn't a place that the train's passengers would have any reason to visit. Until Olly was found, most passengers didn't even know that such a place existed."

"When Olly returned, he wasn't quite the same." Rasmus cast a glance back at the thin sous chef. "Luckily, we discovered that stirring pots calmed him. We don't know why."

"We should get going. We have a lot to discuss." Lily climbed into the pot of stew.

The Stew, to Q's relief, was neither scalding nor wet. Instead, it resembled a small cottage tucked deep in the woods, a place so quiet that if a tree fell, it would have been terribly ashamed of itself for making a sound. Even the fire casting shadows over the room from the stone fireplace was silent. But what the flames lacked in crackling, the fire made up for in scent. Q lowered his eyelids and took his fill of pine, cloves, and Christmas. He opened his eyes and caught the corners of Raya's mouth lifting the slightest bit upward. She pulled them down. "Why did you change your mind?" he whispered.

"Change my mind?"

"About smiling. It's not wrong to find things to smile about here, you know."

"It is." Raya took a seat on the checkered couch facing the fire.

"When you can't stay." She turned her hand over and checked on the gold knot.

Q sat next to her, stealing a peek at it. It was slightly looser than it was at the island, but intact. "I haven't forgotten, by the way."

"Forgotten what?"

"That you haven't answered my question about why you're so desperate to get off this train." Nor had Q forgotten what Raya's hand had felt like when they had found each other inside the kettle. Going blind had forced him to rely on more than just his sight. His skin noticed and remembered things his eyes did not. Had the kettle not been pitch-black, his memory of her hand might have been made of nothing more than its shape, shade, and size. But his skin recalled the fear they shared and the relief they provided each other in the dark. And something else. A secret that snaked under her flesh, tensing her fingers and chilling her hands, the same secret that was always quick to tear the smallest hint of a smile from her face.

Raya set her bag on her lap and stared into the fire. "Olly must have been just like the others on this train before he got lost. He found his place. He had purpose. He was happy. Then on one random day, he lost everything. I don't know how or why he got lost, but what if it was someone else's fault? Do you think that person should be on this train?" Raya hugged her bag, tears glistening in the firelight. "Do you think someone like that, someone who's caused that kind of harm, deserves to be happy?"

Q knitted his brows. "I don't—"

"So." Rasmus sank into an armchair across from the fire. "What's this all about?"

Lily sat down and clasped her hands tightly over her lap. "Rain."

Rasmus's jaw tensed beneath his beard. "It never rains on the Elsewhere Express."

"We've told ourselves that often enough, haven't we?" Lily opened her satchel and pulled out two small vials containing an inky black liquid.

Raya jumped to her feet. "I'm not drinking that."

"These aren't for you, Ms. Sia. It's for me and Rasmus."

Rasmus stood up and paced in front of the fire, casting massive shadows over the room. He slammed his fist against a wall. "It never rains on the Elsewhere Express," he said, his voice as quiet as his fist was loud.

Lily walked up to him and touched his arm. "You and I don't have the luxury of believing that lie anymore." She looked at Raya and Q. "And neither do they."

"Is anyone going to tell us what's going on or are you going to keep speaking in riddles the whole night?" Q said.

"You're right, Mr. Philips. You and Ms. Sia will have the full story." Lily handed one of the vials to Rasmus. "As soon as Rasmus and I remember it. That's what the serum's for."

Rasmus held the vial up against the light of the fire. Not a sliver of light pierced through its dark contents. "The serum is to help us recall something we chose to forget."

"Your old life?" Raya asked.

Lily shook her head. "An incident that happened on the train a long time ago."

Rasmus stared at the tiny vial in his large hand. "Remembering the events of that evening posed a threat to this train. We decided that it was best to erase them."

"How can a memory be a threat?" Q said.

"Thoughts are fragile things." The fireplace's glow softened Lily's face. "Great ideas are born every day and killed by a whisper or a shred of doubt. People talk themselves out of thoughts as fast as they create them. The thoughts that make this train as limitless as our imagination also make it vulnerable to our insecurities and fears. Rasmus and I could not keep a memory that terrified us. It was too dangerous."

"Fear spreads." Rasmus rolled the serum between his fingers, making the liquid crash against the vial's glass walls like dark waves. "The Elsewhere Express has very little room on board for our past and even less for doubt. If passengers questioned this train's ability to keep them safe then—" He squeezed the vial.

"Then what?" Raya's eyes darted between Rasmus and Lily. "What would happen?"

"The train would shatter." Lily's face lost the illusion of softness. "And all its passengers would cease to exist."

"Hold on." Q waved his hand as though erasing all that Lily and Rasmus had laid before them. "Hold on. That sounds terrifying, but aren't we getting ahead of ourselves? You don't even remember what the incident is. How do you know that we're in danger?"

"We know because we kept one part of the memory as a message to ourselves," Lily said. "Rain."

"It never rains on the Elsewhere Express." Rasmus clenched his jaw, pulling his thick neck muscles taut. "Except when there's something on board that the train desperately needs to wash away. We retained enough of the incident to warn us that if it ever rained here again, the danger was back."

"And that we would need help saving the train from it." Lily uncorked her vial.

Rasmus flicked his vial's stopper with his thumb and sent the tiny piece of cork into the fire. "Ready?"

Lily tossed her head back, swallowing the serum in a single gulp.

"Why are all the curtains on the Elsewhere Express shut?"

Frequently Asked Questions
THE ELSEWHERE EXPRESS
PASSENGER HANDBOOK

Lily (who was not yet named Lily)
A Memory

Rapid knocking rattled her compartment's door. Lily rolled to her side, groaning into her pillow. Though she had nothing to keep track of time, she still had enough sense of her body clock to know that it was too early to start her day on the train. She had just boarded and had not yet settled on which department to join. She helped whichever department needed an extra hand that day, choosing to hold off on making a decision until she had tried all of them. So far, she enjoyed working at the Lotus the most, learning cocktail recipes and serving welcome drinks to new passengers. She had, however, crossed out the painting department. She had no talent for painting. Today, she was scheduled to assist the train's conductor.

The knocking grew louder.

"Who is it?" Lily's voice scraped the sides of her dry throat. A dream nuzzled her ear, calling her back. Her eyelids grew heavy. Her compartment made it easy to fall back to sleep. The room was large enough to be comfortable, but small enough to make her feel safe. On days that she felt lonely, it gave her a hug by shrinking ever so slightly and adding extra pillows on her bed.

"It's me, Rasmus."

"Which one?" Lily mumbled into her blanket. Getting out of bed was the hardest part about her life on the train. Her compartment cocooned her in every comfort, from the softest of bamboo silk sheets to a lush carpet of fresh grass. Its temperature was always set just right, anticipating her needs before she could shiver or sweat. In the evenings, a night sky stretched across her ceiling, complete with a dimmable moon. Lily usually set it on a waxing crescent. Some nights, she hid it behind clouds. The compartment had originally come with birds to sing her to sleep, but Lily requested housekeeping to remove them, finding their song too loud. But as soon as the birds were gone, she realized what they were for. Without their chirping, there was nothing to mask the sound of the Echoes wailing and scratching at her window. She called housekeeping and asked them to return the birds and sew her curtains shut.

"Other Rasmus," the voice behind the door said.

Lily bolted up, rubbing the sleep from her eyes. She had not expected the conductor to start his shift so early. She jumped out of bed and slipped her robe on. "Come in. The door's unlocked."

Rasmus strode into the room and bent down, his head grazing the top of the doorway. His pale-blond hair, dented by the mark of a cap, fell over his ice-blue eyes. "I'm sorry for disturbing you. I know that we're supposed to meet after breakfast, but there's been an incident that I need your assistance with."

Lily shut the door behind him. "Of course. What happened?"

"We have a stowaway. Someone left the back door unlocked."

"What?"

Rasmus pushed his hair out of his eyes. "I'll need your help finding it."

"It?" Lily tilted her head.

"We don't know exactly what's boarded the train. No one has seen it."

Lily frowned. "Then how do you know it's here?"

"The rain."

There was still a long list of things about the Elsewhere Express that Lily did not understand, but she had not expected that she would need to add the weather to it.

"I'll explain everything later. Right now, we need to find the stowaway. Get dressed. I'll wait outside."

"Shouldn't we just wait until morning? It will be easier to search the train cars then."

Rasmus stopped at the door and turned around to face her. "Do you know how many dining cars the Elsewhere Express has?"

Lily nodded. "Four. The Dragonfly, the Lantern, the River, and the Lake."

"Not anymore," Rasmus said. "Now it has three. The Lake's gone. The stowaway destroyed it."

Lily gasped. The Lake was a wonder on the Elsewhere Express, a dining car where passengers picnicked on lily pads floating on a clear lake and dined on fine plates painted with flowers that danced in the breeze. Tiered fountains dotted the water, serenading passengers with their gentle gurgle.

Lily had not been surprised to learn that the Lake had been crafted from the most inspired thoughts that found their way on board. The latest addition to the dining car was a crystal fountain that spouted stars. It had taken the Elsewhere Express's craftspeople three revolutions of the train to collect the thoughts that made up the crystal the fountain was carved from. The thoughts had all come from a single person, a cleaning lady who had been working on a book of poetry every night on her train ride home. Her words flowed slower than a trickle, but their syllables tasted like sea salt and dark chocolate, each as rich as it was bittersweet.

"Only a handful of people know about what happened to the Lake, and we need to keep it that way," Rasmus said. "We don't want to cause a panic. I've just sent a memo out to tell the passengers that the Lake's under maintenance."

"How long will it take?"

"To what?"

"To repair the Lake."

Rasmus shook his head. "It can't be repaired."

"Of course it can. It might take some time, but I'm sure the maintenance crew will be able to gather enough songs to patch it up. It will be as good as new. Everything on this train can be fixed."

"Everything"—Rasmus slipped his conductor's cap on—"except this."

Rasmus helped Lily through the Lake's door and they emerged from a jade snuff bottle lying on the ground. A sickly sweet, putrid smell tainted the air. Lily grimaced, covering her nose and mouth. The once-clear lake festered like an abscess, bubbling with reeking, dark pus. No trace of its fountains or lily pads remained. Rotting vines crawled out of the lake to strangle withered trees. Beneath the choked branches, the songs that had been used to repair the train car over its immeasurable lifetime decayed into inky black pools. The foul soup soaked the ground, turning it into a sludge of mud and rot. Lily vomited over her shoes.

"Are you all right?" Thunder rumbled over Rasmus's voice.

Lily wiped her mouth on her sleeve and managed to nod.

"Luckily, there weren't many people around when the stowaway struck." Rasmus surveyed the car. "The few that were here managed to escape."

"And no one saw the stowaway?"

Rasmus shook his head. "That's why we're here. Hopefully, we can find clues before we have to decouple the Lake from the rest of the train."

"Decouple?" Lily choked. "There has to be another way."

"Nothing can save this place. Not all the songs in the world. Let's get to work. I think we should—"

The black sludge gave way under Lily's left foot, swallowing it up to her ankle. Lily grabbed on to Rasmus and yanked her foot out, leaving her boot behind. Decay consumed it. Lily screamed.

Rasmus cursed and scooped her up. "Hold on."

A song crawled out from a pocket in the mud, flapped its wings until they glowed, and escaped to Lily's shoulder.

Rasmus carried Lily through a doorway and into one of the train's game lounges. "Are you hurt?" He set her down on a giant mahjong tile.

"I . . . I'm sorry I panicked." The song flew from Lily's shoulder and settled on top of her head. "We should go back."

"No. The Lake is lost. We need to decouple it before the rot spreads. I'd do it myself but it's a two-person job."

Lily had never witnessed a car being decoupled but imagined that it was going to be a matter of pressing a button or flipping a switch. "Tell me what I need to do."

"We need to go outside to access the coupler."

"*Outside?* But what about the Echoes?"

"That's why it's a task for two people. One of us will have to keep the Echoes away while the other decouples the train. The Echoes can't enter the train, but they can make our task a lot more difficult. We mustn't let them distract us—or worse, make us fall. The Elsewhere Express may break a lot of rules, but not those that govern blood and bone."

The train car adjacent to the Lake was one of the few cars where the Elsewhere Express revealed its true form. Glass walls enclosed a vintage train carriage furnished with polished antiques. Plush, emerald-green velvet seats were arranged around low dark wood tables on top of which rested backgammon boards and brass ashtrays. At the far end of the car, tall lit shelves displayed wooden boxes filled with cigars. Stars twinkled above one half of the carriage's clear ceiling. Daylight, muted by a thick mist, shone through the other. Inside, the train car was split into day and night too.

Lily had never been to this part of the Elsewhere Express. Before tonight, she had come to believe that the train was simply a metaphor, a way to put the impossible into words. But now she saw that she was wrong. Silver tracks glowed through the car's transparent floor, as visible as the glass wheels, gears, axles, and coupling rods that kept the train speeding forward. "I didn't expect it to look like this."

"Like what?" Rasmus said. "An actual train? You're new. You've barely seen anything. I've been here much longer than you and I'm still discovering places to visit. New train cars are constantly being added. You could live a thousand lifetimes and never see all of them. This one is called the Belvedere. It's a cigar lounge built from the thoughts people wear plainly on their faces, whether they're aware of it or not." He ran his hand over a clear wall. "This panel is made from a wide assortment of guilt." He looked up at the see-through ceiling. "And the roof is a marriage proposal a young man composed in his head while on his way to meet the love of his life. The Belvedere is one of the most beautiful train cars on the Elsewhere Express. It's a pity that it hardly ever has any visitors."

Lily stared through a glass wall. If the Echoes were outside, the mist hid them. "Is it because people are afraid of seeing the Echoes?"

"I'm sure that's part of it, but even when there weren't as many Echoes as there are now, and this car enjoyed long stretches of track without them, passengers still didn't come by here often."

"Why?"

"No one wants to be reminded about how fragile the Elsewhere—" Rasmus angled an ear toward the floor. "Did you hear that?"

"Hear what?"

"Listen." Rasmus pressed a finger to his lips.

Lily closed her eyes. A faint cracking sound sent a chill up her spine. "What was that?"

Rasmus peeled back the corner of a Persian rug. A hairline crack crawled across the floor. He balled his large hand into a fist. "It's started."

"What's started?"

"The passengers who escaped from the Lake are telling the others about what happened. Fear is spreading through the train." Rasmus traced the crack with his finger. "And so are cracks."

"What? How?"

"Ideas and dreams aren't broken by hammers. They're shattered by worries and doubts."

Rasmus disappeared through the Belvedere's window and climbed the ladder to the roof.

Lily turned to the song on her shoulder. "Wait for us here."

The song folded its wings, refusing to leave its perch. Its melody wound its way to Lily's ears. She shut her eyes, compelled to listen.

The song bore the melancholy of the grayest of days, when people huddled in blankets by their windows, waiting for the excuse of rain to let their tears fall. Lily guessed that the song had been used to repair a leak in the Lake. Sadness clung to most surfaces, making it an excellent sealant. And now it clung to her.

"No. You can't come. It's not safe," Lily pleaded. The song was all that remained of the Lake and she would never forgive herself if it followed her to the roof and got hurt. "Please. You're the only one left."

The song flew off to an armchair with heavy wings.

Lily stuck her head out the window and squinted in the wind. There were no Echoes in sight. Lily reached for the ladder, glanced back at the song, and climbed up.

"Grab on to me." Rasmus pulled her up to the roof.

An endless chain of crystal train cars snaked along the mountainside like a serpent. "Where are the Echoes?" Lily glanced around.

"That's the advantage of climbing out of an unpopular train car," Rasmus said. "The Echoes prefer to gather where passengers congregate. We'll need to move quickly before they notice we're here." He led the way to the end of the train car, pausing every few steps to steady himself. He crouched at the edge of the car and pulled two unlit torches from his satchel. They ignited in blue flames. He handed one to Lily. "Whatever you see next, you need to stay calm."

Lily nodded and looked over the edge of the car. Between the cars lay a metal statue of two naked bodies sleeping next to each other, locked in an embrace. One body's back was fused to the train car Lily was on while the other's was melded to the Lake's. Their skin shone in the torches' blue light like burnished steel. The metal lovers stirred, holding each other tighter. They smiled in their sleep. "Who are they?"

"Not *who. What,*" Rasmus said. "That's the coupler, the mechanism that links the train's carriages. There's a pair between every car. They're thoughts, just like everything else on this train."

"But why do they look like people?"

"Couplers keep the train together. They need to be incredibly strong. They're melded from the solemn vows that people have made to themselves or others. The thoughts took on this form on their own, eternal words in the shape of eternal lovers."

"How do we unlink them?" Lily's chest tightened.

"The coupler is strong but not unbreakable. These torches are made from distrust and lies."

Whispers swirled in the wind. The torches' blue flames flickered.

"The Echoes. They're coming. Decouple the train now." Rasmus ran down the car, waving his torch in the air. "Over here!" Phantoms grabbed at his arms and legs, howling as they coiled around him. *Let me in. Let me in. Let me in.*

Lily forced herself to look at the coupler. *They're thoughts. Not people. They're thoughts. Not people.* She hurled the torch at the body that was attached to the Lake and struck its hip. It stirred. Blue flames engulfed it and rapidly spread to the rest of the train car. Metal melted, releasing the vows the statue was made of: *Never again. Always. I swear, I won't let this beat me.*

The train car exploded into a galaxy of stars and for a moment, it was beautiful. In the next, it was gone. The remaining half of the coupler curled into a ball and cried metal tears. Lily wept with it.

The uncoupled train cars caught up to the Belvedere. A metal body, identical in every way to the one Lily had burned, lay on its side, fused to the front of the approaching car. It dried its tears and smiled, extending its arms to its other half. The lovers pulled each other into an embrace, renewed their vows, and made the train whole.

Lily watched the pair fall back to sleep, her heart thundering over the train's roar and the Echoes' screeches. Between the carriages was a truth as terrifying as the cracks spreading across the Belvedere. Lily had given up her past to live forever without baggage, but now she saw that eternity was not a covenant that the Elsewhere Express could keep. No one could. Vows were as flimsy as wishful thinking, promises as breakable as the people who made them, fragile, just like everything else on the train.

THE THIRD LEG

NOWHERE

I thought how unpleasant it is to be locked out; and I thought how it is worse perhaps to be locked in.

—Virginia Woolf

YOUR ITINERARY

MAP READING
TUTORIAL AT
THE ARCHIVE

"Where can I borrow a map of the train?"

Frequently Asked Questions
THE ELSEWHERE EXPRESS
PASSENGER HANDBOOK

Lily

A frothy scum blurred the memories bubbling to the surface of Lily's mind. She tried to skim it off but could not keep up. Shapes, shadows, and sounds rose in a turbulent stream, obscuring the events that transpired after the Lake had been decoupled from the rest of the train. Lily hurled the serum's empty vial into the fire. "It didn't work."

"Mr. Goh warned us that this could happen," Rasmus said. "We knew retrieving a memory wouldn't be as easy as getting rid of it. Serums are much better at washing things away than bringing them back."

Lily sank into her chair. Every version of the pharmacist had hated the thought of breaking the train's rules when Rasmus requested they make the serum. The passenger handbook clearly stated that retrieving lost luggage was strictly prohibited. Mr. Goh gulped down his excess baggage serum as soon as he had completed Rasmus's order to rid himself of his guilt.

"How about you, Rasmus?" Raya leaned forward on the sofa. "Do you remember anything else?"

"No. I've told you all that I remember about that night. Everything that happened after we decoupled the Lake and regrouped at the Belvedere is a blur."

"Are you going to ask the pharmacist to make more serum?" Q said.

Rasmus shook his head. "The poems Mr. Goh used to create the serum only blossomed at the Lake. We don't have any left to make more doses."

"And even if we did, it's now obvious that retrieving memories isn't really Mr. Goh's forte." Lily sighed.

Q kneaded his nape. "This was just a huge waste of time then."

"Not entirely." Lily sat straighter. "Now we know for sure that the stowaway we're dealing with is extremely similar to, if not the same as, the stowaway we dealt with last time."

"We do?" Raya said. "Did I miss something? You don't know what either of them even look like."

"But I remember what the stowaway left in its wake. The rotting vines. The foul water. The stench in the air. I also remember what it was like to be around it. It was the same feeling I got when that storm began brewing this evening."

"You sensed the stowaway on the deck?" Raya said.

"And so did you, Ms. Sia. I saw it in your eyes."

Raya frowned. "What are you talking about?"

"The stowaway feels like old sorrow." Rasmus stared at his hands. "The unshakable kind."

Q slid his fingertips down the front of his neck. "Like a rock that's stuck in your throat . . ."

"And in your chest." Raya pressed her hand over her ribs.

"That jagged heaviness isn't a feeling you can mistake for something else." Lily sighed.

"If all three of you felt it, then the safest course of action is to assume that the stowaway, or something like it, is back." Rasmus drew his shoulders back and seemed to double in size. "We may not recall how we stopped it, but the fact that we're alive means we succeeded. What we did once we can do again."

"I don't understand how Raya and I fit into all of this," Q said.

"We obviously won't be of much help. We don't know our way around the train. We'd only slow you down, or worse, get lost. Why choose two people that could turn into Echoes at any moment to help you? The more experienced people you have searching for the stowaway, the sooner you'll be able to find it."

Lily shook her head. "And the faster the cracks would spread. I don't want to involve more passengers than necessary. That would only create panic. I'm sorry, but whether you like it or not, you and Raya got involved in this from the moment storm clouds gathered over the deck. You may not have known what it was at that time, but you felt the stowaway's presence. There's no need for anyone else beyond the four of us to know what's going on."

Raya scoffed.

"Did I say something wrong, Ms. Sia?" Lily said.

"You never stop lying, do you?"

"Why would I lie about something like this? The Elsewhere Express is in very real danger."

"That's not what you're lying about." Raya looked Lily in the eye. "Why don't you just tell us the real reason why, out of all the passengers on this train, you picked me and Q?"

Raya

Raya knew the difference between precious things and spare parts. Dangerous work required expendable tools and there were few things that were more disposable than two passengers who had yet to find their place on the train. Until she and Q located their compartments, they were just as much outsiders on the Elsewhere Express as the Echoes were. "Admit it, Lily. You chose us because we don't matter. I don't want to be here and Q wasn't even on tonight's manifest. If we fall off this train or rot like those songs you told us about, no one will notice or care in the slightest that we're missing."

Lily shook her head. "Ms. Sia, I—"

"And it's not like we have a choice in the matter, do we?" Raya said. "We obviously can't just wait for the Elsewhere Express to decay or shatter."

"You're right," Rasmus said. "You can't. Not if you want to live."

"Just tell us what we need to do." A tempest gathered in Q's voice. This man, Raya thought, was not going to have his sight or life ripped from him twice.

"We need to search the train." Lily stood up. "I lost the stowaway's trail somewhere between the art gallery and the opera house so that should be your starting point."

"Have you forgotten that we don't know our way around this train?" Raya said.

"I haven't. You'll need a map. We store them at the Archive. Rasmus can take you there."

"And what will you be doing?" Raya asked.

"I'll be putting on a smile, running this train, and making sure that no one on board has any reason to doubt that everything on the Elsewhere Express is anything less than perfectly normal."

"How do I use the Archive?"

Frequently Asked Questions
THE ELSEWHERE EXPRESS
PASSENGER HANDBOOK

Raya

Concentric layers of carved white jade formed the Archive's domed ceiling. Moonlight trickled through a pattern of chiseled trellises and flowers, painting a delicate lace of light and shadow on the jade floor. Apart from a pair of black onyx pedestals beneath the center of the dome and a handful of red lacquered reading tables and chairs, the only other thing that occupied the cavernous room was a silky, contemplative quiet.

"This place looks like a cathedral." Raya's voice echoed through the train car. "Or a temple."

"It sounds like one too." Q gazed up at the ceiling.

"I've practically moved in here since I retired," Rasmus said. "The Archivist position is vacant at the moment and so I'm filling in. I assist the occasional visitor, and in return I get the space to work on my little hobbies. My projects have taken over my compartment. I don't remember the last time I saw my floor."

He gestured to a miniature railway that looped in the shape of the train's eternal knot over four reading tables that had been pushed together. Tiny crystal trains, three cars long, quietly made their way to nowhere, little puffs of steam rising from their faceted smokestacks.

"That's quite the setup." Q's eyes followed the little trains on their endless route.

"Thank you." Rasmus smiled. "I built it out of the childhood memories that board the Elsewhere Express. The train didn't have much use for them, and it was a shame to let them go to waste."

"You made these?" Raya raised her brows.

"If we can't shape our thoughts, what can we shape? But this train set is quite literally child's play. Wait until you see how the Archive works." Rasmus made his way to the onyx pedestals.

Raya followed him.

Q held her back. "We'll catch up," he called after Rasmus.

Rasmus nodded and walked on until he was out of earshot.

"I think you're right," Q whispered.

Raya lifted her face to meet his eyes. "About what?"

"About why Lily chose us. I hate to admit it, but we *are* expendable."

"I was hoping you were going to disagree with me." Raya sighed. "But disposable or not, we need to stop the stowaway."

"That's where you're wrong." Q glanced over his shoulder at Rasmus.

"What are you talking about?" Raya narrowed her eyes. "The stowaway will destroy this train if we don't catch it."

"But that's just it. That's not going to happen. Rasmus said it himself. He and Lily may not remember how they caught the stowaway, but that doesn't change the fact that they did. There's no reason they'd fail now. I'm going to help them because I'm desperate to stay on this train." He clasped her hand. "But you shouldn't have to." He turned her hand over, exposing the knot unraveling over her palm. "You're running out of time, Raya. Lily told us that finding our compartment is about finding our true selves. I highly doubt that's something any map in the Archive can point you to. Is chasing the stowaway around the train a risk you want to take when you have no idea how much time you have left?"

Rasmus stood behind the twin onyx pedestals. A carved white jade sphere nested on a simple wooden stand on top of one of them while a blue notebook that had seen better days was displayed on the other.

"Welcome to your crash course on how to use the Archive." He gestured to the sphere. "Do you know what this is?"

"My grandmother had one," Q said, "but it was a lot less intricate. I believe it's called a Generation Ball."

Rasmus nodded. "Correct."

Raya stared at the frayed knot on her palm, half listening to Rasmus and Q. The gold flecks floating around the knot had doubled, bumping into the name of her subway station and the date and time she had boarded her train. She gripped her bag. The only way she was getting home was if she bought herself more time.

Rasmus pointed to the notebook on the second pedestal. "And this is a warning."

"A warning?" Raya looked up from the loosening knot. "About what?"

Rasmus handed the notebook to her. "Have a look."

Raya flipped through its pages, Q by her side. Drawings of walls made of phones and wallets and furniture built from eyeglasses and gloves were scattered throughout it. A few pages were devoted to sketches of a door that resembled a leaf and a crooked tower that touched the clouds. But what stood out from all these drawings were the images that grew darker with every turn of the page. Spirals of all shapes and sizes overlapped one another, some sketched so deeply they ripped through the paper.

"It belongs to Olly." Rasmus returned the notebook to the pedestal. "Passengers who borrow the Archive's maps are required to look through it to remind them what happens when you stray from the map and open locked doors."

Q glanced at Raya, silently prodding her to tell Rasmus that she was backing out of the search. She drew a deep breath. "Rasmus, I won't—"

"I know," Rasmus said. "You won't make the same mistake Olly did. That's what everyone says when I show them this notebook. Olly was the last person anyone thought would get lost. He worked in maintenance and knew the train like the knot on his hand. But the truth is, no one can know everything about a train made of ever-changing thoughts. This Archive can barely keep up with all the knowledge that boards the Elsewhere Express." Rasmus plucked the carved jade sphere from the pedestal. "Take a look at this."

The sphere was made up of a series of free-moving spheres enclosing smaller spheres. A carved dragon and a phoenix slept beneath swirling clouds on the outermost sphere while circular holes on each layer of jade simultaneously hid and revealed the scene carved on the inner balls. Fine jade dust scattered in the air. Raya sneezed. Minuscule carvings appeared on the outermost sphere as though an artist, too tiny to be seen, busily chipped away at the stone.

"This is an exact model of the Archive," Rasmus said. "Thoughts are etched into the jade as they arrive. What you're seeing is what's presently happening on the Archive's outermost sphere."

Raya's gaze flew to the Archive's domed ceiling, her mouth hanging open. "If this is a model, then that would mean—"

"That we're inside the Archive's innermost sphere." Rasmus pushed the side of the onyx pedestal. A seamless drawer soundlessly slid open, revealing a thin gold rod resting on a black velvet cushion. Rasmus took the rod and inserted it through the Generation Ball, maneuvering the inner spheres. The giant layers of jade surrounding the room silently moved as the model did.

Q gaped at the shifting ceiling. "Incredible."

Rasmus peered into the Archive's model, checking the positions of its spheres. "Every invention, discovery, and story started out as someone's daydream. All their beginnings are kept here. Layers are added with every generation of knowledge that finds its way onto the train." He slipped the gold rod through another carved hole and moved more layers around. He looked up at Raya and Q. "I hope the two of you get along."

"Why?" Raya said.

"The map's too large and heavy for one person to carry. You'll have to share its weight."

"Rasmus, about that . . ." Raya glanced at Q.

Q gave her a nod.

"Yes?" Rasmus said.

"I—" Raya dropped her eyes to her bag. Its contents appeared as ashen as the cadavers in her anatomy class. She wondered if they had always looked like this or if they had dulled in comparison to all the brighter things she had seen since she boarded: The songs on the beach. Q's star. His eyes when he painted it. "I just want to say that sharing the map's weight with Q won't be an issue."

Q's brows shot up.

Raya did not expect him to understand her choice. She could not deny that it was the wrong one under their present circumstances. But decisions were time travelers, living in the past, present, and future all at once. This one grew from the roots of the sense of responsibility that lived inside her like a twin absorbed in the womb. It ivied across the unraveling knot on her palm and stretched as far as it could toward tomorrow. Raya had not made the decision as the person who stood beside Q, but as the person she wanted to wake up as in the morning. Choosing herself over a train might keep her alive, but it was not going to save her.

"Good. I'm glad to hear that." Rasmus adjusted the inner spheres until a series of holes from the outermost to the innermost sphere aligned to form a tunnel. "The Archive will lend you the map shortly." The model floated off his palm, drifted back to the pedestal, and hovered over its stand. The tiny phoenix on its outer sphere burst into flames and flew around the carved dragon. The dragon yawned and shook itself awake, rippling the scales from the top of its head to the end of its tail. The dragon crawled across the sphere and dove into the mouth of the newly formed tunnel. "It's coming."

The sound of slithering scales reverberated through the dome. Raya's eyes followed it across the ceiling to the tunnel's mouth directly above her. A gust of wind howled through the opening, riffling the pages of Olly's old notebook. A jade dragon's head burst out of the tunnel, locked eyes on Raya, and charged at her. Q lunged, shoving her from its path. The dragon stopped inches from Q's face and roared, its breath shrouding the Archive in an impenetrable mist.

"Raya—" Q's voice quivered. "I can't see."

Blinded by the thick fog, Raya felt around for his hand. "You're okay, Q," she said, finding and squeezing his trembling fingers. "You're okay."

"Deep breaths." Rasmus's voice echoed. "Draw it inside you."

Q

The air cleared, lifting the blindfold of mist from their eyes. Q exhaled, his clammy fingers wrapped tightly around Raya's hand. He released her, heat spreading over his neck. He cleared his throat of imaginary grit. "What just happened?"

"The Archive lent you the map of the Elsewhere Express," Rasmus said.

Raya glanced around. "Where is it?"

"A train made of thoughts isn't mappable on paper. Thoughts move and morph inside the Elsewhere Express just as they do in your head. The train's map is a collection of these thoughts. It will be obsolete by morning. Until then, it will suit our purpose."

"The dragon's breath was the map?" Raya said.

Rasmus nodded. "And now that it's inside both of you, you'll be able to see how the train cars are connected and find the fastest routes to each car."

Q squinted. "I don't see anything."

"Neither do I," Raya said. "Did something go wrong?"

"Give it a moment. The map will reveal itself when you're ready to see," Rasmus said. "Or hear it."

"How do you hear a map?" Q asked.

"Wait." Raya closed her eyes and angled her head. "I think I hear something."

"Those are the door's songs," Rasmus said.

"I see it." Raya's eyes widened. "I see the map."

"Where?" A tug on Q's ribs drew his attention to the center of the room. Silver specks glinted in the moonlight. Tiny translucent train tracks looped, twisted, and crisscrossed beneath the carved dome. "My god . . . it's beautiful."

"Q," Raya said breathlessly, her gaze on the space between their chests. "Look."

Q glanced down. An eternity knot, as diaphanous as the tracks, dangled between their bodies, one end of its rope disappearing into the space over his heart, the other into Raya's. He reached out to touch it. It passed through his hand, sending a current racing up his arm.

Raya clutched her chest.

"You felt that?" Q said, his eyes large.

Raya pressed her palm over her heart. "What was that?"

"It feels like sharing a body, doesn't it?" Rasmus said. "But don't worry. You can't read each other's thoughts. Being tethered simply gives you a greater sense of how the other person feels."

"Tethered?" Two heartbeats raced in Q's chest.

"Tethering is how you share the weight of the map. The two of you are now linked, like the train's cars."

Q pressed his lips together. Painting was solitary work. As was living in the dark. Feeling Raya's heart pound through the tether was something he wasn't sure he was going to get used to.

Raya ran her eyes over the swaying tether. "It doesn't look very sturdy."

"It's tougher than it looks," Rasmus said. "As long as both of you have a breath inside you, it will hold."

Raya clenched her fingers over the knot unraveling on her hand. "And if something happens to one of us?"

"The person left holding the map will be crushed by it. So I suggest that you take care of each other." Rasmus looked from Raya to Q. "And yourselves."

"We will," Q said, his voice as steady as a paintbrush in his hand.

Rasmus nodded. "I don't expect that you'll find the map too difficult to use. Artists such as yourselves are usually pretty good at this sort of thing." He looked over Q's face and hands. "You're a painter, am I right?"

Q jerked his head. "How did you know?"

"When you've been on this train as long as I have, you get pretty good at reading people." Rasmus turned his attention to Raya. "And you're a song—"

"Med student."

"Really?" Rasmus raised a barely visible brow behind his eyepatch. "That's too bad. If you were a songwriter, it would have made learning how to use the map a lot easier. We could use more musicians on this train. Lily's one of the few we have on board. She can hear the train's songs so clearly, she no longer needs a map to find its doors."

"Where can I catch a tiny train?"

Frequently Asked Questions
THE ELSEWHERE EXPRESS
PASSENGER HANDBOOK

Raya

Rasmus tucked a small jar containing a swarm of swirling lights into his satchel and handed an identical one to Raya. "Use this to signal me in case you find the stowaway first."

Raya examined the jar's contents. "How do we signal each other with fireflies?"

"Not fireflies. Flares. The jars are filled with flashes of brilliance, the little lights that switch on in your head when a great idea pops inside it. Just give them a good shake to wake them up."

"How will you see them if we're in different train cars?" Raya squeezed the jar into her tote.

"Don't worry. I'll see them. What you need to focus on is mastering the map. It will allow you to get to the exhibit area in the gallery car in no time. The key is to keep your destination firmly in your mind. Think about the gallery and nothing else. It's that simple."

"Simple? Are we even talking about the same map?" Q frowned at the tangle of silver tracks that extended from one end of the Archive to the other. "I can't even hear a single song." He looked at Raya. "Can you?"

"Not anymore." The faint melodies Raya had initially heard had fallen silent, leaving her as empty as the day she had smashed her old guitar into pieces.

"Try listening with something other than your ears," Rasmus suggested.

"Sorry?" Q said.

A memory stirred in Raya's hands. She had lost track of the times that songs had raced through her guitar strings and found her when she wasn't looking. She traced the gossamer tracks with her fingertips. A looping track grazed her knuckles. A melody shot up her arm and burrowed behind her ribs. Two tethered hearts jumped.

"The gallery's song." Q's hand flew over his chest. "You found it."

"I knew it." Rasmus smirked. "I knew you had music inside you. You found that song faster than anyone I've taught to use the map. Well, except for Lily. That would have to be a tie."

Raya stared at the map as though she were looking at it for the first time. Tracks untangled in her mind, freeing their songs. Each melody was distinct and waited patiently for their turn to be heard. Raya would have been happy to live in this moment she was standing in, relishing every note.

"Now that you can see and hear the tracks"—Rasmus interrupted a ballad about midnights and ghosts—"you'll be able to travel across them."

"How?" Q said.

"You'll need to catch a much smaller train."

To describe what it felt like to board a train the size of her thumb, Raya thought, was as difficult as getting someone to imagine a song they had never heard. There was one person, however, who would never require her to give such an explanation.

Q's heart jumped as high as hers did and ran as fast as hers raced as they entered Rasmus's crystal train. Their tether stripped their boundaries beyond their bones. Raya had never felt more naked while fully clothed.

Inside the crystal train was a playground with swings and a faded blue slide. Raya strode over to it, keenly aware that Q knew that her heart had stopped.

"Are you going to tell me what's wrong?" He walked alongside her.

"Do I even need to?"

Q took a seat on the double swing. "Knowing how you feel has little value when I don't understand the reason behind it."

Raya set her bag on the grass and sat next to him stiffly, gripping the swing's chains.

"Not a fan of swings?" Q said.

"Let's just say that my brother and I grew up being fully indoctrinated on the dangers of rusty swings and tetanus."

"Your parents didn't allow you to go on swings?" Q stretched his long legs over the grass.

"Not just swings. Playgrounds."

"What? Why?"

"My brother was sick for a very long time."

"I'm sorry," Q said.

"Even after Jace got better, my parents refused to take any risks with his health. They basically covered us in Bubble Wrap and kept us indoors as much as possible."

"They isolated both of you? Were you sick too?"

Raya's gaze drifted to her bag and all the forbidden, sugary things straining its seams. "Being sick wasn't allowed."

"What do you mean you weren't *allowed* to be sick? I—" A high-pitched whistle cut Q off. The crystal train slowed to a stop. He swallowed hard. "We're here," he said, standing slowly.

"I don't know if I want to find the stowaway and get this over with"—Raya choked, sharing the lump lodged in Q's throat—"or if I wish that Rasmus has better luck than us."

"Neither do I." Q stared in the direction of the crystal train's doors. They slid open, splitting the faded blue slide in half and unleashing a hurricane's roar.

YOUR ITINERARY

A PRIVATE VISIT
TO THE GALLERY

“What happened to Olly?”

Frequently Asked Questions
THE ELSEWHERE EXPRESS
PASSENGER HANDBOOK

Q

The only thing that Q hated more than being blind was being lied to, but as he stood inside the gallery’s brutally bare receiving room, he had never been gladder to be fooled.

The room’s sole adornment, a water feature located in the middle of the room, masterfully mimicked the sound of rain. Q reluctantly called the square hole cut into the room’s concrete floor “a fountain,” but his vocabulary did not include a word for a pool where water floated to a cement ceiling in shimmering drops, crawled across it, and fell in a downpour of color.

In the miniature train, the fountain had sounded like a storm. But inside the gallery it filled the room with a steady drumming that, in the comfort of his own bed, might have lulled Q to sleep. He tilted the single umbrella provided by the gallery to keep Raya from getting wet, ignoring the rain splattering on his shoulder.

“This fountain nearly gave me a heart attack,” Raya said.

“Unfortunately, we can’t relax just yet.” Q plucked the crystal train from a rainbow puddled on the concrete floor and stuffed it into his coat pocket. “The stowaway could still be in this train car.”

A woman emerged from the door to the gallery's exhibit area and opened a burgundy umbrella that matched her chunky sweater. "Oh, hello. I didn't hear you come in." She walked over to a rain-soaked desk. "Welcome to the gallery. How can I help you?"

"We're here to see the exhibit." Q wrestled with the sentence, speaking it as though he were pronouncing words like otorhinolaryngologist or floccinaucinihilipilification. Seeing an exhibit—or anything for that matter—wasn't something he had done in a very long time.

"I'm sorry. Could you repeat that?" the woman said. "I thought you said that you wanted to see the exhibit."

"We do," Raya said. "Why? Is it closed?"

The woman let out a squeal. "This is so exciting. You're the first guests I've had since I started working here. I was seriously considering putting in a request to transfer to another department. Everyone who comes to this car just wants to see the fountain."

"Why?" Q asked.

"Because of the rain, of course. This is as close as you'll get to the real thing on this train."

"It never rains on the Elsewhere Express," Q said, not realizing he had said it out loud.

"But passengers also come here for that *other* thing." The woman winked. "Even if no one admits to it."

"What other thing?" Raya said.

The woman creased her high forehead. "When did you board the train?"

"Very recently." Q cast a glance Raya's way to see if the umbrella was still shielding her.

"That explains it." The woman smiled. "Otherwise, you would have known that this place is where passengers come to get the latest gossip. Not that anything exciting ever happens on the Elsewhere Express, but when you're stuck in one place for eternity, you take what you can get." She let out a laugh that reminded Q of birds chirping. "I'm Han, by the way."

"Q," he said.

Raya gave Han a small wave. "Raya."

"If you're interested in the gossip here, you'll have to toss a few secrets of your own into the fountain in exchange. The conductor likes to say that everything on this train is complimentary, but things aren't free just because you don't know what its price is." The light in Han's eyes flickered for the briefest of moments. "Allow me to demonstrate." She cupped her hands and whispered into them. She opened her fingers, revealing a coin on her palm.

It was a clever trick, but nothing Q had not seen nor had time for. He fidgeted, his eyes on the door to the exhibit area.

"This is how you toss your secrets into the fountain." Han offered the coin to Q.

"Thanks. But we're actually in a bit of a—"

"It's a one-sided coin," Han said. "Have a look."

Q lifted a brow and took the coin from her. He held the coin between his thumb and forefinger and flipped it around. It vanished. Though he felt the coin's weight and shape, he could still see Han's grin through it. His eyes and fingers argued with each other, each insisting the other was lying. Q flipped the coin back, restoring its silver face.

"Clever, right?" Han said. "This side carries my secret, which, to be honest, I'm not sure even qualifies as a secret. But returning a book a day late to the train's library is the most exciting thing that's happened to me in a while."

"And the other side?" Raya said.

"It doesn't exist yet." Han tossed the coin into the fountain. It twirled in the air, disappearing and reappearing as it spun. "Not until you make the exchange."

The coin landed in the pool with a small splash. The rain twinkled like fairy lights.

"Hold out your hand," Han said.

Q stuck his hand out from under the umbrella. A raindrop fell into his palm and turned into a coin upon touching his skin.

"That's the coin's missing side." Han gestured to the desk. "Give it a twirl so we can see what secret I got in return. Hopefully, it's something more exciting than an overdue book."

Q sent the coin spinning over Han's desk. The rain swirled around them, blurring into a moving wall of water. Han shut her umbrella. Q followed her lead. Colors spread over the liquid wall like paint in a cup of water, creating a mural of a dimly lit bar inside a giant lotus flower. A man stood behind a granite counter, mixing drinks.

Raya gasped. "It's Aki."

"It really must be my lucky day." Han beamed. "Aki always has good secrets."

Aki poured a petal-pink liquid from a cocktail shaker into a tall glass embossed with the Elsewhere Express's eternal knot. He reached for a silver tin, its contents pasted on its side with a black-and-white label: *Broken Promises*. Aki lifted its lid. Gold powder shimmered inside it. He sprinkled it into the cocktail and topped the drink off with a fresh cherry blossom. The rain wall collapsed with a splash. The silver coin stopped spinning, melted into a tiny puddle, and floated off the desk in colorful drops.

"All secrets surface." Han opened her umbrella. "Before they rain down on you."

Rain poured. Q scrambled to open his umbrella and hold it over Raya's head. She huddled closer to him, a raindrop dripping down her cheek. Q stopped himself from reaching over and wiping it off. Being tethered made their bodies feel like one, blending the slightest discomfort and pleasure. Raya doubled the warmth that flowed through Q and made every step he took lighter. And even though he was aware that this was merely a temporary bond forged from necessity, there was no convincing his heart that it did not pump for two nor his mind that the magnified awe it felt about the gallery was not entirely his own.

"I always suspected Aki used a pinch of powdered broken promises in his Sakura Surprise. It adds a nice kick." Han smiled. "Now, let me get your tickets to the exhibit before you change your mind."

"Why would we change our mind?" Q reeled from the idea of secrets falling around him like rain. "Is the exhibit that bad?"

"I couldn't tell you. I've never seen it. That's why I asked to be assigned here. I was hoping that one day, someone would come along and tell me all about it."

"Why don't you just see it for yourself?" Raya said.

"See it?" Han stepped away from the desk, shaking her head. "No, no. I couldn't do that."

"Why not?" Q said.

"Well, because of . . . um . . . you know, what happened to Olly." Han lowered her voice. "There's never been any official announcement about what happened to him, but everyone knows that this is where he went missing. I've heard that the exhibit can be a bit uncomfortable for some visitors. Olly might have accidentally exited through a locked door in his rush to leave. At least, that's my husband's theory."

"Your husband is on the train too?" Q said. "The conductor told us that only one passenger boards the train per night."

"Oh, we didn't board at the same time. No one does. We met at one of the train's Scrabble nights. He's been the reigning champion since he boarded. You might have seen his name on the leaderboard at the lounge. His name's Rasmus."

"Other Rasmus?" Q said.

"No, just Rasmus. Or Han's Rasmus, as some people like to call him." Han laughed. "He's version number three. Anyway, I hope you don't change your mind about seeing the exhibit because of what I've told you. I mean, how terrifying can an exhibit about your deepest secrets be?"

"What's on display at the gallery?"

Frequently Asked Questions
THE ELSEWHERE EXPRESS
PASSENGER HANDBOOK

Raya

Han stood by the door that led to the gallery's exhibit. "You can't imagine how excited I am." She pulled the door open and slapped her forehead. "I almost forgot." She pointed to a sign on top of the doorway. "I'm supposed to make sure that all visitors read that before entering."

Welcome to the Portrait Gallery. Please note that food, drinks, and flash photography are not allowed.

A smaller, newer sign was posted, slightly askew, next to it.

And never open locked doors.

"That part was added after Olly got lost," Han said. "I won't tell anyone if you sneak a snack in, but please make sure you follow that last rule strictly."

Raya nodded. "Of course."

"I'm about to start my break, but I should be back by the time you're done." Han took the umbrella from Q and waved them through. "Enjoy the exhibit. I can't wait to hear all about it."

Arched stone bridges ventured over ponds and gurgling streams fringed by rushes and blooms in every shade of scarlet. A crisp evening breeze laced with pensiveness and hints of citrus and spice escorted Raya and Q down a winding path. Paper lanterns, nestled among the flowers, woke up and then floated to the sky, illuminating the water garden like hundreds of low-hanging moons.

"Han did say that this was the gallery, right?" Raya said.

"I trust your hearing more than mine." Q smirked. "I can't even hear the songs in the map."

They stepped off a bridge and followed a pebbled path through a lush grove of heliconia, orchids, and elephant ear plants. A lagoon shimmered beyond the greenery, a mirror of the lantern-lit sky.

"Han's luck might have rubbed off on us." Raya looked out from the water's edge. "There's no sign of the stowaway."

"Or the exhibit." Q's voice slipped out in a half sigh.

"You sound disappointed."

"I'm not going to lie. I was curious to see what an exhibit that puts secrets on display looks like."

"A disaster, probably." Raya stuffed her hands into her pockets. "I don't blame Olly for panicking and running away. Who wouldn't? It's one thing to reveal a cocktail's secret ingredient or share that you returned a library book late. But having your darkest secret on display? No, thank you. How would you feel if we had found all your secrets framed and hung on walls?"

"Honestly? A part of me was hoping that we would."

"Why?"

"Because when I told you my biggest secret, it was like I had burst free from a dark locked box and felt the sun on my face for the very first time."

Raya looked away. Still liquid eyes gazed up at her from the lagoon. Her reflection was calmer than she was. Raya was not a stranger to envy, but this was the first time she was jealous of herself. The Raya in the water existed only in the moment, content to hold her breath and watch the lanterns in the sky. Color swirled over the reflection, rippling its peace.

Raya gasped. An invisible hand ushered the colors in several directions, capturing her surprise with brisk strokes. With a few more, a watercolor portrait of herself stared back at her.

"Hiraya," Q said.

Raya jolted. "What did you say?"

"Hiraya." Q read the word scrawled over the bottom-right corner of the painting in the water.

Raya's breath caught in her throat. "My name . . ."

Q's eyes flashed. "You're the subject of the exhibit."

"No." Raya grew lightheaded. "No. I didn't agree to this."

Her portrait mouthed her words. *No. I didn't agree to this.*

Raya's legs shook, threatening to buckle under her. "We should go."

We should go. The portrait copied her silently.

"But we haven't found the stowaway," Q said. "We can't leave before searching the whole car."

Raya looked up from her portrait. "There's no sign of rot or rain. It's not here."

Q eyed the liquid painting. "But don't you want to—"

"—see my secrets on display? No. Absolutely not."

"But what if it helps you find your compartment?"

"Help? How?" Raya's words sliced her teeth. "Lily never said anything about public shaming during the orientation."

"No, but she did say that we needed to reveal our truest selves to find our place here." Q gazed out at the still water. "What if this isn't a lagoon?"

"What do you mean?" Raya said.

"What if it's a reflection pool? What better place to think about who you are than a gallery that forces you to look at yourself? Maybe it's the gallery car's way of helping us find our place on the train."

Raya stared hard at her reflection. "Or it's trying to confuse us."

Or it's trying to confuse us. Her portrait mimicked her movements.

"Why would it do that?" Q said.

"So that we start to believe that we want to"—Raya closed her fist around the knot on her palm—"stay."

Stay. Her portrait grabbed hold of her.

Raya screamed and dropped her bag.

Q clasped her hand. "Raya!"

The painting yanked her from his grasp and dragged her screaming into the lagoon.

Q

People were born from two wombs. The first birthed their bodies, the second, their souls. Q gazed into the black depths of the lagoon, deciding which of two mothers would give birth to the man he was going to be from this moment forward: circumstance or choice. An old, icy dread lapped at his toes. He shivered, tearing his eyes from the dark water.

But living in the dark was circumstance. Living in fear of it was a choice. The tether trembled but Q could not tell if it shook from Raya's terror or his own. The only thing worse than being lost was being lost in the dark, and the only thing worse than being lost in the dark was being alone in it.

Prussian blue. Viridian. Vermilion. Red ocher. Charcoal black. And a splash of cadmium yellow. The lagoon drowned Raya's voice but could not hide the colors her scream had clawed into the night. Q tore off his coat and kicked off his shoes. Ice coiled around his spine, anchoring him to this liminal space.

He looked at the water, unable to remember the last time his vision had been good enough to study his reflection. His watery face stared back at him, waiting for him to choose the soul they were to share. Q pulled his shoulders back. He filled his lungs with as much air as he could and caught the scent of a looming storm.

"How deep is the gallery's reflection pool?"

Frequently Asked Questions
THE ELSEWHERE EXPRESS
PASSENGER HANDBOOK

Raya

The lanterns grew smaller and vanished entirely as Raya's portrait dragged her to the bottom of the lagoon. She kicked and flailed, stirring silt that turned the water murky, but left the terror surrounding her crystal clear. The only wall that stood between her and death was the fragile flesh she wore, all that she relied on to keep blood, bones, and breath inside her. It was an utterly pointless suit, which, instead of armor, came with a mouth, a built-in breach. Lips were the most unreliable of gates through which the air she desperately needed exited in gurgling bubbles of every size. Raya was not surprised by the betrayal. Lips were weak, easily unlocked by sweet whispers and soft kisses or burst open by screams of rage or pain. Earlier, just before her portrait had pulled her into the water, her lips had let a secret she was keeping from herself slip out in one word: *Stay.*

Abandoning her old life to stay on the Elsewhere Express was not an option Raya had thought she would ever consider, but the constant pull of the tether made it difficult to keep from being tugged in its direction. Q's desperation to remain on the train at all costs flowed across their invisible bond as though they shared arteries and veins. And now that death was close to breaching her walls and flooding her lungs, she could think of nothing other than how the Archive's map would crush Q when she was gone. She couldn't let that happen.

Raya's last breath escaped just as the portrait's painted fingers finally let her go. Raya pushed off the muddy floor and swam toward the memory of light and Q. Both remained out of reach, like all things that lived only in your mind. Her lungs burned. Raya clawed at the water, rapidly losing the strength to hold on to the last of her will and her secrets. The more she thrashed, the more her secrets slipped from her grasp, frothing and floating away.

Han, she thought, was right. All secrets eventually surfaced, and as Raya swam up, she braced herself for the downpour. Warmth flowed through her tether and cut the lagoon's chill. It hugged her heart, slowing its wild pounding. Q was close. Raya twisted around, searching for him in the dark. He hooked his arm around her, their tether binding them as tightly as the train's couplers linked its cars. They swam upward, their fears halved and their strength doubled, each of them trying to save the other.

A kaleidoscope of raindrops sliced through the water, infusing it with color and light. Aqueous paintings appeared around them, a labyrinth of watercolor portraits of Raya at every age. Raya flailed, searching for a way out. The underwater gallery extended in every direction. A current circled Raya's waist and wrenched her from Q, pulling her toward a portrait of her fifteen-year-old self. The younger Raya sat at a white dresser, applying a tube of deep red lipstick.

Raya tried to swim away but the current surged, hauling her and Q into the gallery's latest show.

Q

It was dry inside the painting of Raya's childhood bedroom. Under different circumstances, Q might have wanted to linger in it. Paintings had always been his refuge, regardless of how little of them he could see. A sanctuary was a sanctuary no matter what size it was. But this painting did not provide any comfort. Though the painting of Raya's bedroom offered air, it was difficult to take a breath with the tether trembling as much as it did. Q shivered as though the secrets that the gallery was about to reveal were his own.

Raya ran to the lavender bedroom's door and tried to open it. It was locked from the outside. She pummeled it with her fists. "Let us out!"

"That's not going to work." Q drew her away from the door. "Your portrait pulled you into the pool and a current dragged us into this painting. I think we aren't going to be allowed to leave until we see the exhibit."

"We can use the map." Raya's eyes flashed wildly. "Where's the train?"

Q reached for his pocket and froze, remembering that he had torn his coat off before jumping into the water. "It's in my coat."

Raya dropped into a painted bed, groaning into her hands.

"I'm sorry." Q sat next to her.

"It's not your fault." She glared at her fifteen-year-old self. "It's hers."

The painting came to life. Raya's younger self looked into the dresser mirror and swiped a dark shade of red over her lips.

"That's my mother's lipstick," Raya said. "I stole it. I thought it would make me look older."

Her painted version layered on mascara. She checked her reflection and added another coat.

"I lied about my age when I auditioned for a gig at a neighborhood coffeehouse," Raya said. "I don't think the manager believed me but she hired me anyway. This is a painting of the night that I was going to sing there for the first time. Before this evening, I had only ever performed at the children's hospital."

"Rasmus wasn't lying about being good at reading people, then," Q said. "You *are* a musician. That's why you can hear the train's songs."

Raya's younger self reached for a makeup wipe, brought it to her lips, and tossed it into the bin before it could touch her mouth.

"She should have changed her mind." Raya stared at the painted girl's red lips.

"About what?" Q said.

"Everything." Raya walked over to the dresser and stood behind the girl she used to be. "She should have wiped that lipstick off. She should have forgotten all about performing her songs. She should have called Jace and told him not to drive home from college that night to watch her sing."

"Why?" Q said.

Raya gripped the back of the chair her younger self was sitting on.

Q stood up. "What happened, Raya?"

"Jace didn't come. He—"

A current swept through the painting and carried her, Q, and the rest of her confession away.

"What time does the gallery close?"

Frequently Asked Questions
THE ELSEWHERE EXPRESS
PASSENGER HANDBOOK

Raya

The current weaved through an underwater labyrinth of Raya's life. She was young in some paintings, older in others, laughing, sobbing, and everything in between. Raya's music filled each scene, and her heart knew every note. Thanks to their tether, Q learned the songs too. After winding through corridors of her childhood, the current released them in the corner of a dark room.

"Where are we?" Q looked around.

"We're back in my bedroom. This is the same night as the first painting we were in." Raya pointed to a shadow outside her bedroom window. "That's me sneaking back after performing at the coffeehouse."

Fifteen-year-old Raya hauled her sticker-covered guitar through her window and rested it against the wall by the door. She crawled into bed, pulled her blanket up to her chin, and stared at the watercolor ceiling. Though the dark hid her younger self's painted face, Raya knew that she was smiling. Raya touched her cheeks, remembering how much they had ached from grinning ear to ear all the way home. She wasn't even disappointed that Jace hadn't shown up.

For the first time in her life, she caught a glimpse of what it was like to have a purpose other than being his sister. She performed a new song she had written for him to finish her set and let its notes carry her away. The audience in the half-filled room traveled with her, the warmth of their applause lingering in her chest as she lay in bed, thinking about all the rules she had broken just to find out what she was meant to do beyond being born. Raya sprinted to the door and barricaded it with her body. "She can't open this door." Frantic knocking rattled the door against her spine. "I won't let her."

"Hiraya," her mother yelled. "Get up."

"Raya . . ." Q reached out to her.

She turned away from him, tears flooding her eyes. "You wanted to know my darkest secret? Here. This is it. Are you happy now? I live in this night, Q. I remember every second of it." The knocking grew louder, making the entire painting shake. "Jace died because I asked him to watch me sing my stupid songs. He shouldn't have been in his car. He shouldn't have been on the road. He should have been safe in bed with all his dreams."

Painted Raya bolted up. "Mom? What's wrong?"

"It's Jace." Her mother broke into sobs through the door.

Raya grabbed her old guitar. For as long as the door was closed, her mother could not burst into her room and tell her that Jace had been in a car accident or ask her if she knew why her brother had decided to drive home. For as long as the door was closed, she could keep all her guilt behind it. Her painted self ran to the door. Raya swung the guitar at her. The portrait shattered in an explosion of paint, staining Raya's face with blood-red streaks of stolen lipstick.

Her mother's sobbing stopped. The bedroom dulled and darkened. A sickly sweet, foul smell seeped into the room. Raya retched and dropped the guitar. Rotting vines crept over the windowsill.

"It's the stowaway." Q covered his nose with his sleeve. "We need to get out of here." He grabbed hold of the doorknob and twisted it. It refused to move. Q rammed the door with his shoulder.

Raya yanked her desk drawers open. She rummaged through them, pushing aside pencils and pens.

"What are you doing?" Q rammed the door again.

Raya grabbed a paintbrush and half-used tubes of paint. "I'm not doing anything." She thrust the supplies at Q. "You are."

Q

Tendrils of rot crept through the gap beneath the locked door to Raya's childhood bedroom. It crawled over the lavender carpet, spreading decay. Q stood on the bed, painting a hatch on the ceiling.

"How much longer?" Raya glanced down at the rotting floor.

The piece was not Q's best work, but he did not want to keep the brush in his hand any longer than he had to. He had not forgotten Astrid's warning about dark thoughts. He shaded a corner of the hatch and flung the paintbrush to the carpet. Rot devoured it. "I don't know if this will even work."

"If you can paint a star over thin air, you can paint us an exit," Raya said.

"I hope you're right." Q drew a deep breath and pulled the painting's handle. It slid open, revealing a wall of water suspended above his head.

Raya clutched his arm. "I see the lanterns."

Circles of light shimmered through the depths of the lagoon. Q poked at the water. It rippled around his finger, making the lanterns dance. "I'll boost you up." He laced his fingers to form a step. "Hurry."

They climbed out of the lagoon, gasping for breath. Q collapsed on his back, exhaustion dulling the smell of rot.

Raya crawled to her bag and pulled out the jar of flares Rasmus had given her. She shook it and twisted its lid open. A swarm of lights shot out of the jar like fireworks. "I hope Rasmus sees that." Raya shivered in her wet clothes. "We should"—her teeth chattered—"search the rest of the car while waiting for him."

Q grabbed his coat from the grass and handed it to her. "Here."

"But—" Her lips trembled.

"We're not going to be able to search for anything if you go into hypothermia."

"Thank you." Raya peeled her wet coat off and slipped Q's on.

Raya's warmth radiated through their tether, returning color and heat to Q's lips and cheeks, and he found he'd never needed a coat less. He scanned the garden. Lightning clustered beyond the halo of the reflection pool's lanterns, illuminating a double-eave pavilion. "I think I know where the stowaway is."

A torrent broke through the clouds, hiding the pavilion's tiled roof behind sheets of rain.

A figure, veiled by darkness, stood at the far end of the pavilion, its back toward Raya and Q. Black, spidery vines extended from its body and slithered over the pavilion's stone floor like snakes. Whatever they touched decayed. Q crept up the pavilion's steps. Each breath he took tasted rancid, a sour mix of spoiled sorrow and dust. Lightning ripped through the sky and chased the shadows from a humanlike form covered in tiny black insect wings. The figure turned, then broke apart, scattering into multiple swarms.

A blur of wings flew past Raya and Q, catching on their hair, ears, and clothes. Raya squeezed her lids shut to keep them from getting into her eyes. She and Q huddled, taking refuge in each other's arms.

The hum of wings faded. Q peeked over Raya's head. "I think they're gone."

Raya looked up from his chest. "What were those things? They looked like moths."

"I know moths." Q tugged his collar, exposing the inked reminder on his skin. "Those things may look like moths, but they're not. They're monsters."

An eclipse of moths swept back into the pavilion, swirling into the shape of a man as tall as Q. It took a step forward and extended a hand toward him, grazing his jaw with fluttering black wings.

Q froze.

The stowaway withdrew its hand and cupped Raya's face, stroking what might pass for a thumb over her cheek. Raya flinched. The stowaway screeched. Black vines snaked from its body and burrowed into the floor. The pavilion shuddered. Fissures raced up columns and shattered the ceiling. Roof tiles tumbled over them.

Q grabbed Raya's hand and sprinted to the exit, leaping over cracks. They jumped from the pavilion's steps onto the rain-soaked ground. The pavilion crumbled behind them. They stared at the rubble, holding their breath. Moths burst from the debris.

"Let's get out of here." Q backed away from the ruins. "The train's in your pocket."

Raya pulled the crystal train out and squinted through the rain. "I can't see the map."

Q strained to see the silver tracks in the storm. "Can you hear the doors?"

Raya closed her eyes.

Q glanced back. The moths re-formed into a man's shape. "Anything?"

Raya shook her head, keeping her eyes shut. "Wait." She turned slightly to the left. Her eyes flew open. "Over there. A track. But I don't know where it leads. I can barely hear the song over the rain."

The stowaway made its way toward Raya and Q, mimicking the motions of walking without its feet touching the ground. Its screech curdled the air.

"It doesn't matter," Q said.

Raya set the train on the track.

Q stepped between her and the stowaway. "Get in."

Raya clambered into the crystal train. Q jumped in after her, landing in the playground's sandbox. The train's door shut behind them. Raya leaned against a jungle gym, breathing hard. "I hope Rasmus saw the flares."

"He did," Q said, willing it to be true. He stood up, the rumbling of the tiny train shaking the sand from his jeans.

Lightning struck the railway and broke it apart. The miniature train careened off the track. A fissure ripped open beneath Q's feet. He fell into the jagged hole faster than he could scream. A blue-and-yellow seesaw tumbled after him, wedging halfway through the gaping hole.

"Q!" Raya ran to him, slipping and stumbling on the quaking ground.

Q clung to the seesaw, his legs dangling over a black void. Raya lay on her stomach and grabbed his hand. He clung to her and climbed onto the grass, knocking the seesaw into the darkness. "Thank you," he panted.

Pieces of broken crystal fell around them. Q looked up, shielding his face with his hands. The sky cracked open and ripped the moon from the stars.

"How do the train's flares work?"

Frequently Asked Questions
THE ELSEWHERE EXPRESS
PASSENGER HANDBOOK

Rasmus

Rasmus liked broken things. When he was a child, his room was littered with the skeletons and innards of toasters, radios, and alarm clocks. He had discovered early on that the best way to learn how to make something better was to take it apart. But nothing held his interest long. Not school. Not his work. Not even the woman he thought he had loved enough to marry.

His fiancée disappeared from his life after he had left her at the altar, and there were times, though infrequent, that he wondered how she was doing and where she was. The same questions rolled in his mind like tumbleweed on the day he had resigned from his latest job and boarded the Elsewhere Express.

Rasmus would have found the answers to these questions if he had been able to remember his fiancée when he bumped into her at the train's gallery years later. She had changed her face and had swallowed the same vile-tasting tonic as he had. They nodded politely whenever they saw each other around the train with no inkling of who the other was. Their only connection was her husband's name. He was called Rasmus too.

The Rasmus his ex-fiancée loved, Rasmus admitted, was more likable than he was. This explained how this version of himself came to be designated Han's Rasmus and he merely as the Other. Though he and Han's Rasmus were one and the same person, the little left and right turns they had taken since they had boarded the Elsewhere Express changed them in a hundred invisible ways. Han's Rasmus was the train's reigning Scrabble night champion, and he was the Rasmus that tracked down monsters and kept the train safe.

Rasmus had thought that his monster-hunting days were over when he retired as the train's conductor. Beginnings and endings, however, were the most common illusions on a train running on infinite tracks. Days started when the painting crew hung the sun in the sky and ended when a painted moon took the sun's place. Passengers found it easier to accept this arbitrary demarcation than to live in a single, eternal moment. Forever was easy to drown in if you couldn't see the shore.

Rasmus exhaled, concluding his search of the opera house without finding any rot. The train's opera troupe was set to begin its new season in a few days, and he was relieved that he did not have to decouple the opera train car. He looked out from center stage, admiring the train car's elegant interiors. Excerpts from an award-winning crime documentary made up the proscenium while a judge's deliberation on a custody case was sewed into the stage's rich red curtains. Fair thoughts did not distort sound, but were unfortunately notoriously difficult to come by. It would take a very long time to collect enough clear, objective, well-balanced thoughts to rebuild the opera house from scratch.

Rasmus held a gilded frame in front of him. It would have been easier to use one of his crystal trains to travel around the Elsewhere Express, but he had no one to share the train's map or, for that matter, anything else with. As the train's former conductor, Rasmus knew attachments were distractions from duties no one else could perform. Keeping an entire train running smoothly and doubt-free was a job that demanded all of one's attention. The Elsewhere Express existed because its passengers believed that it did and ran exclusively on a fuel of faith.

Flares flashed in Rasmus's good eye. He staggered back, blinded. The flares faded, their light burning what Raya's eyes had just seen into his iris: lightning, rain, and rot.

YOUR ITINERARY

FREE TIME

"What do I do if I damage items I've borrowed from the Archive?"

Frequently Asked Questions
THE ELSEWHERE EXPRESS
PASSENGER HANDBOOK

Q

Jagged pieces of crystal littered the uneven ground, glittering in the pale light of a full moon. Raya and Q sat on their heels, gathering what remained of the miniature train. Q dropped a piece that looked like it could have been its chimney into an empty bag of gummy candy Raya had found in her tote. He reached for another shard, but his fingers refused to stop shaking long enough for him to pick it up. A nervous energy charged the air, making it impossible to breathe without trembling. He stood up, abandoning the bag of broken crystal. "What are we even doing, Raya? This is pointless. We need to find a way out of here."

Raya grabbed the bag and got to her feet. "This *is* the way out."

Q rubbed his forehead. "The only thing those shards are going to do is shred our hands. It's a miracle that the train managed to hold itself together for as long as it did. And even if we found all its pieces, how in the world are we going to put it back together?"

Raya sighed, shoving the bag of shards into her tote. "You're right."

"We'll find another way," Q said.

Something round and soft bounced off the side of Raya's head. She jumped. "What was that?"

Q spotted a balled-up gray object by her left foot and picked it up. "A sock," he said, questioning his answer as soon as he heard himself say it out loud. A blue sock pelted his shoulder.

A set of house keys fell on Raya's foot. "What in the world?"

The sound of metal rattled across the sky. Q looked up. A penny struck the bridge of his nose. He grimaced. More coins rained down, pockmarking the ground. Q shielded his head with his hands. "Run!"

Holes of varying depths and sizes dimpled the valley. Raya and Q snagged their feet in them, tripping and stumbling in the hail of coins. They kept their heads down, darting past stacks of wallets and mounds of car keys, searching for a place to shelter from the storm of loose change. A five-yen coin hit Q's ear.

"Q." Raya raised her voice above the clatter of coins. "There's a light up ahead."

A light flickered in the distance. The outline of a gently sloping hill emerged from the dark. A large tree watched over the valley from the top of the hill with a canopy so wide, it was a forest all on its own. Sprawling branches concealed the light's source but let enough of it shine through to give Q and Raya a destination.

Thick aerial roots trailed down from the giant banyan tree's branches like gnarled trunks, completing the illusion of a forest. Q and Raya sheltered beneath the tree, panting from the sprint up the hill. The banyan's dense canopy muffled the downpour of coins, softening its clatter to a chime-like tinkling.

Raya touched the red mark a coin had left on her temple and winced. "We're going to be quite the sight tomorrow."

Tomorrow. Q rolled the word around in his mind. Growing up, he had hated it. It didn't matter if tomorrow was his birthday or Lunar New Year. All tomorrows ever did was bring him a day closer to a life in the dark. But from Raya's mouth, it sounded different, its syllables holding a promise of all the colors of the morning he missed: the roasted brown and burnt umber peeking from beneath swirls of milky foam in his favorite green glazed mug, the creamy sunrise streaming out of a broken yolk, the languid, buttery yellow puddle melting into amber syrup over golden toast. The word also conjured a palette he had never seen: Raya's brown eyes at midday, her lavender hair in the afternoon, the blush on her cheeks at twilight. The "tomorrow" that Raya uttered was both so alien and familiar that it compelled Q to feel it on his own lips. He spoke it beneath his breath.

Tomorrow.

It tickled his tongue, sparkling and sweet. He had forgotten what anticipation tasted like. Fighting to make it through a night where no second was promised, Q had never longed for tomorrow more. But though the tether told him that he and Raya were both desperate to reach this day's end, he knew they wanted it for different reasons. Raya wished to leave the train as much as every cell in his body ached to remain on it.

"Did you say something?" Raya said.

Q shook his head, making his way to the banyan's trunk.

Raya gasped. "Stop."

"What is it?"

She pointed to a faint light drizzling over his face. "The light." She lifted her gaze to the branches above Q. "It's coming from up there."

They climbed a ladder carved from the banyan's hanging roots into the tree's canopy and stood at the doorstep of a small house growing out of its trunk. Branches intertwined to form the tree house's living walls, its leaves weaving together to roof it. A light shone through the house's windowpanes of crystallized tree sap, casting prismatic flecks over Q and Raya. A green door in the shape of a banyan leaf stood half open between two windows, inviting them in.

"That door," Raya gasped. "I saw it in Olly's notebook."

A jar filled with light sat on a dresser at the far end of the tree house's only room. The tree house, unlike most things on the Elsewhere Express, was just as small on the inside as it appeared from the outside. Q crossed the doorway and shut the leaf-shaped door behind him.

Raya gripped the windowsill, watching the downpour of lost coins and missing socks. "Out of all the tracks on the map, I just had to find the one that led us to the Missed and Misplaced Department. This place doesn't have any frames to help us find the exit. We're stuck here because of me."

"What you did was save us from the stowaway," Q said. "And I don't think the track you chose brought us here. I felt the train go off the rails before it shattered. We must have crashed into a locked door. But we're safe now."

"And lost." Raya sighed. "The air here makes my chest feel tight. It's like the anxiety I get when I realize I've left the house without my wallet or keys. Can you imagine feeling this way every second of every day for god knows how long?"

Q did not have to imagine it. He could navigate his apartment as though he could see, but the world outside was different. He couldn't walk out his door without feeling like he had left something behind, but sight was not something he could run back to retrieve. He walked over to the window and looked outside. Remote controls and eyeglasses clattered over the ground. "Unless Olly kept some umbrellas in here, we're going to have to wait this out before we go searching for the exit."

"If Olly did leave anything, there's only one place he could have kept it." Raya eyed the tree house's lone piece of furniture, a dresser set against a windowless wall.

"Fingers crossed." Q made his way to the dresser.

"Being stuck here must have been miserable." Raya heaved a sigh that echoed in Q's chest. "This place doesn't even have a bed or a chair."

"Which might have worked in Olly's favor. Comfort has a way of making people believe they're content," Q said, recalling the portraits he painted. "It's the most common lie people wear on their faces. It looks like a dead spot in the eyes even under the brightest studio lights. It was tricky to capture during my first few attempts, but after painting it so often, I sadly became quite good at it."

Raya stopped midway to the dresser. "How about here?"

"Here?"

"What have you seen in the eyes of the passengers we've met?" Raya looked directly at him. "They all seem so happy and grateful to be on this train, but are they?"

Q narrowed his eyes. "You don't believe that they want to be here?"

"Like you said, comfort can trick people into being content. What's more comfortable than a train that lets you leave all your troubles behind and allows you to live forever in a magical paradise without paying rent?"

Q shook his head. "That's different."

"Is it? I genuinely want to know what you've seen on their faces because for as many wonders as this train has surrounded us with, this train car has given me just as many reasons to doubt that the Elsewhere Express is what it presents itself to be."

"Why? Because Olly got lost here?"

"Because in all that time that Olly was gone, not a single person on this train thought to look for him here," Raya said. "No one cares if this department exists or not because no one here misses anything or worries about things they've lost or left behind. But look outside, Q. Look at the sheer number of thoughts people devote to thinking about things that have gone missing from their lives. It's part of being human. How can passengers spend an eternity on this train and never once think about loss? How much of them really remains after they drink Mr. Goh's remedy?" Raya locked eyes with Q. "Are they as happy as they claim to be or are they smiling because they're as hollowed out as the Echoes and no longer have anything they care enough about to feel sad?"

Q walked ahead, unable to give Raya an answer. Apart from Lily and Raya, he had not looked at anyone closely enough to see anything other than what he wanted to see. Olly did not count. Wherever he was behind his eyes, he was too far away.

Q had broken his own cardinal rule. Never had he been so willing to be lied to. The train had given him his sight back. If not questioning it was the price of his ticket, he was happy to pay it in full. Painting within the lines did not seem so terrible if it allowed him to see the colors on the page. He stopped in front of the dresser and reached for its top drawer.

Raya inhaled sharply.

"What is it?" Q looked her way.

"The wall."

Q's gaze flew to the wall behind the dresser. Scratches that had not been visible from afar covered every inch of it like the marks left by fingernails in damp dungeon cells. Q traced the dents.

"I wonder if it happened gradually or fast," Raya said quietly.

"What did?" Q withdrew his hand from the wall.

"The way Olly lost his mind. Did it drag out or did it drop on top of him like a downpour of coins?" Raya turned her hand over, exposing the knot on her palm. "I can't decide if it's better to go mad before the knot unravels or after. And if it makes any difference."

Q clasped her shoulders. "Look at me, Raya. We're going to find a way out of here long before that knot comes undone."

"Are we? We don't know that." Raya backed away from him. "We don't know anything about this place, this tree house, or even this stupid dresser." She pulled the dresser's top drawer open a sliver and shoved it shut. She sank to the floor. "I don't want it to be empty, Q. It can't be."

Q sat on the floor, leaning his head against the dresser. Though it wasn't a box, the dresser wielded the same magic any box that was home to Schrödinger's cats did. For as long as it remained closed, the dresser contained three custom-made and dust-free pieces of hope, the exact shape and size of its three drawers. Apart from hope, they could also hold anything Q wished. He filled the first drawer with the exact directions to the train car's exit, the second with two sturdy umbrellas, and the third with a flashlight. He threw in his favorite pork belly buns because he was hungry and added a bottle of Shiraz and two glasses to his imaginary stash. "Have you tried gua bao?"

"Pork belly buns? Yes. Why?"

"They're my ultimate comfort food," Q said. "If you could fill these drawers with anything, what would you put inside them? So far, I have a map of the valley, umbrellas, flashlights, some gua bao, and a bottle of wine."

"Sour gummies. Candy bars. Cake. Any kind. And chocolate chip cookies. Chewy ones with big chunks."

"They do teach you about diabetes in medical school, right?" A smirk dimpled Q's cheek.

"Blame Jace. He used to help me steal—" Raya hugged her knees.

"I'm sorry about what happened to your brother."

"White or red?" Raya said without looking at him.

"Sorry?"

"What kind of wine did you put in the dresser? White or red?"

"A Shiraz."

"I'll take the whole bottle."

"Take two, if you want. Or three. What happened at the gallery couldn't have been easy."

Raya ran her thumb over the gold knot on her skin. "I just wish that this place would let this damn thing unravel faster instead of playing all these games."

"I don't think that the exhibit was meant to be a game."

"You're right. It wasn't a game. It was torture. This train enjoys being cruel."

"I don't believe it was trying to be cruel either," Q said softly.

"That's easy for you to say. The gallery didn't put your life on display."

"Maybe it's because it didn't have to. When I plan a collection, I don't select pieces that I've showcased before. I showed you my secrets before we went to the gallery. There was no need for you to see them up on a wall."

"Need?" Raya said. "Why would the gallery care if I knew your secrets or not?"

"Like I told you, I'm beginning to think the train cars are designed to help us find our way. The Painting and Maintenance Department gave us a glimpse of what was possible if we mastered our thoughts. The Dragonfly taught us how to traverse worries and grudges. The Archive's map showed us how much weight we could carry if we shared it."

"And the gallery?" Raya sat up straight. "What did it teach you apart from Aki's secret ingredient for his Sakura Surprise and my shame? How exactly did putting my life on exhibit for your entertainment help me find my compartment? Tell me, Q, what earth-shaking insight did you get from that little show? That my brother's death was an accident? That I shouldn't blame myself? That living his dream instead of my own won't bring him back? Don't you think I know that?"

"I'm sorry. It was none of my business." Q stood up.

"Wait." Raya jumped to her feet. "I was being a jerk. I'm sorry."

"It's okay."

"No, it's not. You didn't deserve that."

"Raya, it's fine. Really." He glanced down at the space between their chests where the invisible tether connected them. "I can't lie to you even if I wanted to." He flashed a small smile.

"That tether's quite the snitch, isn't it?" Raya sighed.

"It is. Which is why, as embarrassed as I am about what I'm about to tell you, you'll know that it's the truth." A breath deflated his chest. "Do you know what my first thought was when I imagined Olly being stuck here? I didn't think about how scared he must have been or how lonely his days were. I thought about myself. I went on a little trip down memory lane, remembering what it was like to be trapped in the dark."

"Why are you telling me this?" Raya said.

Q met her eyes. "Because I want you to believe me when I tell you that I understand why you said all those things earlier. And it's not just because we're tethered. I understand you because I've stood in your shoes. I'm still standing in them. You said that you knew what each painting in the gallery contained. I don't doubt that. I know as many things about being blind. I know that my experience of losing my sight isn't even remotely comparable to Olly being trapped here. I know that blindness isn't a life sentence in solitary confinement. I know that people have built incredible lives without their sight, lives with more than enough worth and weight to keep them from floating away and boarding this train. I know all of these things." He turned from the window and looked at Raya. "But knowing and believing—"

"—are two very different things." A tear escaped Raya's lashes and streamed down her cheek. She dried her eyes on the sleeve of Q's coat and stopped. "Oh no. Your coat. I forgot I was wearing it. I'm sorry," she said, shrugging her shoulders out of it.

"You didn't read the passenger handbook, did you?"

"No, why?"

"It clearly states that it's against the Elsewhere Express's rules to return a coat."

"It does, does it?" Raya let out a small laugh. "Is this something you know or believe?"

"The latter. With my whole heart." Q walked behind her and helped her back into his coat. "Now it's your turn."

"To what?"

"To practice believing. We can start with this drawer."

"And what am I supposed to believe about it? That it contains a bottle of Shiraz or an umbrella?"

"Either would be great, but since we're starting small, maybe you can just try to believe that no matter what's inside it, you and I are not going to give up opening every drawer, digging through every mountain of pens, and turning every sock inside out until we find a way out of here. Who knows? Today might even be the day that someone just happens to lose an empty picture frame."

"Fingers crossed." Raya drew a deep breath and pulled the drawer open. The tree house shook violently, sending the jar of light tumbling into the drawer, abandoning them in the dark.

"Who should I call if a pipe leaks?"

Frequently Asked Questions
THE ELSEWHERE EXPRESS
PASSENGER HANDBOOK

Rasmus

Secrets poured down on Rasmus from the gallery's fountain, showering bits and pieces of the lives passengers had made for themselves on the Elsewhere Express. Rasmus ignored them, not caring about whether Astrid from the painting crew had a crush on Dev from maintenance or if Min from the Dragonfly had cheated at Scrabble during the train's last game night. The putrid scent leaking into the room made it difficult to focus on anything other than trying to take a breath without gagging.

"Han?" Rasmus covered his nose with his hand. "Are you in here?" His eyes fell on a note on the desk.

On Break. Will be back shortly.

Rasmus would have breathed a sigh of relief if he had breath to spare.

"What is that smell?" Han grimaced, walking up behind him.

Rasmus spun around.

"Other Rasmus?" Han held a handkerchief over her nose and mouth. "What are you doing here?"

"Get out of here, Han."

"I can't. There are two guests at the exhibit."

"I'll handle it. You need to leave right now. There's a pipe leak in the reflection pool."

"Should I call maintenance?" Han said.

"I've already called them. Just go."

"Rasmus." Lily burst through the door. "I got your message."

"What did Olly write in his notebook?"

Frequently Asked Questions
THE ELSEWHERE EXPRESS
PASSENGER HANDBOOK

Raya

Thuds, cracks, and creaks filled Raya's ears, but darkness hid the destruction taking place. Raya imagined the tree house crumbling as the pavilion did and could only pray that whatever happened next was going to be swift. She found no comfort in dying in Q's company and did not wish to prolong it. He deserved to live and see, even if she deserved less. Her only consolation was the small hope that the stowaway might get lost in the Missed and Misplaced Department and never find its way out.

Q held her to his chest. Their tether bound them tighter. "Don't let go."

Raya closed her eyes and waited for the end. Rustling leaves joined the cacophony. Light spread behind her lids. Raya opened them, wondering if the end had come without her noticing. Branches parted from the tree house's window, allowing moonlight to pour over the truth. What Raya had believed to be chaos was construction.

The tree house expanded like a pop-up book, unfolding and growing in width and height. The wall covered in scratches split into smaller square sections that were pushed upward as the tree house grew. Furniture popped up from beneath floorboards and hidden compartments in walls, breaking and multiplying to fill the enlarging space. Cabinets, bureaus, and bookshelves balanced on top of one another, creating a circular atrium determined to touch the stars. Two rolling ladders, guided by wrought iron rails, spanned the atrium's height. Makeshift lamps cobbled together from flashlights and phones lit the atrium's lopsided shelves.

"What just happened?" Q glanced around. "Was the dresser some kind of switch?"

Raya strode over to a textured wall. Odd-shaped stones revealed themselves to be remote controls, coins, and books mortared in place. "Olly's scribbles weren't meaningless . . ." Her fingertips roamed over a plastered table, finding the shapes of wallets and pens. "They were designs. This is the tower from his notebook."

Q gazed up at the atrium's shelves. "Which means that our search for an umbrella just expanded to a whole lot more than one dresser."

"Any luck?" Raya called over her shoulder from a ladder across the atrium.

"Define luck." Q clung to his ladder and pushed a drawer shut. "Because if it means finding more socks than the human population of this planet, I am, without a doubt, the luckiest person alive."

"I hate to break it to you," Raya said, "but that would have to be me." They had examined every shelf and drawer on five levels of the atrium and had yet to find a single umbrella, helmet, or hard hat.

Q chuckled, making his ladder shake. "I just want to know how people lose this many socks."

"I'm just glad they're clean." Raya climbed higher. She stood on tiptoe, balancing on a rung to reach for a large storage box. "Please, please, please do not be socks." She lifted its lid and peeked inside. Notebooks filled it to the brim. "Q, you need to see this."

The box was too large and heavy to carry while climbing down the rickety ladder. Q and Raya loaded their arms with as many of the notebooks as they could and emptied the box in three trips. They set the dusty books in a pile on the floor.

"I hope inhaling all that dust was worth it." Raya coughed and flipped through a notebook. Spirals filled every page.

Q looked up from a notebook. "From the look on your face, I'm guessing that we found the same thing. Spirals?"

"Everywhere." Raya thumbed through a second notebook. Then a third. A fourth. And a fifth. She tossed a sixth aside, adding it to the growing mound of notebooks filled with nothing but spirals. She cracked a seventh open. A bold red line divided its first page into two columns. The first contained a list of items, the second, a series of symbols. Raya knitted her brows.

"Find something?" Q said.

"I'm not sure." Raya handed the notebook to him. "What does this look like to you?"

Q scanned the notebook. "It looks like a list of the objects in the valley."

"Yes, but why list them down like that? And what do those symbols mean?"

"Why fill a notebook with spirals? Why build this tower? Olly was going mad, Raya. Who knows why he did the things he did?"

Their last hope was empty, dimly lit, and smelled like must. Raya surveyed the tower's topmost level, covering her nose with the upturned collar of Q's coat.

"This doesn't look promising." Q's palm muffled his voice.

"What happened to all that talk about believing?" Raya said.

"Sorry." Q wrinkled his slightly crooked nose. "Can I blame the smell?"

"I'll open a window." Raya strode to a large circular window made from eyeglasses. A familiar shape, partially hidden in shadows, caught her eye. "It's the dresser."

"How'd it get all the way up here?" Q walked over to her.

"I saw a lot of things being shuffled around," Raya said. "Including the wall that was behind this dresser. It broke into squares and scattered."

"I wonder if that jar is still in here. We could use more light." Q pulled the dresser's top drawer open. A faint glow spilled out of it. Q took the jar out, its halo barely bigger than his hand. "Well, that didn't help much."

A tiny flickering light flew around inside it, reminding Raya of the flares Rasmus had given them. She pushed away the image of Olly going through a full jar of flares, his hope dwindling with each one that fell to the ground, unseen. "Give it a shake."

Q shook the jar and set it on the dresser. It grew brighter, casting its light over a large spiral etched into the wall. Various symbols were carved over it.

"These symbols—" Raya's eyes darted around the etching. "They're the same as the ones we saw in the notebook."

Q shut his eyes, laying his hand over the wall and feeling his way across the marks. "They're the scratches we found earlier." He looked at Raya. "They've been rearranged."

"That means that this is where the wall originally was when Olly carved the spiral," Raya said. "When the tower was folded into a tree house, the spirals and symbols got jumbled up."

Q looked at the round window made of eyeglasses. "I imagine that this spot gets a lot of light during the day. I would have chosen this place too if I needed a studio."

"Or," Raya said, "Olly etched the spiral and those symbols here so that he could see what he was trying to re-create. Remember those mounds of watches and wallets we saw? What if these symbols on the spiral correspond to where they're located in the valley? What if the notebook we found isn't a ledger? What if it's—"

"—a map legend." Q's eyes flashed. "Raya, look at this." He pointed to two leaf designs etched over the spiral. One was located on the outer edge of the spiral above a tree, the second at its center. "It's the same shape as the tree house's door. If the tree on the map refers to this banyan tree and the leaf is its door, then the second leaf in the center of the spiral could be a door too."

Raya pushed the window open and surveyed all that the night hid. "If our exit's out there"—she glanced over her shoulder at the jar of fading light—"there's no way I'm waiting until morning to find it."

Q

The single flare they had found in the jar flew in an arc toward the valley, taking all of time with it. Q held Raya's hand, certain that the seconds had stopped. He kept his eyes on the tiny light, willing it to burn bright.

The flare flickered and died.

Two hearts sank behind Q's ribs. "It's okay." He squeezed Raya's hand. "We'll find the door when the sun's up."

Raya squeezed his fingers back. "We will."

A small spark flashed and glowed as bright as the sun. It set just as quickly, but not before Q had caught a glimpse of the valley. The tether tugged his heart. Raya had seen the valley too. The mounds of lost objects were arranged in a giant spiral as they had suspected, but what lay at the center of the spiral made their hearts stop. Then race.

"You saw that, right?" Raya's breath quickened. "I didn't just imagine it?"

Q stared out the window. "I saw the whirlpool too."

"Why aren't passengers allowed to go outside?"

Frequently Asked Questions
THE ELSEWHERE EXPRESS
PASSENGER HANDBOOK

Lily

Lily balanced on the gallery car's rooftop, reliving a night that, thanks to Mr. Goh's serum, felt as if it had happened moments ago. Like the retrieved memory, she and Rasmus were, once again, too late. The stowaway was gone by the time they searched the gallery and the most they could do was stop the spread of decay.

Rasmus ran down the train car's roof, luring the Echoes away from the coupling. Lily lay on her stomach and held a torch over the metal lovers, shining its blue flames over their slumbering faces. She remembered how she had felt about tearing that first pair apart, but tonight, her eyes were dry and her hands were steady. She hurled the torch at the lover attached to the gallery car.

Rasmus screamed.

Lily's heart jumped to her throat. She twisted around. "Rasmus?"

The Echoes wailed, swarming over him.

"Why are certain doors on the train locked?"

Frequently Asked Questions
THE ELSEWHERE EXPRESS
PASSENGER HANDBOOK

Q

They climbed down from the tree house amid a drizzle of wedding rings. The tree house clinked and clanked, refolding itself into its original form. Q handed a flashlight he had taken from one of the atrium's makeshift lamps to Raya.

"I hope we're right about the whirlpool being an exit." Raya directed the flashlight's beam ahead of them.

Q switched a second flashlight on. "We've seen doors that look like everything from rice wine kettles to clay pots. A doorway that looks like a whirlpool isn't that much of a stretch."

"True, but I can't help but wonder why Olly took so long to find it," Raya said, making her way out from under the banyan's canopy. "A whirlpool in the middle of a valley is pretty hard to miss."

"I don't think Olly missed it."

"What do you mean?"

"The valley is huge, but it's not so massive that it would take decades to search it." Q held the lone umbrella they had found in the dresser's bottom drawer over their heads. "And a whirlpool that size isn't just hard to miss. It's impossible."

"So you think that Olly found the whirlpool but chose not to go through it?"

Q nodded. "I think that's why all those notebooks we found were filled with spirals. It's almost as if Olly was contemplating a decision, you know?" he said, recalling the sketchbooks he had filled with the eyes of the imaginary woman who visited his dreams. He drew them over and over, unable to decide on their color, size, or shape. His memories of her were slippery and unreliable at best, more changeable than the Missed and Misplaced Department's weather.

"But why would Olly hesitate to go through it?" Raya said. "If the whirlpool was a door, wouldn't he have jumped right in?"

"If the weather holds, we should get answers soon." A silver ring bounced off their umbrella. "Just keep your fingers crossed that no one loses a car."

Raya

The drizzle of wedding rings slowed to a trickle. Raya stepped over a gold band, thinking how careless it was to wear something as important as a vow on a place where it would easily slip off. But this was the nature of promises. Nothing bound people forever. Not gold. Not bone marrow. Not even an invisible tether that tied two souls. Raya hated that she could not keep her secrets from Q nearly as much as she was going to miss sharing them once their tether cut them loose.

Q stuck his hand out from under the umbrella. "It looks like that was the last of it."

"And not a car in sight," Raya said.

"Don't jinx it." Q laughed, closing the umbrella and hooking it over his arm. A silver ring sparkled on the ground. "I wonder what its owner is thinking about right now?" He bent down and picked it up.

Raya kept her eyes in front of her, gripping her bag. "I'm pretty sure that whoever lost it is too busy feeling lost themselves." She knew, more than most did, about the truth behind the things people held on to. At one point, they stopped being objects and turned into limbs.

A weighted breath escaped Q's lips.

Raya stopped and plucked a coin from the grass. "Ten baht for your thoughts?"

Q chuckled and looked at her, utterly focused, as though he was certain that whatever she was going to say next was worth nothing less than his full attention.

This, Raya thought, was a quality that set Q apart from most people, herself included. It had not taken her long to notice that Q was a person who honored the present, taking care not to stray into any second before or after the precise moment he was in.

"I was just wondering if she was here."

"Who is 'she'?"

"The faceless woman I told you about, the woman in my dreams." Q took the coin Raya offered with a smile and tucked it into his pocket. "I lost her every morning when I woke up." The wedding ring wriggled between Q's fingers. It jumped from his hand and onto the grass. "Whoa."

Raya swept the flashlight's beam over the ground. The ring flipped on its side and joined the herd of rings rolling past them. Raya hopped out of a diamond-encrusted band's path. It sped off and settled on a shiny mound of rings.

Q grinned at the rings. "I was wondering how all these lost items got organized."

Raya watched the rings roll up the mound, wishing her own thoughts could sort themselves into neat piles.

Q took the sketch he had made of Olly's spiral from his pocket and directed his flashlight over it. "Once we pass that mountain of white socks, we should be in the inner whorls."

The unfinished train tracks looked more lost than the pens and credit cards they had passed. Without a train to travel over them or stations to mark their beginning and end, the tracks seemed to be aware that while they may have been conceived as part of a grand railway plan, their journey had come to an end.

"I'd love to know how one manages to lose a train track," Raya said.

"Things like that don't get lost." Q stared at the tracks. "They're abandoned. We must be in the 'missed' part of the Missed and Misplaced Department."

From the tower, Raya had not been able to tell the difference between the objects that were lost, left behind, or longed for. They were just like the valley's pockmarked ground. It wasn't until you fell into the holes that you discovered how deep each one was. From a distance, all loss looked the same. Walking through the spiral's inner whorls, Raya saw them up close. Here, the holes were deeper and darker, the mountains of paper, framed photographs, and children's toys surrounding them shrouded by a blacker night. Raya kept her eyes from straying beyond the borders of her flashlight's beam. If this part of the valley was where the deserted and discarded were kept, she was bound to run into a hill containing half of her life.

Q plucked a piece of paper from a mound of assorted stationery, ran his eyes over it, and put it back.

"What was it?" Raya said.

"I don't know. It contained one word."

"What was the word?"

"Once."

Raya walked on, thinking about all the phrases that could have followed it and the infinite ways they could have steered a story's course. The abandoned thought could have been anything. A poem. A short story. A long one. Maybe a song. But the scribbled thought had boarded a train car to nowhere, and no one, including the thought's owner, was ever going to know what it could have become. Raya pressed her lips together harder than she should have to keep a breath from escaping. Metal, salt, and honey coated her tongue. Raya's first thought was that she had bitten it, but teeth were too sharp to not notice. Sadness was stealthier, and tasted of guitar strings, tears, and all the sugary things she wasn't supposed to have.

Q stopped, his gaze on an assortment of musical instruments. "Isn't that your guitar? The one behind the cello? I remember its purple stickers."

"No." Raya walked ahead.

Q caught up with her. "You didn't even look at it."

"I didn't have to. I know it isn't mine. I destroyed the guitar you saw at the gallery after Jace's funeral. It can't be here."

"But that's not the image you picture whenever you miss it, is it? In your mind, your guitar is whole. Pristine."

"How did you—"

"Look around you, Raya. None of the things in this valley are shattered. We long for things, people at their best, not at their worst. As much as I hated how my father's smile was a lie, I can't paint him in my mind without one. The man with a bright smile was and always will be the father I knew. That's the person I miss even if the happy and content man I thought he was might have never really existed. Maybe . . . that's why your guitar is whole too."

Raya shook her head. "Even if you're right, it doesn't matter. This valley is a cemetery, Q, and all these mounds are graves. I could walk over there and find my guitar as good as new, and nothing would change. My own dream would still be dead, and I would still be stuck on this train."

The knot on her palm tingled as more threads frayed and came loose.

The whirlpool spanned the width of six backyard pools. Or maybe sixteen. It was impossible for Raya to pay any attention to it while Olly's twin stood by its edge. The man with Olly's face stared into the swirling current as intently as the Olly they had met at the Dragonfly lost himself in pots of stew. Raya crouched next to Q behind a grand piano, the maelstrom of questions in her eyes putting the whirlpool to shame. "Is that a version of Olly?"

"I can hear you, you know." The man turned in their direction. "Why don't you come out and ask me your questions yourself?"

Raya and Q stood up, their tether as taut as their spines.

"Hello. Welcome to the Missed and Misplaced Department." The man walked over to them. "My name's Olly."

"I'm . . . uh . . . Raya, and this is Q." Raya studied his face. This man and the Olly at the Dragonfly were identical, down to the reddish birthmark on their chins.

"It's great to meet you." Olly extended his hand.

Raya's fingers closed around air. She jerked her hand back.

"Sorry about that," the man who called himself Olly said.

"Who are you?" Raya backed away from him. *"What are you?"*

He smiled. "I'm Olly."

"You're not." Q drew his shoulders back, his eyes sharp. "We met Olly at the Dragonfly."

The man shrugged. "That doesn't mean that I'm not Olly too."

"Are you a version of him?" Raya said.

"You mean like the versions of Mr. Goh?" The man shook his head. "I've only boarded the train once, as far as I know."

"Then are you wearing Olly's face?" Raya kept her distance. "Or is he wearing yours?"

The man laughed. "That sounds like fun, but you can only wear the faces of people who aren't on board the train. You should suggest it to the conductor, though."

"Then what are you?" Q's voice drilled into him.

"Why is it so hard for you to believe that I'm Olly?"

"Maybe it's because my hand just passed right through you?" Raya said.

"Fair enough. But I promise you, I am Olly. And so is the Olly that you met at the Dragonfly. We know each other rather well."

"You can't both be Olly," Q said, his neck and jaw stiff.

The man turned his back to them, returning his gaze to the whirlpool. "Isn't it funny how the stiller your body is, the farther your mind wanders? Olly used to spend his days gazing at the swirls, but he wasn't really here. He liked to reminisce about his time in maintenance. He thought about his friends on the crew a lot too. In the early days, those memories made him smile. As time passed, his old life grew farther and farther away, almost as if it belonged to someone else. One day, it did." He looked at Raya and Q. "That was the day I was born. I'm the Olly that—"

"—Olly lost." Raya's eyes grew large. "You're Olly's thoughts."

"There aren't other piles of thoughts that are like me around here and so I don't really have a place to go. I spend most of my time here." Olly glanced back at the whirlpool. "I like to stand at the exact spot Olly used to stay for hours without moving, just looking over the edge. That's when I feel closest to him, when I feel whole."

"That must be why Olly stirs and stares into pots. It reminds him of this place." Q locked eyes on Olly. "And you."

"How did you get left behind?" Raya asked. "Don't the thoughts in the Missed and Misplaced Department come from people outside the train?"

"Most do," Olly said. "Except for those that circle the drain."

"Drain?" A chill spread through the tether. Raya shivered. "What drain?"

"That drain." Olly chuckled, casting his gaze to the whirlpool. "Last I checked, it was the only thing here that swirled and carried things away."

Raya, Olly, and Q sat on piano stools by the collection of abandoned instruments. "I'm happy that I learned how to do this." Olly patted the stool. "When I first arrived, I fell through everything. I wasn't like any of the thoughts here. They bounced, rolled, and tumbled to whichever mound they belonged to as soon as they landed. But not all of us can be lucky enough to be pens or watches. I imagine that it's quite peaceful when you can't think or worry about who you are or where you belong."

Olly cracked a small smile. "Do you know what I used to do before I got lost? I worked in maintenance as a plumber. I had just unclogged the pharmacy's drain when a leak was reported in the gallery's fountain. The leak turned out to be a simple fix. Since I finished early, I decided to see the exhibit while I was there. That's when I . . . panicked."

"Because you saw your secrets on display," Raya said quietly.

"My secrets?" Olly shook his head. "I don't have any worth putting in an exhibit. The secrets I saw belonged to the conductor."

"*What?*" Q jolted. "Which conductor?"

"The only conductor the train has. I don't recall their name. It was so long ago. What I do remember is being so terrified of their secrets that I bolted through a locked door and found out firsthand why we're told not to open them."

"So we don't get lost," Q said.

"They like to say that, don't they?" His eyes dimmed, making him resemble the Olly that stirred pots even more. "The truth is, they tell us to stay away from locked doors to keep us from seeing things they don't want us to see."

Raya's shoulders stiffened. "Like what?"

Olly set his eyes on the whirlpool. "Like drains."

"Should I be afraid of the Echoes?"

Frequently Asked Questions
THE ELSEWHERE EXPRESS
PASSENGER HANDBOOK

Rasmus

Rasmus had not expected to be blinded by a flare nor to slip on the gallery car's roof. If he had caught a glimpse of the train car the flare had illuminated, he could no longer remember it.

The Echoes swarming him consumed his newer memories first. After erasing whatever location the flare had burned into his eye, they moved on to his afternoon tea and biscuits. They swallowed the memory of a steaming cup in one gulp without getting scalded or tasting it. Pleasure required knowing pain, both of which were beyond an Echo's grasp. Some Echoes moved on to ripping off pieces of the hours Rasmus had spent tinkering with his miniature trains. Others devoured the plans that he was drafting for a portable gilded frame passengers could carry in their pockets. Rasmus lay still and silent, resigned to his fate. Soon, he would know nothing about who he was, other than being the first and last course of a frenzied feast.

"Where do the Echoes go?"

Frequently Asked Questions
THE ELSEWHERE EXPRESS
PASSENGER HANDBOOK

Q

The whirlpool offered Q an invitation with every swirl, promising him calm and quiet if he came just a little bit closer. He took a step forward, lost in the whorls.

Olly pulled him back. "Don't look at them."

Q blinked, clearing his mind of whispers. A current of spectral faces spiraled in the whirlpool, their murmurs mimicking the sound of rushing water.

Raya stared at the Echoes, her lips pale. "I thought Echoes couldn't board the train."

"They can't." Olly shook his head. "They're on the way out. The past needs to go somewhere."

"What are you talking about?" Q said.

"Where do you think memories go after Mr. Goh's excess baggage serum purges them from passengers?" Olly slipped his hands into his pockets. "There's a drain in the pharmacy that needs to be regularly unclogged because some memories are too bulky or sticky to flow through it. I never really gave much thought to where memories went when they were flushed out." He shrugged. "No one here gives much thought to anything, really."

"But Echoes aren't memories." Raya frowned. "They're passengers with excess baggage."

"That's what I thought too," Olly said. "Until one of the memories I had unclogged turned into an Echo in front of my eyes."

Q rubbed his forehead. "I don't understand. Why would the conductor lie about something like that?"

"Why *wouldn't* they lie?" Olly said. "Mr. Goh's tonics are like the poems they're made from. They'll only find their way inside you if you let them in. If passengers don't willingly drink it, every car on this train would essentially turn into the Missed and Misplaced Department, each filled with passengers who were as lost as the day they boarded. There would be no one to run the Elsewhere Express, and in time the train would fall into disrepair. I would lie too if I were the conductor, and my responsibility was to keep this train running and intact. The lie convinces even the most reluctant passenger to let go of their past. No one wants to get thrown off the Elsewhere Express and trail it around for eternity, begging to be let in. I'm willing to bet every thought I'm made of that passengers wouldn't be as eager to cast their old lives away if they knew that what was scratching at their windows each night wasn't a stranger but a part of themselves."

"No." Q stood up. "You're wrong."

"You saw the Echoes. You heard them calling you. If I hadn't stopped you, you would have joined them. Your past was drawn to them as they were drawn to you," Olly said. "Do you know why I built the tower? I thought that if I built it high enough, I would stop feeling their pull. I didn't. They called to me every second of every day. They followed me into my dreams. I drew a map so that I could find a way to avoid the drain while I searched for a way out of here. I never did. It became clear that the only way I could silence them was to . . . drown them out."

"You jumped into the whirlpool . . ." Raya's voice died in her throat.

Olly nodded.

"And found your way back," Q said.

"Did I? Tell me, what was I like on the other side? Why do I miss myself so much that my thoughts gathered here among the lost? How much of myself was able to return? I know how much you want this drain to be an exit, but it's not. Don't make the same mistake Olly did."

"But if this is a drain," Raya said, "then why did Olly wind up in the cloakroom? Shouldn't he have been flushed outside together with the Echoes?"

"As someone who has worked with pipes and drains for a very long time"—Olly picked up a pebble and threw it into the current—"I can tell you that this isn't the first drainage system to exist that efficiently separates waste."

"What makes us human?"

Frequently Asked Questions
THE ELSEWHERE EXPRESS
PASSENGER HANDBOOK

Raya

Phones and wristwatches rained down on the valley. Raya and Q sheltered beneath a grand piano, crouching in silence. Olly strolled back to his spot by the whirlpool, phones and watches falling through him and crashing to the ground.

Raya imagined that she could stride into the downpour with as little care. Nothing could shred her more than Olly's words had. The frayed knot twisting over her palm was the only thing they had left intact. "They didn't overlook this place when they were searching for Olly." She looked out at the mounds of lost objects. "They left him here to keep the truth about the Echoes from getting out."

"We don't know that," Q said.

"Don't we? Do you really believe that a conductor of this train wouldn't have any idea about where memories drain out from?"

"That presumes that Olly is telling the truth."

Raya frowned. "Why would he lie?"

"Because"—Q lowered his voice—"that thing isn't really Olly. It can insist that it's Olly all it wants but it doesn't change the fact that it's no different from the bench you're sitting on or any object in this valley. It's just a collection of Olly's thoughts."

"Isn't that what we are too?" Raya said. "A collection of our thoughts? Beliefs? Values? Fears? Isn't that what's beneath our skin? What makes us human?"

"That's different."

"How? What could be more real than our thoughts? You and I have built our whole lives on them. They've set our limits and direction. They drove you to the edge of a train platform and convinced me to carry around a dead dream. You and I were trapped long before we ever set foot in the Missed and Misplaced Department. Olly has no reason to lie to us. Unlike Lily."

Q shook his head. "Olly may believe what he's saying but that doesn't mean he's right. We both know that thoughts can be wrong."

"I'll tell you what I know," Raya said. "I know that you want to believe the best about this train because it's your second chance. And I want that for you too. But you can't find your place here by waiting to be rescued. Even if I'm wrong about Lily leaving Olly here on purpose, the stowaway is still out there. This train could rot away before we ever find our way out."

"And how are we supposed to leave, Raya? We can't go through the whirlpool unless we want to end up like Olly, and we haven't found a door."

Raya pulled a bag of shattered crystal from her tote. "We still have this."

"A bag of broken crystal? Unless Rasmus's train magically reassembles itself, it isn't going anywhere. And neither are we. Nothing's changed, Raya. We're still stuck."

"One thing has." Raya looked out at the rows of guitars. "Now we have a way of putting this train back together," she said, her voice wavering between hope and dread.

Raya ran her hand over her sticker-covered guitar's neck. It was mended seamlessly and smoothly, without a single scratch or dent.

Longing was a meticulous craftsman and had buffed out all the guitar's imperfections. Even its glittery heart stickers were new.

Raya emptied the bag of broken crystal over the grass and sat down. She set her guitar over her lap. She closed her eyes and strummed, humming, slowly and softly, like someone wading into the sea, unsure if they remembered how to swim. She cobbled together a simple but sturdy song, a raft of memories light enough to float: Q's eyes when he smiled. The warmth of his laugh. Their invisible tether. The melody was small, but had just enough space to ferry a tiny, timeless hope.

Live. Breathe. Be.

The song flowed from Raya into the guitar and took flight on glowing rainbow wings. It flitted around the broken crystal, burned bright, and left an immaculately restored crystal train in its place.

Q scooped Raya up and twirled her around. "You did it."

Raya laughed. Then cried. Nothing cut deeper than loss, but finding what you lost hurt too. You couldn't hold it without grieving for all the years your arms were empty.

A tiny moon rejoined the constellations over the playground's sky. Beneath the stars, grass grew over all the places the crystal train had cracked. Raya's newest song did not leave any stitches or scars. Q admired the healed sky from the swing. "You must admit, this would have been impossible to do with a scalpel."

Raya smiled stiffly, leaning forward on the swing's seat, listening for cracks.

"You can relax," Q said. "You fixed the train and we're on our way. We're safe. The song you found on the beach was beautiful, but it doesn't come close to the one you just wrote."

"The song on the island fixed a leaf." Raya gripped the swing's chains. "This is a train. What if it breaks apart again?"

"Is that what you're really worried about?" Q said.

"Why?" Raya turned to him. "Did our snitch tell you any different?"

"I know what worry feels like, Raya. My stomach twisted itself into knots at every doctor's appointment. Your fear feels *different*."

"How?"

"I don't know."

"Then the tether told you the truth." Raya pushed off the grass, setting the swing in a wide arc. "I don't know what it feels like either." The song that had fixed the train had opened a door to a place that she could not have wanted to flee faster or live in more. She had not expected to find her place on the Elsewhere Express in a valley of the lost and it terrified her to think that if she ever held her guitar again, she would not think twice about paying the true price of her free train ticket. "It's like I've been split in two." Like Olly.

The train came to a stop, the sound of water lapping outside it.

"Which Raya boarded the crystal train?" Q said as the train car's doors slid open. "The one who wants to go home or the one who wants to stay?"

"What kinds of remedies does the train's pharmacy offer?"

Frequently Asked Questions
THE ELSEWHERE EXPRESS
PASSENGER HANDBOOK

Lily

Abandoned teacups perched on almost every surface of the Archive's office, waiting for Rasmus to notice them. He did not. He lay on the cot by a bookcase, staring up at a jade ceiling with unblinking eyes. Lily dabbed a wet towel over Rasmus's forehead, not because it helped, but because doing nothing would hollow her out too. Neither the train's oldest healer, the phoenix that lived on the Archive's outermost sphere, nor Mr. Goh could mend a mind that had been eaten alive.

YOUR ITINERARY

THE
WANDERING CITY
BOAT TOUR

"What's rarer than a banana?"

Frequently Asked Questions
THE ELSEWHERE EXPRESS
PASSENGER HANDBOOK

Raya

The flat-bottomed boat floated down a languid river bordered by a curious mix of mismatched Haussmann architecture, Spanish villas draped in curtains of red bougainvillea, and terraced wooden homes half hidden by cascading tropical gardens. A row of cast-iron streetlamps illuminated the eclectic buildings and set the river on fire. Sampans bobbed over the shimmering reflections while waiting for passengers at wooden docks. A version of the Arc de Triomphe, carved from red jade, stood at the end of the river, presiding over a roundabout of twelve waterways radiating from the monument like the rays of the sun. There was no sign of rot or rain. Raya looked out from the sampan's bow, her heartbeat undulating as the river did. "Where are we?"

"My boat," a voice, as calm as the river, said. Its owner, the sampan's bald pilot, waved from the end of the boat. A low, curved thatched roof covering the rivercraft's midsection stood between them. "Welcome aboard." He smiled, steering with a single sculling oar attached to the stern. "My name's Alain."

Raya managed an awkward wave. "I'm Raya."

"Q. We apologize for . . . um . . . dropping in on your boat like this," Q said.

A grin crinkled Alain's leathery cheeks. "No need to apologize. I had thought the Elsewhere Express had run out of ways to surprise me. I had no idea that there was a doorway on my boat. It must have just recently hopped aboard."

Raya scoured the sampan's floor for the crystal train. It glinted behind the heel of her right boot. She scooped it up, her hair falling over her face. Somewhere between the MMD and this river, she had lost her hair tie.

Alain craned his neck over the boat's roof. "Is that one of those trains that travel on the Archive's maps?"

"It is." Raya slipped the miniature train into her bag.

"I've never seen one in person." He smiled. "Two surprises in one evening. What a treat."

"You didn't happen to notice anything else unusual tonight, did you?" Raya searched the sky for storm clouds.

"Everything on the Elsewhere Express is unusual. Can you be more specific?"

"Has it rained recently?" Q said.

"Rained?" Alain laughed. "That's not unusual. That's impossible. It never rains on the Elsewhere Express."

"How about rot?" Raya said. "Or moths?"

Alain chuckled. "Sorry. It's just been another typical day on the river. Nothing as exciting as rot or moths, I'm afraid. Oh, wait. I did see a bee, or rather a hatpin shaped like one. Does that count?"

Raya exhaled, the tension in her neck and shoulders exiting with her breath. "Bees are great."

Q grinned. "They're absolutely wonderful."

"Well, if you like hatpins and sparkly things, maybe I can interest you in a trade for that little train of yours?" He gestured to the baskets arranged beneath the boat's roof. Each was large enough to fit a small child and overflowing with everything from jewelry to colorful scarves. The largest of the baskets contained uncut rubies, some the size of a baby's fist. "Take your pick. Except for the bananas. Those are rare."

"Sorry," Raya said, "but the train isn't ours. We just borrowed it for the evening."

Alain clucked his tongue. "That's too bad."

"What would you take for that scarf?" Q pointed to a pale purple scarf sitting on top of one of the baskets. A tiny butterfly flitted on a corner of the scarf, delicately embroidered in gold thread. Alain rubbed his chin, his hooded eyes glinting in the light of a streetlamp. "How much is it worth to you?"

"If I were to answer that honestly"—Q smiled, casting a glance at Raya—"I don't think I'd ever be able to afford it."

Alain laughed. "Deal. It's yours. Take it."

"We haven't agreed on a price yet," Q said.

"You've already overpaid. Truth and a good laugh are priceless. You're a terrible negotiator. I was only going to charge you two questions for it and you could have haggled it down to one." He took an emerald ring from the pile and tossed it to Q. "Take this too."

Q caught it with one hand. "What's this for?"

"I don't want you to leave feeling like you were cheated. Scams are for the world outside the train. Here, you get what you pay for."

"Isn't everything here supposed to be free?" Raya said.

Alain pulled the oar as though he had not heard her.

"How would I have paid you with a question?" Q took the scarf from the basket and tucked it, along with the emerald ring, into his pocket.

"First time in the Wandering City?" Alain scratched his bulbous nose.

Q nodded.

"We do things a little differently in this train car. Here, we use questions as currency."

"Why?" Raya said.

"Because they're even harder to come by than bananas. It's a crime how people hardly ever think about them. Very few thoughts about bananas ever board the train." Alain sighed. "I never thought about them much either before becoming a passenger. Now that they're so scarce, I've never craved them more."

Raya nodded, unsure of how to respond. Bananas did not occupy much space in her mind either.

"The longer you've been on the Elsewhere Express, the less you question things," Alain said. "Like anything you stop doing, in time, you forget how to do it. But residents of the Wandering City like to stay sharp. We have to. This train car keeps us on our toes. You never know where you're going to wake up. This morning, I tumbled off a counter in the bakery." The sampan rocked.

Raya grabbed hold of Q's arm.

"Like I said, it keeps us on our toes." Alain pointed to one of the carved stone bridges spanning the river. It shook, casting large chunks into the water. "Hold on tight."

The bridge crumbled. Waves surged toward the sampan. Raya dropped to the floor, a pavilion crumbling in her mind. "Oh god. Not again."

Q clutched her hand.

The river rippled as though coming to a boil. Tiny rocks shot out of the water. One flew past Raya, stopped, then hovered between her and Q. What she had thought was a stone was a small long-billed bird carried by a blur of wings. Hummingbirds. Hundreds of them.

One perched on Alain's shoulder. "This is what happens when the Wandering City changes its mind. The thoughts in this train car are restless. They can't stay in one place or shape for too long."

A shimmer of hummingbirds flew over the boat. Raya gaped at them. "The birds are thoughts?"

"The fleeting kind," Alain said. "Everything in this train car is made from transient thoughts, the sort that dash through your mind so swiftly that often, you're not aware you've had them."

The birds descended over a dock, churning the wind. Raya's hair whipped against her face. The birds flew faster, blurring into a single form.

"This train car used to have other names," Alain said, "but it was difficult to keep up with each time it changed. Yesterday, it was a Nordic version of New Orleans. The day before that, it was a cross between Tudor London and Taipei. Everything changes. Buildings. Streets. Even the weather."

The whirlwind of wings settled, leaving a lighthouse where the dock had once stood. The new structure stood watch over the river, sweeping its beam across the water. Raya shielded her eyes.

"Those thoughts will shift shapes a few more times before the night's over," Alain said. "They make the Wandering City an exciting place to live in, but it's not for everyone. I can show you around, if you'd like."

"Thank you, but we can't stay," Raya said. "We were headed to the Archive, but I chose the wrong track on the map by mistake."

"You didn't." Alain smiled. "Everyone finds this train car by accident. It moves around so much that passengers inadvertently end up taking detours here. The car hops around the track, forcing the other train cars to make way for it. It annoys the conductor, but there's nothing she can do about it. The Wandering City does as it pleases."

"The city's sentient?" Q said.

"Not exactly. How each car behaves is driven by the thoughts that fill it. They're like people that way. Transient thoughts, transient train car," Alain explained. "It's a pity you can't stay long. Until they finish renovating the Lake, this train car, without a doubt, is the queen of the Elsewhere Express. I hope you can come back for a visit when you have more time."

"We will." The reply rolled off Raya's tongue, surprising her more than the detour to the Wandering City had. She had only wanted to be polite but found herself meaning every word. Each came wrapped in possibility like ribboned presents under a tree. Raya unwrapped them slowly, revealing the shiny little futures they contained. She turned them over in her mind, admiring them from every angle. A queue for breakfast at the Dragonfly. A day of collecting songs at the beach while Q painted stars. Happy hour at the Lotus, sipping rice wine cocktails under a sparkling sea. Raya dismissed these imaginings as the effects of lingering in a train car made of fleeting thoughts. She kept her eyes on the river, waiting for them to go on their way.

"Wonderful," Alain said. "I'll be more than happy to give you a tour."

Raya took the crystal train from her bag. The map's silver railway appeared, spilling from the boat's deck and stretching out over the river. Raya closed her eyes, listening for the Archive's song. A dock broke apart and rocked the boat. Raya wobbled. Hummingbirds burst from the water and crisscrossed the tracks, filling the air with low-pitched buzzing. "We can't do this here. I can barely hear the songs."

Q nodded and waved to Alain. "Would it be too much trouble if we asked you to drop us off at a dock?"

"Not at all. Where would you like to get off?"

"Anywhere that's convenient for you," Raya said.

Alain pulled the oar. "We'll be coming up to a dock shortly."

"Thank you." Raya smiled. "We really appreciate this."

"My pleasure." Alain glanced at a basket of rubies. "Since you'll be getting off at that dock, I was wondering if you could do me a small favor? A friend of mine lives very close to where you'll be disembarking. I've been meaning to drop off a present, but I haven't had the time. Would it be possible for you to deliver it for me before you leave for the Archive? It should take no time at all."

"Of course," Raya said without having to think. "We'd be happy to."

"Thank you." Alain steered the boat toward the dock. "Her compartment is right on top of her perfumery."

YOUR ITINERARY

DESIGN YOUR OWN
FRAGRANCE AT
THE PERFUMERY

"Why can't I find any perfume on the train?"

Frequently Asked Questions
THE ELSEWHERE EXPRESS
PASSENGER HANDBOOK

Raya

At the end of a quiet street, nestled between an antique furniture store and a vintage art shop, Madame Manon de Lambilly's perfumery hid behind a peeling door that, over its lifetime, had been painted every shade of wine.

With neither a window display nor a sign to announce its presence, the small shop seemed to be trying its best not to be found. It might have succeeded if the spicy and warm fragrance wafting from the open window on its second floor did not betray it. It drifted down the cobbled street and beckoned Raya to follow. Raya walked up the worn steps to the shop's door, breathing in the scented invitation. A door knocker in the shape of a hummingbird perched on a brass flower at the center of the red door. Raya clutched its wing. The metal bird stirred and flew away. It circled Raya and Q, hovering by the tips of their noses. It looked into their eyes.

Q stared back at it. "I think it's trying to decide whether or not to let us in."

The hummingbird flew to the perfumery's open window and slipped inside.

Raya looked up at the curtained window. "I hope that doesn't mean it didn't like us."

"I hope so too." Q checked the door's knob. It was locked. "But if it does, then we can always try knocking the old-fashioned way." Q tightened his grip on Alain's gift. "I have no idea what things are worth on this train, but I don't feel comfortable leaving a basket of rubies on someone's doorstep."

"Neither do I," Raya said. "Thank god he didn't ask us to deliver bananas."

They locked eyes and burst into giggles, their laughter ringing through the street.

The perfumery's door creaked open. Raya clamped her lips over a chuckle. Q did the same, but with less success. His eyes watered. He dabbed at them with his sleeve.

A woman opened the door, her dark hair tucked into a loose chignon. A bemused smile played over her bright-red lips. Raya struggled to guess her age. Her pale skin was supple and smooth, but her kohl-lined eyes seemed to have seen more than she cared to remember. A draft tousled her hair's loose wisps, sweeping the fragrance from the curve of her neck through the perfumery's door. Sandalwood, citrus, and a story about lost love. The brass hummingbird flew past the woman's shoulder and perched on the door.

"Merci." The woman blew a kiss to the bird and cinched a flowing floral silk robe around her narrow waist. "That little one is very thoughtful. She knows that knocks startle me and so she flies up to let me know when I have visitors. How may I help you?"

"We're looking for Madame Manon de Lambilly," Q said.

"Congratulations," she said in a voice touched by smoke. "You have found her. Please, call me Manon. We are all friends on this train, no?"

"It's lovely to meet you, Manon. I'm Q and this is Raya. We apologize for disturbing you at this late hour."

"Late hour?" A throaty laugh escaped her full lips. "I was just about to open the shop. I cannot be bothered to get out of bed before the sun sets. Please, come in."

Raya and Q followed her inside. The shop's faded façade gave way to decadent walls dressed in a hand-painted silk mural. A peacock, rendered in brushstrokes of brilliant blue, strutted across the silk, its eyes never leaving Raya and Q.

"Beautiful, isn't he?" Manon scooped a small handful of roasted pumpkin seeds from her pocket and offered it to the peacock. The bird stuck its head out of the painting and pecked at her hand. The pumpkin seeds transformed into a painted version of themselves as soon as they touched its beak. "There are two other peacocks in the mural, but they are shy. They hide whenever there is company." Manon dusted her palm over her robe. "But Pavo loves it whenever we have clients. I'm not sure if it is because he loves people or knows that he will have the pumpkin seeds to himself."

"Oh, sorry. We're not here to buy perfume," Raya said. "Alain sent us."

"He asked us to give this to you." Q handed Manon the basket of rubies.

"How lovely." Manon's eyes lit up. "Thank you. I hope that you didn't have to go out of your way."

"We didn't." Raya smiled. "But we really do need to get going. It was nice meeting you."

"It was lovely meeting you too." Manon opened the door. "And thanks again for delivering Alain's present."

"Good night." Q stepped back from the doorway to let Raya through.

"Enjoy the rest of your evening," Manon said. "And, as I'm sure you know, if you happen to run into the conductor, it would be best not to mention that you were here."

Raya turned. "Sorry?"

"You have had your orientation, no?" Manon's dark eyes narrowed slightly.

"We have," Q said.

"Then you should be aware that you're not supposed to go through locked doors. The perfumery's front door was locked when you arrived, was it not?"

Raya shot a glance at the peeling red door. "Well, yes, but—"

"You're lucky that no one saw you." Manon clutched the small perfume bottle she wore on a gold chain around her neck.

Raya quirked a brow. "Visiting a perfumery is against the train's rules?"

"Sadly, yes." Manon coiled her necklace's chain around a finger.

Raya frowned. "Why?"

"I'll be more than happy to answer all of your questions inside." Manon stuck her head out the door, her eyes darting around the empty street. "This is not the kind of conversation you want overheard."

"We really should be going," Q said, looking at Raya.

"If being late for your next appointment is what you're worried about, you can put your mind at ease," Manon said. "I had a customer who spent a whole year trying to choose between two perfumes for his wife. He left with the perfect gift and was not a minute late for his wife's birthday party."

"How's that possible?" Raya said.

"Time stopped the moment you entered this shop." Manon smiled. "So, tell me. Would you care to stay and have some coffee with the truth?"

Raya bit her lip, stealing a glance at the knot on her palm.

Pavo led the way to the grand salon while Manon went to make coffee. A jacaranda tree in full bloom grew in the center of a hexagonal room that could not possibly fit into the little shop they had just entered. Gilded mirrors along the salon's walls reflected the flowering tree, propagating it into an infinite purple forest. Warm, earthy, and green scents drew Raya deeper into the woods.

The jacaranda's blooming branches dipped to the salon's moss-covered floor, twisting themselves into seating and shelves. Faceted perfume bottles sparkled on the branches, clinging to the tree like dew. Heftier colorful bottles sat in nests of spun gold. Each bottle was uniquely adorned with precious stones and metals, teasing the story of the fragrance within it. Raya stuffed her hands into her pockets to keep herself from picking up and smelling every perfume she walked past.

"How do we know that Manon isn't lying about time stopping?" Q looked back at the hallway that led to the door. "I think we should leave."

Raya turned her hand over, showing off her knot. It was frozen in place. "If you believe this knot, then Manon's telling the truth."

Q looked at the knot on his palm. It had stopped moving too. His shoulders softened. "I suppose we could use a break."

"When you welcome catching your breath in what could possibly be a contraband den, you know you're tired."

"Tired is an understatement," Q said.

Raya caught her reflection in one of the salon's mirrors and grimaced. She attempted to retie her hair and glanced at the empty spot where she kept her spare hair ties. She groaned, letting her hair fall.

"Allow me." Q smiled, plucking from his pocket the scarf he had bought from Alain. He walked behind Raya and smoothed back her hair, his fingertips flitting over her nape.

A current ran across Raya's skin, quickening her pulse. "This . . . um . . . was not how I imagined spending my evening," she said, forcing herself to ignore the heat spreading up her neck and over her cheeks as Q's long fingers combed through her hair. "I thought I'd be curled up in bed, eating an entire pint of chocolate ice cream. With a drizzle of salted caramel sauce if I was feeling adventurous."

"Daring girl." Q smiled. "This wasn't how I imagined my evening would go either. This is infinitely better."

"Better?"

"I can see."

"Oh god. Right. Of course. I feel like an idiot for even asking."

"Don't. With everything that's happened tonight, I'd understand if you forgot my name. Besides, I can't wait to start my life on this train and forget that I was ever blind too, Rachel." He grinned.

Raya laughed. "I deserved that."

"There." He secured Raya's hair in the scarf. "All done."

Raya looked into the mirror, her hair neater than she ever wore it. "Wow. This actually might be more impressive than your painting skills."

"There were days after my father died when my mother couldn't bring herself to get out of bed, eat, or even brush her hair. I couldn't make her smile, but I learned to do what I could."

"Oh," Raya said quietly.

He tucked a loose strand behind Raya's ear, looking at her and nothing else.

Raya's face grew warm beneath his gaze. "What are you staring at?"

"Nothing." His cheeks flushed. "I was just . . . um . . ." He cleared his throat and plucked a perfume bottle from a nest. He examined it, seemingly intensely enamored by its faceted stopper. "I was just thinking about how these scents are going to have a difficult time living up to their bottles."

"Oh." Heat receded from Raya's face, leaving her cheeks cold. "I know what you mean. I would hate to have that kind of pressure."

"That's not something you have to worry about." Q winced. "That didn't come out right. I didn't mean you're a dull bottle. You're beautiful. Breathtaking, really. Which is not even the slightest bit important. God. Words. I hate them. I'm going to shut up now."

Their tether tugged at their ribs, making them laugh.

Q's gaze returned to Raya, reticent, then smiling, like someone coming home. She smiled back. "Your bottle's not too bad either."

"Not bad?" he said, pretending to be offended. "That's all I get?"

Raya rolled her eyes. "Fine. You're recyclable too."

Manon glided into the salon carrying a French coffee press and three cups decorated with a hummingbird motif on a silver tray. She set the tray on a branch that had twisted itself into a small table. Notes of dark-roasted coffee, chocolate, and cinnamon wafted up from the tray. Manon walked over to Raya and Q, the hand-painted chrysanthemums on her robe rippling behind her. "Have you had a chance to look around?"

"You have a lovely shop." Raya tried to ignore the current buzzing through the tether and down to her toes. She kept her eyes from Q, reminding herself that however tingly and warm their laughter and banter were, it was an illusion. When the train's map became obsolete and returned to the Archive, their connection would vanish too.

Manon smiled. "Thank you."

"Which makes it even harder to comprehend why a perfumery would be considered an illicit business," Q said.

"Perhaps this will make it easier to understand." Manon took the small perfume bottle hanging from her neck and spritzed it in the air. Black pepper, patchouli, and damask rose bloomed around them.

Raya breathed it in. Piano music, mellow and smoother than good whiskey, flowed over the clinking of glasses and hum of conversation. An elegantly dressed crowd sat around a pianist's small stage, chatting quietly and sipping pretty drinks. A man's hand entwined its fingers through hers. Raya jumped in her seat, yanking her hand from the stranger's grasp. The scene parted like a curtain, restoring the perfumery's salon.

"Did you see that?" Q's mouth hung half open.

Raya stared at her hand. Though it did not retain any marks or warmth from the fingers that had just weaved through it, her skin remembered the stranger's touch. "I . . . I felt it."

"That was a whiff of the night I met my husband." Manon's voice dimmed. "Unfortunately, he wasn't lucky enough to get a ticket to the Elsewhere Express. I created this fragrance so that I could revisit that night whenever I missed him. There is nothing quite like the moment two souls find each other in life's maze. Being lost together is the rarest of pleasures.

"My clients wear my nostalgia on their necks and wrists to experience what it's like to long for someone you will never see again."

"Why would anyone want to do that?" Q said.

"Why do people watch sad movies?" Manon's gaze roamed over Raya's face. "But this isn't a fragrance you would ever select for yourself. You already know what loss is like. I can smell it on your skin. But this grief is not for a lover, no? Perhaps a parent? Or a close friend? Maybe a sibling?"

Raya stiffened.

"Do all of these bottles contain memories?" Q jumped in, plucking a bottle from a nest.

Manon nodded. "Memory is a perfumer's trade."

Warmth rippled from Raya's end of the tether to Q, delivering her thanks. His eyes acknowledged it with a quiet smile.

"Memory is a place outside time." Manon waved her bejeweled hand around the salon. "For as long as you are in this perfumery, all your worries are on pause. It is quite peaceful here, no?" She looked up at the tree's canopy. "I always liked the thought of having an indoor garden, but my old perfumery could fit nothing more than a couple of flowerpots by the window. Here, there is no distinction between what you can grow in your mind and in the middle of a small perfumery."

"You were a perfumer before you boarded the train too?" Q said.

"Yes. But my old atelier wasn't anything as fancy as this. I sold it when my husband got sick so that I could care for him."

A breath stopped midway to Raya's lungs. She gaped at Manon and blinked.

"Is something wrong?" Manon said.

Raya released the breath and choked on it. "You're not like the others on this train. You remember your past. How is that possible?"

Manon stared back at her, her eyes mirroring the questions darting through Raya's. "When did you board?"

"This evening."

"That explains why you are the first visitor to ever ask me that question. All my clients have been on this train for a very long time, so long that they've forgotten how to look at things closely. But to be fair, it's a lot easier to sit through an endless journey when you don't notice the lumps on your seat. Sadly, not everyone on this train has the luxury of being comfortable. As a perfumer, carrying extra baggage is a job requirement. To create fragrances, it is not enough to have a good sense of smell. You need to know what different scents conjure. This is not a skill you can learn overnight. It is knowledge that can only be acquired over time by using all your senses. I could not drink Mr. Goh's tonic and find my place as a perfumer on the Elsewhere Express at the same time."

"You kept your memories . . ." The gold knot on Raya's palm burned into her skin. "And didn't turn into an Echo."

Manon closed her hand around the perfume bottle dangling from her neck. "No, I did not."

"Is it because you found your compartment quickly? Did it anchor you to the train before your excess baggage could drag you off it?" Q's words sounded less like questions than pleas for answers he wanted to hear.

Manon shook her head. "I boarded the train long before Rasmus invented a way for passengers to carry train tickets on their palms. I'm not sure if I would have had the courage to refuse to drink Mr. Goh's tonic if I had to watch my knot unravel. But I would have tried. As much as I wanted a new beginning on this train, I was not going to lose my husband again."

"That's why the perfumery is behind a locked door . . ." Raya pressed her hand over her mouth.

"Rasmus's invention is very clever, no? People obey fear better than they obey rules. Come, while you're here, let me show you how I make my perfumes." Manon walked over to an oval mirror adorned with an etched border of hummingbirds in flight. "All my clients find the process fascinating."

Raya followed her. The tether twisted around her heart, yanking her back. She grimaced, gripping her chest.

Q gasped. "I'm so sorry. I didn't realize—" He hung his head, shaking it. "I wasn't thinking. I'm sorry. I just got so angry because—"

Raya clasped his hand. "It's okay. You have every right to be mad. I know how much you wanted to believe in Rasmus and Lily."

"What else are they lying about?" His eyes muddied into overlapping shades of rage, disenchantment, and despair. "Can we really find our place here or are we just worker ants that keep a lie running?"

"Look at me." Raya gripped the sides of his arms. "So what if they're lying? It doesn't change the only truth that matters. You can see."

"Maybe more than I want to." He pulled away from Raya. "There are so many things about this train that I've been trying to push back into the shadows, trying to overlook, just because I told myself that there was nothing more important than regaining my vision."

"Like what?" Raya said.

"The train's rules. The lies." He balled his hands tightly. "For a place that's supposed to be limitless, I can't shake the feeling that we're trapped. Is it really possible to find your purpose if you're forced to follow a single track?"

Manon pulled the mirror open like a door. A black-and-white field of flowers stretched into the horizon beneath a starless sky. Not a leaf or petal rustled. Not even the wind made the slightest sound. If they were not looking at it through an opening in the salon's wall, Raya might have believed she was watching an old silent film.

"People don't speak when they replay their lives in their minds." Manon reached through the hole and plucked a flower that resembled a large cabbage rose. "The flowers in the Silent Garden grow from these thoughts." She handed the ebony bloom to Raya. "Smell this."

Raya closed her eyes and breathed in the flower's fragrance. A vision of two hands hanging a gold medal around her neck bloomed in her mind. She exhaled, scattering the scene.

Manon took the flower back. "What did you see?"

"A medal."

"How did it make you feel?"

"Nothing. Was I supposed to feel happy? Or proud?"

"I would have been surprised if you did. A memory that belongs to someone else has no color or meaning to a stranger. It is simply one of the ingredients in a long list required to make a perfume. This is why I cannot leave my past behind." Manon sniffed the black bloom. "Erasing it would be like stripping the taste buds from a chef's tongue."

Manon plucked a filigreed perfume bottle dangling from one of the jacaranda's low-hanging branches. "Without a lifetime of memories, I could not possibly know that if I extracted a drop of exhilaration from a winning moment such as the one you just smelled, added it to the curiosity and excitement of cracking open a new book, and mixed in a splash of a memory of chocolate melting in one's mouth, I would be able to make a fragrance that re-created the sweet, tingling heat of a first kiss." Manon squeezed the bottle's tasseled bulb. "Like this one."

A petal-soft kiss drifted in the air and found Raya's mouth. A current ran through the tether, jolting her heart. She gasped and touched her lips and looked Q's way. His eyes fled to the floor. He kept them there, color spreading over his cheeks. The same blush washed over Raya's.

"In the world outside the Elsewhere Express, perfume is one of life's little joys," Manon said. "But for my clients, my fragrances are more than just simple pleasures. They are essential. Like air. While some passengers amuse themselves by borrowing faces, perfumes allow my clients to borrow the one thing that this miracle of a train is unable to offer."

The brass hummingbird flew into the salon and hovered by Manon's ear as though whispering a secret.

"Thank you." Manon smiled at the bird. "Please tell him that I'll be there shortly."

The bird disappeared through the corridor.

"I'm sorry, but a client just arrived. This shouldn't take long. He's here to pick up an order." Manon turned to leave, her robe billowing behind her.

"Who do I call to have my towels replaced?"

Frequently Asked Questions
THE ELSEWHERE EXPRESS
PASSENGER HANDBOOK

Rasmus

A wet towel had not helped Olly. And it did not help Rasmus. But Rasmus understood why Lily dabbed it on his skin. He had patted it on Olly's forehead for the same reason. To survive, hope needed things to do. It puttered, prayed, and paced, doing anything and everything to keep moving, even if it was just in circles. Rasmus stared up at the Archive office's ceiling, wishing he could tell Lily that he could see and hear her, but had been stripped of the memory of too many words to say anything that didn't sound like nonsense.

"Are there consequences for breaking the train's rules?"

Frequently Asked Questions
THE ELSEWHERE EXPRESS
PASSENGER HANDBOOK

Raya

Dev strode into the salon, looking as surprised as Q and Raya were to see him. "Oh, hello." He waved. "You're the last two people I expected to find here. New passengers don't usually need Manon's services."

"They aren't clients." Manon followed him into the salon. "At least, not yet. Maybe you can convince them."

"I think your perfumes can speak for themselves. Anything I say could never do them justice."

Manon smiled. "You're too kind."

Pavo strutted over carrying a small velvet pouch in its beak. Manon took the pouch from it. "Thank you, Pavo," she said, offering pumpkin seeds in exchange. Pavo pecked her palm clean and made its way back to the mural. Manon handed the red pouch to Dev. "Enjoy."

"Thank you." Dev loosened the pouch's string and drew out a small round bottle with a crystal stopper shaped like a hummingbird. "Beautiful as always." He looked at Raya and Q. "Have a sniff."

The bird-shaped stopper took flight, leaving a scented trail in the air. Raya closed her eyes and followed it, leaping on stepping stones of memories. She skipped from a bedtime story to a hug, from the funniest joke she had ever heard to a deep bow met by rapturous applause. Each vanished as quickly as they appeared. Raya exhaled the scent, her fading smile the singular proof that the perfume had once been inside her. No trace of the fragrance or the moments it conjured remained. The only thing Raya was sure of was that it left her lungs and heart empty.

"The Elsewhere Express gives us everything we want, but not the one thing we need to appreciate all that we have," Dev said.

"Absence," Raya said quietly.

Dev nodded. "We never stop. We never mourn. We never look back. Manon's perfume is the gift of goodbye."

"I only use the most fleeting thoughts," Manon said. "As they pass, my clients get to remember, if only for a moment, what it feels like to have something slip from their hands."

Raya looked at Dev. "But you told us that you were happy here, that you didn't miss your old life."

"Two things can be true at the same time. I meant what I said about enjoying what I do here. And I find the strength to do it every day for an eternity when I'm able to remember, even just for a moment, what loss is like."

Manon returned from seeing Dev to the door. "I trust that I've answered all your questions about the perfumery?"

"I can see why some passengers would require your fragrances," Raya said.

Q nodded. "And why you go to the lengths that you do to provide them."

Manon smiled. "So, is there any fragrance here that interests you?"

"No." Q shook his head. "But thank you for your time. Raya and I will be going now."

"Perhaps I can offer you something else." Manon walked over to a mirror on the wall. "I would hate to disappoint Alain."

"Why would he be disappointed?" Raya said. "He asked us to deliver his gift to you and we did."

"And what fine gifts you are." Manon clasped her hands, smiling broadly. "You are both lovely. Exquisite, in fact. Alain knows my tastes. Both of you are carrying a scent that I have never smelled on this train."

Raya frowned. "What are you talking about?"

"You smell like rain. Except for the smell of my husband's skin, there isn't a scent that I miss more. I wish to add your scent to my collection."

A squall whipped through Q's eyes, churning gray clouds. "All of this was a trick?"

"No one has been tricked. I have not told you a single lie. Alain is one of the perfumery's agents. His job is to whisper. And listen."

"And fool people into coming here so that you can take their scent," Raya said.

"I have no intention of taking anything from you that you are not willing to part with. Theft has no place on the Elsewhere Express. That's why I asked you to browse the shop. Go ahead. Choose any scent you want in exchange for yours. I'm always on the lookout for new smells. Scents can get tiresome here. People without a past tend to smell the same. To my nose, they smell sterile. Antiseptic. But you are different." She inhaled deeply, closing her eyes as though savoring a fine wine. "You smell like rain. And tears. And laughter. And fear. And . . . guilt." She wrinkled her nose slightly. "Perhaps a little too much guilt, no? But that can be fixed."

"We're not interested in any of your perfumes." Raya clutched Q's arm. "We're leaving. Let's go, Q."

"Wait." Manon pulled the mirror open, revealing a shelf with a single unadorned bottle sitting on it. "Not even a fragrance that can bring back any moment you've forgotten?"

Raya shot a glance at Q.

"This fragrance can retrieve lost baggage." Manon took the bottle from the shelf. "I made it for myself in case I was ever tempted to take Mr. Goh's tonic and erase my past. I love my husband as much as I always have but he is still a ghost and all ghosts are hungry. They consume you from the inside out. If the conductor even suspected that I had such a thing, I would be thrown off this train faster than the thoughts that fly through this train car. I have never offered it to any other passenger. But I am offering the only dose I have to you."

Q

Manon had promised that the process would be painless. All Q had to do was sit down, tilt his head to the side, and hold still. Manon plucked a white petal from a flower in the Silent Garden and used a golden tweezer to swipe it down the curve of Q's neck and along his clavicle. A shiver ran over his skin.

"Done." Manon dropped the petal into a small glass jar and closed its lid.

"That was it?" Q looked up.

"I told you it would be quick." Manon handed the simple transparent bottle to Q. "Your payment, as promised."

Q examined the bottle and frowned. "It's empty."

"You may not be able to see it, but I promise you that it's filled to the brim. It may even be a bit more than what you need. The scent is in its purest form, extracted from the rarest memories of discovery. It is equal parts gasps and the most electrified air. A single whiff will restore any memory you've lost. A fragrance can flow through you and breathe life into memories in a way no pill, serum, or draft ever could."

"I hope you're right." Q squeezed the bottle. "But the perfume isn't for me." Regardless of the lies Rasmus and Lily had told them, the only way he was going to keep his sight was by helping them stop the stowaway. To do this, they needed to remember how they had done it once before. Truth was useless if the Elsewhere Express ceased to exist.

"Perfumes always make lovely presents, but this gift comes with a warning," Manon said. "Be careful of the memories you exhume. Even the prettiest things, when buried in the damp and dark, will rot."

THE FOURTH LEG

ANYWHERE

Most people are other people. Their thoughts are someone else's opinions, their lives a mimicry, their passions a quotation.

—Oscar Wilde

YOUR ITINERARY

MEET THE
ARCHIVIST

"Why is the Archivist's position still vacant?"

Frequently Asked Questions
THE ELSEWHERE EXPRESS
PASSENGER HANDBOOK

Raya

The cadavers in Raya's anatomy class looked more alive than the man lying on a foldable cot a foot too short for him.

Though Rasmus's wall of a chest rose and fell with his breath, his unblinking eye was empty. Had Jace's eyes been open, Raya imagined they would have looked the same way right before the machines that pumped air into his useless lungs were switched off. Rasmus might have lied about Olly, but he had told the truth about putting the Elsewhere Express above all else. Including himself.

Raya stood over what remained of him, thinking it strange how a bear-sized man could look so small. "Can't Mr. Goh help him?"

"What the Echoes did to Rasmus can't be fixed by a tonic or balm." Lily patted a damp towel over Rasmus's forehead, her voice as hollow as his gaze.

Raya riffled through her bag and pulled out the bottle of fragrance Manon had given them. She drew a deep breath. "How about perfume?"

Lily wrung the towel over a silver bowl, turning her fingertips red and her knuckles white. Water dripped from the towel and into the bowl, its plips, plinks, and plops resounding in the cavern between

Raya's question and Lily's answer. Lily lifted her eyes, throwing a glare at the perfume bottle that would have shattered it if a look could hold shape and weight. "Where did you get that?" she said, hurling her words with equal violence and velocity.

"It doesn't matter where it came from." Raya steeled her jaw.

"What matters is what it can do," Q said. "We were told that it can restore lost memories."

Lily tossed the towel into the bowl and stood up, her neck and cheeks flaring as red as her hair. "Going to the perfumery is against the train's rules."

"And so was asking Mr. Goh to make the serum to retrieve your memories of the stowaway." Raya held the perfume bottle out to Lily. "Do you or do you not want to save Rasmus?"

Lily clenched her teeth and swiped the perfume bottle from Raya's hand. She knelt by the cot and pulled the bottle's stopper off. She waved the fragrance in front of Rasmus's nose.

Raya stood over them, her tether to Q wound so tight, every breath she and Q took made it quiver.

"Rasmus?" Lily clutched the edge of the cot. "Can you hear me?"

Rasmus lay silent, his eye a window into the nothingness inside him. His chest moved up and down, but only to mimic life.

"I hope you didn't trade anything you'd miss for this." Lily stood up and threw the empty perfume bottle on the floor. It rolled beneath the cot. "Manon calls herself an artist. And she is one—the kind that cons you. Nothing good ever comes from opening locked doors. You can never trust what you find behind them."

"Maybe it . . . um . . . just needs some more time." Raya chewed a ragged cuticle on her thumb.

"I'm very familiar with how fragrances work, Ms. Sia. They fool you with pretty illusions as quickly as they fade—" Lily's eyes rolled to the back of her head.

"Lily!" Raya gasped.

Lily dropped like a dead weight. Q lunged and caught her. He cursed, holding her head in the crook of his arm. "Were we tricked?"

Ice slithered up from Raya's ankles. "I—"

Air hissed between Rasmus's teeth. He bolted up. "What happened?" His gaze froze over Lily and Q. "You," he grunted, flinging himself at Q. Q toppled backward, dropping Lily on the floor. Her cheek slammed against jade. Rasmus wrapped his hands around Q's throat.

"Rasmus!" Raya pulled on his arm. "Stop!"

Rasmus tightened his grip. Q wheezed.

Lily's eyes fluttered open. "Rasmus?" She blinked and jumped to her feet. "Rasmus! Let him go."

Rasmus threw a glance over his shoulder. "Lily . . ."

Q choked and coughed.

Rasmus looked back at him and blanched. "Oh god." He let go of Q and scrambled off him. "I . . . I'm so sorry."

Q sat up, gasping for breath.

Raya ran over to him. "Are you okay?"

Q nodded, clutching his throat.

Rasmus burrowed his face in his hands. "I don't know what came over me."

"Come with me." Lily led him to a leather chair behind a mahogany desk. "Sit. Everything will be okay."

Rasmus sat down, making the chair squeak. "I'm sorry, Q."

"You don't have to apologize." Q coughed and drew his hand away from the red finger-shaped marks on his neck. "You were confused, that's all."

Rasmus nodded slowly. "I was."

"How are you feeling now?" Raya said.

"I . . . I'm not sure."

Lily clasped Rasmus's shoulder. "You need to rest."

He inhaled sharply. "The stowaway—"

"—will be stopped," Lily said. "But first, you need to get your strength back."

"I'm remembering things." He bent his head, cradling it over his desk. "So many things." He squeezed his eyes shut. "Too many."

"How about you, Lily?" Raya said. "What happened to you? Did you smell Manon's perfume? Is your memory coming back too?"

Lily looked away. "You should never have gone to Manon's perfumery."

"*What?*" Raya frowned. "Rasmus would still be lying on that cot if it weren't for Manon. Her fragrance brought him back."

"Did it?" Lily said.

Raya looked at Rasmus. He sat in silence with his head bowed, wringing his hands. She chewed the corner of her mouth. "He just needs more time to—"

"I have to go." Lily buttoned up her blazer. "I need to make sure that maintenance locks all the doors to the gallery car and make an announcement about the car's 'renovation.' And I must speak with Han. The last thing we need is rumors." She set her cap on her head, tucking her hair into it. "Can you stay with Rasmus?"

Raya nodded. "Of course."

"Thank you, Ms. Sia." Lily smoothed her features into the pleasant face that had greeted Raya when she boarded. "I'll be back soon."

Water splashed over the rim of the tall glass Raya was carrying back to Rasmus. She stopped and steadied her fingers. The seeds that Lily had planted were tiny, but it was the smallest things that found their way into the deepest cracks. Doubt was no exception. It sprouted swiftly, creeping over Raya's memory of Manon and Olly like the stowaway's rotting vines. She had been convinced that they had been telling the truth. Now, she wasn't so sure. She set the half-empty glass in front of Rasmus. "You should drink this."

"Thank you." Rasmus drained the water in one gulp.

"You're looking a lot better," Raya said. "How are you feeling?"

"Embarrassed." He avoided Q's eyes.

"It wasn't your fault," Q said. "You were swarmed by Echoes and lost your memory. Anyone would have been disoriented."

Raya took a seat across the desk from Rasmus. As much as she wanted to ask him about the Missed and Misplaced Department, this was not the time. Discovering what really happened to Olly could wait. Surviving the night was a more pressing concern. "We're just glad you're all right."

"Thanks to you," Rasmus said. "It felt like I had sunk to the bottom of the ocean. Everything was muffled and dark. And then I saw a light. Felt it. Smelled it. It flowed inside me like a breath, buoying me home."

"Manon's perfume," Q said.

Rasmus nodded. "But my memories are jumbled up, mixed in with the memories the Echoes took. They're like hundreds of old and faded photographs strewn over the floor. I'm still trying to sort through them."

"You shouldn't strain yourself," Raya said. "Take your time."

"I can't." Rasmus shook his head. "I remember the cracks spreading quickly from the Belvedere. That's the one thing I do recall very clearly. We need to catch the stowaway as soon as possible." He closed his good eye, his forehead wrinkling as though he were trying to wring memories from it. "The cracks were everywhere. And moths. So many moths. We were overwhelmed. Lily and I came up with the idea to—" He gripped his desk.

"Rasmus?" Raya said.

Rasmus tore through the desk's drawers, tossing out crumpled pieces of paper, broken pencils, and pens missing their caps. He tugged the last drawer. It was locked. He searched his pockets and pulled out a ring of keys. He shoved a gold key into the drawer and twisted it, flicking his tongue over his dry lips. The lock clicked. He slid the drawer open, holding his breath. A dusty jar, the same kind he used to keep his flares, rolled inside it. He picked it up and wiped it on his sleeve. A round metal object clinked against the glass.

"What is that?" Q said.

Rasmus tapped the jar's lid. The object inside it stirred, unfolding eight silver legs. "Q and Raya, I'd like you to meet Abbie, the Archivist of the Elsewhere Express."

Rasmus

Rasmus was tending bar at the Lotus when he made Abbie, along with countless numbers of her kin. Crafting spiders from the thoughts that gurgled out of the bar's back room sink had been a hobby to pass the time during the bar's slow hours and a way to keep the sink from overflowing. He soldered worries and grudges into eight little legs and hammered them into tiny heads and eyes. Before long, he had large clusters of them, the worries multiplying on their own as worries often do.

In the beginning, the spiders helped tidy up the bar. Later, they ventured outside, building bridges to places they wanted to explore. Only Abbie stayed behind, preferring the warmth of Rasmus's pocket. She enjoyed his trips to the Archive during his days off, going on her own adventures between the pages of books and scrolls. No one was surprised when she was chosen as the train's new Archivist when its old Archivist retired. She meticulously inspected each layer of the jade sphere, making sure that thoughts carved into them were well-preserved and keeping a detailed catalog of every idea that boarded the train. Abbie consumed so many morsels of knowledge that she may as well have been the Archive itself. But her real gift was assisting the Archive's visitors, never tiring of helping them navigate the train's trove of information, a twinkle in all of her eyes.

Abbie was so well loved that every version of Mr. Goh needed to work overtime to make enough serum to erase her from passengers' minds. Rasmus had required twice as many doses as everyone else. The first dose to forget who she was, the second to forget what he had done to her.

The metal spider crawled up the onyx pedestal and disappeared through a hole carved into the model of the Archive.

"What's it doing?" Raya peered inside the jade sphere.

"*It* has a name," Rasmus said, his tone as sharp as the edges he filed on Abbie's legs. "Abbie is reacquainting herself with the Archive's collection. It's changed quite a bit since I trapped her in that jar."

"*You* put her in the jar?" Q jerked his head. "Why?"

"For the same reason Lily and I erased the stowaway from our memory. Abbie helped us catch the stowaway, so I trapped her to keep cracks from spreading through the train. But unlike the passengers, we couldn't erase her memory. She wouldn't be a very good

Archivist if it were that easy to clear her mind. She's the repository of all the knowledge the Elsewhere Express has accumulated."

"I'm shocked she's forgiven you so quickly after what you did to her." Q watched Abbie through the sphere's holes.

"It's because the train's spiders don't hold grudges. They *are* grudges. And a whole slew of other stubborn thoughts. They build all the bridges on the Elsewhere Express. Nothing is stronger than their webs. We wouldn't have been able to catch the stowaway without her."

"Now that Abbie's back, stopping the stowaway shouldn't be a problem." Raya breathed easier. "Right?"

"Not quite." Rasmus watched the metal spider crawl around the model's innermost sphere. "Abbie wasn't the only one who helped us."

"Then we should find whoever helped you and get them to do it again," Raya said.

"We can't." Rasmus's dark pupil constricted, sinking into the sea of his iris as though unwilling to hear what he was going to say next. "They're dead."

Raya

There are limits to how far a mind can stretch. Raya pushed beyond those limits to comprehend the sacrifice Rasmus and Lily had asked of the train's songs.

"We asked the dragonflies for help to find the stowaway first. They refused." Rasmus sighed. "They weren't always that stubborn, but I suppose, over time, you can't help but become the thoughts you carry."

Raya shifted her weight on her feet and hiked her bag higher over her shoulder.

"When the dragonflies turned us down, we turned to the songs for help. Lily asked as many songs as she could to change back from palm leaves and plumbing and whatever else they had fixed or replaced on the train and grow back their wings. They flew off and scoured the train for us. Only one of them made it back." Tears dampened Rasmus's voice.

"Can't we just gather more songs?" Q said. "Raya and I were at the maintenance department. The beach was filled with them."

"Those won't be enough." Rasmus shook his head. "Not if we want to search the whole train. That's why we needed the other songs to grow back their wings."

"How did Lily do it?" Raya said.

"She was different then." Rasmus's tone, Raya thought, was like a note in one of Manon's perfumes, a more bitter than sweet mingling of lilac and loss. "Lily didn't just hear the train's songs. She spoke to them. Not just in the way the maintenance crew gives them simple directions and points them to the things that need to be fixed. Lily conversed with them. Deeply. After we decoupled the Lake, Lily, with the help of the song that had survived the Lake, convinced more songs to help us find the stowaway. She can't do that anymore."

Raya glanced down at the purple notebook peeking from her bag. Inside it was a dead language she could no longer speak either. "I'm sure if she practiced . . ." Her voice trailed off, unable to commit to the lie.

"It won't make any difference," Rasmus said. "This isn't a skill that Lily's forgotten. Her love of music is a part of her that she threw off the train."

Q frowned. "Why would she do that?"

"The stowaway destroyed the songs that Lily sent after it. When they died, Lily felt their pain. She couldn't bear to keep the part of herself that she believed was responsible for their deaths. And so now, while she can still hear the songs on the train, they no longer share the same language."

Raya understood that kind of guilt. It picked at grief's scabs, refusing to let them heal.

Q looked up at the jade ceiling. "We're surrounded by an unimaginable amount of knowledge. There must be something in this Archive that can help us track the stowaway."

"Maybe we shouldn't track the stowaway down," Raya said, her eyes on her purple notebook.

Q shook his head. "We can't just give up."

"I didn't say that. What I'm saying is that we should do things differently this time around." Not once in all the evenings that Raya had tried to run after songs had she been able to catch one. She learned it was better to keep a notebook at the ready and wait for the songs to come to her. "Instead of chasing the stowaway, what if we stayed ahead of it?"

"How?" Q said. "We can't read its mind, assuming it even has one."

"We may not be able to read its thoughts, but I'm pretty sure that we can read the weather. If we can predict where and when it will rain next, maybe we'll have enough time to set a trap before the stowaway shows up." Raya turned to Rasmus. "If my brother could construct a working barometer as a child, it shouldn't be difficult for someone who can build tiny crystal trains and mechanical spiders from thoughts to come up with a way to find a brewing storm."

Abbie shifted around the layers of the miniature Archive, her eight legs blurring at the speed she manipulated them. The Archive's concentric spheres followed the movements of the model, aligning themselves to form a tunnel. A scroll fell through the tunnel and landed on the jade floor. Rasmus unrolled it.

"Good news?" Raya chewed on her thumb.

"No." Rasmus rolled the scroll up. "Very good news." He grinned. "We have the instructions to build what we need."

"A barometer?" Q said.

"A special kind." Rasmus tucked the scroll under his arm. "Remember how the air was heavier and harder to breathe when the stowaway was near? The storm absorbed the stowaway's sorrow. A regular barometer wouldn't be able to predict it. We need one that measures sadness instead."

"Brilliant," Q said. "How can we help?"

"Leave this to me. You and Raya should rest while you can. You'll need all your strength to catch the stowaway."

"Are you sure?" Raya said. "Maybe we can build it faster if we work together."

"Let me worry about the time." Rasmus strode over to the bookcase by his cot. "People are born at the mercy of the passing hours, but there's one place where our roles are reversed."

Rasmus plucked the thickest book from the bookcase's top shelf. "Within the pages of a book, time serves us. It can move faster or slower at the author's whim. Well-chosen words can even bend it. Finding the hours we need to build the barometer is a simple matter of choosing the right book and stepping inside it." He cracked the book open. "I'll work on our little project in here. It reads slower than molasses in winter. It should give me more than enough time to fabricate our device. It's also a great place to take a midday nap. But just like stories, seconds are on a constant march forward. We can control their tempo, but we can't make them stop. Stories will always come to an end. You're welcome to join me in this book or you can choose another one to wait in while I work. I'll come and get you when I'm done."

Q browsed the shelf. "Any book?"

Rasmus nodded. "Short. Long. Fiction. Nonfiction. Poetry. Prose. Good. Bad. All that matters is that it's bound between two covers and has words you don't mind spending some time with. Did you have anything particular in mind? If I don't have it here, it might be in one of the Archive's storerooms."

"There's a purple notebook I'd love to spend some time in." Q looked at Raya. "If its owner agrees."

YOUR ITINERARY

DAY TRIPS

"Can the *Elsewhere Express* slow down?"

Frequently Asked Questions
THE ELSEWHERE EXPRESS
PASSENGER HANDBOOK

Q

Q and Raya were ribbons of ink, traveling through the twists and turns of Raya's handwriting. They looped through a hopeful lyric and, at the end of the chorus, disappeared into a verse. Q had thought that he knew what it was like to get lost in the pages of a book, but nothing he had ever read had taken him into the heart of a song. He crossed its bridge and bobbed over an ocean inside a glowing sphere. Glittering snowflakes fell around him, dancing to the rhythm of the music that filled the globe.

"This has to be a mistake." Raya looked out at the ocean, her palms pressed against the sphere's curved crystal. Identical luminous orbs floated by, riding the waves. In the distance, she caught sight of the small crescent-shaped island where they had met Dev. The shining orbs washed ashore, making its pinkish sand shimmer. "This can't be my notebook. This is the maintenance department."

"But this is your song, isn't it?" Q said. "I remember it from the gallery."

"It is. And so are the others outside."

"Then it makes perfect sense we're here. This is where songs board the Elsewhere Express. Your songs must have come here after you wrote them."

"All these years"—Raya swallowed tears—"I had imagined this notebook as their coffin, and inside it, they had all turned to dust."

"When was the last time you opened this notebook?"

"Do you have to ask? You saw my whole life on display at the exhibit." Raya sat down and held out her palm to catch snow. The golden knot on her skin barely moved as snowflakes melted over it. "I couldn't bear to look at any of my songs after Jace died. And yes, I'm very aware of the irony of lugging around something I can't stand everywhere I go. Pathetic, I know."

"Not pathetic. Human." Q sat next to her. "The hardest things to let go of are the things that hurt us the most. Believe me, I know."

"Touché."

"But—"

Raya wiped the melted snow on her jeans. "But what?"

"Whatever you decide to do with your songs is entirely up to you, but I'm hoping that you get to hear them, at least once, the way I do."

"And what do you hear, Q?"

"Magic." Snow clung to his eyelashes and hair. "I hope there's at least a small part of you that's happy to hear them again."

Raya looked up at the painted sky. "I don't know if I should be grateful or mad at you for taking us here. Out of all the books that we could have killed time in, why did you want to come here?"

"I didn't."

"But you told Rasmus that—"

"I didn't *want* to come here, Raya. I *needed* to. Who knows when and how this night will end? Who knows if we'll make it to morning? I don't want to kill time. I need to make the most out of every second we have left and use them to get to know as much about you as I can." Q shifted his gaze to the ocean. "I almost ended everything on a train track surrounded by strangers. If I'm going to die tonight, I'd like to spend my last moments with a friend."

Raya closed her eyes, letting the snow fall over her lids. It melted on her lashes and ran down her cheeks like tears. "I'd like that too."

"Are we friends, Raya?"

"I'm not sure." Raya smiled. "Maybe something stranger."

Q chuckled. "I'll take that. Considering how we met inside a giant flower—" His eyes flew to the ocean and back to Raya.

"What is it?"

"We . . . we didn't meet at the Lotus."

"What are you talking about? Of course we did."

Q shook his head. "A part of us met here before we ever boarded this train. On this ocean. Surrounded by your music."

"You dreamt about my songs . . ."

"And painted them." Q gently turned her face toward him and held her gaze. "The best parts of ourselves have known each other our whole lives."

"And we didn't even know it." A sad smile flitted over Raya's lips. She tugged it higher to form a happier one. "We don't have to worry about spending our last moments with a stranger then. Just strange friends."

"I don't want these to be our last moments at all."

"That's not something we can promise each other, I'm afraid."

"Then let's not make promises. Let's just make up a story with a happy ending. We're inside a book. What better place to play make-believe?"

"Sure." Raya smiled. "Why not? It's not as if we have something better to do."

"I'll start." Q grinned, sitting up straight. "What would be the first thing you'd do on your first morning as a certified passenger on the Elsewhere Express? I'm dying to try the buffets. Did you see the honey-garlic spareribs at the Dragonfly? And the drunken prawns?"

"I'll have that bottle of Shiraz that you offered at the tree house," Raya said.

Q laughed. "For breakfast?"

"Says the person who wants ribs and prawns." Raya elbowed him. "I'm not judging. Snow globes are supposed to be safe spaces."

"Okay, okay." Q chuckled, holding up his hands in surrender. "Sorry. Please, continue."

"Thank you." Raya bowed her head with a smirk. "Well, after

finishing my lovely Shiraz, I'd ask you to paint me something. The train's bared my soul to you and all I've seen of your work is a star and a hatch."

"I'd show my work to you if I could, but—"

"You know what?" Raya rummaged through her tote and pulled out a notebook and pen. "You can. Rasmus said that all we needed to have a place to wait in were words bound between covers." She handed the notebook to Q. "Here. All that's missing are words. Write your address down."

"My address?"

Raya nodded. "And make sure you put the right date. It has to be a time before you sent your last painting to the gallery."

"Why?"

"Someone you've known all your life deserves a private tour of your studio, don't you think?"

Q walked around his home studio, reacquainting the tips of his fingers with the corners of furniture and walls. His steps were cautious, as though he were feeling his way around with a walking stick. Being able to see in a place where he had only ever lived in the dark was as disorienting as navigating an unfamiliar location when he was blind.

"These are incredible, Q." Raya lingered over the paintings leaning against the studio's white brick walls.

"Thank you," Q mumbled. His paintings looked different now that he could see them in their entirety. The desperation and anger in each of his brushstrokes were on full display. Turpentine stung his nose. "Can we go?"

"Go?" Raya glanced up from a painting of a woman's lower lip. "We just got here."

"You've seen everything." The studio had been his sanctuary, a place where he knew he wasn't going to trip and fall. Now, its walls closed in on him, pressing his old life against his bones. "There's nothing left."

Raya touched his arm. "What's wrong?"

Q sat on a paint-splattered couch, resting his elbows on his knees and cradling his head in his hands. "I'm sorry, but I can't stay here."

"Why not? Your work is amazing, Q. You should be proud."

Q lifted his head, surveying his failed attempts to know the woman who visited his dreams. "I can't help but feel that at the flick of a switch, everything will go dark."

"It won't," Raya said. "I promise."

"I thought we weren't making any promises." Q watched the sun stream into his studio but could not feel its warmth.

"I'm making an exception for this one. You won't lose your sight, Q. You'll never leave anything unfinished again. You'll be able to paint anything you like. The sky, the stars."

You. Q was grateful that their tether let him keep his thoughts to himself. If he were braver, he would ask Raya to sit for him and gently tilt her chin to catch the light. She didn't need to know that posing for him wasn't necessary. He could paint her with his eyes closed. He had hoarded all the details he needed. The real challenge was painting her with his eyes open. Two women lived in her skin: one whose songs could heal, and one who refused to be healed by them. With a single canvas to tell two stories, Raya's portrait would be the hardest one he would ever paint.

"Q?" Raya said.

He stood up. "I'm sorry. I should never have agreed to come here. It feels too real. Too close. I already feel it dragging me back."

"I understand." Raya nodded. "Let's go."

"But there's something I need to do first." He shoved a table and easel aside, clearing a space in the middle of the room.

"What are you doing?" Raya's voice tightened. Her heart clenched next to Q's, but he had no words to soothe it.

"Cleaning up." Q settled on an answer that was the closest to the truth. He gathered his paintings and tossed them over the floor. He marched to a supply closet and took out a box of matches.

"With matches? What are you really doing, Q?"

"Decoupling myself from all of *this*." He struck a match and flung it to a crumpled drop cloth he never used. A flame flickered and grew within its folds. "I'm never going back, Raya. Ever."

"What about everything you said about my songs?" Raya coughed from the smoke. "You didn't want me to throw them away, but here you are, making a funeral pyre of your work."

"Your songs heal." Q's eyes followed the coils of smoke on their path to the ceiling. "These paintings were my disease."

Raya's eyes flew over the scattered paintings. She ran to the drop cloth and stomped the fire out.

"This is my choice to make, Raya." Q glared at the extinguished flame and took another match from the box.

"I know why you can't remember her face." Smoke curled around Raya's boots. "Look at your paintings."

Q shook his head. "No."

"Look at them, Q. *Please.*"

Q sighed. "I'm looking." He poised the matchstick over the side of the box. "Now, can I burn them?"

"Do you see it?" Raya glanced at him expectantly.

"See what?" Q's eyes traveled over his work. Tips of noses. Eyes. Several brows. A few lips. Cheeks and chins. Temples. He juggled them around as he often did, trying to assemble a face.

"Her."

Q furrowed his brow at the pile. "I don't see anything."

"Neither do I."

"I told you." Q kneaded the bridge of his nose. "I don't remember what she looks like. All these paintings are just fragments. They're unfinished."

"That's not why I couldn't see her face," Raya said. "I've built songs from smaller pieces. What I can't do is create a song from lyrics and riffs that don't belong together. When I looked at these paintings, I had to keep asking myself, Which eye do I use? Which mouth? Which ear?" She reached for a painting. "And then I saw this. This piece isn't from a face at all."

Q took the painting from her. It was one of the earliest ones he had made. It had leaned against one of the darkest corners of his studio, forgotten. A name, painted in a delicate cursive, circled a slim wrist on the canvas like red thread.

"You couldn't remember the face in your dreams, Q," Raya said, *"because Lily wears many."*

Two loud knocks on the studio's ceiling echoed through the room. "Q? Raya? Are you in there?" Rasmus called down. "I've finished our barometer."

"Can a crystal train take you anywhere you want to go?"

Frequently Asked Questions
THE ELSEWHERE EXPRESS
PASSENGER HANDBOOK

Raya

"Voilà!" Rasmus set a large wooden box down on the Archive's marble floor. A silver hand crank jutted from its left side. Abbie clambered down his sleeve and over the box, examining every corner.

"How does it work?" Raya said.

"Watch." Rasmus turned the crank, opening the box's lid. Abbie crawled off the box and sat on his shoulder.

Raya held her breath.

Released it.

And held it again.

"Is something supposed to happen?" Q said.

"It . . . um . . . needs a little adjustment." Rasmus kicked the box. An enormous flock of red balloons flew out and into the mouth of the jade tunnel over their heads. "I've assigned each of the balloons a train car." Rasmus reached into the box and pulled out thick bundles of strings. A tiny gold bell tinkled from the end of each. "The balloons are filled with laughter. If the level of sadness in the car a balloon is in rises, the balloon will burst, jingling the bell tied to its string. Do you mind helping me hang the bells up?"

Abbie made quick work of weaving a silver web across the Archive. But even with the spider's help, hanging each string on the web took longer. Raya tied the last of them and rubbed the back of her neck, looking out at the sea of bells.

Q groaned and stretched his arms over his head. "I never want to see another piece of string again."

Raya smirked. "That might make flossing a bit difficult."

"You've never flossed with your eyes closed? You forget. Seeing things in the dark is my superpower."

Raya chuckled.

Q shut his eyes. "I can even see the question written all over your face. You want to know how I feel about Lily being the source of my dreams about the Elsewhere Express." He peeked through his lashes. "Am I right?"

"Did the tether snitch on me again?"

"It didn't have to. I'd want to know the same thing if you were the one on the receiving end of Lily's discarded dreams."

"You've lived with this mystery twisting inside you for so long, Q. It must feel strange to finally have an answer. And have that answer be 'Lily.'"

"What's stranger is that I'm relieved that it's her."

Raya arched a brow. "You are?"

"When Astrid said that the strange dreams I had as a boy came from a passenger on the Elsewhere Express, the first thing I thought about was finding that person. Now that I know who that passenger is, I can thank her."

"Thank Lily? For what?"

"Without those dreams, I would never have picked up a paintbrush. Lily's dreams might have just been excess baggage for her, but to me, the paintings they inspired shared the weight of a life I couldn't have carried on my own."

"I'm glad you found the answer you were looking for, Q," Raya said.

"Except that it brought a friend. Another question I need to answer."

"An interesting one, I hope." Rasmus carried over a tray of fragrant tea and ginger biscuits. Abbie peeked out from his shirt pocket. "Good questions always go well with tea. It will give us something to do while keeping watch on the bells." He set the tray down on a reading table. "Drinking and eating aren't allowed in the Archive, but tonight, I think we can make an exception, right, Abbie?"

Abbie rolled her eight eyes.

A garden of green tea buds, jasmine, yellow chrysanthemums, and a single deep-crimson amaranth bloomed inside the glass teapot. "You're in for a treat." Rasmus poured the tea into cups. "This tea is made from the sweetest daydreams of a man who liked to reminisce about his long career as a librarian. There was nothing he loved more than the smell of books and the sound of rustling pages."

Steam, in the shape of petals, floated up from the cups, carrying the scent of ripe pomelo and a spring afternoon spent curled up with a good book. Raya breathed it in. "It smells lovely."

"Wait until you taste it." Rasmus turned to Q. "Now, about your question. Is it something I can help you with?"

"It's about dreams I used to have," Q said.

Rasmus picked up a biscuit. "What sort of dreams?"

"The kind that get tossed off the train every night."

"Ah. Night dreams." Rasmus took a bite of the biscuit and chewed. "I'm listening."

"My dreams came from Lily."

Rasmus raised his brows. "How do you know they came from her?"

"I saw her face, or I should say, faces, in my dreams. Including the face she's wearing today."

"And you'd like to know how you could have dreamt of a face she only wore today." Rasmus took a sip of his tea. "That's a very interesting question. With a very simple answer." A bell hanging next to the onyx pedestal rang. Rasmus jumped from his chair and sprinted to it, Abbie clinging to his shirt.

Raya and Q hurried after him.

Rasmus squinted at the tinkling bell as though reading something in fine print. He swallowed hard. "The storm's gathering in the engine."

Raya pulled the crystal train from her tote. "We'll head there now."

"You can't." Rasmus hung his head and kneaded his thick nape. "It's the one car on the Elsewhere Express where the crystal train can't take you."

No one visited the engine because no one ever needed to. The Elsewhere Express did not require any assistance to keep the engine running. In time, the doorway to the engine was forgotten, its existence preserved by a single footnote in a dusty first edition of the train's manual. The edition had fallen into disuse, leaving its designated spot on Rasmus's bookcase only when he needed a place to take a nap or fill red balloons with laughter.

Rasmus cracked the book open over his desk and flipped through it. "Here it is." He tapped the bottom of a yellowed page. "It says that the doorway to the engine is—" He reread the line and frowned. "That can't be right. This must be a misprint."

"What does it say?" Raya said.

"According to the manual, the doorway to the engine is in the Dragonfly's ravine." Rasmus rubbed his chin. "But that's not possible."

"Why not?" Q said.

"Because the only way you can get to the ravine is by jumping from the bridge two thousand feet above it."

YOUR ITINERARY

BRIDGE JUMPING
AT THE DRAGONFLY
RAVINE

"What happens if you fall from the train's bridges?"

Frequently Asked Questions
THE ELSEWHERE EXPRESS
PASSENGER HANDBOOK

Raya

The sea of clouds obscuring the dining car's ravine did not make the idea of leaping from the cobweb bridge swaying above it any less terrifying. Climbing over the bridge's railing was the quickest way for Raya to hurl herself from it, but there was only a small window when you could let go of things before they clung to you. Though jumping through the hole Rasmus's metal ladybug was cutting into the bridge would take longer, this option kept Raya from getting stuck. All she had to do was close her eyes and let herself fall. "Thanks, Beatrice," Raya said as the ladybug crawled away from the newly cut hole.

"I can go first, if you want." Q peered down at the clouds rolling beneath them.

"I'll lose my nerve if I have to watch you fall," Raya said, her palms like ice.

"And I'll lose mine if you jump ahead of me." Q held out his hand. "Together then?" Raya gripped his fingers. "On the count of three."

Jump.

"Thou shalt commit adultery" was an unfortunate misprint in the 1631 King James Bible just as the footnote about the doorway to the Elsewhere Express's engine was. Like the Bible, the train's operating manual had missed a rather important word. "Falling from" a bridge versus "falling up from" it involved two very different ways your insides were tossed about. The screams that accompanied them, however, were identical.

Raya hurtled back through the hole in the cobweb bridge as quickly as she had jumped through it. Her hand slipped from Q's grasp. She tumbled toward the painted sky and crashed into a constellation, scattering stars. Her hip grazed the moon and knocked it an inch to the left. By the time she landed softly on her feet by a gurgling brook, she had run out of breath to scream. Broken stars splashed into the clear water and dissolved into twinkling swirls of paint. Raya clutched her bag to her chest. The limestone cliffs surrounding her gave no hint that they hid behind a painted sky.

"I'd like to have a word with whoever reviewed the operations manual." Q walked up from behind her, raking his hair back from his face. "How do you feel about forgetting the stowaway and chasing down a copy editor instead?"

"Lead the way."

Abbie poked her head out of Q's pocket and narrowed her eight eyes at them.

"Relax, Abbie." Raya smiled. "We're kidding."

The spider crawled back inside.

"That felt like a flashback from boarding school," Q said. "Our librarian gave us the same look when we got too loud, but with fewer eyes."

Music drifted past Raya's ear. She turned her head in its direction. "This way."

"You're getting good at this," Q said. "I'll be out of a job as your map porter soon."

"Don't worry." Raya followed the song's trail. "I'll give you a good reference."

"Thanks. And don't forget, the snitch will need one too."

Raya tried to smile but the corners of her mouth were too heavy to hold up. To be tethered to Q was to live in a glass house next to a neighbor who lived in one too. She had gotten used to looking over and waving hello. "I won't."

"Make sure it's a glowing one." Q smiled. "I'm sure you'll want the snitch to be on its way to its next employer as soon as possible."

"Right . . . um . . . can't wait." Raya stopped in front of a tree that was bent so low, its leaves kissed the grass.

A wordless lullaby, sweet and warm like honeyed milk, poured out from a hollow in its trunk. Raya reached inside and pulled out a small hexagonal lacquered music box. Three tiny travelers, carved from mother-of-pearl, rode on horseback over the box's shiny black lid. An inlaid full moon watched over them from a cloudless sky. Raya wondered if the travelers noticed that their voyage was without an end. She reached for its lid.

The box unfolded before she could open it, turning into a miniature mirrored ballroom on her palm. Porcelain dancers glided over an invisible track in the shape of an eternal knot, twirling, leaping, and pirouetting to a song and wish taking root inside Raya's chest.

Live. Breathe. Be.

A freestanding black door, so plain that it was a stain against the ballroom's glitter and gold, stood silent at the center of the whirling porcelain crowd.

YOUR ITINERARY

EXPLORE THE ENGINE

THE ELSEWHERE EXPRESS

Operating Manual

SECTION 12:

ENGINE MAINTENANCE

The key to safe and reliable operations is regular maintenance. To prevent breakage, stripping, and wear, it must be ensured that all moving parts are kept well lubricated. Special attention must be paid to the gears. Note, however, that excessive oiling may result in damage and so it is important to strictly adhere to the prescribed amount and frequency of application.

That is, if you are on any train other than the one for which this manual is written.

The Elsewhere Express is an engineering marvel built by the hours people have spent staring out of the window, wishing they were somewhere else. It is in constant motion, fueled by a steady stream of wandering thoughts. Every inch of the train writhes with reveries and vibrates with the con-

stant chatter of conversations people have with themselves. Its engine cannot spare a moment's rest and the only maintenance routine it requires is peace and quiet. Out of the countless cars, the engine is the only place the Elsewhere Express has requested to keep for itself. We would do well to respect its wishes.

“Where is the engine located?”

Frequently Asked Questions
THE ELSEWHERE EXPRESS
PASSENGER HANDBOOK

Q

Not a single event in the history of the world was ever remembered the same way by everyone. This rule applied as much to wars as it did to high school. While some people cherished memories of fake gold crowns and satin sashes, others recalled lunch tables they weren’t welcome to sit at and stretches of hallways that made them feel small.

Q had a complicated relationship with his defining memory of boarding school. On the one hand, it taught him everything he knew about handling anxiety. On the other, it was impossible to remember a lesson without remembering its teacher. Fear was not a member of the boarding school’s faculty, but Q sat in its class at the headmaster’s office all four years of his stay.

The first rule for surviving Mr. Bailey’s interrogations about his latest disciplinary violation was to not move. Guilty people fidgeted. People who got away with their crimes did not. The second rule was to freeze his features in a mix of shock and indignation while ignoring the icy beads of sweat dripping down his nape. Feigning ignorance and offense for as long as possible allowed Q to determine whether there was any actual evidence against him or if the headmaster was just fishing for proof.

None of these techniques, however, slowed his pulse in the slightest when he stepped into the lacquered music box and onto its dance floor. Navigating the bustling path to the engine's black door required the opposite of being still. What he did need was a sense of grace and timing he did not have.

Porcelain dancers moved as one, following a dance choreographed to a lullaby and a rhythmic, mechanical hum. They weaved through one another, wearing faces that changed with every twirl. "Wasn't that Alain?"

"It was," Raya said. "And now it's one of the chefs we saw at the Dragonfly."

"Why do the dancers have the passengers' faces?" Q scanned the swirling crowd.

"I don't know, but whatever the reason, it looks like we're going to have to find a way through them to get to the engine. How's your sense of rhythm?"

"Let's just say that you're about to find out the real reason I have mismatched shoes." Q winced. "I have two left feet."

The swirling dancers forced anyone who wished to cross the ballroom to follow their flow. Each time Q bumped into any of them, the glittering ball's attendees moved faster. One knocked into Raya's back. She yelped.

"Sorry." Q grimaced. "Left feet."

Raya gracefully weaved her way to him, in sync with the music's rhythm. "I have an idea." She clasped one of Q's hands and led the other to her waist, locking them in a dancer's embrace. "Follow my lead," she said, plunging them back into the path of the porcelain dancers, twirling as they did over the tracks.

Q did his best to keep in step, moving stiffly and holding his breath. He tripped over Raya's foot and hit a dancer wearing Rasmus's face. Dancer Rasmus wobbled, then twirled down the track, unwavering in its direction and purpose. The crowd of dancers spun twice as fast. "Sorry." Q groaned. "Again."

"Close your eyes," Raya said.

"Huh? Why?"

She gently squeezed his hand. "You don't need them."

"But—"

"Do you trust me?"

Trust was something Q reserved for his paintbrushes and walking stick, objects that couldn't lie or lead him astray. But Raya's hand felt as familiar as any of his brushes and their tether as solid and sure as any cane. Q drew a breath and shut his eyes, bracing for the ballroom's frenzy to be amplified in the dark.

It was not. The ballroom in his mind emptied, leaving only the sound of Raya's breath and heartbeat as his guide. He followed them, easily and willingly, unlocking a door he had kept barred since his father died. Behind it beat the softest part of his heart. But for now, he kept the door closed, having mustered only enough trust for a dance in the dark.

Raya brought their dance to an end. "We've reached the door. You can open your eyes."

Q kept his lids closed, holding Raya in his arms.

"Q?" Raya said. "You can open your eyes now."

"Wait." His heart raced but not from the dance. "I'd like to remember this." He released her, holding his hand up between their faces, tracing the air as gently as he would have touched her cheek if they were more than just strange friends. But he did not need to touch her to memorize the shape of her face. The warmth Raya radiated was enough to meld her memory into his palm. He opened his eyes. "Thank you."

"For what?" Raya's cheeks flushed.

Their invisible tether heaved with their chests. "For not letting me fall."

Raya smiled. "Maybe I can be the train's dance instructor."

Q bit his lip, waiting for her to tug her smile down and take her words back when she remembered how much she wanted to leave.

She didn't.

Raya left her words hanging in the air as though she had not regretted them and walked around the black door. "There's nothing behind it."

Q gripped the door's crystal knob. "Then I guess we better hope that the engine's inside."

A sparsely furnished living room welcomed them through the door. Raya stepped inside. Q followed her in, shutting the door behind him. Creamy white gardenias bloomed in a wallpaper garden that made Q wonder what he might see if he pushed their petals and leaves aside. Two butter-yellow wingback chairs sat across the room, arranged at the perfect angle to enjoy the midnight garden. Between the chairs, a pedestal table was set for tea.

"I think the operation manual didn't just miss printing a word." Q's eyes roamed over the room. "It got the directions to the engine completely wrong. We should regroup with Rasmus." He turned on his heel.

Raya laid her palm against a wall. "Q." She drew her hand back. "I think I know why the dancers look like the train's passengers."

"You do?"

"What do they remind you of, Q?"

"Nothing. I've never seen anything like that ballroom in my life. Why?"

"Do you remember what Lily said about the Elsewhere Express being run by passengers?" Raya said. "And what Rasmus said about faith being the train's fuel?"

Q nodded. "Every passenger has a place on the train and a part to play."

"Just like those dancers." Raya glanced back at the door to the ballroom. "Each dancer knows its steps and its position on the dance floor. They never deviate from the choreography or their assigned track."

"So?" Q said.

"What else on a train works with such regular, choreographed precision?" Raya pressed her palm against a printed gardenia. "Feel the wall."

"Why?"

"Just do it."

Q rested his hand over the floral wallpaper. It vibrated against his palm, conjuring images of pistons, valves, and gears moving in perfect sync.

"What does it feel like to you?" Raya said.

"An engine's hum . . ." Q looked around the room, his eyes widening. "We aren't lost." His gaze fell on the blue-and-white teacups. Wisps of steam curled from their rims, neither rising nor falling. He touched the side of a cup. "It's still hot."

Raya picked up the second cup and flipped it over. Not a drop spilled. She set the cup down an inch from its saucer. It slid over the table and hopped back onto its little blue plate. "No wonder no one needs to operate the engine."

"Because nothing changes," Q said.

Raya stared at the black door. "And to keep the train running, passengers need to stay the same too."

The scent of rain wafted through the room. Abbie crawled out of Q's pocket, leapt to a wall, and began setting their trap.

The Archivist admired her work, rubbing her legs together.

"Well done, Abbie." Q angled his head to see the nearly invisible web, making a mental note of its location to avoid getting stuck in it. "Thank you."

Abbie scuttered back to his pocket.

The scent of rain and sadness weighed the air down.

"The stowaway's close." Q slipped behind a bookcase.

Raya joined him, glancing down at the crystal train tucked into her tote. "I really hope Rasmus is right about this train being strong enough to hold the stowaway."

"It is." Q refused to entertain any other possibility. If Rasmus's faith in the little train was misplaced, they were all dead. It was their only way of getting the stowaway to the empty train car Rasmus was preparing to decouple. Assuming Lily received Rasmus's message, she would be on the train's rooftop waiting with him.

Lightning crackled. Q peeked out from the bookcase, holding his breath. A downpour broke, drenching the room. Abbie's web held fast. A lone moth flitted past the bookcase, weaving its way through the rain. Q's tether trembled.

A dark swarm burst into the engine and straight into Abbie's web. They tried to free themselves, tearing off their wings and legs. A humanlike figure took shape amid the turmoil of wings. It opened its newly formed mouth and screeched.

"Now." Q sprung from behind the bookcase.

Raya jumped out, clutching the crystal train. She closed her eyes and cocked an ear. "I've found the track."

Soon, Q thought, this would all be over. The stowaway and the dark he had lived in would be cast off the train and forgotten. Tomorrow, he and Raya would wake up to an eternal day, each holding the time they had bought. Raya would use her purchases to find her way back home. He would use his to convince her to stay. The gallery had shown him what she wanted to return to and he could not bear the thought of barbed ghosts shredding her as they had torn his mother.

Moths fell away from the stowaway's head.

"Oh god." Raya staggered back. "It's Jace."

Raya

Raya's whole body shook, her eyes locked on the mass of fluttering dark wings. "That's my brother."

Q jolted. *"What? Where?"*

"Don't you see him?" Their tether twisted, tangling like the string of questions Raya saw in Q's eyes. "He's right there."

"What are you talking about, Raya?"

"The stowaway is my brother. That's his face."

"What face?" The crease between Q's eyes dug deeper.

"Hiraya." Jace's voice echoed in Raya's head.

"Did you hear that?" Raya gasped. "It's Jace."

"Raya . . ." Q reached for her arm. "It didn't say anything."

"What?" Raya pulled herself free. "He just said my name."

"Help me, Hiraya."

Raya ran toward Abbie's web.

"Raya, stop!" Q pulled her back. "That's not your brother."

"It is." Raya struggled against Q. "It's Jace."

Q gripped Raya's arms. "Jace is dead."

"Save me, Hiraya."

"Can't you hear him?" Raya's hand trembled around the miniature train. "Can't you see him?"

"*I do see it.* I see the stowaway."

"No." She shook her head. "It's Jace."

"Hiraya, please. I don't want to die. Not again."

Tears flooded Raya's eyes. "I need to save him, Q."

Q

Their tether grew slack. Though Raya stood no more than a few feet from him, Q balanced at the edge of the chasm the stowaway had ripped between them. As much as he wanted to believe what Raya's eyes told her, he trusted the eyes he had trained to see the truth more. A part of him wished that he were blind. He had spent half of his life bound to a cold anger and only a sliver of it tethered to Raya's warmth. But that fraction was enough for every cell in his body to scream for it as it slipped away.

"Raya, listen to me. That isn't Jace. It's the stowaway. It doesn't have a face."

"I don't understand." Raya broke into sobs. "Why can't you see him?"

"Because it's a trick," Q yelled over the storm. "The stowaway is trying to save itself."

Rotting tendrils burst from the stowaway's body. Abbie bound them to the stowaway, containing the rot.

"Raya, this is the engine." Q gripped her arms. "If we lose it, we lose the train."

Raya lowered her eyes and nodded.

Though their tether remained slack, Q felt Raya's heart quicken through it, pounding with the same determination he had trusted to lead him in the ballroom. He let go of her, choosing to trust her again.

Abbie scuttled to the wall and cut the web free. The stowaway dropped to the floor, Abbie's web falling over it like a net.

"The train, Raya. Now."

Raya set the crystal train on a silver track, her tears lost in the rain streaming down her face. The stowaway wailed. Raya looked away.

The train's tiny door slid open. Q wrestled the stowaway through it, silver threads clinging to his clothes and skin. Abbie cut him free. The train's doors slid shut, trapping the stowaway behind them.

"We did it." Q exhaled. It was over. They were safe. Q imagined what his first painted sunrise on the Elsewhere Express would look like. Or maybe he would skip it and sleep in. He had infinite mornings to wake up ahead of the sun and watch ripening shades of warm red and orange blend into violet and cobalt blue.

Raya yanked the train from the railway and set it on another track.

Q gasped. "Raya, stop! Don't do this. You're making a mistake."

"No, Q." Raya let the train go. "I'm fixing one."

"Are the train's spiders dangerous?"

Frequently Asked Questions
THE ELSEWHERE EXPRESS
PASSENGER HANDBOOK

Raya

The silence hanging over Rasmus's office amplified the blood drumming in her ears. Raya was grateful for it. She did not care to hear her thoughts talking over one another, offering excuses for what she had done. She had no intention of defending herself. Nothing she could say would make Rasmus, Q, or Abbie understand what her soul screamed to be right.

"Where did you send the stowaway?" Rasmus sat stone-faced across his desk. Abbie stood, all eight eyes on Raya, on his shoulder.

"I told you." Raya shook her head. "I don't know. I put the crystal train on the nearest track I could find. I have no idea where Jace is now."

"That wasn't Jace, Raya," Q said. "I know how much you want it to be, but it's not."

"You're lucky Lily didn't get my message about decoupling the train car," Rasmus said. "She would throw you off this train if she knew what you did. And she never has to know, if you tell me where the stowaway is."

"How many more times are we going to do this?" Raya rubbed

the back of her neck. "Asking me the same question over and over again isn't going to change the truth. I don't know where Jace is."

Rasmus swiveled his chair, turning his back to her. His fingernails dug into its leather arms.

"What now?" Q said.

"The balloons are still in the train cars so the bells will ring, but—" Rasmus glanced at Abbie.

"But what?" Q said.

Rasmus turned to face him. "The stowaway will be expecting us." Abbie jumped onto Rasmus's hand. "It will be too dangerous for Abbie."

"But I'm sure if you asked her to, she'd be willing to try again."

"She would. And that's the problem. Abbie will do whatever I ask. It wasn't the jar's glass or lid that kept her inside the prison I made for her. It was her word. A word she will keep at all costs." Rasmus slipped Abbie into his shirt pocket. "I refuse to put Abbie in any more danger."

Raya stood up. "Let me talk to him. Jace will listen to me."

"I'm sure your brother would," Rasmus said. "But the stowaway isn't your brother."

"I saw him, Rasmus. I saw Jace."

"But Q didn't. Did you, Q?"

Q shook his head. "I'm sorry, Raya."

"I know what I saw." Raya folded her arms over her chest. "I'm not crazy."

"You're not. You're just wrong," Rasmus said with a heavy breath. "Just as Lily was. The stowaway tried to manipulate her too by trying to make her believe that it was one of her friends who had passed. But the simple fact is, the dead don't board the Elsewhere Express."

Raya's eyes hardened. "How do I know that this isn't another lie?"

Rasmus frowned. "I've never lied to you."

"You lied about Olly," Raya said.

"I have no idea what you're talking about. You're confused. And I don't blame you. Just regaining my memories disoriented me enough to attack Q. I can't begin to imagine—"

"I'm not confused," Raya said. "Q saw Olly's thoughts at the Missed and Misplaced Department too. We know about the Echoes and the drain in the valley. You left Olly at the MMD on purpose, didn't you?"

Rasmus got to his feet and drew himself to his full height. "A conductor's job is to keep the train and all its passengers safe."

Q clenched his hands at his sides. "So you did lie to us."

Raya held out her palm. "Even this knot is a lie. Manon didn't turn into an Echo even after she kept her memories. This knot isn't our bond to the train. It's a leash to make sure we don't stray from the train's rules. Why should I believe anything you say, Rasmus? Nothing out of your mouth will ever convince me that the person I saw at the engine with my own two eyes wasn't Jace."

"The same two eyes that saw what the stowaway did to the gallery and what it was about to do to the engine," Rasmus said. "The stowaway would have destroyed this entire train if Abbie hadn't caught it in her web. Do you really believe that your brother is capable of that kind of destruction? Do you really think he's a monster?"

"Jace isn't a monster." Raya's voice faltered. "Maybe he's just lost and scared. Maybe he's just trying to ask for help but doesn't know how. You told us yourself. The storm is heavy with sorrow because it's absorbing the stowaway's sadness. Monsters are evil, not sad. What if—"

"That's a lot of maybes and what-ifs to wager the lives of everyone on this train," Rasmus said. "Let's look at the facts. Your brother is dead and the Elsewhere Express is a train for the living and their thoughts."

"It's also a place for second chances," Raya said. "Or was that a lie too?"

"It's the truth." Rasmus jutted his chin. "The Elsewhere Express gives its passengers everything they need to find their place and purpose here."

"I agree." Raya nodded. "It gave Q his sight. And even if you've locked Manon behind a door, she still gets to live an eternity in the little heaven she's made for herself with her husband's ghost. But I searched for my compartment unable to imagine what the Elsewhere Express could possibly give me. And then I saw Jace at the engine. He isn't on a rampage, Rasmus. He's here so that I can do what I was born to do. He's here so that I can save him and set things right."

A tiny bell rang. Rasmus jumped up from his chair. "We need to go, Q."

"How do we trap the stowaway without Abbie?" Q said.

"I have another—" Rasmus glanced at Raya. "I'll tell you outside."

"Don't do this, Rasmus," Raya said. "Please, just hear me out."

Rasmus pulled out a chair for Raya. "Be quick."

Raya sat down, her heart racing. "Thank you. I—"

Abbie peeped from Rasmus's pocket. Rasmus gave the spider a nod. Abbie jumped from his pocket and onto Raya's shoulder.

"Abbie?" Raya said.

The spider swiftly spun a web around her and secured her to the chair.

"This is insane, Rasmus." Q ran over to Raya. "Let her go."

"Is that really what you want me to do?" Abbie leapt onto Rasmus's shoulder. "Do you believe that the stowaway is her brother?"

"I—" Q shook his head. "I don't know."

"Then answer this question instead. Do you believe that whatever the stowaway is, it's a danger to the train and must be stopped?"

Q drew a heavy breath. "Yes."

"Rasmus lied to us, Q," Raya said. "He's lying now. Jace would never hurt anyone."

"Raya will be safer if she stays here, Q." Rasmus looked at Abbie. "Keep her bound."

Abbie nodded and hopped off him and onto the desk.

"Let me go!" Raya tried to pull her arms free.

"I'm sorry. This is for your own good." Rasmus buttoned up his jacket. "You let the stowaway go once. I can't allow you to do it again."

Raya strained against her silver bonds.

"You'll only hurt yourself," Rasmus said. "The only way you are getting out of Abbie's web is if she frees you. She won't. Not until I tell her to. The only thing stronger than a spider's web is its word."

"We can't just leave her like this," Q said.

"You know I'm right, Q. You know what will happen if Raya comes with us. We'll lose another train car. Maybe more. Is that what you want?"

Raya struggled against her bonds. "Q, look at me. I can talk to Jace. I won't let him hurt anyone. He'll listen to me."

"If you want to stay with her, then stay, Q." Rasmus gripped Q's shoulder. "It's your choice. But if you want to save this train and everyone in it, you know exactly what you need to do."

Raya didn't blame Rasmus or Q. Had their roles been reversed, she would have left them tied up under the guard of a spider too. Rasmus wasn't wrong about her. She was not going to let Jace die a second time.

Abbie crawled up her arm and offered her a ginger biscuit, flashing a small smile as best a mechanical spider could.

Raya shook her head. "Thanks, Abbie, but I'm not hungry."

Abbie nodded, left the biscuit on Rasmus's desk, and crawled away.

Raya's eyes scoured the room, searching for a way to cut Abbie's web.

"Ms. Sia?" Lily climbed out of one of Rasmus's abandoned teacups. "Why are you tied up? What's going on?"

"Lily! Help!"

Lily ran over to Raya. Abbie scuttled toward her and launched herself into the air, slicing Lily's cheek with the point of her leg. Lily winced. "What the—"

Abbie leapt onto Raya and spun more webs around her. Lily swatted her away. Abbie landed on her back. She flipped herself over, getting ready to jump toward Raya. Lily stomped on her with her heel with a loud crunch.

Raya gasped. "No—"

Lily picked up one of Abbie's metal legs from the floor and slashed at Raya's binds with it. The web fell away. "Are you all right?"

"What have you done?" Raya stared at the leg in Lily's hand.

"My job. A conductor's job is to keep the train and all its passengers safe."

Raya's eyes fell on Abbie's metal remains. "But—"

"Spiders are not passengers. You are, Ms. Sia. My duty is to you. I apologize about what that spider did to you. That's never happened before. But then again, that is the danger of anything built from grudges. They can be silent and invisible for so long then suddenly—" Lily glanced around. "Where's Rasmus and Mr. Philips? Rasmus needs help *now*."

"They . . . uh . . . went after the stowaway," Raya said without looking at her. "Rasmus thought it would be safer if I stayed behind."

Lily furrowed her brow. "Which bell rang?"

Raya pointed to a bell by the miniature railway.

Lily rushed to it. "The storm's brewing in a very large train car. Rasmus and Mr. Philips are going to need all the help they can get. We can't afford to let the stowaway escape again. You should catch up with them. I'll follow as soon as I can. Tell Rasmus to send out a flare to let me know if the train car needs to be decoupled."

"But I can't see the map without Q," Raya said.

"Why do you still need the map, Ms. Sia? The train's songs have found their way inside you."

"What are you talking about?"

"I can hear the door's songs wherever they pass through. Wood. Metal." She steered her gaze to Raya's chest. "Hearts. Yours is beating to them now. I heard it from four cars away. If your heart can hear them, there's no reason that you can't. If you listen well, you may even find a shortcut that will take you straight to the storm."

YOUR ITINERARY

SIDE TRIP TO THE
SUPPLY CLOSET

"Where can I get more stationery and pens?"

Frequently Asked Questions
THE ELSEWHERE EXPRESS
PASSENGER HANDBOOK

Q

Rice paddies climbed up the side of a mountain range and shimmered in the light of bamboo torches like a glass stairway. Q surveyed the train car from the topmost terrace. "This place is huge. How are we supposed to set a trap here?"

"We're not." Rasmus walked over to a bamboo bench. "This isn't the train car where the balloon burst. It's the supply closet. We need to get the things you'll need to make the trap."

"The things *I* need?"

Rasmus pulled off his boots and arranged them next to the bench. "You're the painter."

"What exactly do you expect me to do, Rasmus? Drown the stowaway in a ten-liter can of cerulean blue? Build a cage out of easels?"

Rasmus rolled up his pants to his knees. "Did you know that most of the train's painting crew had never painted anything before boarding the Elsewhere Express? None of them were selected for their talent. They were chosen because out of all the train's passengers, they were the most content."

"What does that have to do with making a trap for the stowaway?" Q said.

"A person that's happy to be on this train can be trusted to color within the lines and follow the approved templates for clouds and constellations." Rasmus looked at Q. "Unlike you."

"If you don't trust me, then you should have just left me tied up with Raya."

Rasmus pushed up his sleeves. "That's not what I meant. What I'm trying to say is that to stop the stowaway, we need someone who knows how to break the rules. Someone who isn't afraid to paint with darker shades of gray."

"How do you know what I'm capable of?" Q folded his arms over his chest. "You don't know anything about me."

"I know enough. I've seen the updated passenger manifest and it contains more than just your name and food restrictions. The Elsewhere Express likes to know its passengers. And so do I."

Q set his boots next to Rasmus's. He rolled up his sleeves and pants and stepped into a shallow rice paddy. Mud swallowed his feet past his ankles, squishing as he trudged between rice stalks. "For the record, I think this is ridiculous."

"Your objections have been noted." Rasmus followed him into the paddy. "Now, can we get the job done? Choose a stalk, picture what you need, and pluck it. Remember what I told you. The stalk can be whatever you want it to be. If you require a paintbrush, imagine one. If you need a palette, harvest it."

Q rolled his eyes and yanked a stalk out. Water dripped from its roots and slithered down Q's arm. "This isn't going to work."

"Try again."

Q tossed the stalk aside. He pulled out a second stalk and hurled it off the mountain. Q groaned. "We don't have time for this, Rasmus."

"If you don't succeed, we won't have anything at all. You expected to find nothing and so that's exactly what you found. There is no room on this train for an ounce of doubt. The Elsewhere Express exists because every single passenger believes with every fiber in their body that it does."

Q raked his hair off his face. "Look, Rasmus, if you're asking me to paint some kind of trap, I will. I've painted a star in the air and a trapdoor over water so who am I to say that I can't? But turning rice stalks into paintbrushes and tubes of paint is a completely different story."

"You think you can paint a trap for the stowaway just because you've painted a star and a hole? Any painter here can do that with their eyes closed. You're not painting a piece for your latest collection, Q. You're stopping a monster that will destroy every life that's been rebuilt here."

"I understand that," Q said.

"I don't think you do. If you did, then you would be able to do this." Rasmus pulled out a stalk and opened his fingers. A tube of yellow paint sat in his palm. "And this, and this, and this," he said, harvesting an assortment of brushes and paints. "The supply room isn't built like this for the sake of being odd. It's meant to make you look at all the laws that used to govern your life and tell them to get the hell off this train."

"I'm sorry." Q shook his head. "I can't. Find someone else."

"I wouldn't have asked you to do this if you hadn't already done this very thing a hundred times before." Rasmus looked directly at him. "Everything your hands have ever created was born in your mind first. All I'm asking is for you to do it again." The torches set the blue sea in his good eye on fire. "And to be clear, I'm not talking about the faces your clients commissioned you to paint."

"You're talking about the anger I painted on walls." Q's voice turned as cold and gray as the mud he stood in.

"I want you to find whatever rage has been simmering inside you and paint a void so dark and deep that no monster can ever climb out of it."

"But what if the stowaway isn't a monster? What if Raya was right? What if the stowaway really is her brother? How sure are you that the dead don't board this train? Raya seemed to be very convinced that—"

"So was Lily," Rasmus said. "We almost died because she refused to see the truth."

"But you survived. And so did the train. How?"

"Darkness needs a cage. Built from darker thoughts."

Astrid's warnings ricocheted in Q's skull.

"I don't have a safety waiver for you to sign, Q. There are no emergency exits for any of us to take if something goes wrong. All I know is if you don't find a way to do this, every soul on board the Elsewhere Express is lost."

Only one face filled Q's mind, her features frozen in anger and desperation. This was the last memory of Raya he would ever have whether he succeeded or failed. Q grabbed a stalk by its root. His tunnel of vision shrank the more tightly he squeezed the limp plant. Through it, he saw the lie his father wore from ear to ear, his burning moths, and the train tracks that had invited him to lie down on them and escape. He pulled the stalk out. An obsidian bouquet of paintbrushes bloomed in his hand, dimming the light around them.

"Excellent." Rasmus's face crumpled. He doubled over, clutching his chest.

"Rasmus!" Q dropped the brushes.

Rasmus toppled into the mud. Q dragged him out of the paddy, laying him over the ground. Rasmus mumbled, his words lost in his labored breath.

Q leaned over him. "Rasmus?"

"The tether." Rasmus coughed. "It's gone."

Q glanced down at his chest. Though he could not see his link to Raya, it tugged weakly on his heart. "No. It's still here."

"Not yours. Mine. And Abbie's. We shared the weight of the Archive." He wheezed. "I'm being crushed."

Q's heart lodged in his throat. "Should I get Lily? Mr. Goh?"

"They can't help." Rasmus coughed. "My pocket. Get—"

Q shoved his hand into Rasmus's pocket and pulled out a tiny pouch. "What do I do with this?"

"Plant it."

"Plant it?" Q said, unsure if Rasmus was delirious. He opened the pouch and peeked inside. It was filled with small black seeds.

"The seeds." Rasmus wheezed. "Plant them."

"Where?" Q poured the seeds into his palm.

Rasmus coughed. "Anywhere."

Q dug a small hole in the mud and dropped the seeds into it. An explosion of lavender flowers burst from the ground, overflowing from it and draping the mountainside in a fragrant blanket of powdery florals, evergreen woods, and vibrant herbs. The wind swept the perfume away.

"Now go, Q." Rasmus closed his eyes. "The door to the train car where the storm is brewing is by your boots. It will take you directly there."

"No." Q shook his head. "I can't just leave you here."

"Don't worry about me." Rasmus smiled weakly. "I've sent for the love songs. They'll smell the lavender and come."

"What are the duties and responsibilities of the train's conductor?"

Frequently Asked Questions
THE ELSEWHERE EXPRESS
PASSENGER HANDBOOK

Lily

Lily gathered the fragments that had once been a metal spider from the Archive's floor. She picked up an eye and added it to the pieces of the spider inside her cap. She walked over to Rasmus's desk and sank into his oversized chair. She set her cap down on top of an obsolete operating manual of the Elsewhere Express. She laid the broken fragments of metal on the desk, shuffling them until they resembled the spider. A leg was missing. Lily crouched and spotted it next to the chair that Raya had been tied to. She retrieved it and laid it next to the spider's broken body with a sigh. This was the best she could do. Maintenance would have to take care of the rest. As for Rasmus, she could only trust that the songs would do their job.

She pulled a small notebook from her satchel and reviewed her to-do list. A ham-and-cheese omelet sat at its top. Lily had promised to personally deliver the omelet to Mrs. Pierce's compartment. She scribbled a note next to it, reminding herself to ask the kitchen to add extra cheese just the way the elderly woman liked it. Lily shut the notebook and stood up, smoothing down her blazer. She placed her cap on her head. Though the cap was made from wool felt, it dug into her skull, weighed down by responsibilities she alone could carry.

It was Rasmus who had taught her that a conductor had many duties that could only be done in the shadows—and crushing the spider under her shoe was a duty Lily wished she could have done in complete darkness. That way, she would not have had to see its eyes before she brought her heel down on its head. She had no choice. The train's passengers always came first. Luckily, the guilt of crushing the spider wasn't anything Mr. Goh's excess baggage serum couldn't fix. But relief would have to wait. She was the train's conductor and had secrets to keep, a job to do, and an entire train to keep running and safe.

YOUR ITINERARY

MEETUP IN
THE LOBBY

"Do I get my own compartment?"

Frequently Asked Questions
THE ELSEWHERE EXPRESS
PASSENGER HANDBOOK

Raya

The song was rough around the edges and slightly out of key. It was not a song that Raya would ever choose to listen to, but its faults made it stand out from the river of songs flowing through her. Though she did not know which of the train's doors sang it, Raya could not let go when it took her by the hand and led her to one of the Archive's dust-filled back rooms. Raya followed it blindly, caring only that it took her as far away from Abbie's broken body as it could. She had no choice but to trust Lily's promise that Abbie could be fixed.

Raya made her way through a maze of shelves groaning with yellowing books, scrolls, and an array of artifacts. Rasmus's forgotten teacups, abandoned on shelves, stools, and stepladders, provided the only evidence that someone other than her had visited this secluded part of the Archive before. Raya sneezed, knocking the handset off a French-style brass rotary phone wedged between a hand-crank eggbeater and a tin of flashcubes. The song grew louder. Raya lifted the handset and held it to her ear. The song skipped, startled it had been found.

"Good evening, Ms. Sia." A voice, as warm as fleece and just as soft, poured out of the receiver.

"Oh . . . uh . . . hello. May I know who I'm speaking with?"

"This is the shortcut to the lobby. How may I help you?"

Contradiction. It was the secret behind the best hotels. Exclusive, yet inviting. Elegant, yet comfortable. Private, yet not lonely. The Elsewhere Express had curated people's most interesting and conflicting thoughts to build a hotel lobby—one unlike anything Raya had ever seen but that she somehow remembered fondly.

She stood in the shadows of the giant fire trees that held up a glass ceiling, their flame-red flowers in full bloom. Her eyes followed a winding stream that took the place of a floor. Velvet couches meandered along the stream like boats, circling the fire trees and drifting past water lily–shaped crystal chandeliers. Soft piano music blended with the stream's burbling. The lobby's grand double doors swung open, interrupting the duet. Raya jumped, nearly slipping off one of the stepping stones dotting the stream.

Q froze at the doorway, water flowing by his toes. *"Raya?"*

Raya's eyes darted from Q's face to the satchel slung across his chest. It belonged to Rasmus. Her heart thundered. She could not let either of them get to Jace first. "Where's Rasmus?"

"He's not here." Q closed a fist around the satchel's strap. "He's hurt."

Raya choked on a breath she had meant to exhale. "Is he okay?"

"I don't know. Rasmus could barely breathe when I left him in the supply closet. He . . . he was being crushed."

"What?"

"He shared the Archive's weight with Abbie, but their tether broke. Did something happen to her?"

Raya's heart clenched.

Q winced, pressing his hand over his chest. "What happened to Abbie?" he said, his voice wound as tightly as their tether.

"She'll—" Raya's lips quivered. "She'll be okay."

"What do you mean she'll be okay? What happened?"

"Lily—" Raya drew a breath deep enough to push the truth out. "She found me trapped in Abbie's web. She—" The chill running from Q's end of the tether into her heart told her that no other words were wanted or required.

Raya made her way across the path of stepping stones to the hotel's reception area, grateful that the stones were too small for more than one person. It was easier to avoid looking at Q if she walked behind him, keeping their unspoken truce. A woman with eyes a shade lighter than the emerald silk scarf she wore around her neck smiled at them from behind the marble-topped front desk. The gold knot twisting over the receptionist's scarf glinted in the light of a chandelier floating across the lobby's stream. "Good evening. I'm Isla. How may I help you?"

"Hi." Q rested his palms on the marble. "I know this will sound strange, but I was wondering if you have smelled anything like rain recently?"

"Rain? I'm afraid not. It never rains on the Elsewhere Express. But we can arrange for housekeeping to add a rain-scented diffuser to your compartment if you'd like."

Q jerked his head. "My compartment?"

Raya gasped. "You did it, Q."

"Congratulations." Isla smiled. "You both did."

"What?" Raya said.

"The Elsewhere Express's compartments are located in different parts of the train, but all passengers claim their keys at the lobby. The conductor sent a memo telling us to expect two new passengers this evening. May I see your tickets so I can fetch your keys?"

Raya's palm trembled over the counter as Isla ran her eyes over it. "Thank you, Ms. Sia."

Q extended his hand, his fingers shaking as much as Raya's. Isla wrinkled her forehead. "Is something wrong?" Q said.

Isla bit her lip. "May I please see your ticket again, Ms. Sia?"

"Why?" Raya held out her palm. "Is there a problem?"

Isla stared at Raya's hand, her brows knitted tight. She straightened, adjusting her scarf. "Just a moment, please."

Raya waited for the receptionist to disappear behind the wooden wall emblazoned with the golden knot. "Do you hate me, Q?"

"Why would I hate you?" Q said, his eyes on the eternal knot.

"Because I believe that the stowaway is my brother. And you don't."

Q turned to face her, his eyes soft. "How can I hate you for wanting to save your brother? Between the two of us, you have more reasons to hate me. I left you at the Archive."

"I don't hate you." She just wished that she did. It would be less complicated that way. She couldn't hate Q for doing what he thought was right. Even if he was completely wrong. "I would have done the same thing if I were in your shoes."

"I guess that puts us in a strange spot then," Q said. "Two people who completely understand why we need to stop each other from doing what we absolutely must do."

"Thank you for waiting." Isla walked back to the front desk. "As you know, your train tickets don't specify your compartments. This is because your journey to find your place on the Elsewhere Express is what determines the compartment the train assigns you. The story of this journey is written on your hands. That's why I asked to see them. It tells me what you've held on to and let go of, who you've touched and who you've pushed away. What you find at the end of your search is, after all, entirely dependent on what you're looking for and how you went about finding it." She placed a silver key on the counter between Raya and Q.

"Whose key is this?" Raya asked.

"That is a decision that the train is leaving up to you."

"What do you mean?" Q said.

"The Elsewhere Express has a very strict policy on accommodations. One passenger. One compartment. One bond." The receptionist gestured to the silver key. "And one key. I thought that I had made a mistake when I saw your palms. But, as it turns out, I hadn't. Your search for your place here has led both of you to the same compartment."

"Does that mean we'll have to share until you find another room for one of us?" Raya said.

The receptionist shook her head. "The Elsewhere Express does not reassign compartments just as it does not reissue tickets. Place and purpose don't have duplicate keys. You have until the end of the evening to decide which one of you will stay and which one will leave. In the meantime, will you be needing assistance with your baggage?"

Six passengers attempted to squeeze into an old-fashioned birdcage elevator meant for two. Raya and Q boarded first. Two choices, waiting to be made, followed them inside. Time, the fifth passenger, strode over to a corner and stood still. Silence slipped in after it and took up every available space. The elevator's scissor door slid shut.

Raya and Q stood side by side, their eyes on the door's crisscrossing metal bars, ignoring the decisions pressed against them for as long as they could. Once the elevator opened its door, the time that had waited patiently until then would elbow everyone in the ribs and run out.

"So should we talk about it now or later?" Q said.

"What's there to discuss?" Raya kept her gaze ahead of her. "We have choices to make that are as impossible as they are cruel. You're going to try and kill my brother and I'm going to do whatever I need to do to save him. Assuming we survive that, we'll then have to decide who stays on the train and who jumps off it. There is no scenario where any of us gets a happy ending."

"Then can we make a deal, Raya?"

Raya looked at him. "What kind of deal?"

"Can we pretend that the two people who walk out of this elevator aren't us? Those people are going to hurt each other. Terribly."

Raya hung her head. "I know."

Q reached for her hand. "So can we agree that our short story ends here instead?"

FROM THE LIBRARY OF THE ELSEWHERE EXPRESS

The Short Story of a Kiss THAT NEVER TOOK PLACE

The old-fashioned elevator remembered everything it witnessed and everything it did not. In such proximity to its passengers, it could not help but overhear their conversations and observe every move they made. It learned that words not spoken could say more than words that were, and that the distance people kept between them could feel closer than an embrace. Passengers were open books while traveling between floors, revealing who they truly were when they thought no one was looking. The two exhausted passengers that it gave a ride to one evening were no exception. The elevator lost itself in the pages of their short story and was not too proud to admit that it had deliberately slowed down to read more.

The elevator had witnessed its fair share of kisses. Stolen ones. Short ones. Kisses that made

it blush and look away. But the kiss the two passengers shared was the first one it had seen that did not take place. On a train of thoughts, longing replaced lips, eyes could touch like hands, and two people, who were neither lovers nor friends, could forgive each other and say goodbye with a kiss that never happened. Alerting them to their arrival at their floor had never pained the elevator more. But this was its purpose, the sole meaning of its life. If it failed in its task, it would be no better than all the lost passengers who rode it. It sliced the air with a sharp ding and watched the two walk out its door.

One day, it thought, when it found the right words, it would write their story.

YOUR ITINERARY

COMPARTMENT TOUR

"Does the Elsewhere Express provide toiletries?"

Frequently Asked Questions
THE ELSEWHERE EXPRESS
PASSENGER HANDBOOK

Raya

As little as the Elsewhere Express cared about time, it seemed to care about distance even less. The length of the carpeted corridor between the elevator and the hotel floor's sole door seemed to double with every step Raya took toward a compartment that wasn't meant to be shared. "How do you plan to do it?"

"Do what?" Q said.

"Kill my brother."

"Raya—"

"I want to know."

"It's better if you don't."

"All right. But I think you should know that I will do everything in my power to stop you."

"I understand." Q walked on.

"You should also know that if the stowaway isn't Jace, I'll end it myself. Whatever the cost."

A sweet, crisp, and earthy smell drifted down the corridor.

Q steeled his jaw. "Rain."

The scent of rain snaked up Raya's nose. Her eyes flew around the compartment. A cloud-free night painted above the king-size bed twinkled with stars. Behind the bed, silver words, inlaid into rich, dark wood, borrowed the moon's light.

> *I dreamed I was a butterfly, flitting around in the sky; then I awoke. Now I wonder: Am I a man who dreamt of being a butterfly, or am I a butterfly dreaming that I am a man?*
>
> —*Zhuangzi*

Q strode across a carpet of fresh-cut grass toward the bed. He plucked a scented oil diffuser from the nightstand and sniffed it. "I found our 'rain.'" He returned the bottle to its spot beneath a lamp. "Housekeeping's very efficient."

Raya explored the compartment, grounding herself in every second and step, pretending, while she could, that nothing existed beyond now. She took a passion fruit bonbon from a crystal candy dish though she wasn't hungry and didn't like passion fruit. A cherry-and-cream bonbon appeared in its place. She stared at the candy in her hand.

Q pulled the coin she had given him at the Missed and Misplaced Department from his pocket. "Ten baht for your thoughts."

Raya looked up from the candy. "Why couldn't it have been this way?"

"What way?"

Raya returned the bonbon to the dish. "Why couldn't we have boarded the train like everyone else? Why couldn't we have just found our own compartments like the other passengers, slipped off our shoes and enjoyed the grass tickling our feet, and let chocolate melt in our mouths without worrying about anything other than which candy we were going to try next?"

"Is that really what you would have wanted?" Q said. "I thought that all you ever wanted to do was find a way off this train and go home."

"I . . . I don't know." Raya's eyes sought sanctuary in a little wooden library of incense that told bedtime stories when lit. A passenger, Raya thought, would have to try very hard to be unhappy in a place that provided you with every comfort. The only thing the train lacked was a true sense of time, which was only a problem if you were counting on it to heal your wounds. "I just know that I don't want *this:* an impossible choice."

"An impossible choice doesn't have a right answer," Q said. "But one of us is right about the stowaway and the other isn't. So, if it's any consolation, it's not an impossible choice. Just an extremely difficult one. We at least have a fifty-percent chance of getting it correct." He forced a lightness into his voice. "That doesn't sound too terrible, right?" he said, trying to smirk but not quite managing it.

Raya returned his sad smile and sat down in front of the dresser. "And how about the decision we need to make about who gets to keep this compartment and stay on the train? Does that have a right choice too?" She scanned the items on the dresser.

A box of tissues.

A brush.

A jewelry dish.

A zippered pouch adorned with the train's gold knot leaned against a potted orchid. Raya opened it. A silk eye mask, fuzzy gray socks, and travel-sized toiletries were neatly arranged inside. A small vial containing a thick blue liquid nestled between the lotion and shampoo. She pulled it out and gazed into the tiny sea inside the bottle, thinking how pleasant it would be to dive in and never come up for air.

Q walked over to her. "May I?"

Raya handed him the tonic.

Q pulled its stopper off.

"Are you thinking of taking it?" Raya said. If Q forgot about hunting Jace, she would not be forced to stop him.

"No." He shoved the stopper back. "Yes." He sighed. "Maybe." Q slipped the tonic back into the kit. He looked up at the mirror and gasped.

"What is it?"

He squinted. "I thought I saw something."

Raya leaned closer to the glass. "What did you see?"

The compartment shook, tossing Raya to the floor. Furniture tumbled around them. The painted moon fell and struck Raya's shoulder. She yelped, clutching her arm. A lamp flew across the room and shattered the mirror, exposing an inky void. The compartment tilted sharply, hurling Raya and Q through it.

"Does the train offer adjoining compartments?"

Frequently Asked Questions
THE ELSEWHERE EXPRESS
PASSENGER HANDBOOK

Raya

Raya opened her eyes, her cheek pressed against a hospital room's cold floor. Machines beeped and blinked, monitoring the bandaged figure in the center of the room. Raya knew every detail of this dream by heart. Tonight, however, was the first time it had begun with her lying on the floor.

She got up, her cheek throbbing, and walked over to Jace. She sat on the chair by his bed and began the long watch until morning came to wake her.

"What is this place?" Q said from the other side of the bed.

Raya jumped. "What are you doing here?"

"Shouldn't you be asking what *we're* doing here? And where 'here' is? A second ago, we were being tossed around a train compartment."

"This is real?" Raya leaned over the bed. "Jace? Can you hear me?"

"That isn't Jace, Raya. It can't be."

"Why the hell not, Q? The Elsewhere Express breaks every natural law. Why not the laws of death? You got your miracle. Why can't I have mine?"

Rasmus burst through the door. "Step away from the bed. Now."

"Can songs fix everything?"

Frequently Asked Questions
THE ELSEWHERE EXPRESS
PASSENGER HANDBOOK

Rasmus
Earlier

Winged songs could only do so much. Cuts and broken bones were easy to mend but a broken man required more than colorful wings and wishes. The four songs that caught the scent of lavender and flew to Rasmus's aid split the task. Two went in search of the other end of his tether, another fetched the train's healer, and the fourth stayed behind, offering the tiny comfort of its company while Rasmus was crushed alive.

The songs found Abbie's broken body meticulously arranged over Rasmus's desk. They flitted around the metal corpse, taking an inventory of its parts. Eyes. Legs. Body. Heart. Abbie's murderer had been considerate enough to ensure that the carcass was complete. Fixing Abbie would have been more complicated if they needed to fabricate parts. One of them descended on Abbie, engulfing it in light.

The third song flitted through carved jade trellises, flowers, and vines. It found the train's healer asleep next to a jade dragon on the Archive's outermost sphere and hovered by its ear. It whispered a request into feathers of flame. The phoenix stirred and stretched its fiery wings. It flew to the mouth of the jade tunnel and dove in.

Hitching a ride on the phoenix was faster than flying back to the supply closet. The songs huddled behind its neck, shielding themselves from the wind. Abbie, shiny and whole, rode with them. The phoenix flew through the supply closet's door and spotted Rasmus by a waterfall of lavender flowers. It nudged him with its beak. He didn't move. It nudged him again. Abbie scuttled over to him and curled over his fading heart. The phoenix embraced Rasmus with its wings, wrapping him and Abbie in healing fire.

Now

"Rasmus!" Q said. "I thought you were dead."

"I was." He walked into the hospital room. "Sort of." He pressed his hand over his chest. Metallic clicks and whirring vibrated inside a mechanical heart that had once been his oldest and dearest friend. He tore his hand away, blinking back tears.

Raya blocked his way to the hospital bed. "Stay away from my brother. Jace isn't dying tonight."

"You're right, Raya. He won't," Rasmus said. "Because that isn't your brother. It's the first stowaway. Lily and I trapped it here."

Rasmus

A Memory

The air in the carpeted corridor thickened with the scent of rain and sadness. Rasmus drew a weary breath. He had forgotten what nightmares were like. Mr. Goh's draft was extremely effective at casting away all his night dreams by the time he woke up. This nightmare, however, was not something any of the pharmacy's tonics could fix. The Lake was decoupled and countless songs were gone in one dark night that seemed to have no end. Tiny glowing wings carried their last hope down a long corridor to a shiny black door at the end of the hall. The song paused, turned around, and perched on Lily (who was not yet named Lily), looking from her to Rasmus as though asking them if they were sure they wanted to proceed.

"You can leave us now," Rasmus said, fully aware that he and Lily had already asked far too much of it. It had survived the destruction of the Lake and had been the lone song to return after scouring the train for the stowaway. And now it was leading the way to the monster that had killed all of its kin. "Thank you for everything."

"Go," Lily whispered to the song. "Go to the beach. You'll be safe there."

The song folded its wings and remained on her shoulder.

"Please," Lily said. "Just go."

The song did not move.

"We don't have time for this," Rasmus said. "You can't force the song to do anything it doesn't want to do."

"No. All the other songs are dead because I asked them to help us. I'm not going to let this song die too."

"It will die along with everyone else on this train if we wait any longer." Rasmus marched ahead.

Lily clutched his arm. "What if you're wrong? What if the stowaway really is him? I saw his face."

"You saw what the stowaway wanted you to see. But the dead do not board the Elsewhere Express. It was a trick. If it were real, I would have seen him. But I didn't."

"I don't understand. I drank Mr. Goh's serum. Why do I still remember him?"

"Some memories are harder to erase than others. Especially fresher ones. Some need a second dose."

Lily wrung her hands. "I'm sorry. I don't think I can do this. Not while I can see his face."

"You can and you will." Rasmus steadied her shoulders. "Unless you want to set another train car on fire, you need to pull yourself together." He drew a knife and sake bottle from his satchel. "Abbie will trap the stowaway and you and I are going to throw the stowaway out the back door if it's the last thing we do." He handed the knife to Lily.

The song clung to Lily, refusing to abandon her.

They were too late. A swarm of moths gathered in the passenger compartment before Abbie could spin her web. The moths formed a man's shape and flung Abbie against a wall. The spider dropped to the grass carpet, silent and still.

"No!" Lily ran to it.

Rasmus lunged at the stowaway with a roar. It grabbed Rasmus and hurled him across the room, slamming his spine on the floor. The sake bottle containing the back door shattered next to him. Rasmus groaned weakly. The stowaway exploded into a swarm of moths and surged toward him. The swarm re-formed into a man with a frenzy of moths for a face. It pinned Rasmus down on his back. Rotting tendrils burst out of it and coiled around Rasmus's neck. Rasmus choked and wheezed.

"Rasmus!" Lily scrambled to him, the song flying by her side. Lily raised the knife over the stowaway as it strangled Rasmus and plunged the blade into its back. The stowaway's body broke apart into moths. The blade went through the swarm and struck Rasmus's right eye. Lily screamed and stumbled backward, leaving the knife wedged in Rasmus's bloody socket.

The song dove through the moths toward the wound. It was not a love song like the healing songs that lavender summoned. It was a sad song that had only ever fixed a leaky pipe in a lake. Still, it had to try. Moths knocked it around. The socket was close. But before the song could reach it, it found something more damaged than a blinded eye. The song glowed brighter, embracing the stowaway in light. And a wish.

Live. Breathe. Be.

A bandaged man lay on a hospital bed where there had once been a swarm of moths.

Lily knelt on the floor beside the bed, cradling Rasmus's head.

"Lily?" Rasmus peeked through his remaining eye. "What happened? Where's the stowaway?"

"The song . . ." Lily said, breathing hard. "I think it tried to heal the stowaway."

"What? Why?"

"Maybe because sadness is a wound too," Lily said quietly. "And the song felt that it needed to fix it."

Rasmus tried to sit up but fell back into Lily's arms.

"Don't move," Lily said.

Abbie scuttled over and weaved a makeshift patch over Rasmus's socket with her web.

Rasmus coughed. "But why does it look like that? Who is that man?"

"I . . . I think it's the person whom the song is about."

"What?"

"Songs remain true to their nature when they fix things on the train, right?" Lily said. "I've seen the maintenance crew use songs about new beginnings to turn withered leaves into healthy, vibrant ones. I've watched a sweet song about a mother's love soothe a chef's blistered hand like a balm." She cast her eyes on the bandaged man. "This song . . . it was filled with sorrow and grief—which is great for sealing leaks—"

"—but not for healing," Rasmus said. "We got very lucky."

"Lucky?"

"The stowaway's trapped. Once we repair the back door, we can throw—"

"This song saved us, Rasmus. It saved the train. And now you want to throw it out like garbage?"

"A conductor's duty is to keep the train and its passengers safe. That song isn't a passenger."

"Maybe not. But everyone on this train is alive because of it. We owe it, Rasmus."

"I'm sorry, but we don't have a choice. We can't keep the stowaway here."

"Why not? Look at it." Tears flooded Lily's eyes. "It's trapped. It can't hurt anyone anymore."

"And so you just want to leave it in this compartment?"

"No, not this compartment."

"Then where?"

"We'll leave it where we leave everything that we can't take with us. The past." Lily dried her eyes. "And make ourselves forget that any of this ever happened."

"How big are the passenger compartments?"

Frequently Asked Questions
THE ELSEWHERE EXPRESS
PASSENGER HANDBOOK

Raya

The hospital room was too small to fit two truths. Either Rasmus's story about what the song had done to the first stowaway was a lie or what her heart insisted on was. The bandaged man on the bed could not be a monster and her brother at the same time. Raya gripped the hospital bed's railing. "You're lying."

"Listen to the song." Rasmus stepped away from the bed. "Hear the truth for yourself."

Raya clasped Jace's wrist and shut her eyes. Rasmus knew the train, but she knew this hospital room better than anyone else. She had memorized the shade of its walls, every machine blinking inside it, and the lingering scent of chemicals that disinfected everything except for grief. Jace's pulse drummed against her fingers. Then grew into lyrics and notes.

The song seeped into Raya's hand just as it had flowed from her guitar strings years ago when she wrote it for Jace's funeral. It was meant to carry happy memories, but when it left her lips, it was as hollow and cold as the husk she now gripped. Raya dropped the bandaged hand. There was a monster in her brother's bed, wearing

Jace's song like skin. "This . . . this is the song I wrote for my brother."

Rasmus hung his shoulders. "Lily couldn't see the first stowaway for what it was. She could only see the song that saved us."

"That doesn't sound like Lily at all," Q said.

"She was not yet the person she is. She was new and struggled with the train's rules. That night, something broke inside her. I didn't want to be the person that shattered her completely. And so I agreed to hide the stowaway here by building another compartment over it."

"That's why we have the same compartment." Raya looked at Q. "It's two rooms in one."

Rasmus nodded, releasing a sigh that shrank him. "A prison made from the sturdiest thoughts we could find. Rage. Sorrow. Guilt. We broke every rule to build this cage and hide it from the rest of the train. And ourselves. It took two bottles of Mr. Goh's serum to erase the guilt, but I made the mistake of visiting the gallery to check on a leak before taking a second dose."

"And Olly saw your secret," Raya said. "That's why he got lost."

"I've made a lot of mistakes and you're standing inside one of them. No one was ever meant to see this room. Not even me."

"How did I see it through the mirror?" Q said.

"You look at things closely, Q. Perhaps too closely. When you caught a glimpse of this place, it planted questions in your head that set cracks running across the compartment, breaking it apart."

"Did the bell in the Archive ring because it sensed this room?" Q asked.

"I don't think so. This room has never been a problem since we hid it."

"So it was just a false alarm?" Raya said.

Q reached under the hospital bed. He stood up, holding a moth wing. "It wasn't. The second stowaway was here."

"It must have seen the first stowaway and sensed danger," Rasmus said. "And fled. We should head back to the Archive and check on the bells."

"What about this thing?" Raya glared at the bandaged figure. "It can't stay on this train."

"I agree." Q glanced at Rasmus's satchel. "And this time, we have the tools to get rid of it for good."

Rasmus tensed. "But Lily—"

"—is wrong," Raya said. "Like I was. This is still the same monster that destroyed the Lake and killed all those songs no matter what it looks like."

Q

Q closed his eyes and poised a dry black paintbrush over the wall at the foot of the hospital bed. He did not require paint nor his sight for this piece. A dark palette flowed through his veins and the painting's shape lived in his hands. His brush flew across the sterile canvas, guided by all that simmered inside him.

He dropped the brush, panting, empty, and done. Rasmus had asked him to trap the stowaway in a void, but his darkest thoughts had other plans.

Q took a step back from the dark swarm and let it take flight. The painted burnt moths swept across the hospital room, descended on the bandaged figure, and consumed it.

Nothing remained of the stowaway or the hospital room. The moths, having had their fill, fell to the floor and dissolved into specks of paint in every shade of gray. A grass carpet grew over the stains and every piece of broken furniture was replaced. Two chocolate mints and a good-night note lay on a pillow on the freshly made bed. A story coiled up from the incense and drifted in the air.

Once upon a time . . .

Rasmus silenced the incense in a glass of water. It protested with a hiss. "There'll be time for bedtime stories and rest later. We need to find the other stowaway."

"What we need is a song that can trap it in a helpless and broken form, the way my song for Jace transformed the first stowaway. I allowed the stowaway to escape once and put everyone on this train in danger. And Abbie—" Raya's throat tightened. "I'll write the song. I just need my guitar." She looked at Rasmus. "But it's in the MMD."

Rasmus pulled a key from his pocket. "Then you'll need to unlock it."

YOUR ITINERARY

CHECK OUT THE CLOAKROOM

“Where do I leave my coat?”

Frequently Asked Questions
THE ELSEWHERE EXPRESS
PASSENGER HANDBOOK

Raya

“There must be other guitars on the train that you could use.” Q climbed out of the crystal train and into the train’s cloakroom.

“They’re not what I need,” Raya said.

“You don’t need that old guitar either.” Q slipped the miniature train into her pocket. “*You* made the song, not your guitar.”

“I’m not that person anymore, Q. That guitar is all that’s left of the girl I used to be. That girl made the song strong. I’m just the one who’s broken.”

Two loud chimes rang through the hallway.

“Good evening, passengers.” A voice spilled out of the loudspeaker. *“We would like to request Mr. Philips Jr. and Ms. Sia to proceed to the boarding car. The conductor will meet you there. Thank you.”*

“There’s only one reason Lily would tell us to drop everything and head there,” Raya said. “They’ve found the stowaway.”

Q nodded. “But there’s no point in even trying to stop the stowaway without that song.”

“I’ll be quick.” Raya looked through a rack of dusty coats and sneezed. “I wonder why no one comes back for their things?”

Q sifted through another rack. “No one wants to be reminded of the times they felt cold. Not when you're living a perfectly comfortable new life."

"Here it is." Raya pulled out a green raincoat that Rasmus had told them to find. "The side door should be in its hood." She took Rasmus's key from her tote.

Q grabbed an umbrella from a cubby behind the cloakroom's counter. "I'll go first in case it's raining phones."

"No." Raya set her tote down and took the umbrella from him. "You need to stay here."

"Why?"

"Because in case I get lost, I don't have a hundred years to spare waiting for someone to come find me." She hooked the umbrella over her arm and slipped into the coat's hood.

Icy drops struck Raya's face. She fumbled with the umbrella's button, her mind clinging to the rapidly shrinking possibility that she was caught in a downpour of leaky pens. The umbrella sprung open. Raya held it over her head as lightning lit the sky. She swore and ran.

She sprinted past the little hills of socks and wallets, slipping over the slick ground. She spotted her guitar among the instruments arranged near the whirlpool. A swarm of fluttering wings soared behind her. She caught her foot in a muddy hole and tumbled forward, landing on her knees and palms.

"*Hiraya,*" the stowaway said.

Raya pushed herself to her feet and looked its way. The stowaway stared back at her with Jace's face. She steeled her jaw. "Enough."

Jace's face broke apart, scattering in every direction. The moths gathered and molded themselves into the shape of another man. Q's gray eyes smiled at her. "*Raya?*"

"Stay away from me!" Raya sprinted to her guitar.

The stowaway glided toward her, a thousand wings keeping it from touching the rain-soaked ground.

Raya grabbed her guitar by its neck.

The moths scattered and re-formed ahead of her, keeping Q's face. A tendril shot out from its body and yanked the guitar from her grasp. Rot spread over the wood. *"Excess baggage is strictly prohibited."*

"No!" Raya screamed.

The stowaway broke into a swarm.

"Raya!" Olly waved by the whirlpool. "Over here."

Raya ran toward him.

"I'll hold it off," Olly said.

"Olly—"

"Go! Hurry." Olly dissolved into shining wisps of thought. They circled the black swarm like a windstorm, sweeping the stowaway away.

Raya closed her eyes and listened for a door's song.

Raya clambered out of a taupe fedora.

"Raya." Q rushed toward her. "Thank god."

"The stowaway's in the MMD." Raya panted. "And it has your face. Another of its tricks. We need to decouple this car now."

"Maybe we don't have to. Get the raincoat." Q grabbed a paintbrush from Rasmus's satchel and painted a rough outline of a square on the floor. He set his fingers into an edge of the square, staining their tips with paint. He slid the square open. A void gaped beneath it. "Throw the coat."

Raya dropped the coat into the hole. Q shut the door and painted a lock over it. They sat on their haunches, holding their breath. "Is it gone?" Raya said.

"I . . . I think so." Q gathered Raya in his arms. "We did it. It's over."

Their tether had never bound them tighter, making Raya wonder if it was possible to ever let Q go. But she needed to try. She pulled away.

"Is something wrong?"

"No." Raya shook her head, her eyes on the door Q had painted on the floor. The stowaway was gone, but the decision they needed to make before morning remained. She closed her eyes and cupped his cheeks, gliding her fingers over his skin. "I just want to remember this too."

Q smiled and clasped her hand. Moths burst through the door, tearing them apart. The dark cloud of wings swarmed Raya, pulling her into the void, beyond Q's screams and reach.

"Does the train have a disembarkation procedure?"

Frequently Asked Questions
THE ELSEWHERE EXPRESS
PASSENGER HANDBOOK

Q

Paint was like a smile. If brushed on well, it could hide almost anything. Two coats of eggshell white had been enough to completely cover the scorched moths Q had painted on school property, but a hundred layers of paint could not erase the image burned into his eyes. He would see the horror on Raya's face whether they were open or closed. He bolted upright, cold sweat soaking his shirt.

"Good." Rasmus stood over him. "You're awake."

"What happened?" Q's eyes flew around him. He was back in Rasmus's office, sitting up on his cot.

"The cloakroom's bell rang after you and Raya left. I headed there to warn you and found you on the floor. Raya wasn't with you. I don't know where she is."

"The stowaway took her. We threw it out a back door, but it came back. We need to let Lily know." Q stood up. "We were supposed to meet her at the boarding car."

"I know. I heard the announcement over the loudspeaker. She's setting a trap."

Q nodded. "I'll head there now."

"A trap," Rasmus said, "for you. She wants to get rid of you, Q."

"What?"

"She's convinced that you're a danger to the train."

"That's ridiculous. How do you even know that she wants to throw me off the train?"

Rasmus

Earlier

Rasmus's footsteps echoed over the silence of the hanging bells as he paced the Archive, waiting for Q and Raya to return from the Missed and Misplaced Department. A second set of footsteps joined his.

"Rasmus." Lily walked up from behind him.

"Good. You're here. Did you get my message? We need to talk about the first stowaway."

"Yes," Lily said. "We do. I remember everything now."

"You do? How?"

"I caught a whiff of Manon's perfume when I gave it to you."

Rasmus frowned. "Why didn't you say anything?"

"Because I was as confused as you. I wasn't sure what was happening to me. The memories were all jumbled up and I didn't know if I could trust them."

"And now?"

"I do."

"What do you remember?"

"I remember what we did to the first stowaway and how it got on the train."

Rasmus lowered his eyes and sighed. "I'm sorry, but we had to—"

"I also know who brought the second stowaway on board." Lily locked eyes with Rasmus. "I've instructed that an announcement be made to tell Mr. Philips to meet me at the boarding car. Where you and I will be waiting for him."

The loudspeaker chimed.

"Good evening, passengers. We would like to request Mr. Philips Jr. and Ms. Sia to proceed to the boarding car. The conductor will meet you there. Thank you."

Q

"That's insane." Q shook his head, letting Rasmus's words sink in. "Lily's obviously still confused. We know that the stowaway can play tricks on your mind and made both Lily and Raya see things that weren't real. Maybe it's affected Lily's memories too. Or maybe she didn't catch as much of Manon's fragrance as you did and so what she remembers is in disarray or incomplete. Please tell me that you don't believe her."

A bell rang in the farthest corner of the Archive.

"Raya!" Q sprinted to the bell.

Rasmus hurried after him. He checked on the bell, dropped it, and walked away.

"Where are you going?" Q grabbed his arm. "Where is she? Where's Raya?"

Rasmus tugged his arm free. "I'll take it from here, Q. I'll deal with the stowaway."

"What about Raya?"

"If I can save her, I will."

"That's not good enough, Rasmus. Tell me where the stowaway's taken her."

"Go back to your compartment, Q."

"You have no intention of saving Raya, do you? You're going to decouple whatever train car the stowaway's in."

Rasmus pulled a vial of thick blue liquid from his pocket. "Drink this."

Q glared at the vial. "You want me to erase Raya?"

"I want you to claim your place on the Elsewhere Express just as all the passengers have. You can build a new life for yourself here."

"By leaving Raya to rot."

"I promise that you won't feel one ounce of guilt. It will be as if she never existed."

"How can you say that? The first stowaway would have destroyed the train if not for Raya. It was her song that saved all of you. Even if this tonic wipes every trace of her from my mind, I'll hear her songs. They built this train long before she set foot in it. How can I forget someone who's everywhere? If you don't want to help her, fine. But you can't stop me from trying."

"You can't do anything if you can't get to where she is," Rasmus said.

"Lily was right." Q's voice darkened.

"About what?"

Q grabbed Rasmus by the collar. "I am a danger to this train." He shoved Rasmus against a jade wall. "If you don't tell me where Raya is right now, I swear to you that I will paint the walls and floors of this train with cracks so deep, everything you've built will shatter before you can scream."

Rasmus raised his hands and sighed. "All right."

Rasmus

"You're making a mistake." Rasmus folded his arms, watching Q's pencil fly over a piece of official Elsewhere Express stationery.

"Perhaps." Q set his pencil down and folded the paper in half. "But not one that I will regret." He slipped the stationery into a black envelope and sealed it with gold wax. He walked over to Rasmus and handed him the envelope. "Can I trust you with this?"

Rasmus nodded and tucked the envelope into his jacket pocket. "Good luck, Q. I hope you're right. For all our sakes."

YOUR ITINERARY

A MOONLIT
STROLL

"What time does the boarding team begin setting up the boarding car?"

Frequently Asked Questions
THE ELSEWHERE EXPRESS
PASSENGER HANDBOOK

Raya

Except for the storm pummeling it, the moonlit meadow was the same as Raya remembered. Mr. Nakamura and his team had not yet replaced the boarding car's décor. A lifetime had seemed to pass since she floated away from the subway and found herself standing beneath an oak tree's glowing canopy.

But now, she had no feet to stand on. Nor legs. Nor body. Since the stowaway had abducted her, she had unraveled into threads of disembodied thoughts as Olly had. She scattered through a swarm of moths and moved as they moved, a prisoner held in pieces in a thousand winged cells.

When the swarm took shelter from the downpour in the hollow of the oak's trunk, Raya wondered if this was to be her prison or tomb. She peeked through a tiny hole in the bark.

Lily was walking up to the tree. She pulled an unlit torch from her satchel and a blue flame burst from it. Raya tried to call out but had neither a throat nor a mouth to make a sound.

Lily cast the torch's light on the oak. "Mr. Philips, you can come out now, I know you're there."

"Are you allowed to toss things off the train?"

Frequently Asked Questions
THE ELSEWHERE EXPRESS
PASSENGER HANDBOOK

Q

Earlier

Even in a downpour, the meadow inside the boarding car did not disappoint. It was exactly as Raya had described it.

Q sheltered beneath an oak tree's glowing branches. He knew that he had not endeared himself to Rasmus when he had forced him to reveal where the storm was brewing and the fastest way to get to it. He did not doubt that he made Rasmus wonder if Lily had been right about him. He asked himself the same question.

He took a pencil and a piece of paper from Rasmus's satchel and made a quick sketch. He folded the paper and tucked it into his pocket.

The tether tugged hard at his chest. Raya had to be close. Footsteps trampled his thoughts. Q ducked behind the oak's trunk and waited.

Now

"Mr. Philips, you can come out now," Lily said. "I know you're there."

Q slipped his hand into his pocket, his fingertips grazing the edge of his folded sketch. He stepped out from behind the oak's trunk. "Hello, Lily."

"I was wondering when you'd get here." Lily lowered her torch. "I was beginning to worry that you might not have heard the announcement over the loudspeaker."

"We heard it." Q kept his distance from her. "But there were a few things Raya and I needed to take care of first."

"Like discarding the Missed and Misplaced Department through a painted back door?" Lightning streaked over the meadow. "Sadly, your plan didn't work. As you can see, the stowaway's still on board."

"It has Raya."

"I see." Lily's face tensed. "Don't worry. We'll find her."

The weight of Lily's words was convincing. If she had a plan to get rid of him, Q thought, it was on pause. He pushed his sketch deeper into his pocket. They had a truce.

"But we need to act fast, Mr. Philips." Black tendrils slithered from the oak tree like gnarled roots. "This train car is lost but there may still be a way to save Ms. Sia."

A black rabbit hopped into a jar lying on the rain-soaked grass. Lily picked the jar up and covered it, twisting its lid tight. She peered into the seemingly empty jar and slipped it into her satchel. "That should be all of them."

Q sealed an identical jar and handed it to Lily. "Here."

"Thank you for your help, Mr. Philips." Lily stuffed the jar into her satchel. "The sanctuary's thoughts owe you a great debt." She pulled an unlit torch from her bag. "We need to decouple the train now."

"What?" Q stiffened. "We haven't found Raya."

"We tried. None of the thoughts from the meadow have seen her."

"You can't destroy this car if there's even the smallest chance that she's still here."

Lily tilted her head up, her neck rigid. "I will destroy whatever I need to, Mr. Philips."

Q pulled his sketch out of his pocket and unfolded it. His scribble could barely be called a drawing, but he had learned that on the Elsewhere Express, what mattered were the thoughts he poured into what he created. The crack he had penciled was tiny, but it could destroy this train faster than any havoc the stowaway could wreak. He looked Lily in the eye. "So will I."

"Good." Lily nodded. "I was counting on that." She tucked the torch back into her satchel. "I told you that there was a way for us to save Ms. Sia. I lied. We can't save her. Only you can."

"Me?"

"I'm guessing that Rasmus told you not to come here because he believed I was setting a trap. He was right. It is a trap. But not for you. It's for the stowaway." She took a gold key from her satchel, plunged it into the ground, and twisted it. "And I need your help to make it work."

Whirs, clicks, and clanks echoed through the meadow. The horizon parted like stage curtains, revealing the paneled walls of a much smaller room. The night sky folded away, taking the storm with it.

A curved onyx ceiling took its place. Beneath it, the ground flipped over in square-shaped sections, giving way to polished parquet tiles adorned with the train's eternal knot. The oak tree deflated and rolled itself into a prop box, leaving a swarm of moths fluttering in the shape of its trunk. The moths scattered, abandoning an unconscious figure on the parquet floor.

"Raya!" Q gasped.

The swarm took the shape of a faceless man and snatched Raya up. Raya stirred. Tendrils broke out from the stowaway's body and crept across the car's walls.

"It's trapped," Lily said. "For now. This train car is built from grief, one of the hardiest thoughts. But the car is still decaying behind its walls and floorboards. The rot will spread if we don't stop it."

Q grabbed a brush from the satchel. He did not want to risk painting a swarm while the stowaway had Raya. "I'll make a door," he said, painting swiftly over a wall.

"It will only come back."

"Once we get Raya back, I'll paint a swarm and—"

"You'll need to throw yourself from the train, Mr. Philips."

"*What?*" Q twisted around.

Rot seeped through the floorboards.

"If you want to save Raya, you have to jump off the train. You brought the stowaway on board with you. Wherever you go, it will go too."

Q gnashed his teeth. "No. That's not true. You're confused, just like Rasmus was when he attacked me."

Raya opened her eyes, moaning weakly.

The stowaway twisted its black vines into a whip and lashed at a wall. Splinters flew across the car. The stowaway drew its whip back, loosening its grip on Raya. She wrestled free and sprinted toward Q. Q dropped the brush and ran to her. The stowaway aimed the whip at Raya and caught her by the ankle. Q grabbed her hand. "Lily!" Q yelled. "Help!"

Lily pulled the painted door open. A cliff dropped off outside, the sun rising behind it.

The stowaway dragged Raya across the floor toward it.

"Q!" Raya screamed.

Q clung to her. "I've got you."

Rotting vines broke through the onyx ceiling. Shards rained down on the train car, cutting and slicing Q's face and hands. Blood coated his fingers. Raya slipped from their grasp. The stowaway hoisted Raya to the ceiling, coiling its vines around her like a cocoon. Wind wailed through the painted door.

"Why, Lily?" Q clenched his bloody fists. "Why didn't you help her?"

Lily's hair twisted in the wind. "Because the stowaway would only steal her away again. There's only one way to end this and it's through this door. It's morning. The map and your tether have released you. You can leave this train without crushing Raya."

"Give me a reason to believe you, Lily. Give me the smallest reason and I will jump off this train right now. I swear to you that I didn't bring the stowaway on board. I would never hurt anyone."

"Wouldn't you?" Lily narrowed her gaze at the pocket containing Q's drawing.

Q pressed his hand over it, crumpling his sketched threat. It grew heavier as though filling up with rocks.

"You boarded this train from a dark place, Mr. Philips. And you brought this darkness with you." Lily turned to face the stowaway, her eyes on the fluttering moths that made up its body. "A conductor likes to know their passengers. I read the passenger manifest. I know the anger you've been trying to keep inside you. You've failed."

An objection raced over Q's tongue and rammed against the back of his teeth. He could not deny Lily's words. Nothing she had said about him was a lie. He wondered if she was right about him bringing the stowaway on board too. He stared at the stowaway, remembering what Raya had told him about how it wore his face at the Missed and Misplaced Department.

But eyes were laughably easy to trick. They could be shut and opened, forced to look closely or away, ordered to steal a glance or linger. They saw only what their owners wanted, blinding themselves to everything else.

Other senses were not as quick to be fooled. You smelled what you smelled and heard what you heard, and there was no way to convince a tongue it liked something it did not. But there was nothing more honest than touch. Fire was hot, ice was cold, lips were soft, and knives, dull or sharp, could make you scream. Out of all his senses, Q trusted touch the most. He ran to the stowaway.

"No!" Raya squirmed within the stowaway's vines.

The stowaway met Q halfway. Q extended his hand toward it.

"Mr. Philips?" Lily yelled over the howling wind. "What are you doing?"

Q squeezed his eyelids shut and shoved his hand into the teeming moths that made up the stowaway's chest, intent on grasping what his other senses could not. The insects crawled around his fingers and over his palm, their wings fluttering like whispers across his skin. They spoke as one, revealing a truth that was a secret only because no one listened.

Q yanked his hand out and staggered back, teetering on the edge of his painted doorway. He stared down a cliff. It would be quick, he thought, over before he felt any pain. It was a small price to pay to keep an entire train safe.

He glanced back at Raya. He didn't need to say goodbye. Soon, he would be discarded along with the rest of her excess baggage. He imagined her eyes growing wide at the sight of her compartment for the second first time, unburdened by memories of the stowaway or the dilemma of deciding who got to keep the compartment and stay. Raya would smile when the grass carpet tickled the soles of her feet and breathe a sigh when her bed gave her a hug. A stick of incense would tell her any bedtime story she liked. She would drift into sleep and maybe dream about the train, gifting a young boy with a glimpse of glowing spheres and magic.

Q smiled at the thought and threw himself out the door, taking the stowaway's secret with him.

THE ELSEWHERE EXPRESS

Loudspeaker Announcement

Greetings, passengers. We apologize for the interruption at this hour. We would like to inform you that the cloakroom and the boarding car will be undergoing renovations and will not be accessible during this time. We would like to let you know that the furry and finned friends who were displaced from the boarding car are in need of a new home. Please contact Mr. Nakamura if you are interested in adopting them.

THE FIFTH LEG

You are today where your thoughts have brought you; you will be tomorrow where your thoughts take you.

—James Allen

YOUR ITINERARY

ETERNITY ON THE
ELSEWHERE EXPRESS

Day One

From the Passenger Records of Hiraya Sia

Raya

The silver words inlaid on the wall behind Raya's bed swam behind her eyelids like carp in a very small pond.

I dreamed I was a butterfly, flitting around in the sky; then I awoke. Now I wonder: Am I a man who dreamt of being a butterfly, or am I a butterfly dreaming that I am a man?

Raya wondered who she would be when she woke up the next day. Though the "next day" had come, the train's painters had yet to paint over her compartment's ceiling. Until they did, the longest night of her life had yet to end. She stared up at the painted stars, clutching a bottle of blue tonic to her heart. Once she drank it, she could be whoever she wanted to be, and wear whatever face made it easiest to smile.

Lily had promised that Mr. Goh's concoction would give her the best sleep of her life. Raya could only hope this was not another of Lily's lies. If the serum failed to sweep away every trace of Q, she would live in this night for the rest of her endless journey. Q had paid for her ticket with his life, and she was not going to waste her fare. She sat up and brought the bottle to her lips. The tiny ocean inside it washed a memory of a stroll on the beach she had never taken to her mind's shore. On a sampan sailing down a river of fleeting thoughts, she had dared to imagine a future on the train, days of collecting songs that had washed onto pink sand while Q painted stars above her. She chose to pretend that he was in the sky now, preparing the paints he would need for the most magical sunrise the Elsewhere Express had ever seen. Later, they would meet up at the Lotus for happy hour and watch the whales. Q would smile at her from across the table, his gray eyes crinkling over his Sakura Surprise. She reached out to touch his cheek, tracing the remembrance of his warmth in the air.

Raya threw the tonic on the floor.

Blue liquid soaked into the freshly cut grass. She could not erase Q. Yet. He deserved to be mourned. Raya lay down and pulled the covers to her chin. Lily had told her that her compartment would know if she was feeling warm or cold. She wondered if it would also know if she was drowning. She closed her eyes. Two knocks on her door pulled her from the edge of a dream. Raya rolled to her side, pretending she wasn't there. She was not in a rush to have housekeeping teach her how to dim the moon or adjust the height of the carpet's blades of grass.

The knocking grew louder.

"Can we do this tomorrow?" Raya mumbled into her pillow.

"I'm sorry," a soft-spoken voice said through the door. "It can't wait."

"Rasmus?" Raya got up.

"I have something I need to give you."

Raya took her time walking to the door, trying to come up with a polite way to decline another welcome gift. She had received three so far: a basket of bananas from Alain, a box of official Elsewhere Express stationery from Lily, and a voucher for painting lessons from Astrid. Raya drew a breath and opened the door.

"Hello, Raya." Rasmus stood at the door empty-handed. "Have you drunk Mr. Goh's remedy?"

Raya shook her head. "No, not yet. Why?"

"Good. May I come in?"

"I'm sorry, Rasmus, but I'm exhausted. You said that you had something for me?"

"It's not from me. It's from Q."

Raya's heart jumped to her throat. "Come in."

Rasmus tucked his chin and stepped inside, grazing the top of his head on the doorway.

"Would you like to sit down?" Raya said.

"Thank you." Rasmus took a seat in the compartment's small dining area.

Raya sat across from him, laying her hands on the table.

Rasmus pulled a black envelope from his pocket. "Q asked me to give this to you in case he—"

Raya took the envelope from him, unwilling to hear what he was going to say next. She ran her thumb over a gold wax seal in the shape of the train's eternal knot. "Thank you."

"I'm not sure I deserve your gratitude. Actually, I'm certain that I don't. I told Q not to look for you. It wasn't personal. I just thought that it was fair. I read the passenger manifests. Q wanted to be on this train. You didn't. He deserved a second chance."

"And I don't."

"I didn't say that. You have every right to be here too. You have a ticket. You have a compartment."

A compartment, Raya thought, that would always feel like she had stolen it. In a way, that made her and Q even. Q was a thief too. Deciding who got the compartment's sole key was a decision they were supposed to make together. Q robbed her of that choice.

"You'll do great things here," Rasmus said. "I'm sure of it."

"But that's not what you told Q."

"No, it wasn't. I knew that if he went looking for you, he wasn't coming back."

"You were right." Raya's spine hardened like cement against the back of the chair. "And so was Lily. Q had brought the stowaway on board with him."

"It seems that way, doesn't it?" Rasmus said. "Anyway, that's all behind us now. Once we drink the serum and rid ourselves of this baggage we'll move on and never have to think about what happened on this night ever again. Who knows? The two of us might even turn out to be great friends."

Raya gave up on sleep.

Instead, she stepped through every door she could find, moving from train car to train car, trying to stay ahead of her thoughts. If those thoughts caught up with her, they were only going to try and convince her to read Q's letter. But she refused to open it. As long as the wax sealed his words, they were in the middle of a conversation and this moment was just a pause, and she would drag that moment out for as long as she could. Q would just have to be patient and wait his turn to speak.

And if after this pause she thought of something new to say, he was going to have to wait a little longer.

Day Two

From the Passenger Records of Hiraya Sia

Raya

Raya awoke in a train car she did not remember entering. After she had stumbled into the Lotus, helping herself to the welcome drink she had skipped the first time and treating herself to a few more, the rest of her evening was a blur. She had fuzzy memories of visiting an opera house inside a thimble and a speakeasy that served distilled drunken thoughts in shot glasses with sugar and mint. The train car she woke up in was the last page of a book, which she guessed was the reason she had chosen it to fall asleep in. There were very few things that were more comfortable than a happy ending.

"Then," said Poirot, "having placed my solution before you, I have the honor to retire from the case . . ."

The vaguest sense that she had dreamt about Q floated like a cloud in the back of her mind. She turned to her side. Q's letter tumbled off her lap and onto an ellipsis. Its wax seal cracked open like half-parted lips, begging to speak. Q had stayed the night as she had asked, and it was not fair to ask him for anything more.

She broke the rest of the wax seal and pulled a sheet of the train's official stationery from the envelope. A rough sketch of her face filled the page. She traced a finger over it, feeling the urgency of every line. Despite his rush, Q had been kind. Her eyes were brighter, her smile wider, than they were in real life. He had even smoothed her hair, tying it in place with the scarf he had gifted her. An embroidered butterfly, perched on the corner of the scarf, kept her penciled portrait company.

She turned the sketch over and read the note scribbled on its back.

Hiraya,

This is your face and your name. Let the blue tonic erase everything else, but please, keep these.

Your friend
or something stranger,
Q

Day Five or Fifteen

From the Passenger Records of Hiraya Sia

Raya

Keeping track of time mattered only when you ran out of it. Days on the Elsewhere Express, like the train's stock of dark-roasted coffee and excess baggage tonic, were in endless supply. A new vial of the blue serum sat on Raya's nightstand next to the calendar she had drawn on the train's official stationery. Today was her fifth day on board as far as she could tell, but she could not find anyone who could confirm it.

Fragrant steam wafted up from her cup of oolong tea. Raya breathed it in and exhaled it slowly while watching passengers make their way down a cobweb bridge. Raya had avoided the Dragonfly until Dev had requested that they meet at the dining car to discuss his offer for her to join the maintenance crew.

"Good morning." Dev strode up to her table balancing a tray of congee and an assortment of dumplings and sauces. He had changed faces, but Raya was getting good at recognizing people. Their eyes stayed the same. Dev's eyes were playful and kind, no matter their color. Today they were the shade of buckwheat honey and smiled at Raya from the face of a man who was almost surely someone's favorite uncle.

Raya smiled back at Dev, her first one that had felt real since she had moved into her compartment. "Good morning."

Dev took a seat, his eyes on Raya's tea. "Is that all you're having?"

"I haven't had much of an appetite lately." The train's menu was everything Lily had promised it would be, but Raya could not bring herself to eat more than a few bites of any dish.

"That's a shame." Dev arranged his condiments in a neat row. He nudged a little sauce bowl until it was straight. "The Dragonfly has the best congee."

"I've heard."

Dev took a sip of his tea. "So, have you thought about my offer to join maintenance, or do you need more time to think about it?" He dipped a shrimp dumpling into an angry-looking chili sauce.

"More time? Are you kidding me?" Lily had told Raya to take her time deciding which department to join and to try her hand at different jobs before making her choice. But Raya had made her decision on a glowing beach long before Dev had officially invited her to join him. "If I have to spend another day in my compartment staring up at the ceiling, I'll go insane. When can I start?"

Dev laughed. "Most passengers enjoy having a little break before choosing a department. I didn't realize that you were so bored. I would have asked you to join us sooner."

Raya wished she were bored. The night Q leapt from the boarding car ran in a loop in her head. She paused and replayed it, rewatched it forward and back, scouring every second for anything she could have done differently.

Maybe if she had, Q would be sitting across from her at breakfast, smiling up from a cup of tea. Or did he prefer coffee? Raya hated that she didn't know the little things about Q even if what she did know should have been more than enough.

Unlike the rest of the train's passengers, she knew who she owed her life to. When she erased him, there would be no one left who remembered what Q had done for the train. His sacrifice would go unnoticed just like all the invisible battles people waged every day. Getting out of bed. Smiling. Taking a breath. Invisible victories for invisible people with invisible pain, where the only prize up for grabs was the chance to do it all over again the next day.

Lily walked through the mouth of the cave, greeting passengers as she made her way to the congee buffet. Today, she was a middle-aged woman with shoulder-length brown hair. She nodded at Raya and Dev.

"Lily doesn't like smiling much before her shift, does she?" Raya had stopped trying to call the conductor anything else. Even when she looked nothing like the fiery-haired woman who had welcomed her on board, to her, the person behind Lily's new eyes looked the same. "It's almost as if her smile is set on a timer."

"I wouldn't feel like smiling much either if I had to do what she does every day." Dev popped a dumpling into his mouth. "It can't be fun making sure that everyone's happy and following the train's rules."

Raya warmed her hands around her cup and stared into her tea.

"I'm sorry Q got turned into an Echo," Dev said quietly.

Raya nodded, looking forward to the day when she could believe this story. "I'm sorry too."

"I don't think I would have invited him to join maintenance, though," Dev said.

"Why not?"

"Q would make a better conductor than a plumber."

"Really?" Raya tried to imagine Q in the conductor's crisp uniform. She got as far as the third button of his black blazer before the image of him leaping from the boarding car shattered all other imaginings of him like glass.

"It was obvious how much he loved being on the train. Not every passenger feels that way when they board. When I boarded, I—" Dev's eyes widened.

Raya touched her chin. "Do I have something on my face?"

"I knew it." Dev laughed, slapping his knee. "I knew you looked familiar. I did see you when I boarded."

"That's not possible. You boarded the train long before I did."

Dev shrugged. "Since when did the rules of time apply to the Elsewhere Express? I admit that I don't have the best memory, but I'm right about this. And I can prove it. Meet me at my compartment after my shift."

Dev's compartment moved around a lot on account that it dangled from the collar of one of Mr. Goh's cats. The interior of the compartment was identical to Raya's except for its walls. Photographs covered it from ceiling to floor, surrounding them with stolen shots of conversations, smiles, and faraway stares.

"I know." Dev smirked. "It isn't for everyone."

"It looks great." Raya smiled, keeping her eyes away from a photo of her and Q on the beach.

"The hum of the Elsewhere Express is what I enjoy most about it," Dev said. "You can feel it in the air. It reminds me that I'm never alone. And never will be."

"Did you worry about being alone before boarding the train?" Raya said softly.

"I couldn't tell you." Dev's gaze wandered over a photograph of a crystal fountain. Stars flowed out of it like a liquid sky. "I took Mr. Goh's tonic as soon as I found my compartment. That's the clearest memory I have about my first night on the train. The tonic tasted like the worst thing you can imagine, but after I drank it, I had the best sleep of my life. I've heard that he's improved its taste so that it no longer makes you gag. At least, not right away. What did you think of it?"

Raya clutched her tote's strap. "I haven't taken it yet."

"Maybe you should." Dev eyed her bag. "It helps with shoulder and back pain too."

"Don't worry. I'll take it before joining the crew. The job will have my full attention."

"I'm excited for you to join us. You'll make a great addition to the team. And I'm happy you stopped by. Is there anything I can help you with?"

"You were the one who asked me to come over, remember? You said that you wanted to show me proof that you had seen me before."

"Oh. Right. Sorry." Dev laughed, shaking his head. "I'm not making it any easier for you to believe me, am I? Luckily, I don't have to rely on my memory for proof. I have photographic evidence to back me up." He chuckled, leading her to a wall by the dresser.

Raya's eyes flitted over the collage, unsure where to look.

"There." Dev pointed to a photograph of a ship's deck. "See?" Red battened square sails billowed against a halved sky. A woman, standing in profile, looked up at a bamboo mast. The image was small and slightly blurry, but it left no doubt about who she was. Her lavender hair, tied back in the silk scarf Q had given her, stood out. Wind whipped loose strands against her face and scented the compartment with the sea.

Raya gasped, salt air catching in her throat.

"I took the picture during my orientation. I meant to photograph the masts, but as you can see, I captured more than I intended."

"I don't understand." Raya stared at the photo. "How could I have been at your orientation?"

Dev laughed. "Well, that obviously isn't really you, is it?"

Raya inhaled sharply. "Is that the conductor? Was she wearing my face?"

"The conductor?" Dev shook his head. "No. The conductor isn't in the photo, but I do remember what he looked like that night. In those days, he always chose to look like the shortest person he could find—he hated hitting his head on doorways. If you want to know more about this woman, you should ask him. Rasmus has a much better memory than me."

❀

Raya found Rasmus seated by himself at the Lotus, working through his second bottle of sake. He looked up from his cup and gave her a small wave.

Raya walked up to his table. "May I join you?"

"Of course." Rasmus pulled out a chair. "Can I get you anything?"

"I'm good, thanks." Raya sat down without taking her eyes off Rasmus's face.

"The answer is no." Rasmus sipped his sake.

"No?"

"I haven't taken the serum," Rasmus said. "You can stop staring and trying to guess if I still remember what happened with the stowaway now."

"You said that keeping that memory was dangerous."

"I did, but I'm beginning to realize that remembering that night isn't as dangerous as forgetting it." Rasmus drained his sake cup and refilled it. "Not until I find a way to keep another stowaway from putting the Elsewhere Express in danger all over again."

"Isn't that Lily's job? Or does a retired conductor's duty never end?"

Aki walked over and set a fresh bowl of deep-fried lotus root chips on the table. "Can I get you anything else?"

"Another sake, please." Rasmus raised his empty bottle. "Thanks, Aki."

Aki nodded and cleared a nearby table.

Rasmus took a sip from his cup. "Have you decided what department you'd like to join?"

"I met with Dev today."

"Ah. Maintenance." Rasmus popped a lotus root chip into his mouth. "Excellent choice. Dev's a great mentor. I'm glad you're settling in well."

"How about the woman with my face?" Raya said. "How long did it take for her to settle in?"

Rasmus wiped his hand on a table napkin. "What woman?"

"You remember Dev. Surely you remember the only other person present during his orientation. I saw her photograph in Dev's compartment."

Rasmus clutched his sake cup.

"Who is she, Rasmus?"

Rasmus lifted his eyes from his drink. "What does it matter? Passengers change faces all the time for no reason other than they were bored."

"*What does it matter?*" Raya said. "She had my face. I'd like to know who she is."

Rasmus leaned back in his chair. "Why don't you just ask me what you really want to know?"

Raya could think of only one person whose thoughts might have conjured an image of her, picturing her, silk scarf and all, as she looked today. "Did she get my face from Q's thoughts?"

"You know what happened to Q," Rasmus said.

"Do I? The Elsewhere Express doesn't care about time. There are three versions of you on board the train to prove it. Maybe Q didn't die when he jumped from the train. Maybe he leapt into the past. That's the only explanation I can come up with to explain how this woman came to have the face, hair, and scarf I have now. Q is the only person who could have been the source of the daydream that woman took my image from. That means he survived the jump."

Rasmus looked up at the sky, his gaze following a school of luminescent fish. "Do you know what those fish are made of?"

"No, but—"

"They're made of truth. Pure, shining, blinding truth. They're all the thoughts that swirled and swam through people's minds when they considered lying but decided to be honest instead."

Raya fought the urge to groan. "That's interesting, but I—"

"Whoever came up with the idea of using it as lighting for the Lotus was quite clever, don't you think?" He glanced around the bar.

"Yes. I get it. In vino veritas. Very clever. That's not what I came here to talk to you about, Rasmus."

"Isn't it? I thought that was exactly what you wanted to know.

You're asking me who the woman in Dev's photo is and why she has your face, and I am, as we speak, debating whether I should lie to you or tell you the truth." Rasmus clasped his hands over the table.

Raya frowned. "Why would you even think of lying to me about this?"

"For the same reason you didn't tell me that Lily crushed Abbie."

Raya paled.

"You thought that the truth would hurt me more than a lie would, and you were right." Rasmus emptied his sake. "And now I am in the same position as you were. You, however, do not have a jade dragon to reveal everything you wish to know if you ask nicely. I was less fortunate. I would give anything to be able to look at Lily and still see one of my oldest friends."

"I'm sorry, Rasmus." Raya lowered her eyes. "I know that nothing I can say or do will change things."

"You did nothing wrong," Rasmus said. "And neither did Lily. She was doing her duty as the conductor, keeping passengers safe. I can't blame her for that."

"But you still hate her."

"Hate has nothing to do with reason."

"What are you trying to keep me from hating, Rasmus? Who are you protecting with a lie?"

Rasmus stood up. "If you really want to have this conversation, we need to go to someplace more"—he glanced around the empty bar—"private."

They rode the old-fashioned elevator in silence. Raya tried not to blink. If she closed her eyes, even for just a moment, she was going to imagine Q standing next to her.

"The tales this elevator could tell," Rasmus said, his eyes ahead of him. "Did you know that it's the only elevator on this train? It leads to at least a hundred different locations."

Raya's fingers traipsed over the side of the elevator. "Q and I took this elevator to our compartment."

"*Your* compartment, Raya. Your accommodations were never meant to be shared."

The elevator dinged and slid its door open. Raya stepped out into a large room filled with wooden looms and spinning wheels moving on their own. Swishes, taps, and whirs drifted across the room like murmurs telling a thousand stories at the same time. "What is this place?"

"It's the passenger record room." Rasmus made his way down a shelf that ran the length of the room, his eyes running over the embroidered tablecloths, napkins, and bed linens stacked on it. "We spin all the train's manifests into gold thread. Every knot in this room is a passenger's story." Rasmus took a napkin from the top of a stack, showing off the eternal knot embroidered onto it. "See?"

Raya stared at the knot, struggling to imagine how it might hold a passenger's story.

Rasmus returned the napkin and walked over to the opposite shelf. "It's better than letting records gather dust. This way, they have some use. Just like the passengers they belong to." Rasmus scanned a shelf. "Here it is." He pulled out a set of bedsheets and set it down on a wide sewing table. He took a pair of silver scissors from a basket filled with spools of gold thread and pincushions and snipped the sheet's embroidered knot with it. The knot unraveled quickly, eager to be free. Gold thread pooled over the table.

"Why did you do that?" Raya said.

"I've decided to do things differently this time around."

Raya's chest constricted. "What do you mean *this time around*?"

"This isn't the first time you've asked me about the woman in Dev's photo." Rasmus plucked a needle from a pincushion and threaded the unraveled knot through it. "I've tried lying to you and telling you the truth, but no matter what I do, nothing changes." He pulled the gold thread through the eye of the needle. "I've come to believe that it's because a story can never be told without bias. This time, I think you should see the events for yourself. Hold out your hand."

"Why?" Raya said, extending her hand.

Rasmus poised the needle over her skin. "I'm sorry."

"For what?"

Rasmus plunged the needle into her flesh. It disappeared into her palm, sewing a record into her soul. Raya wished that it were the kind of pain that faded, but every stitch burned as much as the one before it. Only the truth the thread told hurt more.

Passenger Manifest

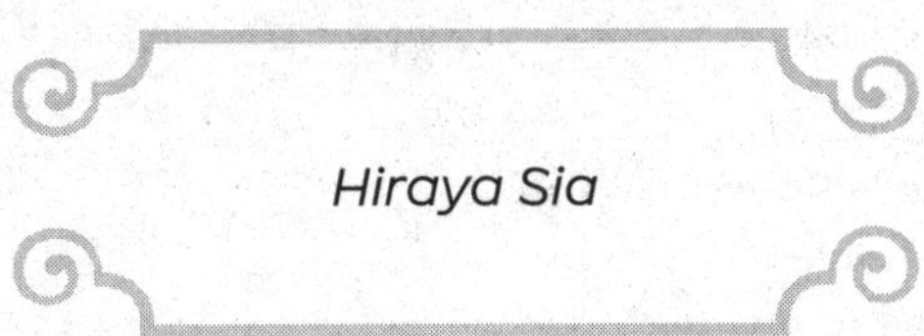

Hiraya Sia

The First Raya

Raya and Q lay on the bed staring up at the compartment's painted sky. "No one is getting thrown off this train," Q said. "We'll sort this out."

"There's nothing to sort out, Q. You found the compartment first. It's yours."

He shook his head. "It's not our fault the train glitched and only assigned us one compartment. We've followed all the rules Rasmus gave us. We searched for our compartment and didn't open any locked doors. This is your compartment too. Who cares who found it first?"

"You heard what the receptionist said." Raya sat up. "One passenger. One compartment. One bond. We can't share it. Only one of us can stay. And it should be you. The train gave you your sight back. It wants you here. It's your second chance to do what you were born to do."

"No. Not at your expense." Q pushed himself up and leaned against the headboard. "I know what it's like to have your dreams stolen."

"You're not stealing anything from me, Q. I told you when we boarded that my place wasn't on this train. Yours is. You've found your purpose here."

"Have I?"

"Of course. Just like the other passengers have."

Q exhaled a heavy breath.

"What's wrong?" Raya said.

"I just can't help but wonder if people have really found their place here or if they've just been assigned tasks."

"And if they have? What's wrong with that?" Raya said. "What matters is that they're happy. And so are you. Look at me and tell me that you don't want to be here, Q."

Q sighed. "I do."

Sharp knocking rattled the door. "Mr. Philips? Ms. Sia? It's me, Rasmus. May I come in?"

Raya stood up.

Q jumped out of bed. "Don't."

"We can't hide in here forever." Raya walked over to the door and opened it.

Rasmus stepped inside. "Congratulations on finding your compartment, Mr. Philips. If there's anything you need to make it more comfortable, please don't hesitate to let housekeeping know." He turned to Raya. "I'm sorry, Ms. Sia. Unfortunately, your journey with us ends here."

Raya nodded. "I understand."

"Allow me to escort you to the exit," Rasmus said.

"She's not going anywhere." Q stepped between Raya and Rasmus.

"The Elsewhere Express has rules, Mr. Philips. Breaking them has consequences that affect the entire train."

Q swore. "You're the conductor. Change the rules."

"I'm afraid it's not that simple, Mr. Philips."

"I think it is," Q said. "I've learned a few tricks from the painting crew." He pulled a brush and a tube of paint from his pocket. "I know what dark thoughts can do and so believe me when I tell you that unless you allow Raya to stay, I will not think twice about destroying this train."

Rasmus shoved his large hands into his pockets. "Then be quick. I don't want anyone to suffer. Go ahead and destroy the train, Mr. Philips. That's what will happen anyway if I allow Ms. Sia to stay. If I break one rule, the passengers will question all of them. Thoughts destroy thoughts. Doubt will spread. And so will cracks. If Ms. Sia stays, the Elsewhere Express will shatter."

"It's okay, Q." Raya gently touched his arm. "I'll go." She gripped her bag. "I'm ready."

Embroidery Lessons

From the Passenger Records of Hiraya Sia

Raya

The gold thread slipped out from Raya's flesh and embroidered itself back into an eternal knot on bamboo silk. No one could tell by looking at it that it had just stitched a tale into Raya's soul. "How many times, Rasmus?" She crumpled the silk in her fist. "How many times have Q and I boarded this train?"

"Too many." Rasmus stared at the shelf overflowing with embroidered silk sheets. "And each time, it's ended the same way. Q dies. You live."

"But Q found the compartment first." Raya's voice quivered. "You escorted me from the train. Why did he die?"

"Q gave up the compartment for you."

"No." Raya shook her head. "That's not true. That's not what I saw."

"You can't see what isn't there. That part of the record has been cut out. The thread couldn't show you how Q begged me to let him join you at the back door to say goodbye, and how, against my better judgment, I agreed to his request. When I opened the door, he threw himself out of it. There was nothing I could do."

"I don't understand." Tears blurred Raya's eyes. "Why would Q do that?"

"For the same reason he chooses to save you and this train time and time again. A moth always flies to the light. There hasn't been a single version of Q that hasn't been a good person."

"So why was the train's record cut? Who cut it?"

"I think you already know the answer to those questions." The bustle of the room nearly buried Rasmus's voice.

"The woman in Dev's photo didn't borrow her face from anyone, did she?" Raya touched her cheek. "Lily was wearing her own."

"Lily was new and wasn't keen on changing her face back then. But I knew that she was going to make a great conductor as soon as she boarded. She was used to carrying heavy loads."

Water splashed around her foot. Raya had not questioned Rasmus when he told her that Lily's office was located inside a teapot stored in a seldom-used pantry. The knee-deep flood she waded in, however, made her fear that she had misunderstood him. A slow, steady dripping sound came from the left side of the room. Raya turned in its direction. Water trickled down a shelf, spilling from the spout of a chipped teapot. Raya lifted the teapot's lid. "Lily? Are you in there? It's me, Raya."

"Come in, Ms. Sia." Bubbles carried Lily's voice to the surface.

"How do I—"

"Jump in."

Raya dove into the teapot and landed softly on colorful woven mats strewn over a slatted bamboo floor. Swaths of gauzy fabric took the place of walls and billowed in the breeze. Round capiz shell lamps, carried by pairs of dragonflies, hovered above and around Raya, bathing the villa in their glow. Raya parted a curtain and looked out. A still, borderless lake surrounded her, the bamboo villa's reflection a ghostly boat floating on a sea of stars.

"Good evening, Ms. Sia." Lily walked up from behind her.

Raya turned, prepared to see a stranger. She had not seen Lily since breakfast and knew that she would have changed by now into a new face to welcome the evening's arrival. A face framed by red, unruly waves met her. "Why are you wearing Lily's face?" Raya said.

"I guessed that since whatever is on your mind couldn't wait until morning, it was something that really bothered you." Lily smiled. "I wanted to make you feel as comfortable as possible. You seem to be rather attached to Lily. You haven't been able to stop calling me by her name."

"I can call you by your real one, if you'd like." Raya stared hard at her. "Or would that be too confusing since we share it?"

"You've spoken to Rasmus, I see. I was wondering when we were going to have this conversation again."

"Again?"

"Every version of us has gone straight to my office after speaking with him. We've had this talk as many times as Dev has shown my photograph to you. I'll have to pay him a visit to make sure he takes his latest dose of Mr. Goh's tonic." Lily strode to the floor cushions arranged in the middle of the room. "Have a seat while I make us some tea. I imagine there are quite a few things that you'd like to discuss."

Raya's tea sat ignored on a low table but did not grow cold. Like the Elsewhere Express, it cared little about change or time.

"Would you like to start with small talk?" Lily picked up her cup. "You've found it helpful in the past."

Raya tried to imagine how all her previous conversations with Lily had gone. No matter how pleasantly this talk began, she could not think of any circumstances where it would end well. "No."

"Are you sure?" Lily took a sip of her tea. "Our other selves were rather curious about why the pantry was flooded with tears. Astrid and Isla were surprised to learn that this lake is where sad thoughts board the Elsewhere Express."

Raya's jaw grew slack. "Astrid and Isla are—"

"Us? Yes. And there are quite a few others too. They all go by different names. No one wants to use the one we boarded the train with. Every version of us is disappointed that no matter what we do or what department we join, we can't stop Q from bringing his darkness on board with him. I've seen it happen over and over again. Once Q boards, the stowaway follows. When he leaves, the stowaway departs too."

"Is that how you remember it?" Raya said.

"How else would I remember it?" Lily frowned. "What did Rasmus tell you?"

"Rasmus didn't tell me anything. I saw the train's records."

"He showed them to you?" The wrinkle between her eyes deepened into a well that seemed to catch all the shadows in the room.

"Yes. He told me that he wanted to do things differently this time. He's tired of seeing Q die."

"And you think I'm not?" Lily's eyes, Raya thought, quivered in a way that made her both unrecognizable and familiar. The face of the woman who welcomed her on board had never showed such pain. The face that greeted her in her compartment's bathroom mirror each morning did. "Respectfully, Ms. Sia, looking at one train record doesn't mean that you know me. You and I are no longer the same person."

"You're absolutely right." Raya lifted her chin. "You stopped being me a long time ago. I would never ask Q to sacrifice himself the way you have."

"That's because you don't have to, Ms. Sia. You aren't the conductor. You don't have to make the hard decisions to keep this train safe. If you did, you wouldn't be able to conveniently ignore Mr. Philips's past and how he's repeatedly threatened to destroy everything and everyone on the Elsewhere Express. Mr. Philips carries an anger inside him, whether you admit it or not, a rage that swarms the train and turns everything to rot."

"And yet there was no sign of the stowaway the first time Q boarded the train, was there, Lily? Not one hint of rot or even the slightest sign of rain. This person you call a monster is, in fact, the very reason why you're standing here. Q threw himself from the train to save you and you couldn't even allow the train to remember him. Why?"

"If you have to ask me that, then you and I really are completely different people now," Lily said. "How could I possibly spend an eternity on this train or even a second in a compartment that Q paid for with his life? Nothing good would come from anyone finding out about what happened that night. Breaking one of the train's most important rules was as good as breaking all of them. The only way I could make sure Q's sacrifice wasn't wasted on me was to make sure that what I did here mattered. I didn't want to be as purposeless as—" Lily bit her lip.

"Go ahead," Raya said. "You can say it. It's the truth. You didn't want to be as purposeless as me. That's why you wanted to be the conductor."

"And I couldn't be a good one if I carried my grief and guilt with me the way you do. I had to let Q go."

"But don't you see? That isn't what you did. You didn't let go of him."

"Of course I did. I took Mr. Goh's serum. The only reason I remember any of this is because of Manon's perfume." Lily took two vials of ocean-blue serum from the tea tray. "But after tonight, neither of us ever have to think about this again."

"Until the next time the stowaway shows up," Raya said.

"Maybe this time it will be different." Lily watched the gauzy curtains ripple in the breeze. "Maybe it won't come back."

"It will."

"You don't know that."

"I do," Raya said. "In fact, I guarantee it. You can throw Q off the train a thousand times and it won't make a difference. The stowaway is still on board the Elsewhere Express. It's never left."

"That's ridiculous," Lily scoffed. "You saw the stowaway scatter into nothing with your own eyes."

"I did. But I also saw what you've cut out from the train's records. Just because you've taken great care to keep that part of your memory buried beyond any serum or fragrance's reach doesn't mean it didn't happen." Raya took a needle threaded with gold from her bag.

"I have no idea what you're talking about, Ms. Sia."

"You will." Raya stabbed the needle into Lily's hand.

Earlier

Rasmus refolded the embroidered sheet and returned it to the shelf.

"That's it?" Raya said. "You just put the truth back and forget about it?"

"It's not my truth to remember. What Lily chooses to do with it is her decision. I can't say that she hasn't made the right choices. She's kept the train safe. When I drink Mr. Goh's tonic, that's what I'll remember. I'll appreciate Lily's service without loathing her." Rasmus smoothed the sheet and turned to face Raya. "And so will you."

"Just like every version of me that's boarded the Elsewhere Express." Raya heaved a sigh.

Rasmus let his eyes fall on the gold butterfly embroidered into the scarf in Raya's hair. "I've lost track of all the times I've sent that away by gifting it to other passengers. But it always finds its way back. All secrets surface."

"What are you talking about?" Raya said.

"The truth you've been wearing. Despite all my attempts to gift or hide it, it seems to know where it belongs and whom it belongs to. The train's records are thoughts just like everything else on the Elsewhere Express. When Lily cut it, it needed a place to go. I sewed it into that scarf. I didn't have enough thread to make a knot and so I—"

"—embroidered a song." Raya pulled the scarf off, remembering with a shiver how Q's fingers had combed through her hair to tie it.

"Thoughts know their owners, just as owners know their thoughts," Rasmus said. "All the other Rayas chose to forget it, afraid of what they might learn about Q."

Raya traced the embroidery. Though gold wings fluttered against her fingers, a dark swarm crawled under her skin. Raya dropped the scarf.

"You can do as all your other versions did." Rasmus took the needle from the pincushion. "Or you can see how the stowaway really boarded the train."

Passenger Manifest

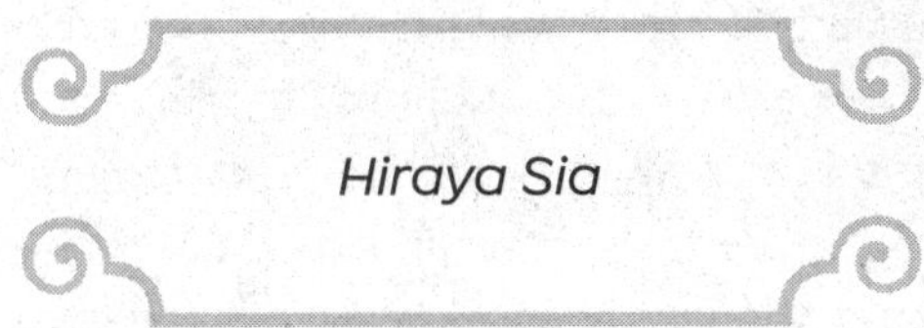

Hiraya Sia

The First Raya

Q didn't scream or flail. If Raya trusted her eyes and ears, she would have called it a peaceful death. But not all silence is calm. Q had said goodbye with two words that would live forever in all of Raya's quiet places, moths in a dark closet, consuming the fabric of her peace.

"Let him go, Ms. Sia." Rasmus pried the sake bottle from Raya's hands and set the train's back door on top of one of the Lotus's tables.

How? Raya wanted to scream. It was Q who held her soul in a chokehold and not the other way around.

"Mr. Philips is gone." Rasmus pressed a silver key into Raya's hand. "Congratulations," he said, speaking as though he was offering her his condolences. "The compartment is yours."

Raya flung the key to the floor. "I don't want it."

"You didn't want your train ticket either, but here you are." Rasmus picked the key up.

"A ticket paid for by my brother and Q. People who mattered and who would have made a difference. I'm a monster, Rasmus." She grabbed the sake bottle and stared into the darkness beyond its mouth. "I don't belong here."

"You think that hurling yourself after Q will fix things?"

"No, but it will make the pain stop." Tears streamed down her cheeks and slid down the bottle's neck.

Rasmus took a vial containing Mr. Goh's serum from his satchel and gave it to Raya. "There are other ways."

Remember me. It was all Q had asked of her, Raya thought, and she couldn't even give him that. Forgetting Q was the only way she would not let the eternity he had bought for her go to waste. She swallowed the serum. It flowed inside her, washing her past away.

But Mr. Goh made his serums in single doses and Rasmus had given it to Raya without realizing that she required two: one for Jace, the other for Q. One dose was not enough for all the blame she hoarded. The blue serum flooded her locked rooms and drawers but could not banish the grief and guilt that called them home. They grew wings to keep themselves from being swept away and took flight to higher ground. A black moth circled the train's back door.

Mary Beth, the nurse on the night shift whose finger Raya had once clung to tightly, had been right about the strength of her grip.

A Meeting with the Train Conductor

From the Passenger Records of Hiraya Sia

Raya

The winged song embroidered itself back on to Raya's scarf. Lily folded her arms over her chest, trying and failing to keep her hands from shaking. "That's not true."

A moth appeared by a capiz lamp and flitted around it, casting shadows over Raya's face. "Q had his demons, but the stowaway wasn't one of them."

Lily stood up. "I think you should go."

A second moth took shape out of thin air and joined the first.

"You tried to erase your past, but clung to your guilt," Raya said. "And it clung to you."

"Please leave." Lily gritted her teeth.

A third moth joined the pair and flew around the lamp.

"Your guilt conjured the first stowaway, Lily. That's why only you and I could see its true face. The guilt that lives inside us colors everything through its lens. And each time a version of Q boards, your guilt brings the stowaway to life." Raya glanced up at the moths. "It's creating another one now."

Lily grabbed a vial and uncorked it. She brought it to her lips. Raya swatted it away. "No!" Lily wept. "I need to forget."

"You can do whatever you want." Raya emptied the second bottle of tonic on the floor. "After we end this." She pulled a sake bottle from her bag. "Permanently."

Lily took a step back from Raya. "Why did you bring the train's back door here?"

Lily peered through the sake bottle. "I suppose that I should be grateful that the train is crossing an ocean. It might hurt less than the cliffs."

"The cliffs you told Q to hurl himself onto?" Raya said. "Yes, I imagine that being broken against them would be a lot more painful."

"What do you want me to say?" Lily's voice thinned. "I did what I needed to do. We may have shared a face and name once, but you have no idea what it's like to carry the responsibility I have."

"Actually, Lily, if there's one thing I've learned, it's that nothing on this train changes much at all. Not its route, not how fragile it is, and most certainly not its passengers. This may be the most wondrous train ever built, but it never truly moves forward. We are no closer to where we're going nor farther from where we left. The Elsewhere Express traps us in thoughts the same way we were trapped in our heads before we boarded it. Nothing has changed."

"Better to have no destination than to be forced to get off at stations filled with disappointment and pain." Lily put her cap on. "Ask any passenger if they are enjoying their trip and if they'd rather be somewhere else. You don't need a destination when you're happy to be exactly where you are."

"But are they happy, Lily? Are you? Drinking a tonic to forget that you're empty isn't the same as being full. Having a to-do list of tasks isn't purpose."

"It's close enough. After you've experienced being responsible for countless souls sheltering inside thin crystal walls, I'll be happy to listen to any other options you care to offer. But not before." Lily glared at the gathering moths. "Right now, all I care about is putting an end to this." She stared into the ocean inside the sake bottle. The wind blowing from the train's back door whipped her cap off. Her red hair tumbled out and returned to its original lavender.

Raya caught the cap.

"Goodbye, Ms. Sia," Lily said, looking back at Raya with Raya's own face.

"Wait." Raya grabbed the sake bottle.

"What is it?"

"I . . . I made a mistake. This can't be the only way. You aren't the stowaway. Your guilt is. Just let go of it."

"All right. I'll let it go if you show me where it lives." Lily's words scraped her throat. "I'll cut myself open right now and throw it from this train. Tell me where my sins end and where I begin, Ms. Sia. I'm listening."

Raya shook her head. "I don't know."

Lily stared up at the moths. Black wings covered nearly all the lamps like a quivering shroud. "Do you know why the dancers at the engine never stop moving? It's because if they pause, even for a moment, they'll realize that after spinning and gliding on a track for an eternity, they weren't dancing. They were just trying not to fall." A small smile, which seemed to have lost its way, settled over Lily's lips. Lily took the sake bottle from Raya. "I've stopped spinning, Ms. Sia. I trust you to carry on where I have left off. The Elsewhere Express cannot be without a conductor."

"*Don't, Lily.* Don't do it. We'll find another way."

"Goodbye, Ms. Sia. It was my pleasure to have served you. This is my stop."

THE ELSEWHERE EXPRESS

Loudspeaker Announcement

Good evening, passengers. We would like to inform you that the conductor has retired after years of outstanding service to the Elsewhere Express. We wish the conductor the very best as she embarks on the next leg of her journey. We would like to assure you that a new conductor will be stepping into the role shortly and request your patience and understanding during this transition period. Thank you and good night.

*Week Six or Month Six or Year Six**

**Maybe Sixty*

From the Passenger Records of Hiraya Sia

Raya

The conductor's day began as it always did with a quick, icy shower and breakfast at one of the Elsewhere Express's dining cars. Today, she craved the Dragonfly's chicken congee. Raya made a stop in the middle of the train car's cobweb bridge. She looked down at the sea of clouds. It was calmer, she thought, than the ocean Lily had leapt into.

Raya had seen her future when Lily sank beneath the waves. She refused to be dragged down by the same weight. She stuck her hand into her upcycled tote and pulled out the only thing left inside it, a candy bar long past its expiration date. She had given the rest of the bag's contents private funerals, sending them off from train cars that suited them best. The last item she had said goodbye to was the binder containing her anatomy notes, in a bonfire on a beach set aglow by songs. She looked over the cobweb railing, dropped the candy bar, and watched it fly up to the painted sun.

"Good morning." Rasmus joined Raya at a rosewood table. "Who are we today?"

Raya's hand flew to her face. Her fingers found her original nose and lips. She punched Rasmus in the arm. "Ha ha. Very funny. I knew I changed before I went to bed last night."

Rasmus chuckled. "Is it my fault that you have a terrible memory?"

"Not terrible, just full. Just like my schedule. Preparing for the reopening of the gallery is taking up every spare second I have." Raya had vowed to rebuild what she could and though she complained that it took up all her time, she welcomed exhaustion. The more tired she was, the easier it was to fall asleep.

"My version of the excess baggage tonic tastes a lot better than Mr. Goh's, you know. It will help you make room for all the things that you do need to remember." He tapped the side of his head.

Raya envied the light in his eyes. Rasmus had drunk Mr. Goh's tonic soon after she had told him about what happened to Lily. He did not want to mourn long. As far as he was concerned, not a single event related to the stowaway had ever happened. Lily had passed on her cap to Raya and was enjoying her retirement, and everything on the train, except for a broken branch on the Leaf Lift, ran as it should. As for the clicking sounds Rasmus heard in his chest, he was certain that it was nothing to worry about.

"I can have the tonic sent to your compartment," Rasmus said.

"Thanks for the offer." Raya opened the flap of her satchel, showing off the single notebook she kept inside it. "But my notebook is perfectly capable of sharing the load."

"How about your songs? Do you have room for them too?"

"Plenty." Raya smiled and sipped her tea. "The ten purple notebooks you harvested from the supply room for me are more than enough. How many songs do you think I write in a day?"

"Not nearly enough. But seriously, Dev says that the songs you've written are excellent. They're speeding up repairs."

"Great. I've been trying to make up for backing out of joining the maintenance crew."

"Dev understands how things work around here. Lily chose you to take over the most important job on the train. You had to accept," Rasmus said, repeating the tale that he had made Raya promise to tell him, the story he had crafted and wished to believe. Raya had agreed because the story was mostly true. She did have the most important job on the train, a job that allowed her to keep an eye on the back door and anyone who might board it.

Later That Evening

The vintage boarding car had been faithfully re-created from the original designs that Rasmus had unearthed in the Archive. Raya had requested only one change. Instead of emerald green, the couches were upholstered in a gray fabric that borrowed its color from an overcast sky. Without any brass plaques to remember Q's sacrifice for the train, Raya made do with a memorial to his eyes.

"Good evening." Raya struggled to keep her smile in place. The face she had chosen for this evening had not smiled in a while. Its muscles were tight and hard, weighed down by years of frowning. Raya slowly curled her lips upward, worried that it might crack like clay. She had spotted a face with an easier grin, but there was no time to change. The evening's new passenger had boarded.

"Where am I?" the passenger said. "What is this place?"

"Welcome aboard the Elsewhere Express." Raya's eyes roamed over the young woman's face and the wisps of lavender hair framing it.

She had spent countless nights imagining what it would feel like to greet another version of herself, practicing welcoming her in the mirror. But rehearsing a spiel with her reflection was different from talking to a person who could talk back.

Raya stared into her old eyes, watching thoughts dart through them like the Wandering City's hummingbirds. Thoughts crumbled as fast as they were constructed, questions and theories about where she was and what was happening to her flying across her other self's eyes. Was she going mad? Was she having a panic attack? Was she dead?

"Don't worry," Raya assured her. "Everything will be clearer after your orientation. But first, I'll need to see your ticket."

"What ticket?" the other Raya said without noticing the rectangular piece of stiff black paper sticking out from her tote.

"You may want to check your bag," Raya suggested.

Her other self glanced down at the paper.

"May I?" Raya took the ticket from her. She had come to realize that inspecting tickets was merely a formality, having yet to meet a passenger who presented a fake ticket or one with the wrong date. Her eyes flitted over Other Raya's ticket.

The Elsewhere Express. Check.

Eternal knot logo. Check.

The passenger's name was missing. Other words took its place. Raya knitted her brows, forcing herself to reread the next lines slowly.

HERE

An Exhibit

By Q Chen Philips Jr.

Raya's other self plucked a similar piece of black paper sticking out from a purple notebook in her overstuffed tote. "Or are you looking for this?"

"Where did you get this?" Raya's fingers trembled over the invitation to Q's exhibit.

"They were handing them out at the subway. It's for some kind of art event or exhibit."

"Who gave it to you?" Raya demanded.

"I don't know. Who cares? It's your turn to answer my questions now. Who are you and where the hell am I?"

Incense scented Raya's compartment with white sage and told the story of a fight between the sky and sea and the kite that had caused it. Raya did not care who won. She wasn't listening. She lay on the floor, pinned beneath words printed in gold ink. The invitation pushed down on her chest and emptied her lungs. Raya sat up, letting the invitation slip to the floor. She snatched it up and reread the fine print on its back, hoping that this time around, it would make sense.

Raya.

On the count of three.

Jump.

YOUR ITINERARY

DISEMBARKATION

Six Weeks or Six Months or Six Years Ago*

**Maybe Sixty*

Q

There is a quiet clarity that only a fall from a train can provide. Death makes all other thoughts seem small. It shoves them out the door like a bar at closing time, shuts the windows, draws the blinds, and when your mind is empty, sits with you in silence. Q welcomed its company. He did not want to die alone.

Q could not think of anything to say to Death. Speaking required him to think, and thoughts, this close to the end, were dangerous. Doubt did not just shatter trains. It broke a person's will too. Q needed to keep his will intact until he slammed into a boulder or the ground. If it cracked, even just a little, he would scream, and Q could not tell if he had fallen far enough to be out of Raya's earshot. He did not wish for her to hear his fear.

Q did not have time to find the courage he needed to throw himself off the train. All he had were a stowaway's secrets to weigh him down. Each moth he had touched when he thrust his arm through the stowaway's chest had been a thought filled with Lily's guilt and told him the story of all the other times he and Raya had boarded the Elsewhere Express. He had not brought the stowaway on board, but if he jumped, he hoped he could take it with him. He clung to the stowaway's truth, needing to believe, up to his last moment, that what he had done to keep the train and Raya safe had worked.

Q landed on his feet, his eyes shut, wondering if he was alive or in hell. He kept his eyes closed, refusing to shed a tear for something he did not regret. A strong wind whipped his coat and hair, carrying the roar of an approaching train. The broken walking stick in his hands told him where and when he was. This was the night he had boarded the Elsewhere Express, the night he would get his sight back and meet a woman with lavender hair. All he had to do was step away from the platform and board his train when it came to a stop. Q turned and walked away from his latest second chance. The only way he could keep the Elsewhere Express safe was by never boarding it and awakening Lily's guilt again.

Live. Breathe. Be.

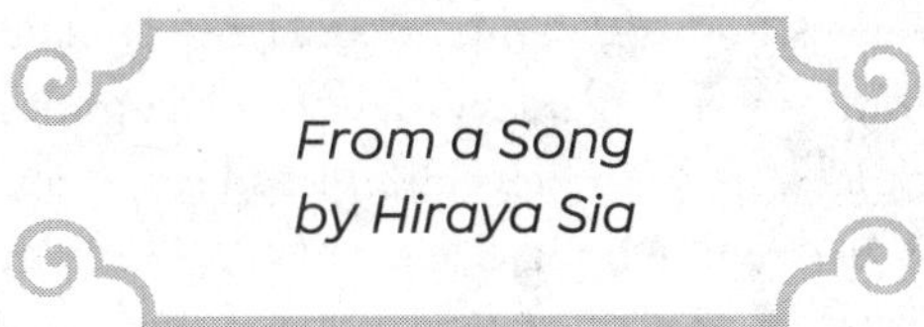

From a Song
by Hiraya Sia

Raya

Without his memory, Rasmus would never understand what she needed to do, but Raya did her best to put her reasons into words. She gave up trying to write them down, realizing that the train's official stationery could only bear so much weight. She crumpled her latest attempt into a ball and threw it into the bin beneath her desk. She pushed her chair back and stood up.

Raya walked over to the guitar she kept in her office. She sat on a floor cushion, cradled the guitar on her lap, and played. Winged songs burst from its strings, carrying every thought Raya could not write or say. They would whisper to Rasmus while he slept and by morning, he would understand why he had a conductor's cap in his hands.

Raya pulled out a sake bottle from her satchel and set the train's back door on the floor. She tucked a black-and-gold invitation into the inner pocket of her blazer, leaned over the mouth of the bottle, and counted to three.

A cat purred. Raya opened her eyes and met the empty stares of passengers whose thoughts were elsewhere. A woman stroked her cat with her acrylic extensions. A math student played Haydn on his headphones. A man stared at his muddy pant leg and thought about a regret named Lily. Something heavy pressed against Raya's ribs. She glanced down. Her arms welded her upcycled tote to her chest. The Elsewhere Express was already beginning to feel like a dream.

The subway car slowed at her station. She hooked her bag over her shoulder and stood up. While the bag's strap still dug into her skin, its load did not feel as heavy. Without the ghosts she used to carry, Raya could walk with her chin up and spine straight, bearing the posture of a person who had learned to shoulder the weight of a train. She stepped off the subway car and rechecked the time on the invitation to Q's exhibit. It opened at midnight, and she had more than enough time to head back to her apartment, take a long, hot shower, and change.

Raya paid for her cab and hopped off. It had started to drizzle, and the art museum was still a block away, but she decided that she needed to walk the rest of the way without an umbrella. She missed the rain. Her stride was slower than those around her. After being on a train without any control over its route or speed, following her own path was disorienting. And welcome. She poured her intention into every step, setting her own course forward.

The rest of the museum was closed and those who wished to visit Q's exhibit were advised to go through the back door. Raya laughed at the joke only she could understand.

The museum allowed two people inside at a time but gave guests the option to view the exhibit alone if they came by themselves. She fell in line and waited for her turn. The queue buzzed with anticipation, but no one's heart pounded as fast as Raya's did.

It set the cadence of questions marching through her mind. What had happened to Q after he jumped? Could he see? How did he know how to find her? She told herself to remember to congratulate him on the exhibit before she allowed any other questions or words to race out of her. Once they started flowing, they wouldn't be able to stop. She had twice as many stories to tell him.

Raya wondered what it would be like to see Q against the backdrop of the everyday and what she would look like to him. She was certain that he would only look brighter. But she would not tell him that. That could be her secret without worrying about a gold tether snitching.

The queue had snaked around the corner of the block by the time Raya neared the museum's back door. She had not realized that Q was so popular. She had overheard as many theories about the exhibit as there seemed to be people in line. Some said its title meant the exhibit changed each time it moved venues. Others said that it was meant to be ironic. Raya put on her earphones to drown the theories out. She wanted to be surprised. Jace's favorite song filled her ears, inviting her thoughts to wander. Raya let go of their leashes and let them run free.

Raya reached the front of the line. She reeled her thoughts back and listened carefully to an usher dressed in a crisp black blazer and cap she had worn until a few hours ago. The usher informed her that guests were free to explore the exhibit as they pleased, but that no phones or flashlights were permitted. Each guest was given an alarm shaped like an eternal knot to wear around their neck which would buzz when their time was up. Guests who broke any of the rules would be escorted from the museum and not allowed to reenter. Raya signed a consent form and nodded that she understood.

The usher took the form from her and ran his eyes over it. "Welcome aboard, Ms. Sia. We've been expecting you."

A night sky was projected onto the high ceiling of the museum's exhibition hall. Though it did not look as realistic as the ones painted on the Elsewhere Express, it had its own magic. Stars were free to chart their course across the galaxy, sailing across the sky as they pleased. Raya did not recognize a single constellation. A full moon cast its halo over drifting clouds and shared its light with the exhibit below.

Raya walked across a gossamer bridge. Q had done away with the dragonflies and made the bridge appear to float over a glass pond on its own. Raya leaned over the bridge. A galaxy of luminescent fish swirled beneath the glass. Raya stepped off the bridge and onto a moonlit beach covered in pink-tinted sand. She followed a path lit by glowing spheres inland. Red paper lanterns floated over an illusion of a lagoon that filled the length of a second exhibit hall.

An usher walked up to Raya. "Good evening, Ms. Sia. I hope that you're enjoying your journey through *Here* so far."

"I am, thank you." Raya silently wished the usher away. The exhibit was a space she did not want to share.

"Before you enter the gallery, you'll need to wear this." The usher offered her a black velvet blindfold.

"Thank you." She took the blindfold from him and slipped it over her eyes.

"Is it comfortable? I can adjust it if it's too loose or too tight."

"It fits fine. Thanks."

"Perfect. I'll lead you into the lagoon now."

The sound of water filled the hall. Cool silk billowed around her and kissed her skin. Though the installation stopped short of submerging her in water, it played with her senses enough to convince her that she had plunged into the dark depths of the Elsewhere Express's lagoon. She resisted the urge to tear off her blindfold and run. She took a deep breath and exhaled it slowly, reminding herself that eyes were not the only way to navigate the space. She softened her shoulders and let her other senses lead the way.

A breeze, perfumed by roses and mint, blew through the lagoon, whispering poems and singing wistful songs. Raya's hands found shapes she recognized and others she did not.

Tables made from coins and pens.

Spiral sculptures constructed from rings and eyeglasses.

Chairs made from socks.

A sculpted face that Raya recognized as her own. She inhaled sharply. Her hands wandered over the statue, trying to find the warmth of Q's hands in the curves he had sculpted from memory without ever having touched her face.

This labyrinth, Raya realized, was not meant to be escaped from, but explored. The alarm around her neck chimed like the Elsewhere Express's loudspeaker did right before an announcement.

"Ms. Sia," the usher said. "Your time is up. You may take your blindfold off now."

Raya pulled the blindfold off and squinted. "That was incredible."

"Thank you. I'm glad you enjoyed it."

"Before I go, I was wondering if—"

"Oh, the exhibit isn't done yet, Ms. Sia." The usher smiled, taking a silver key from around his neck. "There's a special section that's closed to the public. Mr. Philips left specific instructions that it should only be shown to you."

Anticipation was the best part of happiness. Raya read the name of the private exhibit that was painted over a shiny black door.

Locked Doors

Raya slipped the key into a keyhole, turning it until it clicked.

She pushed the door open and stepped inside. The scent of rain, the fresh kind that came in April and made flowers grow, welcomed her. Darkness hid the rest of the room.

The door shut behind her.

Butterflies that glowed in the dark flew across the room and vanished as suddenly as they appeared. A full moon revealed itself over a twinkling night sky, bathing an exact replica of her train compartment in its pale light.

Raya took off her shoes and strode across the grass carpet, smiling as it tickled her toes. A lamp on the nightstand came to life and shone over an incense stick. Raya sat on the bed and took a closer look. She wondered if the stick of incense could tell bedtime stories too. It stood silent and unlit, showing no sign that it had anything to say.

Raya pulled the nightstand's drawer open and looked for a match to light it even as she doubted that it would make any difference. Sometimes incense sticks were just incense sticks and that was okay. The exhibit had already told her the only story she cared about. Q had fallen from a train, picked himself up, and built a beautiful dream that people lined up to see. A pair of earphones sat inside the drawer along with a small note. Raya picked up the note and read it.

On the count of three.

Raya smiled so wide her cheeks hurt. She put on the earphones, closed her eyes, and got ready to jump. Q's voice clasped her hand.

Hello, Raya. How have you been?

I've thought about what I wanted to tell you for a long time. I even made a script.

But as you know, words and I, well, we don't always get along. And so I built this exhibit instead. I didn't plan for it to be this massive, but somewhere along the way, it took on a life of its own.

Thoughts, as it turns out, enjoy building things off the train too. Who knew?

You can probably tell from the exhibit that I no longer create the kind of art that I used to. The Elsewhere Express did not allow me to keep my sight. I can't say that I was happy about it, but in time, I realized that I had brought home a much better souvenir. I thought about the old paintings I had made of the train and why I was never completely happy with them. They only captured what I saw and never how they made me feel. When I had my eyes, I made pictures you could hang on walls. Without them, my paintings allowed you to walk through their world. I wish that I could have been there to see your face when you took your first step inside this one, though to be honest, I feel that I already have.

You were my companion in the dark even before I knew your name and have been present every second of this journey. Even if we no longer share the train's map, I swear that sometimes, I still feel the tug of our little snitch. Maybe it's because I've left a bit of myself on the train, or perhaps I've taken a part of it with me. I suppose it could also be heartburn, but I have been trying to be good at avoiding things that are too spicy. Whatever the case, I think that it was this pull that led me to the train's back door the day I boarded, a moment when time decided to stop pretending that the past, present, and future were not happening all at once.

Today, as I record this message, I am keenly aware that time is back to its old ways. I am a voice from the past, desperate to reach your ears in the future. I'm profoundly grateful for all the dreams you sent my way and beyond happy that tonight, I'm finally able to share one of mine. I hope you like it even if it's not quite finished. It seems that it's my curse to run out of time and this was a project that I couldn't complete without you. This place is merely a rough sketch of a fading memory without your songs. I tried to wait for you as long as I could but our stations were just too far apart. I could not find any trains that stopped in the future. I built this exhibit in the hope that it would travel where I could not and left my estate with instructions to find you based on the details I had glimpsed on your ticket. I've done all this to share a last wish, a single petition that I have borrowed from your songs.

Live, Hiraya.
Breathe.
Be.

Your friend
or something stranger,
Q

Raya pulled off the earphones. They slipped from her hands and bounced on the grass. She walked over to the dresser and sat down, watching her reflection weep. It watched her cry too. One of them shed sad tears, the other, a deep and quiet joy.

It would be a long time before she could say that she truly understood what purpose was, but whether it was a dream, the pursuit of it, or the detours people took because they chose a path of kindness, she knew that Q had found it. She took a purple notebook out of a small purse and left it on the dresser. She scribbled a letter to Q's estate on stationery embossed with a gold eternal knot.

Her songs and Q's dreams would meet in a world where their owners could not, continuing a story that had ended inside an old elevator.

THE SIXTH LEG

A DETOUR

Live. Breathe. Be.

—Hiraya Sia

"Is it possible to disembark from the train at any point during the journey?"

Frequently Asked Questions
THE ELSEWHERE EXPRESS
PASSENGER HANDBOOK

You may choose to end your journey at any time, but due to the nature of the train's route, we cannot guarantee that you will arrive at your intended destination on time, intact, or at all. But not to worry. Time's rules are not passengers. You are more than welcome to try your luck at jumping off again, should the train happen to pass through that day twice.

THE STATION

Q landed on his feet, his eyes shut, wondering if he was alive or in hell. He kept his eyes closed, refusing to shed a tear for something he did not regret. A strong wind whipped his coat and hair, carrying the roar of an approaching train. The broken walking stick in his hands told him where and when he was.

This was the night he had boarded the Elsewhere Express, the night he would get his sight back and meet a woman with lavender hair. All he had to do was step away from the platform and board his train when it came to a stop.

"Hello, Q."

"*Raya?*" he said, recognizing her voice. "What are you doing here?"

Raya led him away from the platform. Q tried to figure out where he was, but Raya kept him from sensing anything beyond her. Her footsteps filled his ears; her scent, his nose and lungs.

"Are you real?" she said.

"Are you?" Q dropped his walking stick and ran his hands over her face.

Raya pressed his hand to her cheek. "Do I feel real?"

"How is this possible?" Q said. "I jumped off the train."

"So did I."

"When?"

"When you told me to. I got your invitation."

"My invitation?" Time, Q thought, had broken some rules when he jumped from the train. He heard Raya rummaging through her bag and pulling out something that sounded like paper.

"To your exhibit." Raya pressed a piece of paper into his hand.

Q ran his fingertips over the raised dots on the ticket-shaped paper and found an invitation in Braille. It was to an exhibit that his hands did not remember making, but that he had sketched a million times in his soul. He saw it as clearly as if he were taking Raya on a tour of the exhibit himself. Eyes were not required to see hope and possibility. Or love in any shape it took. What tethered people was felt in their hearts, a place deeper than eyes could see. The threads of thought, time, and tenderness that bound him to Raya were too numerous to count. They gently tugged inside him and glowed bright, providing all the light he would ever need.

"I see you." He brought his forehead to hers, eyes closed, and cupped her cheeks with his hands.

"Hello," she whispered back, her words flitting over his mouth. "Again." She drew his hands from her face and laced her fingers through his. "Come with me."

"Where are we going?"

"It's a surprise," she said, the smile in her voice ringing like a bell.

Raya led him by the hand to explore a space his senses painted in his head like the most incredible dream. A train terminal, palatial in both elegance and size, surrounded them. Its high, arched glass roof framed the bluest sky. Sunlight poured through the glass and glinted off marble platforms and rows of golden tracks.

Q clutched Raya's hand in case this was a dream and morning tried to rip him away. "Where are we?" he said, feeling her gaze like the sun on his face.

She took his palm and laid it over her heart, the brightest path in the station. "I think it's our stop."

Acknowledgments

This section of the book is usually used to thank the people who've had a hand in bringing it to life. In this case, I would say that everything I wrote preceding this page—the book itself—is my way of thanking everyone who has shared this crazy journey with me. If you see yourself, hear your words, or feel like any of the train cars in the story feel familiar, it's because on this journey of a lifetime, we've sat by one another's side.

And so, with a heart bursting with gratitude, I present the Elsewhere Express Passenger Manifest:

My parents, grandma, and family
My furry and non-furry kids
The Gang
Aueeie and Mina
Jake and Kris
Mia
Amy
Tricia and Imogen
Ayesha

Catherine, whose lived experience and insights were invaluable

The beautiful people behind this book's cover and design: Irene, Alexis, Regina, Haylee

(The AMAZING) Team Elsewhere Express at Penguin Random House and my international publishers

And the man who purchased a nonrefundable train ticket with me more than twenty-five years ago without really knowing where we were going.

Thank you for coming aboard!

About the Author

Samantha Sotto Yambao is a professional daydreamer, aspiring time traveler, and speculative fiction writer based in Manila, the Philippines. She is the author of *Before Ever After, Love and Gravity, A Dream of Trees, The Beginning of Always,* and *Water Moon*.

samanthasotto.com
Facebook.com/samanthasotto
Instagram: @samanthasottoyambao
X: @samanthasotto

Get on board the Elsewhere Express—the train that takes you to your life's purpose. As you color in this illustration, let your mind wander and your heart open. What are the colors of your daydreams? What picture do you want to paint of your future? And what kind of life can you create if you dare to color outside the lines? Enjoy this activity on long train rides and journeys of all kinds.